[Type here]

The Queen of Brazil

Published by Black Diamond Press LLC
Fort Lauderdale, Florida

Printed in the United States

ISBN 978-0-9897740-1-7

Library of Congress 1-970260061

10 9 8 7 6 5 4 3 2 1

Publisher:

Black Diamond Press LLC
Suite 103
4640 SW 42nd Terrace
Fort Lauderdale, Florida 33314

The Queen of Brazil

By

Asa Fisk

Dedication

To all who are being abused or have ever been
abused...
May you never suffer again.

To all alcoholics and addicts...
May you find the strength to conquer.

To all veterans of war...
May peace cover this world.

THE HONOR AND GLORY OF WAR

Oh rally round the flag boys
Our politicians will us to battle with the bad men again
Raise the flag, load your weapon
We shall go forward in honor, courage and glory
To fight the bad men again

It is wonderful to fight for honor, courage and glory
We shall win, we will rock you We are right, they are wrong
We shall protect, defend and defeat the wrongs
We are the champions of all time

This is the manly thing to do
The honor of this mission is great and wonderful
We are right, they are wrong That goes without saying
Our honor, our honor, our wonderful honor

We shall march and fight It is glorious to kill and defeat Oh what
honor
We shall decimate the wrong doers
Our politicians tell us we are right and our enemy is wrong
We shall win Then...

When Johnny comes marching home again Hurrah! Hurrah!
We'll give him a hearty welcome then Hurrah! Hurrah!
The men will cheer and the boys will shout
The ladies they will all turn out
And we'll all feel gay when Johnny comes marching home

Here comes the parade now
Look there is the Mayor
And our Senators and Representatives
Look at all our politicians marching tall
They smile and wave

Look – look! Here comes Johnny down the street Marching tall
with his rifle and all those medals Wow what a soldier - what an
honor! Here comes Billy, he looks great but wait Where's his other
arm? What an honor!

Look, look here comes Paul but wait Why is he so short?
He lost his legs He has a wheelchair now
That's okay - what an honor!

Here comes Jimmy in a box Why does his mother cry?
She wastes her tears - She should not cry
What an honor it is TO DIE!

Hurrah! Hurrah!

Asa Fisk

Chapter One
Trying to Fix the Problem

The waiting room was about twelve feet by ten feet. The walls were painted a brownish yellow, which was starting to show some age. The ceiling was white, and there was a non-descript green area rug covering a brown ceramic tile floor. The room was semi dark. There was a window, but the shades were drawn, and no exterior light shown into the room from outside the building. The door to the room offered the only escape. Only one lamp in a corner was on, and there was also light on the opposite wall coming from an aquarium that was placed upon a stand on the center of one wall. As he sat alone in the room, he watched the fish slowly move about the lighted aquarium. Gives an air of calmness to the place he thought. He smiled and laughed to himself and thought this is good - no sense to having the crazies be upset. Calm, yes calm is best. There was one of those small, opaque, sliding windows, typical of medical offices on the same wall as the aquarium. He could see the blurry top of the head of the ugly receptionist he had checked in with when he first arrived, busy doing her work in the next office.

She had handed him a clipboard and pen, and rudely said "Fill it out and take a seat. Doctor Ray will be with you shortly," slamming it shut after she had done her obligation.

He sat down and filled in the form, getting madder and madder with all the stupid personal questions the forms asked. He finished it quickly hating each question more than the one before. He turned his attention to the room. As usual he would take in every detail of the room and burn it into his memory. There were uncomfortable chairs lining the walls and a few tables which held outdated magazines. 'You would think that for the prices these guys charge they could afford fucking new magazines. What a rip-off.'

He sat in the waiting room wondering if this would be worth his time. He admitted to himself that he was depressed, and it was getting harder and harder to control his anger. The anger was the real problem; when it got out of hand, he just couldn't control it and worse sometimes he couldn't remember all he had done. Why did he do all those things?...they were just automatic reactions...he wasn't

1

wrong…but he had to stop before he did it again…maybe this would help. But how are you going to get help and still not say what you had done to cause what he had done. So why not just get some pills and be on his merry way. Yes, that was the answer…that's what he decided to do – just get the pills, see if they worked and be done with this silly exercise of futility. He really couldn't talk about what he had done to anyone. That would be stupid. Just dance around the questions and be on his way. As he sat there, time slowly passed for him. He had been early for the appointment, but by only fifteen minutes and now it was ten minutes past the hour. His anxiety was making the clock drag seconds across his mind.

"Oh, fuck this!" he said out loud. He got up from his seat and knocked on the opaque receptionist window. It opened with a scraping sound like the glass was being pulled across sand in the tracks.

Before he could say anything, she angrily spit out, "Doctor Pierson is running late and will be with you shortly. Please have a seat." The opaque window slammed shut.

'Bitch' he thought. He returned to his seat and focused on the fish. 'They seem happy or at least as happy as fish can feel being held captive by glass walls. They're in jail, better them than me. I never want to go to jail – couldn't stand that.' The word jail flashed in his brain and it immediately brought back memories of the Army. 'Shit, the Army had been bad enough. Fucking rules and regulations, always someone telling you what to do, when, where and how. How the hell had he gotten away with all the stuff he had pulled?' He just always saluted, said "Yes Sir," and did what he wanted. He smiled at the thought. 'The Army was a system and all you had to do was work the system, work it your way. The Army – idiotic – at best, The Big Green Machine…The Big Green Killing Machine. How we ever won a war is anyone's guess. Maybe other countries' armies are worse; they must be because we always win the war. No that isn't right…we didn't win in Nam, nor Korea. Guess we are on a losing streak… Maybe you can't win against guerillas…'

"Mr. Liberty."

Someone calling his name pulled him from his thoughts. He looked up and saw a tall thin blond standing in the doorway looking at him. She had a halo of light framing her head and body from the lights

2

in the hallway, but it was hard to discern her face or other features due to the glare.

"Please follow me."

He rose and followed her form down the hall. She opened an office door and then moved out of the way, so he could enter. There was a man with sun glasses sitting behind the desk. The man rose and put out his hand to shake James' hand. "Mr. Liberty, I am Ray Pierson, nice to meet you."

James quickly realized that the shrink he had come to see was blind. James walked across the room and shook Ray's hand and mumbled, "Nice to meet you too."

"Please take a seat and if you don't mind please shut the door to my office."

James shut the door and sat in a chair on the other side of the desk from Ray. He quickly perused the room and noticed a computer with a lot of additional boxes attached to it. The walls had a few pictures, mostly portraying Army stuff.

"How can I help you Mr. Liberty?" Ray smiled at him looking in his general direction.

"Look, ah, I guess I am a little depressed or at least that is what my doc at the VA said. He thought it might be a good idea and I thought maybe it might be a good idea to see a shrink and at a minimum get some happy pills, that's how you can help me. I was suppose to see a shrink at the VA hospital, but they said they were booked solid, so they said they wanted me to do an outplacement at a private shrink, so they sent me to you. I guess I just want some happy pills, and I will be on my way."

Ray chuckled, "Well, I will be glad to do that for you, but before I can do that I need to get some medical history and some information from you. Happy pills come in all different shapes and sizes so before I give you some I need to know what is happening to you, why you need them, what dosage and stuff like that. So, if you can stand to work with me a little bit...I can figure out what you need."

3

"Okay, but let's not make this painful. Okay?"

"Do you know why you are depressed?"

James swallowed hard, here come the lies he thought, "Well I think it is really because of my love life. I seem to be making the wrong choices with the women I seem to choose, or they seem to choose me, I'm not sure.

"Well that's a common problem. We all have problems with our love lives. Are you married?"

"No, I am almost divorced."

"Almost? How long ago were you married or how long have you been married?" As Ray asked this question he stood, carefully making his way around the desk and sat opposite James in the other chair.

James watched him expertly navigate himself to the chair facing him on the same side of the desk and sit. "I have been married for about fifteen years to Susan. We started divorce proceedings well over two years ago and it is almost officially over. We have been separated for about three years. She was younger, but Mr. Al Cohol bit her and then she started mixing the vodka with a lot of pills. She went down in flames and I couldn't do anything to stop her. I tried, but nothing worked. I was in love with her – still am – but it is over, and I have accepted it. It has gotten pretty messy at the end."

"So, what is your love life doing now?"

"I am presently sort of dating a woman, Vera, who lives in Brazil. She is divorced, a scientist, has two children. I am also being harassed and chased by my secretary. She is threatening sexual harassment if I don't let her be my girlfriend and if she has her way, she wants marriage. I am still seeing my ex-wife to be, but only to help her on the road to recovery,"

"Wow, that's pretty busy for anyone. I can see why you are depressed. What do you do for work? Or should I say – do you have time for work?"

4

"I am a project manager for a construction company. I am building a site of up-scale homes in Hobe Sound. That keeps me pretty busy, and is rather stressful. I work about twelve hours a day. There are about thirty-five different subs I have to manage plus twenty guys who are my carpenters and labor force."

"I have been given a brief record of you by the VA. You were in Nam. Is that affecting you in any way? I mean since you came to me through the VA system...I mean...well...have you ever been diagnosed with PTSD?"

"No, none of that shit bothers me. I was a tank commander, but all that stuff has long been forgotten.'

"No anger issues... any issues of sadness... any bad dreams... survivor guilt... any physical issues from wounds?"

James was angry when he answered. "I said no. It doesn't bother me...it's over, done, finished."

"Easy James, I have to ask the questions...just to get a background...just to find the answers as to what is causing you to be depressed. There are things bothering you, but you are too close to the problem, so you don't see it and how things affect you. Like the forest and the trees thing...you are in the forest, but you can't see the forest because all you can see are the trees. That's my job, to help you get to see the forest for what it is and not just the trees.

"Ya, but your blind, I take it, and how are you going to get me to see when you can't see yourself?" James was rather nasty with his retort.

Very calmly and soothingly Ray answered, "Yes, I am blind. However, I see through your words. There is nothing for me to physically see...it is only what you tell me. And if I am to be of any help to you I will have to visualize through your words because you have already seen what there is to be seen. We can't recreate what has already happened. You just need to tell me, and I will see...please excuse the pun."

"Ya, I get it. Sorry." James stopped himself. He needed to control himself. His anger might make him say things he shouldn't and that would be bad.

Ray continued, "By the way, I lost my site in Nam. I stepped on a mine and it nailed me. Prior to that, I had twenty – twenty. Have you had any other therapy before this or help from any of the Vietnam Veterans groups or groups like Wounded Warrior Foundation, stuff like that?"

"No, I don't need their help. I don't want to sit around and relive the war and boo-hoo on someone else's shoulder. I don't need a handout. I guess there are many who do and many in need, but I don't. I can and have made my own way in the world. Some of those groups are good and they help many, but they can't help me, and I don't need it. It really pisses me off about the government. You demand people go fight a war, then a lot of them come back fucked up in the body or in their mind, and the government only pays lip service to the problem. Then they, and their families, suffer for their whole lifetime."

Ray paused for a moment, "Well, they are good groups and there are many good people just trying to help. There just aren't enough people willing to help. In addition, a lot of the veterans tend to refuse help, for fear that it is a sign of weakness. For the moment, let's just leave it at that, I would rather discuss your problems. Are there any other issues bothering you?"

"Yes. People who are stupid...people who ask too many stupid questions...people who don't do their work and even if they do it...they do it wrong...people who don't do what I ask or tell them to do."

"James, do you view this as a control problem?"

"No, just as a stupid person problem."

"Have you always taken the lead position in your career?"

"Yes." James snapped, and then thought he had better not get into any long discussions.

"James, I would like to help you and as a result, make your life more enjoyable. However, if you just want the happy pills, that is fine but understanding our reasoning for our actions makes for a better life. We learn how to control and manipulate our actions to make a more plentiful and bountiful existence. I can just give you the pills or you can decide to make yourself a better person. If you don't try to change things – things will never change."

"You're rather insulting," James said calmly. "You have no idea as to who I am…and you jump to conclusions about my life and then want me to walk the path with Dr. Ray, so I will be healed and a wonderful person since I am not that now."

Ray started laughing, "No, I am no faith healer. Just like you, I have been professionally trained. You probably know more about psychology than I know about construction but being able to control the different processes in life makes you smarter. You may even be smarter than me. I haven't formed any opinions yet."

"That's not true. A person usually forms ninety per cent of their opinions about a person in the first ten minutes of meeting that person."

"Yes James, that is correct and very astute of you. Look, let me be straight up and honest with you. My 'quick' opinion of you is you are very intelligent, display strong leadership qualities, a nice guy who has gone through a lot of shit in his life and handled it well. However, I also think you have some anger issues, maybe part of or stemming from military PTSD and from other issues generated throughout your life. I don't know what they are, but you do, and they are locked inside you causing you to act in certain ways. I believe depression is caused by an over-loading of the brain and sensory system. Now the pills will help, but they do not erase the underlying causes, and as such, those issues will come back to haunt you at a later date. If you decide to cleanse your mind, I can help or at least I am willing to help you if you so desire. And I promise not to hurt you," he ended with a big grin.

James was silent, just staring at him, weighing his options. He was trying to figure out if he should do this. He would have to be careful about what he said. "Do you report this case, my case, back to the VA hospital? Does it go on my record?"

"No, all I have to do is say I am treating you for personal issues and that's all I report - period. Anything you say is between you and me and does not go any further."

7

"What about your notes?"

"I can show you all the notes, but they are kept in a general sense. I stay away from actual details."

"And what if I have broken the law? Not that I have, but what is it that would compel you to inform the authorities?"

"Nothing, well that's not true. If you were planning a suicide I can have you committed for your safe, wellbeing. Other than that, everything is confidential and cannot be discussed with anyone. Doctor's notes on a patient are privileged information, and cannot be revealed, even in testimony in a court room proceeding. My only obligation is if I determine you are in imminent danger to yourself or others then I must stop you, protect you or those you could harm. If you have already done something, then that is just history and not reportable. Have you broken the law?"

"NO! And I am not about to, and I am too chicken to commit suicide, so I guess you might say I am a safe bet." James swallowed hard. This conversation was getting too dangerous to continue. "What else do you want to know?"

"How often do you lose your temper?"

"It seems to be a daily thing lately. There is a lot on my mind."

"I will write you a prescription for Wellbutrin and pills called a SSRI for your anxiety. The Wellbutrin will help your depression and the SSRI's will help keep you calm and regulate your moods and emotions. By taking them, it will calm you down and allow you to see things from a different perspective. I will write you a sixty-day supply, but I would like you to come back and tell me how you are feeling after about thirty days. That okay with you? Also think it over about doing some therapy with me and we can discuss your problems. Who knows I might be able to help you." Ray picked up the phone on his desk and told the person who answered to give Mr. Liberty the two prescriptions for the drugs he had mentioned. "There, you can pick them up at the front desk on your way out."

"Okay, thanks. I will give it a try and see if they work. Okay that was good; I have to go now – Thanks." And without conviction said, "Ya, and I will think about doing the therapy." James stood up, quickly turned and went to the door, paused as he grabbed the door knob and looked back at Ray. He thought, 'This is different – a blind therapist? I don't know about this one.' He felt Ray could be someone he could trust, but better to wait and rethink his thoughts. He was already treading in dangerous waters.

During the next month James took the pills while going about his normal routine. He thought long and hard about doing this therapy thing. He called his lawyer to ask if what Ray had said had any validity. If he opened up, could Ray harm him by telling anyone? His lawyer said Ray was telling the truth. Then his lawyer got interested and asked what he had done. James ignored his requests for information.

James decided to try this therapy thing. He was feeling better with the pills and his anger seemed to be subsiding. The people he was working with had been remarking he was different and was in a better mood. He made an appointment and followed up by making an appointment for every other week at the same time. He also made a promise to himself not to talk about anything that could put him in jeopardy. He didn't tell anyone of what he was going to do. That would make him appear weak and maybe mark him as a nut job or a person who was having trouble coping with life. He couldn't show weakness to anyone. That was not him…he never showed weakness only strength. He was the leader not a following sheep. His thoughts were always correct, direct and to the point. The thoughts of others were always muddled and mixed with stupidity and compromises. He made decisions while others always waited for someone else to do it. James thought people are always afraid to take a stand… but he was not.

Chapter Two
The Beginning of the Problem

July 24, 1969 Xuan Loc, South Viet Nam
11th Armored Cavalry Regiment
"The Blackhorse Regiment"
Base Camp

Board of Inquiry

James walked into the room saluted and presented himself in front of the table, where four officers and two sergeants were seated, "Sir, Staff Sergeant James Liberty reporting as ordered."

"Take a seat Sergeant."

James sat in the only chair about ten feet in front of the table facing the six men at the table.

The Sergeant-Major stood and read from a sheet of paper. "Sergeant Liberty, this board of inquiry is investigating the death of Lieutenant Mark MacDonald, who was killed in a fire fight in Tay Ninh Province in the village of Hoc Noi on July 13, 1969. The evidence in our possession shows Lieutenant MacDonald was killed by friendly fire by three 5.56mm rounds from an M-16A1 weapon, which struck Lieutenant MacDonald just below the left ear, in the left temple, and the middle of the left side of the neck. Those rounds exited his body at the same level points on the opposite side of the body. Those rounds attributed and caused his death. Lieutenant MacDonald was commanding an Armored Cavalry Assault Vehicle (ACAV) directly to the right side of the ACAV commanded by Sergeant James Liberty. This board is requesting any and all information in your possession concerning the death of Lieutenant MacDonald from your knowledge and view point during said fire-fight." The Sergeant-Major then sat in his chair at the end of the table.

"Thank you, Sergeant-Major," said Colonel George S. Patton III, Commander of the 11th Armored Cavalry. "Sergeant Liberty, you have heard the summation as read. Now, we would like you to recall the events of this incident and the fire-fight."

"Yes Sir." Sergeant Liberty paused and slowly looked at each person on the panel across from him before he started to speak. "We had been informed by our intelligence section of enemy activity in the village. We were ordered to proceed with a reconnaissance in force into the village. We ran the five kilometers from our gathering point to the village. Lieutenant MacDonald was to take the point with his squad followed by my squad directly into the center of the village and at one hundred meters from the village, fan out with Lieutenant MacDonald's squad to the right of center and my squad to the left of center. Sergeant Fiestas' squad would circle to the north end of the village and Lieutenant Cassons squad would circle to the south end of the village forming an elliptical circle of ACAVs and tanks around the village, with the back side open to prevent a back cross fire upon ourselves but allowing us to see anyone trying to escape. We have practiced and have successfully done this maneuver before during other fire-fights."

Major Baunsen interjected, "Sergeant Liberty, you were out of position during the maneuver, why?"

"Yes Sir, I was. Sergeant Cooper, who commands the lead track in my squad, reported to me he was having engine problems and could not maintain proper speed. I made the decision to move all the vehicles down to the left one position and wait for Sergeant Cooper to get caught up. He was slowly catching up with my column, but since he was late I felt the formation would best be served if I moved my track into the center left position. Filling the spot Sgt. Cooper was supposed to be, thus allowing Sergeant Cooper time to arrive and fill at the end of the left side of the line. That way, we would have the greater fire power directed at the center of the village and the enemy in the beginning of the firefight, which was your desire and directive Sir, at the briefing. Sir, was that not your directive?"

"I'll ask the questions, Sergeant," shot back the angry Major.

"Yes Sir."

"Go on Sergeant," said the Colonel.

"We started taking enemy fire before everybody was in their correct position. Everybody opened fire as soon as possible on the village. There was mass confusion with the villagers scattering and the Viet Cong firing small arms and Rocket Propelled Grenades (RPG's) at us. I finally got into the correct position to the left side of Lieutenant MacDonald's ACAV, only about fifteen meters away and slightly behind him. My crew fired their M-60's and I fired my 50-caliber machine gun into the village.

The fire-fight lasted about ten minutes and the VC who weren't dead or wounded escaped out the back side of the formation. We killed as many as possible including the women, children and animals. After we had shot up the village, I directed the ACAV's in my squad to start forward motion and start chasing the VC. I looked to my right wondering why Lieutenant MacDonald's ACAV wasn't moving. That was when I saw Lieutenant MacDonald slumped over and dead in the turret. I immediately called for a medi-vac chopper, told my squad to proceed forward, and I pulled my ACAV in front of the Lieutenant's for its protection, got out and went to the Lieutenant's ACAV. I directed and helped his crew pull his body from the turret and lay his body on the ground and called for a medic. That's about it Sirs."

"Sergeant, why did you call for a medi-vac chopper before you even moved and without a closer inspection of the Lieutenant's wounds? Don't you think you were a little quick, a little presumptuous in your judgment?" asked Captain Murphy.

"No Sir. Either he was badly wounded or dead. In any event we needed a chopper. However, I could tell he was dead."

"Sergeant, how could you tell at that distance?" said Captain Murphy.

"Sir, when you have been in this fucking hell hole as long as I have and have been in as many fire-fights as I have, you can see, feel, and know these things almost instinctively. No disrespect Sir, you too will get to the same point once you have been here longer, Sir." James had bitterness and hatred in his voice.

"That's enough of your snide comments," snapped the Sergeant Major.

13

Captain Murphy tried again, "Knock that shit off and tell me how you knew he was dead."

"Sir, it was easy to tell. His shirt and flak jacket were already soaked thoroughly with his blood, the wounds were still gurgling and draining all the blood from his head, his body looked lifeless, his eyes were frozen open and there were massive holes in the right side of his head. Wounds like those are never good. He had spilled more blood than anyone can. His head looked more like an exploded pumpkin. Even his como helmet had exploded open and was half gone. I could see half of his head was blown away. I've seen it before, Sir." James delivered his remarks snidely.

Captain Angelo chimed in, "Sergeant, at what point in the firefight did you start firing your M-16?"

"Sir, I never did. I testified earlier I used my 50-caliber machine gun. That was the only weapon I used, Sir."

Captain Angelo came back, "We heard from Sergeant Willis that he saw you using your M-16."

"Sir, I did not use my M-16, only my 50-caliper. Sergeant Willis must be mistaken. I might add Captain; Sergeant Willis was five ACAVs away from my location and to my left. You think you see a lot of things in a fire-fight, Sir. And I believe Sergeant Willis has only been in two fire-fights, Sir. There's a lot of confusion, Sir. A lot of things happen in a fire-fight, and there is no explanation. Newbies firing in the wrong direction, I don't even know half the time. Sometimes you just can't say for sure what is happening. Guns are very dangerous Sir. Just ask the women and children in the village. Oh sorry, you can't – they're dead."

"I said enough of your sarcastic comments," the Sergeant-Major snapped.

"Sergeant, did you shoot Lieutenant MacDonald by accident or did someone on your ACAV shoot the Lieutenant?" Captain Angelo asked.

"No Sir, I did not shoot him, and I am very sure no one on my vehicle shot him. And besides, how to you know it was an M-16 that killed him? Because you said the rounds exited the body? I would imagine as to who did shoot him is anyone's guess, Sir, and with what weapon - is anyone's guess," Liberty said very confidently, angrily and strongly.

A silence fell upon the room. All the men at the table looked down at their notes and then a few started clearing their throats. Something had been said and put into the air, but nobody wanted to make a comment or remark. There was just dead silence. It seemed to last a long time. Finally, the men at the table started looking at each other and then Captain Murphy spoke.

"Sergeant, we were told you and Lieutenant MacDonald got into a fight a month or so ago. Is that correct?" said Captain Murphy.

"Yes sir, well it was more like a little scuffle."

Dead silence fell over the room again. All the officers sat up straight as if they had finally gotten to the meat of the matter. "Tell us about that incident Sergeant," the Colonel asked.

"Yes sir. A couple of months ago I was in Saigon for three days arranging supplies for the Regiment. When I returned, I was told Lieutenant MacDonald had been fucking my favorite whore. When I approached him on the subject, he told me to 'fuck off'. We had some words back and forth and then we got into a wrestling match of sorts. We were separated by some troopers who were nearby. We both laughed at the silliness of the matter once we were separated. I mean it was just a whore. I then apologized to him and he apologized to me. We then went to the NCO club, had a few drinks, talked and laughed about it and from then on nothing more was said. That was the end of it."

"Sergeant, we have learned that Nutan, the girl in question, was beaten up by Lieutenant MacDonald. She ended up in a Vietnamese hospital for over a week. Did you know this when you had the fight with Lieutenant MacDonald?" questioned Major Baunsen.

"Sir, at the time of the scuffle with the Lieutenant I didn't know that. However, Lieutenant MacDonald was always beating up the whores he used. It was like a habit with him."

The Major angrily cut in, "That is not what we are discussing Sergeant. The Lieutenant isn't on trial here."

"Am I, Major?" Liberty chimed back.

15

"This isn't a trial, but an investigation. Just go on with your accounting of the situation," said the Major.

"Okay." James paused, looked at the Major with an icy stare, and finally started talking again. "I found out about the beating he gave Nutan later. I talked to Lieutenant MacDonald about it and he said after he fucked her, he caught her stealing money from him. You know how these whores are Sir; you must watch them every second. We, as troopers, have to stay together Sir, and protect each other. She was just another thieving slope head, Sir."

"Did you visit her in the hospital?" asked Captain Murphy.

"Yes Sir, I did. I visited her and since she was my favorite whore, I felt a little obligated to give her some money to help her out since she is trying to support her family, and she wasn't going to be working until after she recovered. And from the wounds she had, it would probably take a long time. But, all in all, I think she learned her lesson Sir, and I thought I might be able to use her again – she was a pretty good fuck, Sir."

Dead silence fell across the room again. The Colonel finally broke the silence and asked if there were any other questions for Sergeant Liberty. No one spoke. "Okay Sergeant, thank you and you are dismissed. If you remember anything else pertinent to this investigation, please inform the Sergeant-Major and you are not to discuss this with anyone."

"Yes Sir." Sergeant Liberty rose from the chair, came to attention, saluted, did an about face and walked out of the room. After he was out of the building a smile crossed his lips.

*****

Quan Loi, South Viet Nam
August 6, 1969

The 11th Armored Cavalry Regiment was an armored tank regiment. They were the most aggressive and most decorated unit in Viet Nam. They were different because of their mobility and their ability to quickly cover large amounts of territory. Because of their career officers, they always volunteered to act as the point unit for many military actions in Nam. They were strong, they were sharp, and they killed more enemy than other units. They were protected by their so called "Iron Coffin" attack vehicles. They were feared - they were aggressive. They went after the enemy in a way that Congress would not approve...but no one told Congress. They did not wait for the enemy to come to them, they went after the enemy. They went after the enemy in a way that made the enemy go the other way. They were brave, strong, fearless and crazy. They set the example for other units. The North Vietnamese Army and the Viet Cong respected the fire power of the Blackhorse and they wanted to hurt them badly. To kill those that would kill them. The mantra, the desire, the psyche of the 11th Armored - was   TO KILL.

The tank commanders and officers had gathered for a meeting at the rear of the communications ACAV. "Okay everybody, quiet down. QUIET! We expect to get hit tonight," Captain Murphy said sternly. "The 5th North Vietnamese Regiment swung north out of our area of operations two days ago and then yesterday noon swung south for a few clicks then back east and then back to the south toward us. We think they were just trying to get us to believe they were going somewhere else. We believe they are coming back here and getting ready to hit us tonight."

A low whistle came out of someone in the group follow by an "Oh shit."

The Captain continued, "We have three listening posts that called in, and said they are mustering to the south, east and west of us. They will probably start with a false attack from the north. All tanks and ACAVs will man the perimeter with a two man watch. Load all weapons, put up all RPG screens, trip wire flares, put out any claymores and barb wire you have and get ready. Lieutenant Shaw, take the north to east quadrant, Sergeant Liberty, take the east to south quadrant, Lieutenant Casson, take the south to west quadrant and Sergeant Fiestas, take the west to north quadrant. They will hit us with somewhere with between 1000 and 1500 men."

A nightmare was in the offering and everybody knew it. The 11th Armored Cavalry was stuck out front again, out in a clearing, just off the edge of the jungle. The Commanding Officer, Colonel George S. Patton III, was a cowboy, a full bird Colonel looking to make his first General's Star. He had a famous father and a prophecy to achieve. He put his command always out front, in the most dangerous areas and always volunteered his units for the point position for any mission whenever possible. The men hated him because they knew that they were just his fighting pawns in his career plan, and they ended up with the dirty work. They knew during a night operation he would be nowhere to be seen. He would be way back at base camp, so far away from the area the only thing that could hurt him was a runaway cork from a champagne bottle. He was the Pentagon's Manager of Casualties. They loved him because he conducted a war without penalties. You couldn't do anything wrong, as long as you kept killing the enemy.

"Each squad will supply a mortar crew for the willy-peter flares located 25 meters behind each line. Ammo supply will be here at 1300 hours, and a hot meal" the Captain went on.

"Oh hooray, the last supper!" Liberty cracked.

"Shut up Liberty" the Captain barked. "Get everybody ready, ready as you can. Check your weapons and get everybody's mind right – It's going to be a long night. Any questions?"

From the back of the group came "Can I take my R & R now Captain?" The Captain ignored the comment.

"What will we have for air cover Captain?" asked Fiestas.

"They're going to try to keep a few spooky gunships at the ready depending on when we get hit. As to how long it will take to get them to get over us is anybody's guess. But they are prepped and ready. They have at least 10 to 15 minutes in the air after the attack starts and before they can reach us. We may also have some choppers till the spookys start making their runs. Since it will be at night don't plan on the choppers.

18

Make sure everyone gets cover if and when those spookys hit. Let's not lose anybody this time."

The Captain paused and slowly looked around the group. He searched out the eyes of each man, looking for a question, taking each man's mental temperature, looking at some for possibly the last time. He finally raised his right fist and strongly said - "Blackhorse."

"Allons" came the response from the group. The automatic unit slogan response was very weak, even though it came from about fifteen men.

"Okay – go get ready. Wait a minute, one more thing...The decision or I should say the recommendation from the review board regarding the death of Lieutenant MacDonald has been decided. The review board's official determination is the death of Lieutenant MacDonald was an accident due to unknown enemy or friendly fire. This is the decision which will be passed on to central command at MACV. It was decided he was killed, possibly by enemy or friendly fire, but if by friendly fire it was accidental in nature, due to the fact a firefight was occurring at the same time. It is indeterminable as to whom, singular or plural, due to the nature of the wounds caused; any responsibility can be assessed to any one person or group of persons to have done this with forethought or malice. That's all, dismissed." During the Captain's last statement, he never took his eyes off Liberty and James never took his eyes off him. At the end a slight smile appeared on James' face. The group broke up and headed back to their vehicles.

This element of the 11th Armored had deployed in an almost perfect circle. The circle was like the covered wagons from the old west. All the tanks and ACAVs were pointed outward. There were seven M-1 tanks, six Sheridan tanks, sixteen ACAVs, two command ACAVs and a radio communications ACAV. There were about eight vehicles on each quadrant. There was a space of about 15 feet between each vehicle.

Sergeant Liberty and Sergeant Cooper headed back to their vehicles and their positions on the circle. Cooper finally spoke first. "Mutha fucker here we go again. We get into more shit. They outta pay us by the body instead of by the month," he said in a soft West Virginia drawl.

"Look you hill-billy hick – You never give our government any praise for allowing you to practice your killing of people. I ask you, where else can you go - kill people – and not get arrested?" said Liberty laughing sarcastically. "They give us the tanks, planes and guns so America's fighting sons can keep old glory waving in Vietnam now!" he said in a sing song fashion. "Think of all the government officials, Senators, Representatives and the President's cabinet and even the President of the United States wanting to shove democracy down the throats of these meager rice farmers. And we are the forefront of their very thoughts, words and actions. We have to guard these jungles and dangerous rice paddies from the torture which could be inflicted by the communist yellow hoard coming down from the north, and to save democracy for the good people of South Viet Nam," he said with a wry smile on his face. "When we get back to the real world, you can be proud you have saved all those beautiful, round eye, American women from being ravaged by the slope heads, and you prevented the takeover of the United States. When you get home, appreciative women will come to you, rip their clothes from their supple beautiful bodies, crawl all over you and pamper you with more sex than you ever thought possible for saving them."

"Sarge, there ain't a 'supple body' in West - By God - Virginia. There all doublewides! And that's why all the men become miners – to get away from their fat wives, sisters, cousins or whoever they married, then they go underground for as long as they can, and the company will allow. Sarge, what did you think about the decision?"

"Coop, you did tell the board you had engine trouble – right?"

"Ya, I already told you. I said it just like you told me too. Why?"

"Just checking. Come on Coop, let's get the boys ready. We can talk about the decision later. We have three newbies and they don't know their ass from a hole in the ground. Get'em fat, happy and sassy and let's make sure they don't kill us by accident. You take the fat one and the skinny one and I'll take the pretty one."

"Lib that ain't fair. I hate newbies – they're dangerous."

"Life is not fair and certainly war is not fair and I'm in charge. So therefore, you get the two clowns and I get the pretty one. So, let's get em ready. Agreed? Agreed," said Liberty answering his own rhetorical question.

"Hey Sarge, when are they going to put an officer in charge of our squad?"

"Well I think soon. After what happened to MacDonald, I don't think any of these chicken shits are jumping to take over. All these officers are worried that the bullets in our group aren't aimed properly, if you know what I mean. They will find a stupid volunteer soon, probably someone new in country."

They split as they got close to their ACAVs. Cooper went to tell his men while Liberty went to find Richie Hegeman, the commander of the ACAV to his left. "Richie," Liberty called.

"Over here Sarge," came the reply from the side of the ACAV. Hegeman was sitting on an ammo can. His shirt and pants were off, and he was just sitting there in his briefs, socks and boots eating from a C Ration box. "Hey Sarge, I got peaches again in my box lunch. I saved them for you. I know how much you like em." Hegeman was just a happy guy never admitting there was a war going on around him. He just acted oblivious to the whole thing and pretended he was just having a good time. He was just putting his time in, counting the days till he could take the big bird home. "I don't know why you like em. Those warm peaches taste like rotten pussy. No, - they taste more like a dead gook's rotten pussy," he quipped. "What's up Sarge? Those fuckin meetings you go to never seem to put a smile on your face. Let me guess, - Nixon is going to give us some round eyed, Red Cross, Donut Dollies for the weekend, and a ride down to Vung Tau for a weekend R & R and wild sex."

A smile crept across Liberty's face. "Yes! Right again. You are one crazy mother fucker" he said with joy, "You guessed it. But first, we're going to get hit by the NVA 5th Regiment tonight. They want to get the party started early."

"Great," Richie said enthusiastically. "I'll get the ice and glasses. I got some sardines but I'm out of cheese and crackers. What else could we serve our guests?"

21

"Get the whole squad together Richie. We have too many newbies in the squad and not enough body bags to go around. Hustle it up there's lots to do. We are going to get hit hard this time."

"Hey Sarge – we're still having cocktail hour tonight, aren't we?"

"Ya, wouldn't miss it. How can you have a war without a civilized cocktail hour? Now go get everybody."

The group assembled under the blazing, hot, noon-day sun. They were dusty, dirty and soaking wet from the constant sweat which ran from their bodies. They listened. You could read the fear on their faces. Liberty told them what to do and where he wanted them. He told them like it was the very first time. He emphasized there were too many newbies, and if they didn't follow his instructions – they would be wounded or worse. The short timers respected Liberty. He had been leading the squad for almost five months. He was aggressive, careful and cognizant of what it took to keep everyone alert and ready, always ready for the worst. He assigned them specific tasks from laying out trip wire flares to the placement of claymore mines to the correct way of digging in the chain link cyclone fence which served as RPG screens in front of the ACAVS to protect them from a direct hit. "Now, make sure they're dead, always put at least two bullets in them. Those fucking gooks will do anything to crawl back and kill you if you give them a chance." He dismissed them and they all slowly scattered back to their vehicles in silence.

Liberty went back to his ACAV, got his shower bag out, stripped down and started taking a shower with the one gallon of water the bag held. He hadn't had a shower in three days. The water felt good as he danced under the small shower head as fast as possible. Water was too precious to waste. He felt alive again. He braced a small mirror up on the tank and started to shave using a helmet as a sink.

One of the newbies, Wells, came up to him, "Sarge, can I talk to you?"

"Would you mind if I finished my shave and got dressed first? I don't like talking to guys while I'm naked. One of you guys might get a weird idea. Give me a second." Liberty finished shaving, put on shorts, socks and pulled his dirty jungle fatigues back on. As he was pulling on his pants he turned to Wells and said, "Okay, go ahead."

"Sarge, I'm really scared." Wells was so nervous he was shaking. He was a pimply faced kid about nineteen; the sweat was running down his body making red streaks while mixing with the red dust that covered his body.

Liberty looked at him intently then smiled and calmly said, "We're all scared Wells. If you weren't scared, that would make me very nervous."

"Sarge, Sarge, I've never been in combat before," he blurted out. "I don't know what to do. I can't kill anybody. I can't shoot anybody. I'm gonna get killed." His lips were quivering, and his eyes were welling up with tears.

"You're the new driver on Shortround's vehicle, right?"

Wells nodded.

"Look, you're gonna be okay, just do what Shortround tells you to do and suck it up," he said firmly. Everyone has to die someday but today is not your day. I can tell from your face. You're scared but you'll be okay. You've got to be careful and help by shooting your weapon. You *can* kill the gooks. Ever been hunting Wells? You just have to pretend they're ducks and you're out hunting. You shot your weapon in training, didn't you? If you don't kill them - they will kill you. If you don't try to kill them, then they will kill you or one of the guys around you. Everyone has to do the best they can. It's the only way we will all survive but we must depend on each person to do the very best they can. We're all together in this thing and we all want to go home in one piece"

"But Sarge, I'm really scared."

Liberty answered sternly, "Knock it off Wells. Listen to me. We're all scared. The chances of you dying are less than if you were driving a car back in the states. Over fifty thousand people are killed on our nation's highways every year. You're better off here than in the states driving over to your girlfriend's house. Look, I am going to do my job, Shortround will do his job and you are going to do your job. And with everyone doing their job this will be a piece of cake and we all will be laughing about it tomorrow morning."

Suddenly it seemed to register in Wells' mind, Liberty might be right. He stopped shaking. He looked at Liberty, took a deep breath and you could see his whole body relax. "Okay Sarge, I'll try"

"Don't worry; you're going to be fine." Liberty lowered his voice, "Let me give you a secret." Wells leaned forward to hear this valuable secret better. "Get a second weapon. You've got an M-16 right?" Wells nodded. Get a second one and keep it with you and get plenty of ammo. That way, if the first 16 fucks up, you've got another at the ready. Nothing worse than having your weapon fuck up, and you must fight those bastards hand to hand. Even try to get a 45 – just in case. Okay?

"Okay, Sarge, thanks for the secret," Wells said, sincerely feeling better and thinking Liberty was his new God and protector.

"Now go back and get your weapons and listen – really listen to Shortround, he's a good trooper and he's stayed alive for a long time. Now go help him out. And pay attention to him! Got it?"

"Got it Sarge. And Sarge, thanks." Wells headed back to his ACAV.

After he was out of earshot, Cooper came around the corner of the vehicle where he had been eavesdropping and said to Liberty, "He's a dead man. I had to laugh when you told him he would be safer than going to his girlfriend's house. Man, you can really twist those numbers around."

"Knock it off Coop, he'll be fine. Give the guy a chance. If I remember correctly, I think I even gave you a chance once.

"Ya, you're right. You do have a silver tongue Sarge. What's that 2 - 2...expression of yours?"

"Two per cent of the people think - two per cent of the people think they think - and the other ninety-six per cent are waiting for a leader or a Messiah to lead them to the Promised Land."

"What's he?

"He's a ninety-sixer. Did you really have to ask?" Liberty said sarcastically.

At 1300 hours four Huey helicopters arrived, blowing the red dust into a huge cloud everywhere in the clearing next to the circled tanks and ACAVs, bringing in the resupply of ammo and a hot meal. The men gathered for their meal shortly after the Hueys left and the dust settled. The men scooped out hamburger patties, mashed potatoes, green beans and a piece of cake from the food canisters and plopped their food into a single sloppy pile in their mess kits. They made their way back to their vehicle or tried to find a comfortable spot on the ground to sit and eat. A few men had hung hammocks and slung ponchos above to provide shade between the vehicles. They returned to them to eat and catch a nap. The mood was somber and quiet. You could hear the scraping of the spoons on the mess kits. After the food, everybody rested as best they could.

There was no escaping the hot, broiling sun. When you were in the field it was a never ending, always hot, always dusty, always with one hand near a weapon. There was an exception – the rainy season. During that period the rain came by the gallon and everything was always wet and moldy, always with one hand near a weapon. There was never that beautiful spring day. Either it was pouring rain with everything soaked or the hot sun making everything excruciatingly unbearable. Seconds were minutes, minutes were hours, hours were days, and days seemed like months. And with each second everyone had to be always on the alert and ready for the next firefight. There was no rest. If a person could get two or three hours of sleep per day it was a miracle. It was always hot days and nights and even hotter when they went on patrol. They were stuck in their vehicles which were even hotter due to the engines running. Diesel fumes filled their nostrils and lungs. They were just living and working in their iron coffins.

The 11th Armored Cavalry had just seen very heavy action nine days earlier. They had lost eight of their troopers in a heavy firefight just to the south of Quan Loi. The men were well aware that getting hit again so soon was not good. There were a lot of new replacements and replacements were dangerous. The replacements filled the eight vacant slots and the five short timer's slots of those who had rotated back to the states. The newbies were green, not use to combat, didn't know their

25

jobs and never knew what to do. Short timers wanted to stay as far away as possible from newbies.

A whistle blew, and everyone slowly arose and went back to work, digging in their positions. Sergeant Liberty had five ACAVs under his command. He walked from one to the other, stopping to talk to everyone and asking where their position was and checking their weapons and ammo supply. He walked the line checking claymores, flares and trip wires. The day passed slowly. The baking sun made everyone move slowly. Liberty checked in with Lieutenants Casson and Shaw, the other two group leaders to each side of his platoon. Looking carefully to make sure they were ready and talking to the men on the adjoining vehicles.

At five p.m., Hegeman, Cooper, Fiestas and Shortround showed up at Liberty's ACAV. They brought folding lawn chairs, and each had a bottle of their favorite liquor. It was a tradition Liberty had started. It was a time to forget the war and talk of all the things they wanted to do when they got back to the real world. They formed their own circle, made their drinks and the conversation started.

"Hey Sarge – Is college hard?" Shortround broke the silence.

"It's harder than killing people. You barely have to think to pull a trigger and put another body in the ground. Don't worry Shortround; you'll just have to think. Seriously, there is nothing worse then what you are going through now. When you get back to the states, EVERYDAY...WILL BE ICE CREAM! War is just an exercise in futility. Some asshole named Johnson, excuse me, President Johnson, started this war because it was good for the economy and good for his re-election. Then he had a brain fart and realized he was wrong. That's when Nixon took over. I think Nixon is trying to bring this silly war to an end and we will all go home - heroes - well not heroes, just fucken idiots who got caught up in this crazy war. College - ah, that's a drop in the bucket - you'll have more fun and a lot of coeds to suck your dick."

"Heroes? There protesting everywhere. I don't think this lovely experience is something I want to mention to anyone." Shortround said as he sipped his drink.

"Relax my fat little Negro friend" Richie interjected.

26

"Black!" Shortround angrily shot back.

"Whatever, my fat little '*black friend*'. I wish you people would make up your minds as to what your race wants to be called. This is all a just a bad dream, and some day you will wake up and be sitting at the breakfast table with your mother and ask her 'to pass the fucken sugar.' That's when you will know it is over. After she whacks you alongside the head with a frying pan," Richie said laughingly.

"Sarge, what are you going to do when you get back?" asked Coop.

"Well, first, I'm never going to bed at night again without a woman next to me. Sleeping with you guys every night is about the worst thing I can think of. There's no sex and only thing you guys do is fart. To me, that's just no fun," Liberty said in a melancholy way.

"Don't worry Sarge, we're all going home with you, so you won't miss us," said Richie.

"Where are you going home to, Sarge? Shortround asked.

"Switzerland" Liberty said without hesitation.

"Why Switzerland?" asked Cooper.

"Because they forgot to invent wars there. They are really good at chocolate, watches and banking. So that is where I want to be. The murder rate is low there, not like here. Killing people is wrong, but someone has to make that call. There are plenty of bad people everywhere and bad people don't deserve to live. Unfortunately, the people we are killing aren't bad – just trying to have peace in their country."

"How did this war start Sarge?" Shortround asked.

"Well, they have a long history of other countries trying to take them over. I think the Chinese started it, but just before us, France wanted this as a colony for the resources, mostly for the timber and the rubber. Remember when we were in the Michelin Rubber Plantation? That's a French tire company that wanted to own the country. Then the powers in France decided to keep the power, the country and the rubber. Well, the French are good at cooking, but Ho Chi Minh, the Vietnam leader in the north, didn't want the frogs running his country and wanted their independence, like we did against the British. So, Uncle Ho led his boys and beat the shit out of the French at a place called Dien Bien Phu. Then years later, Eisenhower tried to help a little but wanted to stay out. Then Kennedy tried to help the South fight a civil war or some such thing. Then Johnson really escalated the whole thing starting in '64. He needed help with the economy at home – And what's really good for the economy? A good war! So, now we are up to over a half million of us fighting a bunch of aggressive, nasty, militaristic rice farmers, who are trying to take over the world in the name of communism - because some fucking idiot in our government thinks that communism is like some contagious disease...and by God...America's wonderful boys are going to save the world from this terrible infectious disease. Hopefully, our new President Nixon is trying to end this fun excursion to Disneyland East."

"Aren't we going to win the war Sarge?" asked Fiestas.

James started laughing. "Win? Lose?... Winning Losing...There is no difference in war. Remains to be seen, but I don't think we can win like we did WW2. Korea didn't come out so well. We take an area for a while then the gooks come back in and take it over again. There is too much corruption, greed, egotistical politicians, stupidity or something."

James' speech became very serious and pensive. "Oh ya, let's see...politicians...What we should really do is sacrifice one congressman a day until the war is over. Just take one a day out behind the capital building and shoot 'em. Do it by the lottery system so it is fair. If we and all the other countries did wars that way, I'd be willing to bet wars would never get to the second day.
Can't you see the evening news now with Walter Cronkite...?" James lowered his voice trying to imitate Walter Cronkite, *"Good evening, Ladies and Gentlemen. - In the Vietnam War today, Senator Talks Too Much from the state of Stick It To You was selected by his numbered ball being drawn at random in the war lottery. He was the first Congressman chosen by the new lottery system. He was escorted out behind the Senate Office Building by members of his own party and shot by Vice President Agnew. The Vice President needed four shots to kill Senator Talks Too Much because it appears the Vice President is a bad shot.... - In related news. In North Vietnam today; Communist Leader Ho Chi Minh shot*

28

Senator Wham Bam Thank You Mam from the province of Dead Dick. Ho only needed one shot but used a second shot just to be sure the senator was killed properly as specified in the new rules of the Geneva War Engagement Convention Treaty signed by all nations... In late breaking news – The war between the United States and North Viet Nam officially ended today when all elected government officials of both countries signed and agreed to an everlasting Treaty of Peace."

"Now, that's the way a war should be run instead of the way we do them now. And another big problem of this war is the other team isn't wearing game jerseys. You don't know who to kill. The other team, our enemy, the bad guys are made up of men, women and children from the north and south, and they are mixed in with the South Vietnamese men, women and children good guys. So, all you are allowed or can do is kill whatever, whoever is in front of you. That's the fun of war. A whole bunch of innocent men and sadly women and children are going to get killed and they don't deserve it. It's what the military calls collateral damage. Just a fancy label but it is just another term for murder. This is so our great, wonderful, intelligent, military minds – boy that's an oxymoron – can justify the killing of innocents, and then are great and wonderful leaders can sleep at night. It is easier for the heads of governments to go to war, than it is to sit down at a table and talk things out. Instead they throw the people of the countries into a blood bath. I say, put the heads of government in a fire fight against each other and see how they like it. If their asses had to be on the line, I don't think they would be so quick to pick up a gun. I bet they would talk long and hard before they had to spill their own blood. Good people shouldn't have to suffer and die because a group of non-combat participating people make the decisions for those who have to go do the dirty work. From the beginning of time the only thing we have done is kill people. The rest of the stuff we do is just to fill in the spaces between the wars and get ready for the next war. Something is wrong...I just don't know...all I know is I get paid to kill whatever is in front of me..." Liberty's voice faded, and a strange glazed look came over his face... "Just kill the bad guys...don't ask questions...just kill the bad guys...bad guys deserve to die...and in the case of war, even if they are the good guys...War and peace...Too much war and not enough peace." Liberty was mesmerized...he was in a trance...talking out loud but talking to no one...staring into space and only talking to someone in his head. He went silent.

The group just looked at him in awe and was quiet. They started looking at each other not daring to speak. Some did not really totally understand what he had said or meant, and no one wanted to continue his conversation or add to his thoughts. Finally, someone told a joke and the subject changed. Liberty finally stopped staring into space and mentally returned to the group but didn't say anything more and no one dared to say or ask anything of him. The cocktail hour went on with the normal talk of women, sex and future times. Their special grouping for cocktails slowly broke up after a respectable hour. No one spoke of what was about to happen. Everyone headed back to their vehicles and their dinner of a cardboard box of C Rations, after which they prepared for the coming night.

The sun slowly started to leave the sky and head for its night time bed. The sunset was beautiful with streaks of purples and pinks. Shadows grew in length and then the light slowly faded to darkness. Liberty climbed into the turret of his ACAV and started cleaning his 50-caliber machine gun. He talked quietly to his men, while checking out the flat plane of the field in front of them and then studying the tree line some 300 meters on the other side of the field in front of him. He was satisfied everyone was in position and ready. His eyes were becoming accustomed to the dark.

By ten p.m. you could hear a pin drop. Two men stayed awake on three hour shifts while the other two men tried to sleep. Liberty had taken the first shift with Georgia, a young country boy who had been with him on the ACAV for a few months. They talked quietly to each other while studying the field in front of them, looking for signs of movement. Over the radio in James' commo helmet came the order came for a "mad minute" at 10:55 pm. Everyone was to fire outward from the circle of vehicles toward the tree line for sixty seconds. At ten before the hour in a whispered tone he woke Ellis and Bourassa. He told them what was going on and to get their weapons ready for the sudden burst of firing which was about to happen. He warned them not to waste more than about a hundred rounds.

At 10:55 all hell broke loose. The mad minute started. Thousands of tracer rounds suddenly burst outward from the circle of vehicles. A thunderous roar of gunfire came from the weapons. Rounds covered the field in front of them and peppered the wood line. The willy-peter mortar flares were shot into the air and slowly floated down, lighting the area up like a high school football night game. You could not hear yourself think. Liberty first fired his 50-caliber machine gun, then the two M-16s, which hung from the turret and ended the mad minute with firing two clips from his 45-caliber pistol he always kept on his hip. It ended at 10:56 as suddenly as it had started. If there was anyone in front of them before the mad minute – there wasn't now.

Liberty reloaded the weapons and checked his ammo supply. He assigned Ellis the 50-caliber machine gun. He then crawled into the forward area of the ACAV, got into a hammock and immediately fell asleep.

He awoke when he heard the faint radio going off in Ellis' commo helmet. He shook Georgia then pulled himself up by Ellis in the turret. "Another mad minute?" he asked Ellis.

"No Sarge. Fiestas thinks he has got something creeping up on his side. He asked for flares. They're going to launch a bunch of them."

"Fiestas is always a little jumpy. He's probably seeing things again." Liberty stayed and waited, looking into the darkness.

Suddenly there were the sounds of flare rounds being dropped into mortar tubes, scraping the metal sides of the tube as they went down, then the dull sudden explosion of the round as it started its journey upward into the black of night. There were a few quick seconds of silence, then the POP of the flare. The whole area suddenly became day. It revealed hundreds of gooks heading for their encampment.

"Holy shit! – everybody get it going!" Liberty yelled. He had never seen so many gooks in an open field. They were everywhere, charging toward their circle. Once the flares had ignited, the whole world exploded at once; machine guns, claymores, rifles and grenades all going off together. Bullets were bouncing off the vehicles as everyone fired into the oncoming onslaught. Bodies in front of the tanks were dropping but not fast enough. The charging mass of humanity got closer with every second. Liberty grabbed his M-79 grenade launcher fired as many rounds as he could get off then realized they were too close, and then went back to his 50-caliber machine gun.

31

A sting to his right shoulder pushed him backwards. He ignored it and kept shooting. They were like ants – just everywhere. He fired his 50-caliber but realized they were getting too near and there were too many of them. He grabbed his M-16 and started firing. Liberty put clip after clip into his M-16, emptying each one as fast as possible. He couldn't find any more clips. He pulled out his 45 and waited and looked for a shot at the first body he could find.

A gook got to the front of his ACAV. Liberty and the gook made eye contact. An eternity passed between their eyes, both knowing that life was not in the cards for one of them. The gook raised his AK-47 and aimed it toward Liberty. Before the gook got his bead on Liberty, Liberty's 45 fired, hitting the gook in the forehead. He shot him a second time in the head just as he hit the ground. Liberty watched him drop. A huge feeling of warmth flowed through James' body and a massive sense of fulfillment came upon him. He paused for a brief second and thanked God. 'Nothing hard about killing,' he thought, 'it just keeps getting easier and easier with each one.' He then looked for the next closest target.

The shooting was intense. It seemed like it would never end. Bodies were dropping everywhere, some just dropping, some exploding apart, and some being hurled backward. Blood was being splattered everywhere while pieces of bodies were being separated from their owners. The firefight lasted another 10 minutes before the NVA sounded a whistle for retreat. They retreated as fast as they had charged. What seemed to be hours was over in fifteen or twenty minutes, and the field in front of them was empty except for hundreds of bodies. Everyone held their breath, knowing there could be a second charge on their position. All you could hear was everyone scrambling to get more ammo, and the reloading of the weapons. The next charge never came. The flares kept the area well lit, yet there was not another onslaught.

"Is everyone okay? Sound off! Liberty screamed. Everyone answered by name and the replies came back from everyone as okay. They waited with no one talking just listening for any sound. The silence was broken by the static and sounds from the radios and como helmets asking for reports.

Georgia came up to Liberty. "Sarge you're hit. Medic!" he screamed.

"Shut the fuck up," Liberty retorted.

"But Sarge..."

"Pay attention to what's in front of you!"   Liberty pulled out a bandage pack, pulled his shirt back and covered the squirting, bloody wound as if it was a mosquito bite. "Georgia, get me my bottle of scotch." Georgia handed it to him. He took a long swig from the bottle while holding the bandage in place over the wound, then he smiled and ceremonially put the top back on the bottle with his free hand and then when he picked up the bottle - he dropped it. As it shattered on the metal floor plates of the ACAV, Liberty slumped over - passed out.

*****

James slowly opened his eyes. He was looking up at the dim gray sky, which was just starting to see first light. He was lying on a stretcher. "What the fuck happened?" he slowly asked looking for anybody to answer the question.

"You just got grazed in the shoulder, Sarge. I guess you lost some blood and passed out," Richie said kneeling down beside Liberty. "The medic gave you a pint of good scotch to replace the blood you lost and bandaged you up. Sorry, but you're not getting a ticket on the freedom bird for a baby scratch like that. They are going to medi-vac you out on the next chopper back to Long Bien hospital where the sweet nurses will take care of you.

"Fuck that," Liberty growled sitting up. "What happened last night?"

"Nothing more, they turned tail and ran away. We got real lucky. There was a shit pile of them too. The Captain says Cassons squad is going out at point to chase them today."

Liberty got to his feet. "Everyone okay – anyone hit?"

33

"Just you Sarge," Richie said. "Three other guys got wounded, none of our squad. All worse than you, but they will be okay. They will be flying out with you. You pissed me off Sarge." "How's that?"

"Well my dad runs a funeral parlor back home in Maine. I thought after you got hit I had a body I could practice on. I'm gonna work for him when I go home. Since you have been a good friend to me here, I'm gonna give you a great discount when you take the big dirt nap."

"Gee thanks Ritchie. I don't know what to say. I suppose you want payment now."

"Well, I'd appreciate it. It would really make my Dad proud to know I am already out there marketing and making money for the family business. Business is a little slow in Maine...not enough people dying...and the population isn't that great. We've got to get the business anyway we can."

Liberty shook his head, laughed and said, "Get the fuck away from me, you ghoulish bastard." He then walked around checking his men for himself, making sure they were all right. After he checked all the men in his squad, he headed for the command post.

Liberty came upon Captain Murphy. "Hey Cap, how'd we make out?"

"Just four wounded. We are moving south down the road ten clicks. Lt. Casson is going to scout it out and take point. How did you make out? You okay? I hear you're being medi-vacked out," the Captain asked.

"I'm fine and my guys are fine. I'm not going anywhere. It was just a scratch. The medic patched me up. Hey Cap, let me take my guys out for point instead of Casson."

"No, it's his turn."

"Captain, he will get them all killed. That fucken Lieutenant couldn't lead a shit out of his own asshole."

"Look Liberty, he's got to learn and it's his turn. Let him take the point. We're only moving down about 10 clicks."

"Captain, he doesn't know what he's doing. He's an idiot. Whoever gave him that bar on his shoulder should be shot. He has already lost – what- three or four guys in two months. I haven't lost anyone. Let me do it. I need to take a ride and get out of here for a while."

"Liberty you're a hard-headed mother fucker. Okay, go ahead. Move your guys out as soon as you're ready." The Captain realized Liberty would do a better job. Liberty was use to the point and would give them a better recon of the area. "Keep in close contact with me and stay out of the shit. We've lost too many guys lately."

"Got you covered Cap." Liberty smiled as he walked away back to his squad area. He reached his ACAV and told his men they were taking the point and moving out ASAP.

"Wells," Liberty yelled. "Go cut me a couple of heads and put em on stakes. Then paint their faces with the green paint and mount them on the front of my ACAV."

"WHAT? WHAT? I will not. That's sick," Wells said looking like he was going to throw up.

"Just do it Wells," Liberty said sternly.

"I will not," Wells said defiantly.

"Oh yes you will."

"Why Sarge, why?"

"Because you idiot, the gooks scare easily. They have some notion that if we steal their heads and paint them green their souls can't go to the great beyond or some such deal like that. When they see us coming with those mounted heads they will run the other way which is what we want. We don't want any contact today.

"I can't do it Sarge," said Wells in a crying way.

35

Liberty walked over to Wells, put his arm around him and slowly walked Wells and himself away from the others. "Now Wells, you listen to me. You are going to do this because it must be done. This is important, so you will do it. Let me tell you what happens if you don't... First, I put you under arrest for disobeying a direct order. Then I have you staked to the ground, so you can't escape, which just happens to be next to an ant hill. I then have the mess Sergeant, who is a friend of mine, pour honey on you. The ants love honey and after they have their fill of you, I will let you up, if there's anything left of you, and put you on a chopper to fly you to the LBJ ranch – that's the Long Bien Jail - stupid. Then the Military Police will beat you with rubber hoses all day long. After a few months, they may get to your trial and maybe with a little luck you will only be sentenced to one or two years of very hard labor and then given a dishonorable discharge, and no one will ever like you again. So, you see, I am only looking out for your very best interests, so go get a machete and start chopping some heads or save me some time and go get me some honey."

Wells looked at Liberty with fear, very wide-open eyes and looked like he was going to puke and answered, "Okay Sarge, I'll do it but it's going to make me sick."

Liberty shoved him towards Shortround. "Hey Shortround, square this trooper away. Make sure he gets me a couple of good looking heads and make sure he really jams the stake deep into the heads. I don't want them falling off this time."

"You got it Sarge." Shortround and Wells wandered out in front of the tanks to find some bodies.

"Hey Wells," Liberty yelled, "You're just here to kill people - so stop taking it so personally. Get use to it. You just have to relax and learn to enjoy it. Killing people can be fun!"

Chapter Three
Present Day – South Florida

"Hey Boss - you missed something really good," Jason, the electrician, yelled as James walked down the street of the construction site. James had just arrived from an off-site meeting with the project developer. As he walked down the street, everyone seemed to yell at him making some remark or wisecrack. James was confused as to why this sudden outpouring of remarks was directed at him. There were over a hundred workers on the site, each yelling to him, cat calls, jeers, laughing, joking. They all seemed like they had something over him. A secret he did not know about.

James walked the length of the site. There were over thirty buildings, all under construction – some near completion – some just starting. The forty-million-dollar site was a beehive of activity. Located on a sandy, fifteen-acre site in Stuart, Florida, there were thirty-five different construction trades, all working at building an upscale housing project. Concrete trucks, delivery trucks, pick-up trucks, cranes and workers' cars were clogging the twenty-foot-wide road which ran down the middle of the site. He barked orders to them as he walked. The men weren't listening to him – just giving him the business. Whistling, laughing and smiling at him. They were saying he was the luckiest man in the world. "I wish I was in your shoes boss!" "Hey boss – fix me up if you don't want it." James was confused, questioning, wondering why this sudden change had come over the men.

James had his own different, creative management style. He demanded respect from all the workers and got it. All the workers liked him. He was smart and savvy. He was older than most. James' six-foot, rugged, athletic frame, sandy brown hair and clear skin did not reveal his age. He looked ten years younger than his mid-fifties age. Everyone was always surprised to learn he was old enough to have served in Viet Nam. He always had a smile for all and a gleam in his deep, dark, blue eyes. James became your friend first and worked with his people to make sure everyone succeeded at their work. It was his attitude of success for all that made everyone realize; he was your partner and not your boss. He was a winner, a survivor – a trait he learned in Viet Nam which stayed with him his whole life.

His thirty years of construction experience were respected by all. This was his life. He was in control, he called the shots. He could make your life miserable if you were on his bad side. If you stayed on his good side, he would do anything for you to bring you success. James controlled not only the workers, but the flow of work and most important, the flow of money throughout the project. He was responsible as the final word on everything. James reached his large office trailer and went inside to feel the cold blast of air conditioning. Florida construction sites were always hot, but only James and his secretary enjoyed the air conditioning, one of the pleasures of being the boss. He and his secretary, Beth, were the only ones comfortable in the hot, humid, South Florida heat and humidity. He walked into Beth's office at one end of the trailer and grabbed a cold drink out of the refrigerator.

"What's up Beth?"

Beth looked up from her work and gave James an icy stare. "Nothing," she shot back.

"What the fuck is up with everybody? What's up with you? Everybody on this site is acting weird."

"You don't know - you prick?"

"No, I don't. Would you please explain," he asked her? "And don't call me a prick please. I didn't do anything to you."

"Ya - that's one of the problems around here," she said sarcastically.

Beth had only been in the field office for about four months. She had been transferred to the field from the main office to help James as his administrative assistant. She was a short, sexy, fiery, long haired redhead with a very desirable body, accented by large breasts, shapely legs and a cute face that made her very attractive. She had made it very obvious many times she wanted to have an affair with the boss. James had kept his distance. He knew from previous personal experience the problems office affairs created. He knew all too well from many secretaries he had taken to bed in the past.

38

"Would you please knock that shit off and tell me what happened while I was gone."

"Okay'" she sighed. "Mike, the electrical inspector, showed up with these two sluts. He took them all over the site looking for you. Then he brought them in the trailer for a cold drink and let those whores use the bathroom. They couldn't even speak English. I should have made them use the sani-cans on site. They probably put some weird disease on our toilet. I'm going to go Clorox that toilet right now."

"Would you please stop that shit and tell me what the hell is going on."

"He wants you to call him as soon as you get in."

"Was there something wrong with the inspection?"

"No, I don't think so. He signed off in the inspection book, but he was all smiles and giggly. Probably it was something to do with those sluts." Beth paused and sweetly said, "I'll buy you a drink after work."

"I think I have to go home and straighten out my sock drawer," he said with a smile.

"Come on, we'll have a couple of drinks then I'll help you straighten your sex – I mean socks."

"Thank you dearie," he said smiling sweetly, "but I think I have enough problems at the moment, and I don't need the list to grow."

Beth stomped back to her office at the other end of the trailer.

James busied himself with the never-ending stack of paperwork. After an hour of paperwork and making telephone calls, he got a call from Mike.

"Hey Mike, how's it going?"

"You know James, I bring you a present and you are not even there," he said with attitude and male bravado.

39

"Present? What's my present Mike?"

"I told you. My wife's friend was going to visit. Her name is Vera and she's Brazilian, a blond bombshell, she's a knockout, honest. I brought her by the site today to let you meet her, but you weren't there. If she wasn't my wife's friend, I would go after her in a heartbeat. Why don't you join us for drinks tonight? We are going to try the Eagles' Nest for drinks and some dancing. Come on – join us. About nine, okay? Come on, try it, and give it a whirl. I lied and told her you were a great guy. I promise it's a good deal."

"No – You know I swore off women for a while."

"Well its time you got back on the horse. How long has it been since you've been laid, a year, two years? All that cum backs up in your brain and makes you go crazy. You gotta get it out every once in a while. Come on give yourself a break and besides I can't handle two Brazilian women at the same time. Brazilian women are little love machines. They will take you to task.

"Okay, okay, okay Mike," James sighed, "I will, but if she's a dog…I'm not going to stay long."

"Don't worry, she's noooo woof-woof – we'll have fun, honest. We'll be there about nine. Come find us, see you then."

James hung up and thought 'What have I gotten myself into now.' His thoughts turned to his last failed marriage. His life had been turned upside down by his last wife – his second one. He had married Susan, twenty years his junior. Susan was beautiful, intelligent, fun to be with and work with. She was beautiful, thin, and very glib, with a smile for all and a sense of humor that made everyone laugh. Her long dirty blond hair hung passed her shoulders and framed her angelic face with pale blue steel eyes. She carried her five foot-five-inch frame atop two beautifully shaped legs which appeared not to have any knees. Her smile melted everyone. Anyone who met her felt totally at ease in her presence. Along with her beauty she conveyed a feeling of magnetism toward all and all were drawn to her. James had been devoted to her.

Years earlier, Susan had fallen deep into the alcohol, then secretly started taking pills for anxiety and depression. The combination had been deadly. She went from a vibrant and wonderful person to a drunken, pill popping zombie. Drinking, from first thing in the morning till she passed out at night, mostly in secret and right under James' nose.

Once he realized he had a problem on his hands he tried to do everything possible. James put her in rehab centers, took her to doctors, shrinks, AA meetings, Al-Anon meetings and therapists over a two-year period but nothing worked. There had been so many trips to the emergency room at Martin County Memorial Hospital he had lost count. When he took her to the emergency room the staff would greet him by his first name. 'Hey James, what's up with Susan this time?' There had been black outs, sometimes when she fell she would crack her skull open as she hit the tile floor. Other times she would think she was having a heart attack, or she thought she had lost all feeling in her arm or her leg. These feigned ailments were real in her alcohol-soaked brain but were always proven out as not having any merit. It was only her imagination controlled by the pills and booze. When she did try to sober up or stop drinking she would start having convulsions. The doctors would fix her up, keep her at the hospital when necessary, and if she wasn't in too bad a shape they would let James take her home. They would give him Phenobarbital to administer to her to prevent the convulsions. He had to become her nurse, watch her sleep, give her soup when she would finally take some, then clean up the mess when she threw it up. It took days to sober her up. Finally, she could fend for herself and he would go back to work full time instead of running home every two hours to check on her.

It never lasted; Susan would come out of rehab or after a stay in the hospital, be sober for a very short while and then have a drink to celebrate her sobriety. Nothing worked. It was three years of hard work trying to keep her sober. Once he was able to keep her sober for forty-five days, but that was one rare occasion. Normally, sobriety lasted for only three, maybe four days. It had ruined her life and his. During the work day James would call her every few hours. If she didn't answer after ten in the morning, he knew that the liquor had won the day. He would come home from work to find her drunk and passed out.

Their twelve-year relationship was ruined. She responded to nothing, and only kept spinning and spinning downward into a deeper and deeper abyss of pain and anguish. There was nothing left of the beautiful relationship they once had. They couldn't even talk. She played him for the fool he had become. He kept trying to save her but nothing -

41

nothing ever worked. Their relationship was not to be. The sex wasn't even enjoyable even when it did happen. She only had sex because of her expected sense of marital obligation. He did sex to try and instill a sense of love back into their relationship and try to use the thought of their love to get her off the alcoholic train. The life spark of their relationship had been extinguished never to be again, but not in his heart. James kept fighting a losing battle with all his heart and soul.

The cost of her treatment through the years had taken its toll. At the beginning of the problem, James couldn't get insurance for her, at least not insurance that would cover her rehab visits. Susan had been put into rehab by her parents when she was twenty-one, and it was on her medical record. Because of this, the insurance companies would not fund a policy with an alcohol or drug clause. James had to pay everything with cash. He spent their savings and then had to sell their home to cover the expenses. It had been very, very expensive. The big-name rehab centers were thirty, forty thousand a month. The hospital bills were enormous. The doctors and shrinks were hundreds per hour. The medications were out of sight.

James made fun of the rehab places calling them "re-education camps" with a Chinese accent. That's all he could do - it was his way of handling these horrid situations. If he didn't laugh at these situations he knew they would eat him alive. He understood it as survival for himself and his wife. Each of these month long re-hab jailings were thousands upon thousands of wasted dollars always ending with the same no progress result.

James tried to save her and handle the problem without telling anyone their dirty little secret or the craziness of the situation. Susan made him promise never to tell her family. She hated her family and wanted to hide her disease from them. James did for the first two or three years. He suffered silently as she pulled him down to her level.

James tried to save her, thinking his past knowledge of dealing with his own mildly alcoholic father would give him the ability to solve Susan's problem. He thought he could save Susan and bring her back to a normal existence. James would take the car keys, credit cards and cash away from her so she could not get her poison. It was to no avail, because somehow, some way, she would always find a way to keep the booze flowing in her veins like a wild raging river. He did everything and

42

anything possible, even occasionally to drink with her, trying to find and get to or understand the psychological root of the problem to make her see the light. Susan, however, kept losing brain cells and made less and less sense with each drink. As the months of drinking turned into years, the situation just got worse. Then, when the blackouts started, she became more than he could handle.

She would hide alcohol in places only she and God knew. He would find those places, but she was always one step ahead of him in finding a new hiding place. Always finding a way to buy the precious alcohol her body screamed at her to buy. She hid booze from him in the freezer, in the linen closet, in the washer and dryer, and even under the guise of using washed out lotion bottles, Clorox bottles and anywhere else she could find where he wouldn't normally look. James became a cop, a security guard, a jailer and it proved out over the years he was terrible at it. He wanted to save the woman he loved, but he was proving inadequate. She could outfox him at every turn. He worked hard during the day, as he had to keep them financially afloat. She worked harder during the day drinking and had the whole day to find new and better places to hide her stash of alcohol poison.

He finally could not take anymore. Her parents, Nancy and John, were rich – filthy rich. They lived in Houston. They owned an oil company; they owned a bank, houses and yachts. They had maids, staff. They were at the top of Houston society. Against the wishes of his wife, James finally could not take any more emotionally or financially. He called Susan's parents for help. After a week of many conversations, Susan's parents agreed to help, but bring Susan back to their home in Houston. They sent Susan's two younger sisters over to collect her and fly her back to Houston. Susan flew back with them very drunk. James put her in a wheelchair and told the attendants she was mentally sick and heavily drugged, so she would be allowed to fly. After much discussion about a letter from a doctor which was lost and "Oops, I'm sorry I lost it, and this is the best we can do at the moment," they allowed Susan and her sisters to board the plane and head back to Houston.

The stay with the parents only lasted a few months, most of which was spent in a hospital. After Susan did sober up, she somehow talked everybody into giving her a second chance to return and live again with her husband. Six months later and after James had many more trips to the hospital, James and Nancy placed Susan in a rehab center in Ocala.

She stayed there for over nine months, only because she couldn't find a way to escape.

James was heartbroken but knew their relationship was over. He drove the eight-hour round trip every other weekend if only to spend a few hours with her. She was not the person he married. The divorce would be next, and he would end up alone without the woman he loved. He suffered with the depression for two years, never coming out of his shell. He had tried to date a few times, but it did him no good. He couldn't get Susan out of his mind.

Chapter Four
The Queen of Brazil

As James was finishing out the day doing paperwork, Beth came up behind him, and squeezed her large breasts onto each side of his head as he sat at his desk. "Want to see how big and hard you make my nipples?" she said sexily. "Want to see how hard I can make you?"

"I can already tell, you're about to break my eardrums – Thank you very much," he calmly replied. "Beth, maybe someday, but not today, okay? Go home and play with your husband."

"Bill is not my husband."

"Okay your boyfriend – the guy you live with – whatever," he said exhaustively.

"Are you going out with those sluts Mike brought by today?"

"Those *two sluts* were his wife and her friend. Give me a break, will you? Can't you get your mind out of the gutter? You are so crass; can't you clean up your language just a little bit? You would make a sailor blush…And so what if I do go out with them for a drink?"

"No, I can't. I say what I want. It's what everybody is thinking so why not say it. If you took me out for a drink at least you would know ahead of time you would score at the end of the evening," Beth said purring like a little kitten. "Come on let me take some after-hours DICK-tation from you."

"Beth. Look, I need another woman in my life like a fish needs a bicycle."

Beth sulked back to her office.

James worked on paperwork till 5pm. Everyone on the work crew had left by four. Only he and Beth were left on site save the security guard. Beth made one more impassioned plea for a drink after work.

James said no. Then they left the trailer, got in their cars and headed to their respective homes.

James checked his mail then took a long hot shower. He fixed himself a sandwich and decided to take a nap. The hot, humid heat of southern Florida always took its toll on the body. James decided if he was going to go out later, a short nap would rejuvenate him. At eight p.m. he awoke, dressed and got ready for the evening.

James arrived at The Eagles' Nest a little after nine pm. He could hear the rock and roll band as he got out of his car. He walked into the bar and waved at one of the bartenders he knew. He slowly strolled through the bar and went around looking for Mike. The place was jammed with people at the bar and every table was filled. He finally spotted Mike sitting with two women. He could tell right away Mike wasn't lying. The blond was beautiful. Even sitting he could tell she had all the right equipment in all the right places and a pretty face to boot. This might be fun after all he thought. He came up from behind her, bent over and started to give her a kiss on the cheek and whisper an introduction in her ear. Might as well get this party started quickly he thought. He didn't see the left hook coming as he startled her. Luckily her aim wasn't that good, and he took a fist to the shoulder.

"Easy darling...I'm your date for tonight, James said.

"I nao kiss who you are," Vera angrily and defiantly responded.

James apologized and then started an introduction. "I'm very sorry. Mike didn't tell me just how beautiful you really are, and I didn't know whether I should shake your hand or not, but I did have this overwhelming urge to kiss you instead. I'm sorry, I'm James Liberty from Stuart, Florida, USA and you must be Vera from Brazil and I still have an urge to kiss you."

"I let you shake hand and keep kisses to self. I nao kiss men I nao know and I only kiss men when I want," she arrogantly said with a beautiful, sexy accent.

"My apologies again my dear," James said with a big smile.

"I not your dear!"

46

"Look I apologize. I'm very sorry. Let me buy you a drink," said James trying as best he could to turn this situation around.

"I nao drink," Vera said stubbornly.

"Look I can't win for losing here. Can I get a break here?"

"I let you dance with me," she said haughtily without emotion.

They moved to the dance floor and started to dance to the rock music the band was playing. Vera was about five-foot eight inches tall, crowned with long blond hair set off in a pony tail which made her dark, blue eyes stand out. She was a photographer's dream. She had a very pretty soft face with distinct features. Her oval face had beautiful eyes with perfect skin, with a cute turned up nose, with soft and supple lips colored beautifully red. Her body was exquisite with a very shapely and curvy frame. Her breasts were large and moved gently against her body. Her nipples protruded through her bra and forced the dress fabric to reveal their large size. Vera's rear rounded outward, not too far and not too wide. James knew many women and he recognized perfection when he saw it. Her long shapely legs had great muscle tone in the calves going down to thin ankles and lovely feet. Every part of her was in perfect proportion. It was hard to find anything wrong with face or figure. James was fascinated by her immediately.

They danced for three songs. They watched each other dancing while everyone else on the floor and the surrounding area was watching Vera. James knew he was winning her head. She was impressed with him. A smile broke out on her face, she was watching him. She stopped dancing, leaned close to him and whispered in his ear, "You buy me drink – orange juice – now."

They went back to the table and tried to talk to Mike and his wife, Zulma, over the noise of the band. You had to yell but no one could really hear anything over the raucous sound of the band, all you could do was smile and nod. James ordered drinks from the waitress by yelling in her ear, she nodded and went to get them. Finally, the band decided to take a break. Everyone at the table started talking at once, relieved by the sudden quiet. Everyone then laughed and finally started taking turns. James was introduced to Mike's wife, Zulma, who was Vera's friend.

Vera sat back and watched James talk to Mike then she started talking in Portuguese to Zulma.

"Well I see you met Vera," Mike said with a broad grin on his face.

"You didn't tell me she was such a delightful person. Thank God, I still have my head. I thought she might bite it off," James said. "I've never apologized so much in my life."

"And you should," said Vera arrogantly interjecting into the conversation. "You nao polite. You be more polite to woman you never meet."

"I apologize again my dear."

"I not your dear!"

"Okay, okay, okay – I apologize. I am very sorry Vera. Would you like me to leave?"

"Nao, you dance well, I keep you for while," she said with a warm smile. "Maybe you get better."

Vera and James started talking to each other, ignoring Mike and his wife Zulma. James did not fully understand exactly what she was saying but it didn't matter. He was enthralled by her beauty, her intelligence and her cute accent. For the first time in years he felt a connection to a woman.

They danced some more, not touching, just watching each other. Finally, the band slowed the music and James took Vera in his arms. She just melted around him. He felt every part of her body pressing against him. They became one person floating together. He felt her supple breasts, nipples and long thighs press up against him. He felt her lips rub against his neck and Vera's head snuggled tightly into his shoulder and neck. Her hot breath was slowly blowing on his neck. He melted into her and felt a warm sensation in his loins. James felt the stirring and could not hide his erection as it grew rock hard between them. As Vera felt the pressure she just pulled her head back, looked at him, smiled then nuzzled her head back on his shoulder. The slow songs ended, and the

48

band picked up the beat. Vera grabbed his hand and said, "We don't need dance anymore" and led him back to the table with a smile.

During a break of the band, Mike suggested they go to a country and western bar in West Palm Beach. Vera got excited at the idea. James noticed her interest and seconded the motion, quickly found the waitress, gave her a hundred and turned back to the group and said, "Let's go."

They moved to the parking lot and James said to Mike, "Vera and I will follow you." They went to their respective cars as James opened the door for Vera and quickly ushered her into his car.

"Can trust you?" she asked coyly.

"I promise not to harm you."

As they drove, the conversation rushed from item to item. James tried to cover as much ground as possible. He was captivated. He tried to concentrate on his driving, but it was becoming bothersome to him. He wanted to pull over and just talk to this beautiful and glib woman.

"Where are you from?"

"Sao Paulo, Brazil"

"What do you do?"

"I research scientist, study yogurt. I used teach, retire now do research."

"Are you married?"

"If married, I not be in car with you!" she answered in a shocked way.

"How long are you going to be in the United States?"

"For week maybe."

"Do you have any children?"

49

"You are very – how you say – None of business"

James laughed. "I am being nosey. I am sorry. I just want to find out about you and what you are all about. It is just my way and I am suddenly fascinated by you." James suddenly was scared he was pressing the issues to fast. He didn't want to scare her off. He started to back off and started to pay more attention to the driving and following Mike.

"Don't you think me young to have children?"

"Well, I think you are young, but you do not have to be too old to have children," he said diplomatically. "How old are you?"

"You American men not polite. For information, I thirty-nine anos. I have two boys twelve and eight."

"What do you like about the United States?" said James trying to open up the conversation and soften her up. "I love your accent and you look too young to have boys that old."

Her long, blond ponytail bounced as she threw her head back smiling and laughing. "Now I think you are now to be nice. Thank you and I like United States, don't worry I am not trying to get Green Card and you not getting into pants."

"Easy, my dear. I am not like all the other American men. I must first get to know you better before we go there."

"Your country very nice. The roads very good, you have everything you want in stores and everything is easy." It is nice place to come to. I like San Francisco and I want see the cowboys in Texas. My Brazil is too muito beautiful and costs muito less. We have beautiful beaches, beautiful women and good food – I love. Better than Florida." There was a light arrogance and pride to her remarks. "Have you visit my country?"

"No. I have always wanted to see Brazil but have never been there. I have traveled to Asia, the Caribbean and all around the United States. I would like to see South America sometime. I have always thought Brazil would be nice because it is as big, about the same size as the United States, right?"

They pulled into the parking lot of the club and parked next to Mike and his wife Zulma. Mike paid the cover charge as they entered. The club had a big round dance floor surrounded by a drink rail where people could stand and watch. There were tables and three bars strategically placed so you were never far from a bar. The place was full of wanabee cowboys and cowgirls. "This is real west?" asked Vera.

James laughed. "This is just a place where people who like country and western music come to dance, drink, find women and pretend they are cowboys. I think most of these people are accountants and secretaries who work in the office buildings around here."

"I like country western – dance now?"

They moved to the dance floor and spent the rest of the evening dancing and small talk. The night passed in a flash for James. The band stopped playing and last call was announced just before one o'clock. James suggested some food but the other three begged off and said they were tired. They headed for the cars. James didn't want the evening to end. He suggested food again and heard the refusal.

Vera came close to him and said, "You are nice American man. If you want feed me, you take me dinner tomorrow night, if want."

"I want."

"Okay, call tomorrow and tell me time."

"I will."

She put her arms around him, kissed him quickly on the cheek and got into the back seat of Mike's car. Mike held his hands up and shot James a quizzical look as he got behind the wheel. James was still standing in the parking lot as they drove off watching them leave, feeling empty and unfulfilled.

*****

James was late to work the next morning. He went into the trailer and was quickly greeted nastily by Beth. A cup of coffee for him in her hand and a wisecrack, "All fucked out you bastard? Well, did you get some pussy last night? Did you fuck the bitch?"

James looked up and smiled, "No my foul mouthed little helper."

As Beth stormed back to her office she filled the air with stinging remarks. "Probably she couldn't get you up. Those hot Chiquitas are all talk and no action. You missed a great piece of ass last night. After work, I was so horny I came twice in my car – you bastard! When are you going to learn that what you need is staring you in the face every day? You'd rather fuck that Honduran whore than a great 100% American white woman. I'll teach you one of these days – you motherfucker."

James sighed and smiled then decided to let it go and get to work. As the day progressed his mind kept going to Vera. He could not get the remembrance of her face to go away. Her scent was still reminiscent in his nostrils. Her beautiful face, accent, blond hair, long legs, beautifully shaped ass and lovely large breasts were all he could think about. He waited till 11 am to call her at Mike's house. No answer. He went to lunch and tried to eat but wasn't hungry. He called again at one pm.

"Hallo," she answered.

"Hi Vera, how are you," he asked.

"Who call me?"

"This is James. Remember me from last night?"

"Yes, what you want?" she said stonily.

"Well remember we talked last night and we decided to go to dinner tonight."

She paused, "Tomorrow night – No tonight. I have plans, see friend tonight."

"But…"

"We part today - this morning – today, and I say tomorrow night. Okay, you come get me eight tomorrow night. I see you. Tchau James," she hung up.

James stared at the phone. The empty feeling in the pit of his stomach was making him nauseous. Oh well, he thought, at least I will see her then. He wondered who she would see. He wondered the rest of the day. The day dragged on.

His thoughts were only of Vera. He started to plan the next evening. 'Which restaurant?' He went through his list of favorite places. He decided on the 'Jettys.' No, it's in Jupiter; he changed his mind, too far away. 'I should keep it close here in Stuart and better yet, keep it in Port Salerno near the house – easier to get her to my bed. It won't happen if I have to take her back to Mike's place, no privacy. Okay that's it – I'll take her to 'Bare Bones' – good menu – nice table by the water – easy to go back to the house.'

A few minutes after the call, Beth strolled into his office. "Not going out with your Honduran whore tonight?" Beth said gleefully.

"No, I'm not and she's not a whore and by the way, she is from Brazil not Honduras," James shot back.

"Oh, I know all that - and okay - she is just your average Bimbo from Brazzzzille," Beth said stingingly. "So, my roommate is taking my kids out for pizza tonight, so we should get it on. You're soooo – soooo horny and I want to fuck you – big boy."

"How did you know?"

"Honey, this is a small trailer and I have ears like a hawk. So, since you're not going out tonight – let's give me a stab or two, huh?"

"Ain't gonna happen – *Hawk ears!*"

"You BASTARD!" as she stormed back to her end of the trailer.

James thought, I better be more careful around the office, she might be listening on the phone. Beth was good at her work but a real handful to deal with. He thought she must teach sailors how to swear. If he stayed away from her she will eventually get the hint and stop all this desire to have sex. If he had sex with her he would never be able to get rid of her.

James went home and decided to rest up for tomorrow night. He asked himself why did he always pick women who were challenging? Probably, because he appreciated good looks coupled with an intelligent mind. He liked to talk after sex, so he would always pick a woman who had a mind. You need to talk between sessions. To James, there was no challenge to just having sex and then going home. He always wanted to have sex more than once per session and he always tried to make sure the women were satisfied. He would rather make love than have sex. It had been a long while since he had any desire for a romance, but he was quickly remembering his needs and thoughts of what he liked and wanted. He loved to play with their bodies until he heard the moaning female sound of total satisfaction. He would search their bodies with his lips, his hands, and especially his tongue until he found all the spots on a woman that made her quiver in delight and fulfillment.

Through his life he had many women, too many to count. Women were easy. His good looks and a smile made sure he received more than his fair share. He had learned at an early age all he had to do was look them in the eyes and keep smiling. Men are too serious. Women like men who are happy and smiling. Women let their guard down and feel more comfortable with a man who smiles, compliments them on their good looks, tells them how smart they are and looks them square in the eyes. He had been doing it for years. It didn't work every time, but it was a numbers game anyway. A woman would always appreciate a man who smiled at them. It was that special recognition for the woman that she was attractive, desirable and the only one he wanted to look at in the room. Focus on one, smile at her, flirt and tell her how intelligent and special she is. It worked, and it worked well for James.

When he was young he tried many women. As James aged, he realized he preferred quality over quantity. He looked for that special woman, a woman that took his heart away. To share a warm and exciting love with a special woman was his greatest desire. There were so few special women. They were so hard to find. He had found Susan and from that point on she was the only one he wanted. After they were separated he had no desire for anyone. Years had gone by even though they were not divorced yet. But now this was different – Vera brought all those old feelings back in a rush…feelings that had been absent for years.

Chapter Five

Capturing the Queen

The sun rose Friday morning but not until after James had already had a pot of coffee. He went to work early and was on site before anyone else. There was a spring in his step as he walked the site checking the different areas of the work. He had made up his mind to pursue his new Brazilian Queen. She was intelligent, beautiful, spoke two languages, had a scientific mind and put heat in his loins. He had been without a woman for some time and this blond honey had reawakened a desire in him. Tonight could not come quickly enough for him.

As the site came to life, filling with workers, he greeted many of them, asking questions and getting a reading of how their work was going so he could schedule the future properly. He joked and kidded with the workers. A few remarked how happy he seemed. He wandered about the site until the canteen truck arrived. He had a cup of coffee and a doughnut, talked with the workers for a while longer then headed for his office.

The moment he walked in Beth was all over him. "Sounds like you think you're getting laid tonight."

"Are you able to read my mind?"

"Honey, you're an easy read. The only problem is you won't fuck me, or should I say you won't fuck me at this moment, but you will," as she turned and walked back to her office.

James went through the day, ignoring Beth and focusing on his work, trying to wrap up the work for the week. He left early, did some errands on the way home then showered and napped before getting ready for the night.

He was on time for his date only to find Vera "not ready" as he expected. Mike made him a drink and they made small talk. "I told you she was hot, huh?"

"Wow! Yes, she is, thanks. Tell me more. What's her deal?"

"No deal," said Mike. "She's Zulma's friend and she just decided to come and visit for a while. Zulma hasn't known her long. They met in Brazil a couple of years ago. If I could speak more Portuguese I could tell you more. She's a college professor, divorced for about five years and looking for a guy but I don't think it's a hard search at the moment. She's a good house guest, been seeing a few guys. After she meets someone new she moves on. All the guys seem to like her, but she seems to keep moving on to the next."

Vera and Zulma entered the room. To James, Vera looked look like a beautiful vision as she came across the room. She gave James a quick kiss on the cheek and whispered in his ear, "You muito handsome, I think good time tonight."

Zulma wanted to take some pictures and Mike wanted to print them out on his new computer program. James had to keep adjusting his pants, so he wasn't so obvious. Finally, after goodbyes, Vera and James headed for the car. James opened her door and Vera cooed, "I love polite gentleman."

"I'm the only one left my dear." James chatted, and Vera started asking questions of him. He avoided them for a few minutes and then said, "I will tell you everything you want to know after we get to the restaurant and I can look into your beautiful blue eyes."

They were seated in the restaurant at a table by the water. "Will you have a glass of Champagne or wine with me?" asked James.

Vera hesitated for a long pause, "I try one glass of wine."

James ordered a bottle of wine and Vera shot him a mad look. He smiled and said, "It's less expensive by the bottle and who knows you might want a second glass. You drink very little, that is good but is there any particular reason you don't drink more?"

She paused for a second, "Ex-husband drink much and drink more than should. He muito mean and nasty when drink. I nao like. Now tell me about nice polite American gentleman."

James slowly and carefully started to tell his story. "There is not much to tell. I was raised in a good family in Boston. I went to school

56

for Architecture and after I graduated I had to go in the Army and ended up in Viet Nam. I spent three plus years in the Army and a year in Viet Nam, was shot three times, came home and went to work in the construction industry. I married, had two kids, a girl then a boy. They are in their 20's now. I divorced after ten years of marriage. I rarely see my children; they are grown and gone taking care of their own lives. As a result, we don't have much contact. After a while, I remarried to a much younger woman and then after ten years she started drinking a lot and taking pills. I could not stop her. It ruined her and our marriage. Finally, we divorced, and it left me looking again for the perfect woman," as he smiled lovingly at Vera. He had mainly been honest, except for the painful divorce, dancing quickly over many of the details. Talking about his life was okay but he wanted to turn the conversation back to this new woman. During his whole story he watched her face and tried to read her feelings. She was sad about his story and he knew he hit some cords in her and she felt empathetic.

When she wasn't looking he refilled her glass. He wanted to loosen her up a little. When she turned and noticed the full glass, she angrily shouted at him, "What you do? You try take me – get me drunk so you put pinto in me."

James started lightly laughing, "No, no my dear. I am sorry. I honestly forgot you do not drink much. Besides, even if I fill your glass that does not mean you have to drink it. And furthermore, if I wanted to put my 'pinto' in you, I guess that means penis, I would just do that, with your permission, of course. I would not have to get you drunk. It is only a polite, bad habit and I will not do it anymore."

She looked him in the eyes for a few seconds and then laughed, "Okay, believe you - but nao put pinto in me."

Don't bet on that honey, he thought, I'm already there and you just don't realize it yet. "Come on, let's order, have a nice dinner and then I have a surprise for you."

She smiled with the thought of a surprise. They ordered dinner and laughed through the ordering process as James described what was on the menu. Her command of the language was good, but she still asked a lot of questions. Her pronunciation was good, but she could not always find the right word and she sometimes left a word or two out of a sentence. Her accent was cute and sexy. James was having the most fun in years.

They laughed through dinner and he continually complimented her on her language ability and her scientific genius. Occasionally, he would throw in some timely compliments on her intelligence, her beauty and her beautiful body. She just kept smiling and looking at him when she thought he was not looking. He filled some spaces with telling her about his house and his job.

He paid the bill and off they went to the car. "What is surprise for Vera?" she asked excitedly. James just stayed silent and smiled.

They drove toward a beach near his house and as they passed his house he pointed it out to her. He could tell she was curious. She took a long searching look at the house. They parked near the beach and walked across the sand to the water's edge. "You said you liked beaches, so I thought you might like a walk on a nice one." They took off their shoes and James rolled up his pants. They strolled along the water's edge. It was a beautiful night with almost a full moon rising over the water and a light warm breeze. The only sounds were those of the waves gently rolling on the shore and the sounds of bait fish jumping in the water.

He took her hand in his. She didn't resist. It was as if they had done the same thing a thousand times. They walked in silence with the small warm waves rolling over their feet. They reached a point of beach which jutted out into the water. The lights of houses far in the distance shimmered across the water from one direction and the moonlight lit the top of the waves from another direction. They stopped and turned towards each other. James put his hands on her hips, gently and slowly pulled her close. He looked in her eyes. The lights of the night were shimmering and dancing across their faces. He paused, reached up and held her face with his hands. James leaned forward and gently kissed her lips. After a few seconds he stopped and just looked in her eyes. She grabbed him around the waist and kissed him long and hard. He could feel her body relax and mold herself to him.

They kissed a third time holding each other tightly. He stopped, paused a minute then took her hand and slowly started walking back to the car. After a few minutes of walking he turned to her and softly said, "Are all the women in Brazil like you or am I just the luckiest man in the world? My body is trembling. What are you doing to me?"

Vera smiled and said, "I feel same way. Make love here?"

That was easy he thought. "No, not here. Come, we will go back to my place."

Not a word more was said. He helped her put on her shoes and guided her to the car. He opened the door for her as she slid in. He drove back to his house, they walked up the front walk as he fumbled for the keys opening the door. She followed him to the bedroom. He turned toward her and they kissed, a lover's kiss, soft, sweet and gentle. His hands deftly found the zipper to her dress and it fell to the floor. Vera wasn't wearing a bra. Her large breasts were firm with large areolas and hard, large nipples. James cupped her breasts with his hands then kissed each one squeezing the nipples with his lips and sucking them into his mouth. She took a deep breath and threw her head back. He quickly took his clothes off never taking his lips off her and holding her upright, not letting her fall. He kissed her breasts, her neck and her stomach while she breathed in deep sighs with eyes closed.

He held her in his arms and kissed her deeply. His tongue darted gently into her mouth with her tongue responding to his. He slowly pulled down her small panties and then laid her down on the bed. He reached down and gently took off her high heels, slowly kissing her legs and slowly working up her legs. His tongue guided his lips all over her legs, behind her knees then to the insides of her thighs and into the crevices where her legs met her torso. James kissed her vagina as Vera took a deep breath and held it as he continued.

"Please, please stop – put you in me…please now, now," she begged with a whimper.

James ignored her for another few minutes slowly kissing, sucking and licking her till she responded to his every touch. He then gently lowered himself on the bed between her legs, which quickly spread to accommodate him. He put one hand under her back then kissed her waiting mouth. His other hand reached down and felt her ready wetness. He guided himself to her waiting vagina and gently pushed inward. James moaned and then slowly went deeper and deeper inside of her. Vera made little soft whimpers with each deeper thrust. He was kissing her on her lips, neck and breasts while thrusting deeper and deeper.

"Meu Deus!" she screamed. Her legs wrapped around his hips as she quickly pulled him deep inside her. She squeezed him with every muscle in her body again and again. She exploded, her body shaking.

James stopped, still deep inside her and felt her shake and climax again while kissing her neck and lips.

She finally caught her breath and said, "You cum?"

He didn't answer. He started gently thrusting again. After he was all the way in, he started thrusting faster and faster. "Oh, Meu Deus, I cum 'gain," she screamed and her whole body shuttered again.

James didn't stop. Minute after minute he kept thrusting never stopping. Sweat formed on him and her while she kept the rhythm with every thrust. Finally, he came, exploding inside of her and afterwards holding very still and groaning, his eyes closed, and his legs shook. His penis kept pulsating and Vera moving with him. Finally, the throbbing stopped.

They were soaking wet with the lovers' sweat they had created. He rolled to the side getting his weight off her but still holding her tightly and staying inside her. He sweetly kissed her.

"I need smoke," she said.

"But Vera, you don't smoke," he said questioningly.

"I know...but now...know why...people smoke." They both laughed at her comment.

They laid there quietly looking at each other, not talking. James finally got up went to the bathroom and returned with a warm damp wash cloth and a towel. He sat next to her slowly running the wash cloth over different areas then toweling her body and after each area he would kiss her there.

After half an hour she smiled at him and reached down and felt his manhood. "I make pinto feel good." She started moving her head toward his penis.

"No," James said warmly and sweetly. "Tonight was just for you. I just wanted to make you happy tonight. Tomorrow night you can make pinto feel good."

"James, I want know what time is?"

60

"It is one am, Vera. Why do you want to know?"

"I want make sure I love you tonight not tomorrow."

They laughed, kissed and held each other, pressing their bodies so close they were one. They slept a lover's sleep with arms and legs entwined.

It was five am when James awoke. He slowly slipped from Vera's grasp so as not to wake her, went to the kitchen and started making coffee. As he poured two cups, she came up from behind him and encircled his waist. He felt her arms and her warm naked body next to his. He shivered as her hand went down to grab his new erection.

"I think noa Gringos know how make love to woman."

"They don't. Just me, my dear."

"I want thank woman who teach you."

They stood watching the sunrise on the porch, holding each other and sipping coffee. "I go back to house, shop with Zulma. You take me home?" she asked.

"Of course...but I do not want to," James said with a wry grin. He took her back to the bedroom and they made love again. James started kissing her and within seconds they coupled again holding each other tightly, moving together till they climaxed at the same time. She kissed him like he had never been kissed before. He felt warm and loved. He felt dizzy from the love making – like nothing he had ever felt before. Afterwards, they dressed, and he took her back to the apartment. "I will pick you up at eight tonight," as he turned and kissed her goodbye. She smiled.

Chapter Six

Susan

As James entered his house, the phone rang, and he picked it up. Hello," he said.

"Hello Baboo."

"Well hello Babyboo," he said as a warm smile and feeling came across his face and body. He stilled loved Susan. The pain of losing her was still great. "Well I see they are allowing you to use the phone again at the re-education camp. How goes it"

"Same old shit. This place sucks. I've completed my nine-month sentence here next week and they are going to let me out. I am allowed to get an apartment in Ocala on my own."

"Well that's wonderful. What do your parents say to that?"

"They don't know I'm going to do it. I hate those motherfuckers. If they knew, they would try to put a stop to it and keep me locked up for another nine months."

"How are you going to swing it without their knowing it," said James suddenly feeling like he was being used again. A pain started coming across his brain and his wallet. He knew where this was going.

"I was thinking that if you would help me get my feet on the ground, we could make a deal on the alimony once we are divorced."

"Hold it," said James with a serious, almost angry tone. "We've been apart for over two years now while you have gone from one of those re-education camps to another. I have been giving you money the whole time for whatever you needed so you wouldn't have to appear weak to your parents - whatever the fuck that means and it doesn't make sense. That crazy lawyer your parents hired hasn't even gotten the paperwork right while he has been bleeding your stepfather John out of as much

63

money as John can print. I know the lawyer is going to whack me for alimony even though as soon as the divorce is final, John is going to give you a nice big fat trust fund. It really pisses me off. Now you want me to give you more money to get set up behind their backs...NO!"

"Baboo, you know I love you. We can adjust the alimony between us - fuck the lawyer, fuck the courts and my parents. I just need to get set up, so they can't say no. I know, I know, you have been wonderful through all this, but I need the help. I haven't had a drink in over nine months. I'm not cured but I think I can stay on the straight and narrow. I need some help...please...pretty please...you know I love you...and I know you love me. Maybe, well, just maybe, we might be able to put everything back together again."

James went silent and sat down. She pleaded and begged some more but James didn't hear a word she said. His logical mind was racing over the past five years and all the pain he had gone through during her illness. The love lost, the time lost, the money lost, the hospitals, doctors and especially all the promises she had broken.

Then the angel side of him started telling his heart and brain how much he loved her and how sick she is, and it really isn't her fault. Alcoholism is one of the most insidious diseases that exists. The sad thing was she only knew about ten per cent of what he and she had been through. She had been drunk most of the time and never remembered what had happened. She had lived in a fog. Yet, he loved her. She was his wife – for better or worse – in sickness or health...

They had been lovers, business partners and a husband and wife team for over ten years plus five miserable years of pain and agony from the disease. They had one of those strange relationships that comes along only once in a great while, only once in a Blue Moon. They were joined at the hip, they breathed and exhaled simultaneously. They were one; everyone knew it, and many were envious of how wonderful a relationship between a man and a woman can really be. There were no fights, no harsh words, just the utmost of cooperation and respect for each other and for the relationship.

Of their fifteen-year relationship, it was only the third five years that became a train wreck. James had tried to save her. He ranted and raged. He took her to doctors, shrinks, hospitals and AA meetings. He took her to doctor appointments and he physically carried her to the emergency rooms when necessary. He tried everything he could think of to stop her from drinking. He thought he could save her from this menacing disease. What he would never face and would not accept is the fact - only she could stop her drinking, only after she hit bottom and only when she wanted to change her life.

He accompanied her wherever and whenever they went out because he had to drive, she couldn't. But, somehow, she was always able to get her hands on alcohol no matter what he did to prevent it. James had to work to support their lifestyle. This gave Susan time to get her hands on the alcohol and consume it in mass amounts. He would call her all day long and he quickly realized that if she didn't answer the phone after ten am it was all downhill from there. He would come home at night to find her passed out. He would sit in the living room, alone in the darkness with her passed out, trying to figure out what to do next to stop this frightening grip alcohol had on her and how it was killing him.

Once he hired a babysitter to stay with her but on the second day of this plan, he returned to find both Susan and the babysitter drunk. The babysitter said "I don't know how she got drunk. After she got drunk she convinced me to drink with her because it didn't make any difference and we would try again tomorrow. She's a wonderful person," she slurred.

That was the other major problem; Susan could talk people into anything. James saw her do this with everyone. From doctors and nurses to shrinks and just anybody. She had fooled her family for years. Her ability to tell stories and convince the listener she was telling the truth was amazing.

"Look Babyboo, you're just a rehab junkie. You haven't hit bottom yet and I fear that day. I hate to say this, but you scare the hell out of me. Everyone who has any knowledge of alcoholism has said to me they haven't seen anyone as bad as you."

"Baboo, I want you to trust me, no one else will and it is impossible to tell if I can stay clean unless I have the chance to try. Please help me, I can do this, please trust me. We can put our lives back together again, I know we can...Let me do this...I've got to get out of this crazy place."

He knew they would never be together again. James thought for a minute let out a long sigh and agreed. "Okay, one more time...how many times have I said this? What do you want or need?"

"I need you to sign a lease for me and I need a little furniture. First month and last month and I need a bed and a couch and a few odds and ends. I'll get a job right away then I can manage," she made it sound as easy as pie.

"Okay, I'll put the money in the account. Will two grand be enough?... On second thought, make sure that will do it, okay?"

"Yes, that will do it; everything will be wonderful, thank you Baboo. You'll see I'll be the new poster girl for clean and sober. I'll have the landlord send you the lease and just send it back."

"You had this all set up didn't you?" said James, feeling like a fool.

"Well ya, because you love me. Hey, I even feel like having sex again. I'm horny. I should be able to get it all set up by Wednesday next week. Can you come up and we'll have some fun?"

"Oh ya, let me drop everything, get fired and come up for a piece of ass. Hiring a hooker would save me a lot more money than funding you," James was painfully laughing.

"Don't you dare, you know I love you," she said with a sexy lilt in her voice.

"I'll come up as soon as I can. Okay let me go...You got what you want...now let me go cry...Bye-bye," James said with a sigh and hung up. James knew in his heart that it was far from over – her alcoholism or his love for her.

Chapter Seven
Pedro Then Beth

James spent Saturday doing errands. His mind went racing back and forth between the two women on his mind. Was it over with Susan? The pain through the years had been excruciating and the divorce was almost done. He knew it was time to move on with his life. He had been telling himself that for over three years. Now, was it starting with Vera? At least he had ended his sexual dry spell which brought a smile to his lips.

He decided to take a long lunch at his favorite Mexican restaurant, having his favorite dish accompanied by continual Margaritas while watching some nebulous college football game. The bar was empty on a beautiful sunny fall day. His favorite bartender, Pedro, made sure he got excellent service while they chatted. "You look happy boss. Get lucky?"

James smiled, "Ya, if we didn't have women around, we would kill each other. Ah…maybe I have that wrong…maybe if we didn't have women around…we would stop killing each other…Well anyway…You married Pedro?"

"Was." Pedro then went off like a rocket and started talking so fast James was having a rough time keeping up with him. "Went back to Mexico to visit my family last year and a friend of mine convinced my wife I was fuckin around in Mexico and then he told her I also had a girlfriend here. He even got some fuckin whore here to lie to my wife and tell her I was fuckin her on a regular basis. Then he started fuckin my wife. I came back, and she kicked me out, divorced me and now I'm payin child support, alimony and he's still fuckin her on my money, livin in my house. Nice friend huh? Now, my two sons think I'm a pile of shit and he is wonderful, cause he gives them all sort of toys with the drug money he gets – the slimy bastard.

James had never seen this side of Pedro. Pedro got hot and got hot real fast. James had a cynical smile cross his face, "Why don't you take him out?"

"I ain't goin to jail over that bitch!"

"Hey man, that's up to you but…when a man fucks you up don't you think you owe him a favor? You're not going to get any justice in the courts. When I was in Nam, we had our own way of justice. It's just a different way of looking at the problem and dealing with it so you achieve satisfaction. You have to take care of your own problems in life. If you depend upon the law or the legal system to work for you…Well, just don't hold your breath waiting, because you're going to turn blue. Remember the police only show up after the crime, not before or during. Then they try to figure out what happened. A lot of guess work. Sometimes it is obvious and sometimes they don't have a clue.

If you're careful, you won't get caught. Accidents happen all the time. You just have to make sure it looks like an accident and you don't leave any evidence. Or, if it isn't going to look like an accident, make sure…make sure it's a clean hit. Hey, your Mesican brothers do it all the time. And don't tell me you are lily white in your mind. Do it yourself, all alone, then no one knows and make sure the guy is dead. Dead men can't talk."

"Hey boss, that's pretty heavy. If I got caught, I'd be behind bars givin blow jobs and gettin my ass reamed, said Pedro laughing.

"Pedro, let me set you straight. Last year in this city there were 11 murders. Six were solved and that's only because they were witnessed by someone or the idiot who did them, did them out of passion or stupidity and didn't cover his tracks. Five people got away with the deal because they were careful, acted alone, when no one was around and there are also about five other people that just amazingly disappeared without a trace. Don't tell me you can't get even – you just have to be very careful – no evidence. You have to plan, be very patient and be very, very careful," James said this in a monotone voice while staring into Pedro's eyes. "Don't be emotional – Be logical – Be prepared and anticipate."

"You ever do it Boss?" said Pedro now being very serious.

"Look Pedro, if I had and I told you, I'd be breaking the no evidence – no witnesses rule. Then you would know, and it could come back to hurt me later. It just must be my little secret only known to myself. Just remember - plan, be very careful, no one can see you do it and most important never, never, ever tell anyone. Don't leave any evidence. Think it through, no fingerprints, no footprints, no ripped clothing, nothing left behind and no witnesses. And, you can be your own worst enemy by developing thoughts of guilt or remorse about what you have done. A guilty conscientious eventually will make people confess even when they know they don't have too. You have to be strong, control your mind. If it was worth doing, do it right, don't look back and the hell with the rest of the world. Nobody pays your bills. Don't hurt the innocents, just the miserable creeps that roam this earth in huge numbers.

Killing isn't a bad thing; it's all depending upon how you look at it. Men have been doing it since the beginning of time. It is built into your DNA. Look at all the wars there have been. Men like to kill. It proves their dominance and power. In business, adversarial companies will do anything to cripple, maim and put their competition out of business, just another form of killing. We want and have the desire to kill. We like to kill. How many times have you heard people say – 'I'm gonna kill you!' – How many times have you heard parents say it to their children? How many times have you heard it said between lovers, friends, any relationship? How many times have you heard it said on TV or in the movies? We shout it from the roof tops. Our society is designed to kill. Killing is so inherent within us; we really don't have an opposite. How many times have you heard? – I'm gonna let you live. We kill everything we can get our hands on – animal, vegetable and mineral. There isn't anything we don't kill."

Pedro was looking at James in a trance with his mouth wide open. Finally, he started to speak, but he had to swallow hard first, "Ya, I guess you're right but what about the Bible and religion and all that stuff?"

"The Bible pretty much starts killing when Cain slew Able. Then the stories go on and on about all the Kings who killed this group of people or that group of people. Do you want to talk about the killing of Christ? Or David and Goliath? Fuck! - I think the Bible should get pretty bad reviews. We have come two thousand years since Christ and nothing has changed except the weapons we use are getting better and better. We invented the Atomic Bomb – that was a doosie, or how about an M-16 or an AK-47 Assault Rifle. Ya, these things replaced sticks and stones. The society of this world hasn't learned a fucking thing."

Pedro jumped in to say, "Religion says it's a sin to kill. The ten commandments and all that."

69

"Religion, let me think, oh ya. All religions seemed to have failed this world. If they were any good, we wouldn't have the problems we have today. Religions are the same as any other group or nation. They hide under the cloak of righteousness. Religion has been responsible for more wars than countries. Popes have started and conducted more wars than I can count in the name of or the *need* of Religion. We could start with the Crusades or maybe the Romans killing the Christians for fun or how about the Inquisition? That was another goody for history. Too many people have lied in the name of Christ and too many people have died in the name of Christ. Religion just keeps people busy while giving them some kind of weird false hope.

How about Hitler wiping out the Jews because they were an inferior race? How about all the Indians in this country who were wiped out? There were over fifty million people killed in World War II alone. All over this planet, political leaders, religious leaders, tribes, sects, individuals, countries, mal contents, wanna-bees and has-beens kill in the name of money, power, territory, religion...give me a break...I don't have the time in my life to list them all or all their reasons. I haven't even gotten to things like drive-by shootings, gangs wars, cops killing the wrong person or the right person.

My friend, killing is just something we just naturally do. Let the punishment fit the crime. We kill because we want to, and we will rationalize killing somebody or something until we leave this planet. It is just human nature my friend. There are people out there on this orb of six billion people who deserve to die. They are just taking up space and valuable resources, not contributing anything and just hurting others. They deserve to die. Let me say that again. There are people on this planet who are shits, contribute nothing and fuck with good people. Those people deserve to die.

I bet you can very easily come up with a list of five people you would personally like to see dead. You won't do it because it is against your nature. However, I am sure there is at least one person on your list you really would like to see dead and you know that the world would be a better place without them. Fear of getting caught is what keeps you from doing it. Once you get past that fear – then you can do anything. We kill because we finally come up with a reason to kill. We just like to kill. We have to kill – it is part of life." James put a hundred on the bar, smiled and said, "Enjoyed – see you later," walked out of the restaurant, got into his car and drove away.

70

Pedro was still in a frozen trance and sort of nodded and half waved goodbye.

*****

James finished his errands and headed back to the house. The Margaritas made him sleepy, so he decided to take a little nap. He had not been asleep long before a knock at the front door woke him. He shook off his sleepiness, through a towel around his naked body, went to the door and opened it.

"Hi honey, thought I would drop by and have a drink with you," was Beth's opening line.

"Can't I ever get any peace?"

"Honey, now how are you spelling that; P-I-E-C-E or P-E-A-C-E? Don't you realize we were meant for each other? Now, I would like a P-I-E-C-E," she pushed him to the side as she walked right past him.

"Well you better spell it the other way because it ain't gonna happen. Would you please listen to me and stop stalking me? Beth, I just don't think..."

"Don't think sweet cheeks, just do me."

"Beth – Stop it! Beth, I like you but number one we have a business relationship. Number two we...

"The hell with number one, two, three and as many numbers for as high as you want to count. Just stop and really listen to me."

James took a deep sigh and said, "Okay, Beth – I'll listen."

"Look, the main office sent me to you four months ago. When they told me about the duties and all that other crap they also put in my head that you were in charge of the biggest project they had ever had, and you were a person not to fuck with. I must say I was more than interested even before I met you. Someone who is running a forty-

71

million-dollar project in this Podunk town is someone I want to get to know and maybe admire.

I read the file before I showed up on site and I was amazed that someone in this company knew how to write a proper letter and could walk and talk as well. They also sort of told me about your marital problems to that drunken slut of..."

"HEY!" James snapped.

"Sorry, but I was amazed how you could handle the site and all the crap you are going through. I do really have to hand it to you for being as nice as you are to your wife. You can't find a man like you on just any street corner."

James felt betrayed by the office and the confidences he had shared with the owner.

"Once I got to the site I was further amazed by you. Getting to know you and how you handle everything so calmly and completely...I was amazed. Every day I fell deeper and deeper in love with you just watching you, listening to you and knowing all the pressure you were under and then to top it all off – your personal crap you're going through and have gone through. I want you more than...more than anything I have ever wanted. And I also want to throw in – It was me who straightened out that fucking mess of an office you created and, if anything, you have to give me credit for that...

"Okay I give you credit but Beth, stop with the other shit or my head is going to explode..."

"As long as that head explodes inside my juicy cunt..."

"Beth, STOP IT!"

"NO I WON'T! I won't ever stop. I have found you and YOU are the one and only for me from now till the end of time. You are mine and I will do anything to stay next to you forever. I don't care what it takes. I will work my ass off for you, give you all my money, cook, clean...I will fuck you, suck you till you can't walk...anything you want...you want extra women, I'll get them for you...ANYTHING!

72

"Beth, stop. I appreciate all you are saying, and it is sure tempting but there are some flaws in your thinking..."

"Like what?" she said in disbelief.

"If you give yourself to me, like you are talking about, it will destroy you personally. You are unique unto yourself and if you change to accommodate me, with my every whim and desire, you will lose yourself. You will evolve into something you eventually will not care for, because you will become something that is not you. A relationship has to be give and take on an even basis. Not just what I want or what you think is good for me but what is good and best for the both of us, so we both give to a shared relationship."

"You're fucking that BRAZILIAN BIMBO! – Aren't you?" she screamed.

"It doesn't matter whether I am or not. Just listen to me now. I am still married to someone I love. I know it is over because I cannot take any more pain and I am just going through the downward spiraling dance of matrimonial death. I love her, or should I say, I use to love the woman I married. But through the years she has changed because of the alcohol and pills from Hyde to Jeckle or Jeckle to Hyde, whichever. She is not the person I married. She is a totally different person who has caused me severe pain and we both have to go our separate ways. Her drinking and pill popping has caused her to lose more brain cells than I ever had. She is loved by me and at the same time she is pitied by me. I know the end is near. I do not know when exactly it will occur, but I will stick it out to the end. She is still my wife and she will get all the caring, love, dedication, support and most importantly, the respect she deserves, as the woman I wanted and married years ago until the bitter end."

"That's nice. - You're fucking that fucken wet back cunt, aren't you? You are; you son-of-a-bitch!"

"THAT'S IT! Knock it off Beth. STOP IT!"

"NO I WON'T! I'll show you that our relationship will be the best there ever was."

"Beth, stop it. You are going to ruin something great that could have been if you keep on going." James was trying to think as fast as possible. "Give it some time and space, please. You are very pretty, sexy

73

and very desirous but you are going to kill this relationship before it even starts. Let me do what I have to do and when the time is right we will see if you still want to have a relationship with me. I still have a divorce to go through and a whole bunch of other crap. I guarantee you nothing will happen between us until after I resolve a lot of other issues. Okay?"

"You *do* want me, don't you?" she screamed with joyous, Christmas morning excitement.

"Oh, GOD, help me please!" James moaned out loud in exasperation.

"Okay, okay, okay. I will do that. I knew you wanted me. I just want one thing and I will do anything you ask from now on, promise."

"Okay, what?"

"Just give me one quickie now. Just a quickie and then I won't ask again or want you again till the time is right. You can do whatever you want, including that Brazilian hooker you're fucking, you bastard. I promise, I promise, honest."

James was worn out. He was tired of the debate. He was debating with himself. 'What was this - I promise you day?' He couldn't decide. His mother's words came back to him. *'When in doubt – do without!'* Oh, what the hell, maybe this will get rid of her. If I give her a bad fuck, she might leave on her own. That's what I'll do – I'll give her a bad fuck and then I'll be able to get rid of her. "Well…"

Before he could finish thinking or talking Beth jumped off the sofa, grabbed his towel and ripped it from his body. "Oh boy," she squealed in delight at the sight of his naked body. Her eyes opened wide and glistened. She quickly dropped to her knees and sucked his cock deep into her mouth. James started to protest but it was too late. He knew it was too late.

Her clothes somehow fell off her body. She played with him while he just stood there. Somehow, she was all over his body at the same time. She pulled him to the carpet. Her mouth was everywhere, her hands were everywhere. She was putting her breasts in his mouth. She was stroking him with her mouth, she was everywhere. James had become aroused by her actions. He had her large breasts and nipples all over his body. She then did some sort of a body spin. He was confused as to which of her body parts were doing what to his body parts.

She pushed him into the bedroom, never stopping the wild motion on his body. She maneuvered him towards the bed and pushed him over. Beth quickly mounted James. She grabbed him and started to insert him into her. She looked at him panting with eyes wide open. "You're too big," she cried.

James smiled, "Honey, I appreciate the compliment, but you've had kids and you know you can get a 12-pound turkey through that hole. So, I don't think my little cock is going to upset the balance of Nature. Try a little harder."

With a big smile on her face, she slid herself over him breathing hard and panting as she did. Ooooh, ooooh, ooooh she cried in happiness. It didn't take long before she climaxed.

James laid there watching, enjoying, but wondering why women couldn't control themselves better. I go from no sex in years to sex every time I turn around. God these women are fast he thought. I must be out of touch.

Beth started pumping on him again and quickly climaxed a second time, then collapsed on top of him. "Just hold me you bastard," she whimpered.

James put his arms around her and held her tightly. She finally started breathing normally then her hips started gyrating on top of him.

"Hold it! You said all you wanted was a quickie."

Beth looked at him, "As soon as you climax – that's a quickie – and you haven't yet cowboy, so I'm gonna ride you till you accomplish the mission, then the quickie is over. And until you climax, I'm gonna get me some more of delicious you." Her hips increased their motion, rolled her pelvic bone on him then suddenly climax again with a scream. "Oh my, it just keeps getting better and better. This is better than I thought it would be. Baby, I'm gonna Crazy Glue you to me!" A cry of happiness came from her throat and a smile a mile wide came across her face. Then a sheepish look came across her face. "What do you want baby? Do you want to get on top?"

James looked at her for a few seconds then flipped her over on her back and rammed himself into her and laboriously labored on top of her. As he continued she screamed words of encouragement to him. "Fuck me you delicious bastard." Her heels dug into his ass and kept pulling him faster and faster.

It didn't take long before he climaxed. Within a split second after he rolled off her. He was spent. After he stopped, she looked up and smiled at him, a Cheshire Cat smile. She quietly got up, retrieved her clothes from the other room, came back to the bedroom, and dressed while smiling at him. Jumping on top of James, she kissed him quickly.

"Thanks for the quickie honey. Have a great time tonight honey. I hope you have something left for the South American slut," Beth said, faking mock concern with a big smile. She left the room then slammed the front door on her way out.

James laid there wondering what the hell had just happened. He thought, well this was a very tiring day for a day off and it isn't over yet. He rolled to his side and fell asleep quickly.

Chapter Eight
Love in the Air

James picked up Vera and took her to the Jettys, his favorite restaurant, located on the Jupiter Inlet. It is positioned directly across from the Jupiter lighthouse along the side of the inlet where it joins the inter-coastal waterway before going to the open ocean. It is a picture perfect romantic scene. They had a quick drink at the bar while they waited for his favorite table at the front of the deck closest to the water facing out. Then they could watch the boats as they cruised by the restaurant with an unobstructed view.

As they walked to the table through the restaurant, Vera drew the eyes of every man in the place and most of the women. If they had been passing out drool towels they would have run out. There was no question Vera's beauty was well noticed.

"This very beautiful and romantic James. The noite is muito beautiful."

James smiled, "Not as beautiful as you and by the way your dress is a knockout and you seem to be attracting a lot of attention."

"You want be with ugly woman James?"

They sat in the moonlight with a cocktail, conversing with just the interruptions of the servers preparing the table, bringing the bread, condiments and menus. They held hands and just stared at each other during the interruptions, smiling and laughing.

Vera had changed her demeanor from the night before. She was soft, warm, submissive and docile. She was calm and loving when she spoke to James. "My dear, I go Brazil next week on Saturday. Will you stay with me till then?"

"There is nothing I would like better; unfortunately, I must work during the day. I am sure you have shopping to do to fill your day. If you like I will fill the nights."

She didn't hesitate, "I like...I want. Which correct James?"

"They are both right. Those are the perfect answers I wanted to hear."

The waitress arrived, "James, how are you tonight?" She leaned over putting an arm around his shoulder and kissed his cheek then smiled and nodded at Vera.

"Great Patty. Good to see you again. I think tonight we will just have another glass of the good California Chardonnay. For dinner we will have shrimp cocktails, followed by Maine Lobsters boiled and Swordfish grilled, plenty of lemon and butter and a couple of house salads."

"I love a man who knows how to order, and you make it so easy on me. I wish all my customers were like you. I'll be back in a flash."

After she left a concerned Vera turned to James. "James, she know you well. You like her? She kiss you. How many womans do you have?"

He knew right away where this conversation was headed. "Hold it Vera. I have been coming here for over ten years, one, two or three times a month. They know me well, I know the owner well and many of the people who work here. I come here alone or with someone occasionally but no one special. I don't have womans. There have been many moons that have gone by, shining on my empty arms. I have been alone for a long time."

Vera was smart enough to back right down and change direction. "That good, I just want to know if there are many womans in James life. You order for me, I like. How you know I will like?" she said quickly changing the subject.

"If you didn't I would have to find another girlfriend," he said laughing. "Most people, unless they are allergic, love lobster, shrimp and swordfish. It is my favorite meal. I think you will like it and since it is a healthy meal, I am sure it will fit in with your Brazilian diet."

They had fun and laughed through dinner. Teaching a woman how to eat a lobster properly always was a sexual side show of teaching them how to suck and use the tongue properly to retrieve all the meat. "Now I know where you learned how to love me. You have lots practice. This should be subject taught in school. Then all womans be happy."

As they drove back to James' house she cuddled next to him and stoked his leg. He could tell she was getting horny. James wondered if he was going to be able to perform. He had already climaxed three times in the past twenty-four hours and was on the verge of having to perform again. He started to have self-doubt about his sexual ability. He had not had sex like this for many years. He remembered there were some blue pills in his medicine cabinet his Doctor had given him in a sample pack. He had never tried them or had reason to use them but decided taking one might be good insurance.

After arriving at the house, he led Vera to the porch and said let's talk for a few minutes. "I'll be right back," as he headed for the bathroom. He quickly and frantically searched through a drawer and finally found the packet he had received from his Doctor. He took one and read the instructions - *One hour*, - Oh God, this isn't going to work, stall, stall he thought worriedly. He went back to the kitchen grabbed two glasses and a bottle of Baileys, then headed to the porch. He stopped to put some music on and tried to delay as much as possible but there wasn't that much to do.

"This will settle your stomach my dear."

"Don't need – want you make love now," came the reply.

"Well I need to settle my stomach, so let's talk for a minute."

"Okay James. I cook you Brazilian meal this week, you like?"

"Yes, I would like. How about Tuesday night?"

Vera's mind was on something else. She got up and came over to his chair bent over and kissed him long and hard then dropped to her knees. She unbuckled his belt, unzipped him and reached in for his cock. "Oh, my friend is sleeping. I will wake him up," as she sucked him into her mouth. She spent a few minutes sucking on him. "My beautiful pinto is much tired. I work hard to wake up. You not want James? You not like?"

79

"Yes, I want. Let's go in the bedroom dear." This was going to be harder than he thought. Nothing was happening and fear and panic set in. They got to the bed and he slowly removed her dress while gently kissing her. After her dress was off she stopped him.

"My turn," Vera said. She unbuttoned his shirt and took it off. She unbuckled and unzipped his pants for the second time. As she pulled down his pants she started laughing and pushed him over onto the bed. She removed his pants, underwear, socks and shoes in one motion. She stood there in high heels and panties with her hands on her hips. "Now you will know - LOVE OF VERA! I have not had like for man till I meet you. James, I want you." She started kissing him and then slowly worked down his body kissing, licking and biting. She took his manhood in her mouth.

James slowly went hard, he breathed a sigh of relief and as she sucked him to erection a smile crossed his lips. He was back in action but getting this Brazilian Hoover off his cock was a problem. She wasn't going to release him till he exploded. "Vera, Vera, please stop I want my pinto back because I want to put it inside you..."

She said something he couldn't understand because his cock was in her mouth, she wouldn't stop. He could feel the heat building in his loins. He grabbed the back of her head and pushed himself deep down her throat. She put a finger in his ass and James exploded like a Roman candle. James was shocked. She finally stopped and looked up at him and smiled. "Now you put Pinto in me."

"Honey, I don't think I can. You'll have to give me some time."

"I fix...I want pinto now!" She sucked his cock again until he was rock hard. James was amazed. "YES...MY PINTO!" she screamed with glee. She mounted him and put him inside her. She didn't stop till he came again, and Vera had come so many times he could not count. She squeezed him so tightly he thought he wasn't going to get his cock back.

James was dizzy. He was panting. He was exhausted.

"You like Vera Love?"

He couldn't say anything. He just looked at her with mouth open and nodded then fell asleep.

The next morning, he awoke, and she was on top of him again, and he was hard. *'How'd she do that?'* he thought. The sun was up. *'How long have we been at it?'* They kept making love until she let out a shriek and collapsed on top of him.

"How long have we been making love," he asked.

"Ten minutos," she answered. "You very good."

James thought he had the life blood sucked from his body. He pushed her off of him. He reached down to feel his cock and make sure it was still there. He dragged himself to the shower and fumbled with the knobs till he got the right temperature. He was leaning against the shower wall for support as the water washed over him. Then Vera jumped in the shower with him and started washing him.

"What we do, hoje? I make coffee James – you want in shower?"

"I think I want to go back to bed for a while," he said in pain.

"Good, good, good. I want make love 'gain too."

"No darling...I mean I think I need to take a nap...you wore me out..."

"I bring café wake you - we love 'gain!"

He thought, apparently no one is paying attention to my dead body and especially my dead dick.

Vera toweled him off and pulled him back to bed. They lay there quietly. After a while she got up and brought him a cup of coffee. James slowly sipped it and tried to wake up. Eventually, he started to respond but not until after the second cup. James carefully avoided making love again, saying he wanted to save himself for later.

They spent the day walking around the village of Port Salerno, had lunch at one of the harbor side restaurants then went back to James' house to make love again. A very exhausted James accomplished the mission after he consumed another blue helper, but afterwards his equipment was now very dead.

During the next week they played, ate in, ate out, went shopping, went to listen to music, danced, talked and talked. The conversation never stopped. They discussed everything and learned about each other, almost everything. James took some afternoons off, so they could play. The love sessions went on constantly. James had a fear that his pill supply would run out before she left town.

Wherever they went, James noticed how fascinated everyone was with her beauty but also with her persona. Both men and women immediately paid attention to her. They seemed to drop whatever they were doing to help or serve her. At one point, James laughed and said to her, "I think you must be the Queen of Brazil and all the people are your subjects." People sucked up her personality like a sponge sucks up water.

Vera laughed, "No James, I don't want be Queen, I want be Princess, want you be King, then you me marry, then be Queen. If you husband, I Queen of Brazil! Queen of America! Like fairy tale book!"

Friday night arrived. They had a quick dinner and then went to bed. In between the rounds of making love Vera cried. "You want see me 'gain?" she asked four or five times.

The answer from James was always yes. Finally, he said, "Vera, I like you very much. This is not the end but the beginning. I have a vacation coming up after this project is finished. I will come to Brazil and spend some time. We will stay in touch by telephone and computer and plan the trip. After that trip we will discuss what we want to do with our relationship. You must realize I am very taken with you and you have put a warm feeling in my heart. So, we will see, but we need a little more time. Is that okay?"

She was crying and smiling and then they would start making love again. "You make me very happy James."

The next morning, he took her to Mike and Zulma's apartment. They were going to take her to Miami and the plane. The ride to the apartment was full of Vera crying and kissing James. She made him pull off the road and they made love one more time. He smiled because he had taken the last blue pill that morning. They finally kissed goodbye with tears on her cheeks and warmth and happiness in both their hearts.

*****

During the week he was spending with Vera, Beth had been strangely quiet. She didn't say a word about anything personal and did her work quickly, efficiently and didn't come on to James at all. It was a perfect business relationship. It was so perfect it made James uneasy.

James went to work the following Monday to find Beth already there with the coffee made and waiting for him. She brought him a cup and sat down in his office. "It seems to me that I think I give better blow jobs than that Brazilian cunt, don't you agree?"

James choked on his coffee. "Have you been spying on me?" he demanded.

"Well ya...well not...not all the time, just a lot of it. I did catch most of the good parts."

"You fucking bitch! How dare you!" James screamed at her.

"James, you belong to me. If you want to fuck other women, that's okay. I said I wouldn't interfere, but you belong to me. I just wanted to know what was going on and what you were saying. No problem...it's all private between us. Are you going to see her again? I mean if you want to - that's okay. We could even have a threesome. How about that? I don't want too but if you do, I'll go along with it."

James was in shock. They were interrupted by a sub-contractor before he could say anything. The day progressed with one problem to be solved quickly followed by another. Finally, after the workers had left the site, James walked into Beth's office. "Beth, you must stop this craziness of yours. I do not want you to spy on me anymore. I will have to fire you if you don't stop."

She looked up and sweetly smiled, "James, you're not going to fire me. It would be foolish of you to do so. I know too much. Besides you don't want a sexual harassment suit, do you? I said - don't worry, you can do anything you want, anytime. I will always be there, and I will do anything you want – anything.

"You're crazy," he said, walking away wondering what to do with this crazy bitch.

She yelled after him, "Want a quickie after work? Are you horny yet?"

James left the office slamming the door as he left. He went home and sat on his porch wondering what to do about Beth. The phone rang, and it was Susan.

"Hi Babyboo. How are you?"

"Hi Baboo! I wanted to call and thank you for all the money and getting the papers back so quickly. Everything went very smoothly, thanks to you. And I'll have you know I'm all moved in and set up. I am going to start looking for a job this week, that way I won't be a burden on you anymore. When can you come up and see the place?"

"Not till next weekend. Don't take any more money unless you talk to me first. All the accounts are linked and you're still on them till we finalize the divorce. You have to come to the bank with me to sign some papers. A bunch of screwy Florida laws."

"Did I go over the agreed amount?" she asked.

"No but dam close and that's enough and I see where you took $500 in cash, so you should be all right for a long time. Did you hear me and understand that?" he said sternly.

"Yes, I promise to do as you say."

"Babyboo, look I love you and I really want you to succeed this time. Stay away from the booze, please. This is your last chance with me - don't screw your life up anymore. Do the right thing and stay straight. You're too beautiful and smart to throw away your life on booze. After the divorce, I'm not going to be there for you. Your parents will come through with a trust fund for you, just like they did for your sisters and your brother. But you're going to have to stay straight and then you will be set for life." James knew he had given this speech many times however, getting her to accept the concepts in her head was anybody's guess.

"I promise Baboo. I'm really gonna try extra special and extra hard just for you."

"You still don't get it honey. You have to do it for yourself. Don't do it for me or anyone else – Do it for you! This is your life and now you are on your own again. If you screw up and start drinking again, there is no one to take you to the hospital – there is no one to stop you from drunk driving – there is no one who will control you. You know what you do. No, I guess you don't, you've always been drunk when you do those things and you don't remember. Look, just stay away from the booze. If you get depressed, go talk to the people at the re-education camp you just left. They will help you, please, please, please. This time do it and fool everyone, because no one will be betting on your success more than me. Look, you could kill yourself very easily. Or worse for you and me - you could kill someone else, then, we are up a creek without a paddle. I, and you, would lose everything. This is important, so hear me clearly. If you fuck up and kill someone or maim someone in one of your drunken driving stupors, under Florida law, I am still responsible for your actions. And I just can't go through that. I, we, would be sued and lose everything. I would lose everything that's left – not that there's a lot that's left – after paying for your 'treatments' for the past three years. But I would end up working to pay for some law suit and you would never get your hands on the trust fund you're going to get because you would be in jail."

"I promise – I promise. This time I'm really going to do it. You watch! And once I get my hands on that trust fund, I'll share it with you Baboo. You wait and see. This time I'm going to make it."

"I hope so Babyboo, I hope so. Okay, look, stay straight and I'll be up to see you on Friday night. Be good and behave!"

"Okay Baboo, I'll see you Friday and I love you beaucoup buckets. Night"

James went back to thinking about now both problems; the crazy bitch Beth, and his fruit loop, drinking, soon to be ex-wife Susan. Even though the past ten days with Vera had been wonderful, she was gone. The true realities of life had come home to roost.

He had to do something about Beth and get rid of this craziness she brought to the table. I can't rush to fire her that would be stupid. He was very vulnerable to what she could do or threaten to do to him and his career. He had to get rid of this. His thoughts took him back to Vietnam, then to Maine, then to Houston. No, she didn't deserve that. Besides she's a woman. That's against my code, only men. There was no reason to kill her. Maybe I could get her to quit but how?'

The phone rang again. 'What is this Grand Central Station tonight?' he thought.

"Hello"

"Hey James! I just finished this great book on Patrick Henry. 'GIVE ME LIBERTY OR GIVE ME DEATH.' Killed anybody today James? I guess the author didn't realize you get the same result with either one you pick."

"Shut up you baboon!" said James recognizing the voice of his long time, closest friend and only true confidant, Alan French.

Only Alan knew his secrets. Their friendship started in prep school. They kept in continuous contact and constant visiting. They were closer than brothers ever could be. They had both gone to Viet Nam but at different times, yet their experiences and their frames of reference were similar. Alan ran a fishing lodge deep in the western woods of Maine. Alan was a huge, big, burly man six-foot tall and two hundred and fifty pounds. He had curly black hair and strong facial features with a mustache, Roman nose and a smile for all. He was the epitome of the Maine woods lumberjack and fishing guide. He liked to stay in the woods away from society, but if necessary he could don a tuxedo and mix it up with the best of them.

James jumped, "Don't talk like that on the phone you fucking idiot!"

"What's going on with you? You've been real quiet and haven't called in a week," Alan chimed in.

"Ya, well, lots have been happening. Wait till you hear all this." James started with the saga of Vera, the complications with Beth and the ongoing story with Susan. It took him thirty minutes to explain it all.

"Well, well, well," Alan finally chimed in. "You always have led an interesting life. What are you going to do about all that shit? I think

86

you have a real problem with Beth. She sounds like she is wearing you like a glove. You're not going to do THAT again, are you?"

"No, don't be crazy. I have to get rid of her somehow though. She could end up a big problem if I don't get rid of her. For God's sake, I have enough problems with Babyboo. I don't need any more. Hey, I was thinking of going to Brazil after this project is over, wanna go?"

"No. I'll let you go and survey the territory and then if you go back, I'll come along. I'd rather have you set up the women for me," Alan said chuckling.

"Why do I always have to do all the work? Next time I come to Maine, you better set me up with a good-looking thing. You owe me."

"When are you coming up?"

"I'll set up a flight. Let me plan a long weekend. Babyboo just cost me a pretty penny to get her set up. I hope this time it works. She's going to kill herself if she starts drinking again. I've never seen anything like it. She is so bad when she gets on the booze. I have to go forward with the divorce and I don't have any hope for her to get her brain cells back. It will never be the same. I just want her to be safe. Her family is too rich, and they can take care of her much better than me. She just makes me crazy. I love her, but she is not the same woman I married."

Alan paused, "I know, I feel for you. You have put a lot of work into that project and I love her too. She is a wonderful person – the best you've ever had but she really has lost it. The booze is an insidious disease. You are doing the right thing. You've got three years into that project with no results. I don't know how you've done it and frankly I don't know how she has lived through it. What's the next step?"

"Well, John's lawyer will file for a court date. Then it is just a simple appearance before the judge and it's done. I end up paying alimony for two years – that sucks but Babyboo and I will work that out. John will then cut loose with her trust fund and she will be set for life. My only prayer is that she doesn't drink. Only God knows what will happen if she drinks.

"You getting serious about the Brazilian chick? – What's her name?"

87

"Vera. I don't know. Everything is very confusing right now but ya, I think I like her a lot. She is one hell of a woman. Very intelligent, very beautiful, great body and keeps up with me in bed. But it is too soon to tell. I'm just getting back into the game. I've been sitting on the bench too long. I want to play for a while and she is definitely something I want to play with, we'll see."

"Okay cool. Now I have to go shovel some snow. When you come up, we'll go cross country skiing. The trails are great this year. Be good and I'll talk to you later." James was talked out and tired, so he finally decided to go to bed.

*****

The following day Beth began her sexual assault on James again. She did her work but every chance she got, she did something. She would grab him in the crotch when he walked by. She would put her arms around him whenever possible and try to pull him to her. She suggested lunch, dinner, drinks and anything sexual she could. She was relentless. James tried to ignore her, dodge her, stay out of the office as much as possible but he couldn't, she was in his face every time he moved. At the end of the day she turned to James. "James it's time to go home and I'm real horny. How about you stick that wonderful cock of yours into my tiny pussy? I just want a little quickie. I have to go home tonight to that idiot I live with and I'd rather go home with a good feeling inside me. It will keep me happy all night."

"Beth this has to stop!"

She turned and with hostility and rage in her voice, "Well it's not going to stop. I don't ask much of you. Every once in a while, I want you to fuck me. Is that too much to ask? And I think you had better. I've got a letter all written about your sexual harassment and I bet I can get it to the district attorney before you can blink. Now, I'll meet you at your house in a few minutes – got it? I'm not married and you're as good as divorced and a little physical recreation for us isn't the worst thing in the world. Who knows, you might get to enjoy it," she spit out these words with fiery anger.

James decided discretion was the better part of valor. He would play along until he could think of a better course of action. This was just a management problem to be solved. He had to come up with a plan. "Okay, Beth, I give up. If you want to be my bitch, then get your ass to my house and let's get it on."

"Now you're thinking with both heads properly," she said sweetly.

They left the office and went to James's house. James poured himself a drink, took it into the bedroom, took his clothes off and hopped onto bed. "Okay sexy, you're going to have to get me hard because look - I'm just limp. So, start sucking baby. Oh, one more thing. I will agree to your demands, but you have to promise me one thing."

"What's that?"

"From now on we keep the office sacred. No more sexual come-ons, no more remarks. You do your work as the perfect assistant and these sexual romps are a secret, got it?"

Beth happily agreed as she striped down and jumped on the bed. She quickly went to work on him. She started to kiss him on the lips but James pushed her head down to his cock. She didn't resist and started sucking his cock. It didn't take long before she got James rock hard. After she got him erect she just looked up at him and smiled. She straddled him and put him inside of her.

James made minor movements with his hips. He could not stop wondering what it was going to take to make this crazy bitch stop. Beth climaxed and looked at James and realized he had not. She kept going, wanting to please him. Finally, James realized she would keep going forever if necessary. He rolled them over, so he was on top, pumped her hard till he came.

He rolled off and angrily said, "Okay, there's your quickie. I have some things to do. Now get the fuck out of here." James got up and went to take a shower. Beth got dressed silently and left while he showered.

Chapter Nine

Susan and the Divorce

James drove to Ocala to see the apartment he had rented for Susan. It was a cute, little, one bedroom and she had decorated it nicely. They spent the weekend together. They made love a few times but James' heart was not in it. She was trying to show her appreciation to him for having helped her and it was a little bit for old times' sake. They went out for meals and did a little shopping for things for the apartment. He wanted her to be comfortable in her new digs.

The conversation centered on her new life; her attempts at finding a job, all about her AA meetings and temporary cash flow for her. James gave into everything she wanted and needed and then some. She was totally absorbed into her new life and never asked about his life and what he was doing. James was totally bored, but he realized this was part of the recovery process. She was the center of her world and she was the whole world, nothing else really existed for her outside of her world. Susan had lost so many brain cells because of the alcohol she was not the woman he had married, this was not the woman with whom he had fallen in love. The woman he loved had died and been replaced by what was in front of him, the exterior was the same, but it was only the empty shell of his wonderful Susan.

He left early Sunday afternoon saying he wanted to beat the traffic. He only got about an hour outside of Ocala when he pulled off the road and started crying. Feeling empty and lost, tears ran down his cheeks. Finally, he stopped and pulled himself together. He just wanted to save her from a terrible life. He didn't want any more to do with this crazy love he had for Susan. To keep her safe and sober was his only thought. He finished driving back the four hours to his house with a tremendous weight of sadness and loss riding with him.

*****

The months passed. James was absorbed in his work finishing the project. He had not had a vacation in over four years. He visited Susan every two or three weeks on the weekends. He was trying to help her get settled into a new life. She stayed sober, but James had an uneasy feeling that stayed with him. There was something different, something wrong. He could not put his finger on it. He thought it must be part of letting go and the upcoming change of the relationship with Susan.

He decided that if everything went relatively smoothly the project would finish on time, his divorce would be final, and he could take some time off and go visit Vera in Brazil. It gave him a goal to aim for.

Beth had settled into wanting sex with him about once or twice a week. He obliged but without feeling and of no interest except to just do the act. She would come by the house after work, have a romp in bed and go home. She chattered the whole time, but he never heard her. To James, it was just the ramblings of a nut job. She talked about their future together. He just smiled, nodded, preformed his necessary obligation and would then continue his life as soon as she left. James thought at the end of the project she would have to go back to the main office and would be out of his hair, hopefully forever. Time just might cure his problem with her.

The divorce date was set, and the details were worked out. In two months the divorce would be official, and everyone could move on. Susan's parents were happy which meant they were getting rid of James, whom they thought was the main reason of Susan's alcoholism. James inwardly laughed at their stupidity and naiveté. He let them have their thoughts. Good God, they had more money than cents. They thought they could cure Susan once he was out of the picture. What they didn't realize was James had been fighting the Susan battle for years and was tired. Something had to change, and money was power – they had the money, so let them have the power – let them have Susan – let them fix what he could not. It might work, but since Susan hated them, he really did not give it much of a chance of success. He would always be there for her if they failed.

92

He spent hours on the computer, video conferencing with Vera. She tried to teach him some basic Portuguese. They planned his trip. She would take time off and they would travel southern Brazil. She would show him her country and all the spots she loved. They were like giddy teenagers, laughing and enjoying each other's company even with 5000 miles between them. His feelings for her were growing. The magic of a new relationship was weaving the threads of the fabric of a new life. He wanted Vera in his life permanently. She filled the void in his life that Susan had made by the disease she had foisted on them. Vera made him very happy and horny. He tried to think the process through to make sure he was thinking with the right head. James' expectations were rising for the upcoming occasion. It made him happy. It was the first time in three years he felt like a normal man again. He also kept it a secret from Beth and was sure never to mention Vera's name.

*****

James called Susan, "The divorce is set for Tuesday. You have to be there since you are the petitioner. But I guess your lawyer has already told you all this. Why don't you drive here Monday and we will have a good night, a good dinner and hit the courthouse in the morning? Then after we can go to the bank and have you sign all the paperwork to get you off the accounts."

Susan stalled, "I am so nervous about it. I am going to drive there with my friend, Denise. I think it would be best if we stayed at the Howard Johnson Motor Lodge. Denise is afraid of you."

"What the hell are you talking about? Why are you doing that and why is Denise afraid of me?

"Please Baboo. You know how nervous I get, and Denise promised she would stand by me and help with the driving. Denise is just afraid of men. Please just let it go. If I see you beforehand or in court, I will fall apart. Please let me do it my way. You don't have to be there. It will be quicker and easier for me. If you're there, I swear I'll make a stop at the liquor store. Please, please.

James thought for a moment, "Okay, but first they've been having problems at the Howard Johnson Motor Lodge. It's a hotbed of bad activity. Someone was murdered there last week, and I think there is some drug activity going on there. I will make a reservation for you at Pirates Cove. Then, talk it over with Denise and convince her I am not the boogey man and the three of us will have dinner." James thought something doesn't smell right.

"Please Baboo. Just let me do this and stay away." They argued for a while more, but Susan wasn't budging on her stance. Finally, he decided to relent to her wishes. "If I know you're going to be there I will fall apart. Denise will take care of me. Okay?"

"Okay, but when are you going to sign the papers at the bank?"

"I'll sign them on the way out of town - just have them ready for me, okay?"

"Okay, we'll do it your way."

Tuesday arrived, and James went to work. The thought crossed his mind that he should show up at the courthouse, but Susan had convinced him to stay away. Let her go through with it and he could relax and enjoy his new-found freedom. He couldn't – he still loved her. He had wanted so deeply to continue the fifteen-year relationship with her, but everything pointed him in a different direction. The pain of the years of alcoholism scarred him deeply.

The day of the hearing, his thoughts were on the divorce proceedings going on without him. He waited for a call from Susan to tell him the divorce was final. No call came. At the end of the day he called her – no answer, he left a message. An hour later he tried again, still no answer. He called his lawyer. She told him the proceedings were quick and over in a few minutes and done by ten-thirty. He went over a few details with her and then asked if a woman was there to help or stand by Susan. "I didn't see anyone there with her," was the reply. "I wasn't looking for anyone. I really don't remember but I may have seen a man with her."

The following afternoon Susan called him. "I'm sorry Baboo. I was too upset to talk to you. That was the worst thing I have ever had to do. I just high-tailed it back to Ocala. I cried all the way. I forgot to stop

94

at the bank, I'm sorry. Just have the bank send me the stuff and I'll have it notarized, okay?"

"Susan, you worried me sick. I thought you went out and tied one on."

"Baboo, please, I'm the sick one. All the pressure from my family and the psychiatrists at the rehab place to do this divorce and you know I love you and I always will. They all ganged up on me. I hate it – I hate the pressure they put on me. It's done and over with and we can move on. And NO, I didn't tie one on. I told you I am straight and staying straight."

"Okay. I was just worried. Was Denise there or did someone else go with you?"

Susan paused, "No Denise was with me," came her stumbling flat reply.

James let it drop. "Well you are a free woman again, even with your old name back. Now let your family give you the secret trust fund I'm not supposed to know about and enjoy your life. Tell me after you get it, so I don't have to continue this ridiculously high alimony. What a rip off. I'll send the stuff from the bank and please get it back to them as soon as possible. If you had done it on the way out of town like you promised; we wouldn't have to go through all this other work."

"I will. I am going to Houston next week to sign the trust papers. I'll let you know when everything is done. I love you." She started to cry and said she had to hang up because she was too upset.

James hung up and went to his favorite local bar, Shrimpers, to drink away the divorce. After four hours he couldn't remember how many drinks he had. His favorite bartender, Ginny, brought him some food without his asking and then finally shut him off. She sent him home, trying to get him to take a cab but James refused and just left, thinking the car knew the way back to the house.

*****

95

The following morning, Beth showed up at his house. She woke him up. "Good morning darling. Time to rise and shine! You missed your first two meetings. I covered for you. Isn't it wonderful to have such an efficient assistant? And an assistant who just loves to take your DICKtation." She sat next to him on the bed and started playing with him.

"I wouldn't do that - I might just get sick all over you. Oh, my head!"

"Okay, remember tonight is Thursday, our regular night, so make sure you feel better by the time the day is over, cause I'm not going to show you any mercy. And make sure my favorite head is working properly."

"Beth, get the fuck out of here and go back to work. I'm going to take a shower and a gallon of Alka-Seltzer and I will be along shortly. Now, get the fuck out of here!"

Beth left, and James headed for the shower and got ready for the rest of the day. He finally arrived by noon to find a huge bunch of problems to solve with a head pounding like a big base drum. He slowly recovered, then went to the bank and arranged to have the release forms sent to Susan.

*****

Susan called him before she went to Houston. "Hey, guess what?" she said. "The parental units are giving me a new car when I get to Houston."

"That's nice but how are you going to get it back to Florida? Are they going to ship it for you? You can't drive that distance alone. What gives?"

"Oh, they will have someone from the oil company or the bank help me and then they will fly them home. You know how they are."

"Okay. Congratulations and oh, by the way, did you send the papers back?"

"No, Baboo, I will before I leave – promise."

"Okay. Have a good trip. Love you."

"Love you too, Baboo. Talk to you when I get back."

Chapter Ten

Sessions

James had decided that the therapy was helping. He was still lost, and nothing was going right. He was losing his temper too often. He would hide it as best he could. He tried to keep everything inside of himself. He was a human pressure cooker. On the job, his work was going well but he was not one with the world. He was lost because of the divorce. He decided to keep doing the therapy with Ray. What would it hurt? He just had to make sure to keep his mouth shut and not tell about that stuff. The death of his marriage was hurting him the most.

Ray convinced him that no matter what he did to try to save the relationship with Susan - it would be to no avail. He continued to point out to him that his desire to save the relationship, being a male, he was in the smallest minority of thought. The huge overwhelming majority of husbands with alcoholic wives cut and run from the problem. He praised him for his thoughts, honor and deeds for Susan's betterment but slowly tried to make him move on with his life. It wasn't like he was leaving her by the side of the road. Susan had one of the richest families in Houston to take care of her and could do so much better than he because of their money and power. James thought with the sessions his mind would heal his heart. What held his thinking back was that he believed each member of Susan's family was very narcissistic in their personal lives and would not help her beyond a perfunctory attempt. They would not and could not help her and give her the personal attention as much as he had or he could. No matter how much he thought about the problem, he always came back to the same answer; end the relationship and get on with his life.

Ray tried to bring up another subject with him. He wanted to talk about Viet Nam and post-traumatic stress disorder. James kept refusing and didn't want to discuss the war. James had already decided that Nam was over and now it was history. Besides, it had been a different world; it had no bearing on his life now. Ray kept trying and James kept refusing.

"Look James, you have gone through very traumatic life events stemming from Nam. Those events have carved deep scarring recesses in your mind. Now you have gone through some pretty shitty events in your life, and you are now working on your second divorce. Your anger has to go away before it eats you alive. Don't fight the river."

"Look Ray, I'm fine. Yes, I get angry and I find it hard to control myself, but I'll be okay. I'm smarter than the average bear."

"James, I can see something inside of you that you are not telling me, some hidden secret, something you are not letting me see. What is it?"

James laughed at Ray's comment, "Oh you can see again my blind guru." They both chuckled. "Nothing...there is nothing I am hiding." James could never tell what he had done. "Look I think I am drinking too much. But I'm okay and as soon as this divorce is over in my mind, I'll be fine. The anger issues will go away then I will be happy again. Ray, this isn't working for me. And by the way you can't see."

"Oh yes I can. What have you done that you're not telling me?

"The only thing I can think of is that when I get angry I cannot control myself. I just lose it and some other alien being takes over my mind and body. I just react to the situation. I can't control my actions and I don't remember everything that I do or say."

"James do you remember anything you have done?"

"No...there is nothing major. I just go into a fog. Let's just forget it. It's not important. Ray look...I don't think this therapy thing is working for me. Look if I think I need help I'll come back to you and we can start again. Deal?" James decided to quit therapy, he didn't want to talk about it anymore. The whole thing was too invasive. He really couldn't talk about it – he didn't dare – who could ever understand? He wanted to stop these sessions before he said something he shouldn't. Everything was in the past and it was better to leave it alone. Why tell anyone what he had really done? Why let the cat out of the bag? It could only hurt him if he did. Those things he had done were just a can of worms he never wanted to open. Deal with the anger, take the pills. Let's not bring up what he had done.

"Okay James. I can't force you, but I do want to help you. Please don't let the situation get any worse. If you find yourself doing things you shouldn't, come back and we will discuss it."

"Ray, thanks for the help with the divorce. Let me get past it and if there are any instances I can't handle, I'll come back. And I'll keep taking the pills, they seem to help." James shook hands with Ray and left the room thinking therapists are the nutty ones. Fuck the therapy and fuck those pills. I don't need a therapist, I need a drink and off to his favorite watering hole, "Shrimpers," he went.

Chapter Eleven

The Money Problem

The Susan Problem

Over a week later James received a call. "Mr. Liberty, this is Bob Shea at Chase Bank. I'm the Vice President of the branch. We need you to stop by the bank to sign some papers to release some money from your 401K to cover your account. We would appreciate it before five. I will have the papers ready, so just ask for me."

"I know who you are Bob, what are you talking about? Just cover the checking account with the savings account, like we always do."

"Mr. Liberty, there isn't any more money in your savings account, so we must take the balance from your 401K, unless you have some money to deposit from another source. Are you bringing funds with you?"

"Bob, hold it. What are you saying?" James was confused. "Your people must have made a mistake. Check again and just transfer the money I need from the savings account and put it in the checking account – like I signed up for."

"Mr. Liberty, there is no money in the savings account and there is no money in the checking account. You went through all of it last week. Since you are a good customer, I covered all the outstanding charges until I could get a hold of you and since you have the 401K with us, I knew we were covered. Since you went through so many charges I checked to make sure they were legitimate. That must have been some trip you went on."

"Bob, I didn't go on any trip. Your people have really screwed this up."

"No sir, all the charges came through on your wife's cards and I thought maybe there was fraudulent activity. So, I personally called the merchants involved just to make sure. I talked to them and they identified your wife in person, by card and personal identification since the charges were so large. Is your wife not in Texas sir?"

A sinking feeling hit James, "There's something wrong Bob but I will be down to the bank shortly. Freeze the accounts till I get there."

"There is nothing to freeze Mr. Liberty. Your 401K will just about cover the problem. I'll be here sir. I'll wait for you. See you shortly, sir."

James hung up the phone. He then called the bank's computer system to check his balances. They all came back saying overdrawn and the checking account came back with an overdraft of about $8,000.00. He wrote down all the strange charges from when the charges first started to appear. Hotel bills, restaurants, gas stations, a Texas City Sherriff's Department, a bail bondsman, even a car company and check cashing stores were on the list. James was quickly adding the possibilities up in his mind. He quickly realized that Susan had not returned the paperwork. He placed a call to her. He had no luck, just the answering message. He kept trying and trying but she wouldn't answer. He drove to the bank and met with Bob.

James sat down in Bob's office and they went through the charges item by item. Finally, they reached a balance owing of almost eight thousand dollars on top of the almost $22,000.00 already taken from the accounts. James was in shock. "Bob, look, um…, my wife and I got a divorce a couple of weeks ago. I am not legally responsible for these charges and you need to go after her and replace the money back into my accounts."

Bob sat for a moment and looked seriously at the papers on his desk. "Well, I am sorry about your divorce but unless I am mistaken we have no release on file dissolving the union and taking Mrs. Liberty off the accounts. Therefore, the charges have to remain on those accounts and you will have to go after her. Are you going to deposit today to cover the overage or do you wish to dissolve the 401K and cover the charges that way? It would leave you a positive balance of about $3,350.00. If you do not have a deposit right now, I will have to freeze your account. What do you wish to do sir?"

James was still in shock. "First, take her off the accounts. Then Bob, why don't you float me a short-term loan to cover this until I get to the bottom of it and recover the money from my wife? She went to Houston to get a trust fund and I'm sure everything will be fine in a day or so?"

"Now, Mr. Liberty, I cannot do that. Until she signs the papers and has it notarized she has access to the accounts. You have been a wonderful customer of this bank for a long time. However, it would not be prudent or wise for this bank to give you a loan, especially under these circumstances. Until we get that paperwork signed, you and Mrs. Liberty are thought of as a single unit regarding legal liabilities. I thought you may have a way out if the cards were stolen, but I carefully verified that it was Mrs. Liberty who made the charges. I wish I could but it would mean my job since I was the person who called the merchants and I am the one who heard *why* some of the charges were incurred. Sorry."

"Bob, what are you referring to?"

"Mr. Liberty, I can't divulge all that, just let me say that that the charges are not the normal charges we typically deal with and are not the types of business we normally see on a customer's account. The charges are, or bring to mind, that the customer may be involved with questionable activities. That's more than I am suppose to tell you but since you are and have been a good customer, I am saying this to you personally, if you follow me.

James went silent and thought for a minute. "Bob, thank you. Go ahead and cash out the 401K and I will straighten this mess out, unless there is another way to handle it that isn't so painful to me?"

"No sir, I wish there was, unless you can deposit from another source, it has to be this way. And I cannot close the accounts. I guess you better find her and get those cards back. You are still responsible for any and all charges."

"Okay, Bob, go do it. Cover the charges and give me two thousand in cash. I may need it." James signed the paperwork Bob put in front of him then got up and walked out of the bank. He knew what had happened. She was drinking again, and this was worse than he had ever dealt with.

James went home and decided to get to the bottom of this quickly. He started by checking the other credit cards they shared only to find out she had used all the available credit up and they were all at zero. The blood rushed to his head. Panic set in. He tried to think of what to do. He had to stop her. He had to find her. He called a female Sheriff he had a very short but fun relationship with a year or so ago. "Martha, this is James. How are you beautiful?"

"Well, well, well - you fucker, why haven't you called me?"

"Martha, I love you darling, you know that, but I need help right now and I don't need the bullshit."

"You leave me in the lurch and kick me to the curb, then you come back for help…"

"Martha, yes or no, what's it going to be?"

"Okay, anything for you. Whatever you want, and I better get a famous James' dinner out of this…Agreed?"

James laughed, "Okay, you got it. Here's the deal. My sweet, now ex-wife seems to have run amuck. She is running up charges on my bank accounts and credit cards. She is in Texas. She has paid money to the Sheriff's department in Port O'Conner, Texas and Beaumont, Texas. She paid money to A-1 Bail Bonds in Orange, Texas. I need to get as much info as to her whereabouts and what's going on. I think she is drinking again and has gone crazy again. Help me, please. I need to find her and get with her to get the cards back."

"I thought you said she was now your ex-wife. Why do you care?"

"She is, but it's too new and she still has access to my money. It is just legal – smegal paperwork that needs to be signed. Till then I am screwed. I need to find her and get this thing figured out fast."

"Okay what name is she using?"

"I guess Susan Liberty…that's the name on the credit cards…she got her maiden name back…Susan Dunlap…it's got to be one of those…"

"Okay let me see what I can find out. I'll get back to you. I'll call you back if I need any more info."

"Thanks, baby."

The next call was to Susan's mother. "Nancy, this is James. Where is your daughter?"

"Hello James. That is none of your business!" She said icily. "I'm sure she is fine, and I want you to stay away from her."

"Hold it Nancy. As much as you love to hate me I am sorry to tell you, but I think you now have a big problem on your hands. I only want to make sure she is okay and from what I know I think she is in big trouble. I know she went to sign the trust papers with you in Houston. Do you know where Susan is now?"

Nancy stumbled and stammered. "I'm sure she is alright. How did you know about the trust? That's none of your business."

"Nancy look...I have reason to believe she is in some big trouble. She has paid fines to the Sheriff's departments in two different Texas towns and to one bail bondsman in Orange. Not to mention a huge pile of bills to hotels and things that don't make any sense. Knowing her normal ways, I think she is drinking again. If she is with you and you know better, then fine I'll go away. But if she is not with you, then we have a problem and it is only her safety I worry about. Now tell me what you know."

"No James, she is not with us. She and her friend left over a week ago and I thought by this time she would be back in Florida."

"Friend? What friend?"

"Oh, Roger, you know the man she has been dating for the past six months. He is her AA friend. They came here and stayed a few days. We gave Susan the car and they left."

It was more like pulling teeth to get information out of Nancy. "Tell me more Nancy. Did she sign the papers? Did she get any money? Do you know where they went?"

"Well, she signed the papers. How did you know about the trust fund?"

I knew about the trust a year ago when you and John decided to give it to her. I also knew you wouldn't give it to her until after the divorce, so I wouldn't have a claim to it. She told me about it right away and I thought it would be best for her, so we kept it a secret. I am not interested in your dam money Nancy. This doesn't matter, tell me about the rest."

"Well, we didn't give her any money. Roger said he had plenty. They left and said they were heading back to Florida. John and I decided not to give her any money until she has proven to us that she has stopped drinking and doing what she is suppose to be doing. She has to go three years without a drink and we have the right…"

"Excuse me Nancy. From what I know at this moment, during the last ten days, Susan and Roger, have spent over thirty thousand dollars of my money on a bunch of some crazy things, I don't even have all the details yet. They have paid fines or something like that in two or three Texas towns, paid a bail bondsman once and have lived very well at a couple of hotels. I've got a cop looking into it now and when I find out more I'll let you know. I guess I'm the fool and I have been taken for a ride here. I'll get back to you Nancy. If you learn anything more let me know, would you please?"

"Okay, James I will. I don't want anything to happen to her either."

James knew that Nancy sounded sincere, but she was always more worried about her next Pilates class or her social obligations more than her own daughter. He knew she would be of no help.

It wasn't till the next day that Martha got back to James. "You owe me big time James. I think you should take me away for a beautiful long weekend – like to the Bahamas. Here is what I found out so far. Susan is hanging out with a guy by the name of Roger Cleft. They seemed to have started out in Port O'Connor, Texas. It must have been one hell of a party. They wrecked a motel room, trashed it and among other things threw the TV into the pool. After, the cops got involved, they paid a large amount of money to the motel and then Roger got arrested for soliciting an undercover officer for crack. Susan paid the bond money cash and they left, since there was no hold on him. They then went to Beaumont, Texas after a stop at the Hyatt in Houston. They mostly had room service and stayed in a suite while in Houston.

In Beaumont they stayed at the Hilton. During the second day there she had him arrested for assault and battery. He was drunk and high. She was drunk and beaten up. The Beaumont Police took pictures of her – not pretty. She went to the hospital for treatment. He stayed in jail almost two days and then she paid the full bail of three thousand to a bail bondsman in Orange, Texas to get him out.

Then after she got him out, the same night she called the police on him again for abuse. Back to jail he went for the night. She then posted another thousand dollars to get him out the next morning after his arraignment. They smashed the car into a parked car in the parking lot of the hotel and drove off. The desk manager saw them do it, reported it and they were stopped by the Beaumont police only a few miles away. They apparently settled with the owner of the other car and no charges were filed.

Their next town was Lafayette, Louisiana. Is this beginning to sound like Bonnie and Clyde to you? They were stopped by the Lafayette Police and they found pills and a piece of crack on Roger. She was drunk, so the cops took Susan to a motel to let her sleep it off since she was not driving. They checked her in and helped her to the room. Roger spent the night in jail and guess what? She paid the bail after his arraignment the next morning. They hit the road after a day and night at the Hyatt. And that's where the trail goes cold. Don't know where they are. I put a tracer on them in all the states from Texas to here. So, if they sneeze too loudly I will know about it.

By the way my darling, I pulled Roger's record. Wow - as long as my arm. He has done hard time twice. Once for armed robbery, served 14 months and once for assault and battery with a weapon, served nine months for that one. He has been arrested about twenty-six times in four different states. A lot of minor stuff: auto theft, shoplifting, fighting, drug possession and a lot of beating up on women. Five different women got him arrested nine different times on the abuse charges alone. None of the women pressed charges. This guy is a creep and dangerous. He beat up a cop once and got off on a technicality. So many addresses on this guy it looks like the Manhattan phone directory. You'll have more as soon as I get it my dear. Now, how about a beautiful weekend in the Bahamas – just you and me?"

"You've outdone yourself dear. Great work, really appreciate it."

"Well, tell me when do we get on a plane and go relax?"

"Soon my dear, soon. I've got to straighten out this mess first and then Fantasy Island here we come. Love you big bunches. I'll get back to you or if you hear something give me a call. Mucho thanks, talk to you later."

With Martha's information and the charges on his bank accounts James was starting to put all the pieces together. He realized Susan was drinking again and she was with a new friend – boyfriend – lover? She had not signed and sent back the bank papers as she had promised. They went through his money fast and there was little he could do to stop her. He would be liable for all of the charges she made. James kept trying every hour to reach Susan on her cell, but she wouldn't answer.

*****

It was two am when James' phone rang. James rolled over and looked to see that the call was from Susan. "Hello."

A very friendly voice said, "Hello James. My name is Roger and I am a friend of your wife, Susan. I just wanted to have a discussion with you. Susan told me what a wonderful guy you are and how generous you are. She also has told me that you are some kind of a war hero. Got a lot of medals in Nam. She really thinks very highly of you."

"Let me speak to Susan."

"Well she is asleep right now. Boy, she is a beautiful woman. She's just lying here naked as a jay bird on the bed …really pretty. You have great taste man…"

"Fuck you asshole – I said - let me speak to Susan!" James was pissed. He realized that Roger was drunk or high and slurring his words.

"And I said – she's asleep Bro! I called to talk to you…"

James slammed the phone down. This conversation was not one he wanted to have and certainly not when he was half asleep. The phone

110

rang again and James, more awake this time, sat up and decided to take the call. "Hello."

"Hey man, don't slam the phone on me. I'm just trying to be friendly. I mean I am fucking your wife, so we have something in common - like we share – stuff – ya know what I mean?"

"Look Roger, I hate to tell you this, but she is not my wife, we are divorced but you knew that now, didn't you?

"Ya, but she still loves you. I'm just fuckin her for a while. We're on this trip, havin a good time, travelin around. She's a beautiful woman and I just wanted to tell you how much I like fuckin her. She's a great piece of ass."

"Where are you Roger? What town are you in?"

"Hey man, how the fuck should I know…we are somewhere in Louisiana, I think…I think, let me look at the phone here…says…says…oh the match book cover from the liquor place where we bought stuff…says Slidel…ya I think that's where we are…Slidel."

"Well how long are you two going to stay there?"

"Well we are on our way back to Florida…that's where we live…ya know…in Ocala…in an apartment there. It's Susan's place but I spend a lot of time there. Don't tell her but I'm also fuckin this other bitch in Naples…and I go back and forth…"

James decided to play this drunk or stoner for all he could and that meant changing tactics. "Oh Roger, don't worry I won't say a word. Maybe we should coordinate schedules cause I still go to Ocala every once in a while. That way we won't get in each other's way if you know what I mean."

"Ya man that's cool…I will call you when I go to Naples and tell you how long I'm gonna stay there and that will leave the place open for you…Hey I got a question for you…Did she ever let you fuck her in the ass?…She says she's a virgin in the back door…Is that true man? Cause I love to hear em squeal when I ram it in their back door when they don't expect it…ya know what I mean?"

"No Roger, she hates that...don't piss her off...she gets bullshit and she will tear you a new one...ya know what I mean?"

"Oh ya...I slapped her around a few times and she snuck off and called the fuzz on me and they put me in jail...fuckin bitch...I did it a second time and she did it again...I ain't gonna do that again till she sobers up...she's a mean drunk when she gets pissed...isn't she?"

"Yes Roger, she is..."

"See, she said I better not call you but I knew you was a good guy...we need to talk more often...maybe we could meet somewhere...what do ya think?"

"Sure Roger. Let's wait till you get back from your little trip and we can meet."

"That'll be cool. Hey, I look forward to that man...Okay I'm goin to sleep now. I know you couldn't tell but I'm a little fucked up. I had a little crack with my booze, he-he...Hey, you do crack man?"

"Just once in a while. We will get together and split a rock Roger."

"That'll be cool. I'd like that man. Okay, I'm gonna get some sleep. It's been great talkin to ya. We'll talk again soon, I'll give ya a call.

"Okay Roger. You take care now. Good night." James hung up and knew what he was going to do next, he just didn't know when and where...yet.

*****

The next night Susan called James at three am. "Hello Baboo."

"Don't you people realize that normal people are asleep at these hours?"

"Oh, Baboo. I know you will talk to me at any time. You love me and you use to wake me up in the middle of the night plenty of times."

"But Babyboo that was for fun and besides you enjoyed it. Why are you having your new boyfriend call me?" She was slurring her words and James knew better than to try and admonish or attack her because she would just hang up. No matter what, he had to play her like a fish on the line when she was drinking. She was blitzed, and she had been for weeks. There was no telling what her real condition really was.

She faltered for a second, trying to figure out what to say... "I didn't know he was or I mean did, no I didn't know honest. He is not my boyfriend! He is just a friend I met at AA and he is kind enough to help me drive the car back to Florida."

James felt the heat building, but tried to control his words, "Look Susan, don't try and play me for a fool. I know just about everything. You and Bozo there have been drunk for over two weeks. It normally takes two days to drive from Houston to Ocala and you and Bozo have been on the road for over two weeks. You have stolen over thirty thousand from me and you are fucking some dirt bag. I am pissed and disgusted with you..."

Susan cut in, "I'm not fucking him, honest..."

"Knock it off – DEAR – I'm not a fool. You are drunk. You are somewhere in Louisiana. You and Bozo have been raking havoc all over the Southeast and doing it on my money. You never signed the papers from the bank and how dare you use – steal - my money to front your drunk and pay for your travels, bills, bail money, booze, drugs and whatever. What the fuck do you think you are doing?" By the time James had finished, he was very mad and found it hard to control the anger in his voice.

Susan was silent. She started to cry and sob. "I'm sorry, I didn't mean to. I signed the papers in Houston and then they wouldn't give me any money. I was cold sober, honest. John said I had to stay sober for three years and be subject to being tested whenever they want to prove I'm sober. Those fucking hypocrites! They wouldn't give me any money. Then Roger and I left, and he wanted to see some of his old friends in Port O'Connor. We went down there, and I started drinking I was so pissed. We both fell off the wagon and he got caught trying to buy crack. He ended up in jail and when he got out we got into a fight and he trashed the motel room...I didn't do it...he did. Then I had to settle up with the motel, so we wouldn't go to jail..."

"STOP! SHUTUP! Don't say another word. It's all just bullshit. I know the whole story the police already told me. You've been lying to me for months and I was too stupid and too trustworthy of you during this whole time and now look what you've done to me. You're nothing better than a ten-cent cunt. You lie when the truth would serve you better. To make matters worse you have been stealing the money from me to pay for everything you two have been doing. Do you know how much this has cost me so far?"

"Just a few thou...You can take it out of the alimony...I'll pay you back when I get the money from the trust fu..."

James lost it, "Look you drunk stupid bitch. You've crossed the line this time. You've already taken your first year of alimony in two weeks, over thirty thousand dollars! There is no trust fund till you straighten out and that may take...only God knows."

"No Baboo, I couldn't have taken that...I didn't spend anything like that. I just paid for the rooms, gas and some booze. Roger has been paying for a lot of stuff..."

"Shut up! He has been paying for all his stuff with your credit cards, which aren't yours anymore; they're mine, so therefore I've been paying for everything. And the grand total to date is over thirty thousand. Do you here that - thirty grand? Do you know now why I'm pissed?"

"Oh...I don't think...he told me he paid for his bail and a lot of the other stuff with his credit cards..."

"Susan, that fucking idiot with a dick attached can't spell credit card. You - no - I am being taken for a ride. Now where are you and how drunk are you and when was the last time you ate?"

"Slow down. I'm in Louisiana, no Mississippi. I ate yesterday. What day is it?"

James tried to recover, "Okay. Let's take it slowly. Susan, you need to get some sleep and some food in you. Can you drive? Never mind

114

I already know that answer. You can't drive sober, let alone drunk. Where is lover boy now?"

"He's asleep – really passed out."

"Okay first, go get the credit cards out of his wallet and take yours back. Now tell me where you are and I will come and get you."

"I don't know where I am – somewhere in Mississippi, some town along the highway, I-10. Don't come here. I'll be okay. I'll be home soon. Honest. I'm real close to Florida."

"Susan, you're in a fog. Come on, admit it, you don't even know what day it is. Tell me where you are..."

The phone went dead. James tried to call her back but all he got was the answering message. He didn't even bother to try to leave a message. She was blitzed but at least she was alive. How many times had he had to revive her? How many times had he taken her to the emergency room? How many times had he tried to straighten her life out? Too many times to count and he felt sad she had no control over her mind and body. And he could not influence or fix the situation.

This time was bad. Now she had taken a lover, boyfriend, drug taking, drinking buddy, whatever he was, James was mad and upset. For the first time in their fifteen-year relationship she had cheated on him. The anger rose in his body like a gathering storm. She may be done with him - but he wasn't done with her. He still felt responsible and obligated toward his wife – his ex-wife. She and the new boyfriend had crossed the line. James rationalized it was not Susan's fault. She had never ever done anything like this or had never wildly spent money – never. The blame was resting directly on the shoulders of the new man – Roger. He was stealing from James. He had stolen his wife; her credit cards and he had stolen James' money.

There was an anger building inside of James of huge proportions. From outward appearances no one would ever detect it. No one could ever see it happening to him. Slowly the rage was building like that of a pressure cooker on a stove at high heat. The rage, the heat, both coupled with the pressure – the powerful pressure. He knew how to control it. Never let it show, just smile and go on about your business. Be logical, plan, think and act in a deliberate non-associative manner to gain the desired objective.

The next night at two in the morning the phone rang, and it was Roger. "Hey man – how's it goin? That fuckin wife of yours is a great piece of ass, ain't she? I just love fuckin her. Did you like fuckin her?" He was drunk or stoned again and his words were slurred and ran together.

"Hey Roger, she's not my wife anymore," James said as a matter of fact. "She is now your problem. What the hell are you guys doing? – Touring the south – one motel at a time? You guys have made a real short trip into the longest voyage I have ever seen," said James chuckling.

"Ya –ha ha. It is a little long, but we ran into a bit of trouble here and there. And I have had to drive the whole way. Susan gets a little drunk and she can't drive for shit. Tomorrow, I think we're going to Pensacola."

"Ya Roger, you are getting closer. Ya, don't let her drive. Her eyesight isn't that good especially when she's drinking."

"Hey James, I know what you mean. When she drives we spend more time on the sidewalk than the road. I'm just trying to make this trip enjoyable...have a little fun..."

"Well you guys have fun. I'll talk with you later. Bye." James ended the conversation. There was no sense in trying to talk to him, Roger could barely keep the phone to his ear. He kept dropping it while talking.

At eleven pm the next night the phone rang, and it was Susan. "I need some help." She was sobbing, and her voice was full of fear.

"What's wrong Babyboo?"

"Roger beat me up again." Her incoherent words were mumbled and covered over with sobs.

James was about to say 'again' to her as if he didn't know, but he did know. He had pieced it all together so why try and get her to remember what she had said or not said. That would be a waste of time.

116

Her brain doesn't work anymore so why bother and question her. "Say it again...calm down...I'll help you...take a deep breath...start again..."

"We were parked (sob) at a 7-11." Her gut wrenching crying between sentences were the same as he had heard from wounded men dying in Vietnam. "He was trying to buy some crack. He could only get crack...from some Mesicans who were hanging out there." She broke into crying again. "There's something else..."

"What?"

She broke down completely again unable to continue. He did not rush her, all he could do was listen to her. She cried out plaintively with great pain and anguish, "He made me...made me...made me fuck two Mexicans so he could get the rock. I didn't want to...but he just kept hitting me till I had to...I'm sorry. It was horrible...I'm sorry..." Susan started crying with undistinguishable words interspaced in her sentences.

"After he got mad at me when I said...I had to go back to the motel...he then beat the shit out of me again right in the parking lot. Some cops pulled in next to us as he was beating me. They jumped out and arrested him. They found the rock on him, so they told me he was going be locked up for a while since...it's a holiday weekend... Fourth of Revolution thing, and he can't go before the judge till next week. The cops were real nice, and they got another couple of cops to help me up to the room since I was drunk and beat up...but at least I wasn't driving. They wanted to take me to the hospital, but I told them I was okay. Can you come and get me? I can't drive...my foot is all fucked up...I can't walk..." Her sobbing and crying never stopped.

James was silent, amazed by her story. She was still drunk and slurring her words, but sober enough that he realizes she was cognizant enough to make sense. He felt helpless and deeply sorry for her pain. He wasn't sure what to say. "You ready to stop drinking for a while?" was all he could say between the sobs.

"Yes, I will...I promise...I'm hurt pretty bad...I can't walk...Will you please hurry? I don't know how long before he can get out."

"Okay, where are you?"

"I'm at the Traveler's Inn Motel just off I-10 in Pensacola, room 236. When can you get here? I don't know which exit but here is the number and you can call them for directions."

James thought for a moment. "Okay." He took the number down. "I'll get started shortly. I have to get someone to come with me to drive your car back here. It will be a while because I'm five hundred miles away. I'll make it as quick as possible. Don't shut off your phone and get some sleep."

"I won't...please hurry. There's something else..."

"What?"

She started crying again. "He made me fuck the two Mexicans...I'm not a whore, am I? I didn't want to...honest. I mean it really hurt. I tried to fight them off, but he let them hit me too. It was easier to let them fuck me than to let them beat me anymore. At first, I said no but they all just kept hitting me till I had to...I'm sorry...then they were hitting me...It was horrible...I'm sorry. I'm not a whore...am I?"

James went quiet and thought for seconds trying to grasp her pain, "No, – you did what you had to do. Better to save yourself, forget it. Okay, I'll be there as soon as possible. Don't turn off your phone. We'll get through this. Everything is going to be okay." James hung up and stared at the wall trying to grasp what he had to do and what was going to be needed. Flashbacks of firefights from Vietnam were mixed with Susan's story. Then all he could think about was Nutan and how badly she had been hurt. He felt the pain and hurt Susan was going through. The divorce didn't mean a thing to him, he still loved her. Susan was in trouble and he would have to save her. No matter what, he had to get to her and save her from this animal before something else happened.

James was on a mission. He acted in a mechanical way...the way he had been taught by the Army. Don't think – act! He picked up the phone and called Ben. Ben was his field assistant, the second in command. He worked hard during the week. "Ben – can you take a trip with me? I need some help now. We need to take a drive to Pensacola and then I need someone to drive Susan's car back from Pensacola."

"Aw shit boss. Pensacola? Its Fourth of July weekend. I have plans. It's the only three days off I'm going to get for a long time. I'm tired and I need some rest. Can't you find someone else?"

"Ben...I can't trust anyone, especially for this. I'll tell you everything on the way. I'll make it up to you. I'll drive to Pensacola – you can sleep while I drive. We should be able to do the whole thing in twenty hours. You'll be back on Saturday night with Sunday and Monday to rest up."

"Okay. Boy, you talk me into the strangest things. Let me say goodbye to my girlfriend properly okay?"

"Ben, that should only take you about 3 minutes according to her. At least, that's what she told me..." James was trying to add a little humor to the situation.

"Fuck off boss!"

"Okay - I'll be at your place in about an hour and three minutes," James said with a laugh and hung up.

Chapter Twelve

The Trip

James gathered what he needed and headed for Ben's apartment, stopping by an ATM and a gas station to fill up. He reached Ben's place. Ben was outside waiting. Ben crawled in the back seat, growled and said he was going to take the nap he was promised. James swung up onto the Florida Turnpike and headed north. He was wide awake and trying to plan this out. He could not make any decisions until he could get control of Susan. The sun was rising when Ben awoke. James took an exit and went to a pancake house type restaurant, so they could grab some breakfast.

After they were seated Ben turned to James. "Okay boss, this should be good. Tell me why in hell I am now on my way to Pensacola - with you - on a hot – crowded holiday weekend with the highways - jammed with cars - instead of lying with my beautiful girlfriend in my bed in Stuart?"

During breakfast James told Ben everything he knew.

"What a nightmare," was Ben's reaction. "What are you going to do Boss?"

"First I have to get control of the situation. I have to get control of Susan and bring her back to Stuart. Then I'll see from there." There was no reason to involve Ben with his real thoughts. After breakfast Ben said he would drive for a while so James could sleep.

As they neared Pensacola it was about noon time and Ben woke James although he never really slept. James called the motel and got directions. They easily found the motel and pulled around back until they found the right room. James went up to check things out. He knocked on the door of the room and finally had to really bang hard on the door to wake Susan up. She finally opened the door after ten minutes of knocking.

121

James saw his beautiful ex-wife. He almost couldn't recognize her. She was a disaster. She looked more like a dirty, alcoholic, bag lady who hadn't bathed in a month. The stench of booze, beer, cigarettes and rancid BO filled his nostrils with a rush. Susan's face was heavily bruised, smeared with dry blood, her hair was a mess, tangled and matted, her clothes ripped and torn, she was hopping on one leg and she looked worse than he had ever seen her.

James grimaced at the site of her. Suddenly he started to cry. Tears rolled down his cheeks. He helped her back to the bed and sat her down. James went to the door and waved Ben up. Ben was in shock at the sight of her. They started to clean her up as best they could, washed her with wet towels, getting rid of the dried blood. Susan sat quietly sobbing, flinching when they rubbed against a sore or injured part of her body, constantly trying to fall over so she could go back to sleep. She was in a daze. Quietly she made comments, James said yes and agreed to anything and everything she said but was just patronizing her. He told Ben what to do as they cleaned her up. James couldn't stop quietly crying.

They quickly threw her things in a bag, found the keys to her car and then James fireman carried her down the stairs to his car. He laid her down in the back seat where she immediately fell asleep. James and Ben talked and discussed their plan to get back up on the highway and head east back to Stuart. Ben wanted to take her to a hospital right away. James vetoed his thoughts. He knew it would be easier to do in Stuart and besides her injuries could wait, they weren't life threatening. Ben did not understand that James had become a professional medic and doctor when it came to Susan. They stopped first for gas; some things to munch on and soft drinks then drove onto I-10 and headed east. With Susan passed out in the back seat, they rolled across the Florida panhandle in caravan, talking every fifteen minutes or so, on their Nextel radios. After two hundred miles, they had another gas stop and then quickly returned to the highway.

Susan came to and started talking her trash talk, trying to justify this, her latest trip and experience. James just listened as he had so many times before. She pissed him off with each word; he kept it all to himself and just kept driving. He had to get back, so he could sleep and plan what to do next. At midnight they got to the house. Ben split with the car he was driving and returned to his apartment, saying they would meet up later to get the car back to James. James carried Susan into the bathroom. He took off his clothes and then stripped her down and put her in the shower with him. She couldn't stand on her own, so he braced her and washed her. He soaped her down and shampooed her with one hand while holding her up with the other. She kept slumping downward, so he finally had to lay her down in the tub to wash her properly. Her body was covered with bruises and cuts all over with different hues of yellow, purple, blue and red skin tones.

She was slowly sobering up. After the shower she wanted a drink and to talk. James had learned long ago from the medical pros at the hospitals and rehab places not to try to sober her up himself. Each and every one he had ever talked to about her always warned him to let her keep drinking lightly until he could get professional help. She could easily go into convulsions and she was prone to seizures as she had demonstrated many times in the past. He did what they had told him to do – let her drink and try to moderate it down. He gently carried her to a chair and made them each a light drink.

They sat, talked and had a few drinks for an hour. "How come you can drink and stay so sober?" she asked.

"Because my dear I don't make drinking an Olympic event like you do. Your body is allergic to alcohol and it has total control of your mind. Someday you will realize it, hopefully soon, and you will be able to stop. And I hope I live to see it and I hope you do too," James said lovingly.

He discussed with her his plan to sober her up. Let her rest up for the balance of this weekend. He was sure it wasn't broken. When she felt better he would take her to the hospital for an x-ray on her leg. Then he would put her in the dry out clinic connected with one of the hospitals in their town. They would hold her there for 72 to 96 hours and keep a watch on her and give her any medication she would need while sobering up. Then he would decide what was next and best for her.

He carried her to the bed. She started crying and sobbing again. It lasted for about ten minutes. James sat next to her quietly stroking her hair until Susan finally fell asleep. James went back to the porch and had another drink by himself. It had been a long hard trip. He had never seen her in a worse condition. She was a physical wreck and her brain was totally shot. How could she let herself get to this condition? Why had she allowed Roger to physically abuse her? How could Roger do this

123

to her? She knew better. She had two Masters Degrees, she was smart and intelligent. The alcohol was the cause of this problem. The alcohol was the root of the problem and Roger was the manipulator and the devil incarnate. Roger had certainly taken advantage of her and James' credit cards. James was slowly putting the pieces of his next move together. Since Roger was the problem now and could cause more harm in the future, he would remove the problem, permanently. He had only about five weeks before he was to leave for Brazil. He had to come up with the total plan. He had to be careful. There could be many connections made if he was not careful. It had to be done in a manner where it would not come back on him. Somehow, he had to find an alibi which would remove him as far as possible from the action. He started thinking the process through. He had done this before. It was just a matter of being very careful – very careful.

James finally went to sleep next to his Susan. As he crawled into bed, he knew there was nothing left between them sexually, even though he knew at some point she would probably try to start something, he was not interested. He just wanted to get her back to sanity and on the wagon. He did not love her sexually anymore. His pride would not let him. She had stepped outside of their relationship and he did not want her back. He was thoroughly disgusted with her actions. She had crossed that imaginary line. He just wanted her to be able to return to some form of a normal life, whatever normal is.

Chapter 13

The Plan

James tended to Susan over the weekend. They slept late on Sunday and finally got up around three pm. Susan had awoken first and somehow crawled from the bed. James got up to find her sitting on the porch having a drink. He made coffee shaking his head in disbelief and joined her. They talked, as they always had. She was apologetic and remorseful. He easily and slowly pumped her for information about Roger, trying not to raise any suspicion. Where did he live, what did he do and anything else, which could give him clues as to how to handle what he was about to do?

He took her to the hospital on Tuesday and had her leg x-rayed. Susan had a sprained knee and ankle, badly bruised thigh, calf and two broken toes which they put in a walking splint. James brought her back from the hospital and the next day he took her to the dry out clinic. He made sure they stopped at the bank first to have Susan sign off the accounts.

With her in safe hands for a few days he could start planning and looking at his options. He looked at the situation as he would a military operation, looking for the loopholes. Where could he fail? What were the weak points? How could he get caught? How could Susan be used against him? There were many cross points where eyebrows could be raised if he wasn't careful. This operation has to go off without a hitch. This was the most dangerous one he had ever pulled off. He had to have an iron clad alibi. He could not eliminate his desire, reason or motive. Therefore, he just had to be in two different places at the same time, one place to commit what he was about to do and another place to prove he could not have committed any crime.

Four days later Susan returned from the hospital, not looking her former self but a lot better than the condition when James had found her. She spent two more days at the house sober. Susan decided she could handle her life again and wanted to return to Ocala. James followed her to Ocala to make sure she returned safely.

He went with her to the Sheriff's office with her to swear out a restraining order against Roger. The next day, with Susan's promises to stay sober ringing in his ears, he headed home. What he did not realize was - he would never see his Susan again. During the drive he planned his next step the whole way.

*****

"Hey Alan, how goes it?"

"James - good to hear from you pal. Where have you been?" James launched into the story of Susan and what had happened and spared no detail. "It was the worst I have ever seen her." At the end of the story he had to end with one last detail. "I checked yesterday with the Sheriff's department in Pensacola and guess what?" he said rhetorically, "they let the bastard out due to a technicality. Well this sort of changes my plans. Hey listen, I need I big, big favor from you."

"Sure, whatever you need."

"I need you to come to Florida for three or four days. I need to do something and it would be wonderful if you could come, visit and stay with me. Why don't you arrive a week from Wednesday. Maybe we could go fishing. Something like that..."

Alan immediately knew where James was going with this conversation, "Hold on James...no more...you promised me you wouldn't anymore! You are not married to her...it is not your responsibility. You're getting too old for this. You get caught and you're not going to like being some big, black guy's prison bitch with a big asshole. Buddy, you are going to slip up. Don't do this, please don't."

"Alan let me cut to the chase. Yes, I'm going to and I need a cover and you can do that so well for me. We can grab the boat and just go fishing...You owe me big time...do I have to remind you who got you out of that crazy business deal, where you almost lost everything you own including the fillings in your teeth to that fucking guy who was going to clean your clock? Just one more time is necessary, and I need your help."

"James, why don't you just say you're up here and that way I can just stay here? I'll cover for you – very easy."

"Nice thought buddy – would if I could but too many trip wires doing it that way. Too easy to trace stuff. You've got to do this for me. Oh, and by the way, send my little pea shooter I left up there. Just break it down and mail it in a few different packages and let's do this thing as quick as possible. I'm hoping for next week."

"Mother fucker – okay let me see what I have to do. Promise me we will sit down and discuss this and if I come up with an alternative you will listen to me? God, you make me nervous."

"Hey, come on Alan, where's the old Nam spirit?"

"I left it in Nam and you should have too," Alan hung up.

*****

The next week went smoothly. The site was slowly finishing up on schedule. Beth was only coming over to James' house once a week for her sex session. She was calm, happy and a joy to work with. She stopped her advances in the office. There was plenty of work to keep her busy. The site and the buildings would finish on time.

The packages arrived. James assembled his gun, a small, six shot, thirty-two caliber pistol. The numbers had been filed off years before when he had put it in a safe place for future use. Alan was scheduled to arrive on Wednesday.

On Monday, James left at noon and drove to Naples, Florida, a two-hour trip. He drove around and found the AA meeting place Susan said she had been to for meetings, when she had visited there. He found, what was supposedly, Roger's apartment. He visited three bars in the area looking for the right set up. He looked for parking lots. He walked around looking for security; cameras, police points, obstacles that could impede his plan. He drove out of town in two different directions until he found what he was looking for; a deserted area, an orange grove five-miles outside of town. He drove the route twice to fix it in his brain. He found an entrance to the grove and drove in, got out and walked around and found an irrigation ditch. He then went back to town and went to Roger's apartment, parked outside across the street and waited in his car.

A painting company pick-up truck finally drove up about five-thirty and Roger got out. He matched the description Susan had given him. He spoke with the driver for a few seconds, then the truck drove off and Roger went into his first-floor apartment. He was wearing painters' pants, a T shirt and sneakers. At six-thirty, Roger came out of the apartment and started walking toward the main part of town. He went to the AA meeting hall for an apparent seven pm meeting. James slowly drove the area for thirty minutes then went back to the AA hall and waited across the street. At eight pm the meeting was over. It wasn't dark yet, so Roger was easy to watch and follow. Roger went to one of the three bars James had been in earlier. James smiled and thought; – Just a good little alcoholic, just like I thought.' James parked his car and went into the bar.

Roger was sitting at the bar alone, drinking a shot and a beer.

There were very few people in the bar. James took a stool three down from Roger and ordered a beer, never really looking at the bartender. He sat there quietly, sipping his beer and watching Roger out of the corner of his eye. During his second beer he turned toward Roger and asked, "You from around here?"

Roger looked over, "Ya. Where ya from?"

"Miami. I'm over here looking at a job for a client that he wants me to do. This one is just going be a pain in the ass." James sounded discouraged and put out.

"What do ya mean?" Roger asked curiously.

"Well the guy's a good client and just bought another house over here. I've got to paint it for him inside and out. I'm a painting contractor and I do all his work in Miami, so I've got to help him out. I have too much work in Miami. This is just a pain in the ass."

"How so?" Roger's interest rose significantly.

128

"Oh, the job pays well but I have no one I can spare from my crew to send over here to do it. If I could just find a decent painter here to handle the job; you know, prep the job and buy the paint, just do it. But I haven't even got the time to spend looking for someone. Life's a pain isn't it?"

"Well my friend, today is your lucky day" said Roger with glee in his voice.

"How's that?"

Roger picked up his beer and moved over on the stool next to James. "Hi, my name is Roger Cleft and I just happen to be a painter and lookin for my next project. Maybe we could hook somethin up. I could do the job for you. I've been a painter for over ten years. I'm the best painter in town."

James shook his hand and introduced himself as Leon Scorbia then signaled the bartender for another round. "Ya, sounds good to me. You could handle the whole thing, inside and out, beginning to end, no problem?"

"Well ya, no problem, if the money's right. I ain't comin down on my price for anyone. I can get all the work I want, so if we can agree on the money…"

"Well Roger, okay, what the fuck do you want for money?"

"I get eight cents per square foot inside and twelve cents per square foot outside per coat. That's for a one-story house. Now that includes flat on the walls, ceilins and semi on the jambs and base. If there's staging necessary, I charge by the hour to put up and take down, at twenty bucks per hour. If there's a lot of prep work, I charge by the hour for that at twenty per hour. Painting is a flat rate and everythin else is by the hour – like if I have to go get the paint – stuff like that. You pay for all materials and a spray unit rental. I can spray, right?"

James started going over the details, "The house is in good shape, white inside and green outside. It's a four thousand square foot house so it should figure about sixteen thousand square feet inside and another eight thousand outside. Very little prep work and minor staging. A little new color added in some rooms, two coats maybe three depending on the color. You can spray no problem; the house is empty and there are new

129

rugs going in so no problem with overspray. You have to clean up for yourself as part of the price. But here's the trick, Roger; I have to get this done by the end of next month – for sure. You might have to work a few weekends to get it done in time. As long as you think you can handle it – ON TIME – then I'll add a thousand as an on-time bonus. I'll pop you a grand at start and pay for what's done by the week and the bonus if you get it done on time – no exceptions. You should be able to walk away with about seven grand for the whole thing for a month's work. What do you think Roger?"

Roger just stared at him. James knew Roger was trying to figure how many rocks he could buy. He was also figuring how much he could screw Leon out of. "Okay Leon, we got a deal but one thing. I want fifteen hundred up front. I got some bills to pay and I ain't got no time to chase the money owed to me, so if you want it done on time – that's what I need up front. Do we have a deal?"

James took a deep breath looked pensive for ten seconds then said, "Deal" and then shook Roger's hand. "Tell you what Roger. Let's have another beer on it. I've got to get back to Miami. Can we meet on Thursday late and we can go to the job so I can show you where it is and give you the colors, so you can get started?

"What about the money?" Roger was drooling for the money.

Oh ya, no sweat. I'll give you the fifteen hundred and a grand for the materials to start with. How about that?"

"Sure Leon, sounds good. I'll meet you here at six pm. Oh, I will need it in cash to get started."

"Cash, no problem, instead, give me your address and phone number and I'll pick you up at your place about five-thirty. That will be easier for me – that okay with you? Will grab some beer, go look at the job, come to a final agreement and settle up. That way you can get started as soon as possible. Can you start by Monday?"

"Okay." Roger wrote the information down on a scrap of paper and handed it to James. "Now give me yours Leon."

"Well my stupid girlfriend carefully dropped my cell in the water yesterday. I have to get a new one tomorrow. Giving you the number won't help. Don't worry, you just be at your place on Thursday and I

130

will meet you there. If I have a change in plans, I will call you and let you know."

All of a sudden Roger became very serious and instructive, "You need to beat the shit out of your broad for doin that. She won't do it a second time. You've got to keep these cunts in line. Take it from me, if you do not beat them on a regular basis – they won't respect you, they won't fuck you good and they turn into rotten cunts. I always beat them and a few cigarette burns here and there, never hurt either. I just broke one of my girlfriend's legs. Now, she really respects me. Oh, I tell them I love them after and all that cry crap, but you've got to beat them and slap them around. Do it! – You'll see how good it works!"

James wasn't sure what to do. He fought the urge to reach out and just strangle this bastard. That would ruin the plan and put him in jeopardy. He bit his lower lip. He then smiled and said, "I'll try that when I get home and see what happens, thanks, good idea."

James downed his beer, paid both their bar tabs with cash, left a big tip and said he had to get back to Miami. He thanked Roger again, said it had been a pleasure, looked forward to working with him and quickly left. As he reached the door he gave a quick glimpse back to see Roger grabbing the tip off the bar. James smiled, thinking this guy is very greedy and very predictable. James drove back to Stuart thinking that was too easy. This guy was drooling for the money. He thinks he is going to screw me out of some money. He will be there at the appointed hour, of that James was sure.

*****

James called his good friend Bruce, who owned the excavation and utility company, which did all the work for James' projects. Through the years, their business relationship had grown into a very close, personal friendship. "Bruce, I need to borrow one of your trucks on Thursday, okay?"

"Sure James, anything you need buddy, what's up"

131

"Nothing I just have to do something. You don't need to know. How about that white pickup truck? It doesn't have new tires on it, does it?"

"Sure, but new tires? Why do you ask? No, it doesn't have new tires."

"Don't ask. Just leave the keys in it on Thursday and don't lock your yard where you keep it. Okay?"

"Sure, anything for you but..."

"I said - don't ask, just do – Got it?"

"Okay. Are you going to explain this to me?"

"No, I am not. Just remember to leave the keys it on Thursday and leave your yard unlocked on Thursday and it will be back by Friday morning, okay? And you don't know anything. Ya, one more thing, go buy new tires for the truck on Friday and bury the old tires where they can't be found. I'll pay for them but just make sure you do a good job of getting rid of them."

"Not a problem. You got it boss."

*****

James picked Alan up at the airport on Wednesday afternoon. All the way back to the house, all Alan did was try to talk James out of what he was going to do. After they reached the house they made drinks and sat on the porch to talk.

"You can't keep doing this. Please stop James. Something is bound to go wrong at some point and then it will be too late. You will end up spending the rest of your life in the slammer. How many have you done anyway? Tell me the truth."

"Look brother Alan. You are the only person who knows what I have done. It isn't that I am proud of it. It is just that it needed to be

132

done. The men whom I have killed…deserved to be killed. Remember Nam and all the people we killed who really didn't need to be killed except they were in the wrong place, wrong war at the wrong time. We weren't there at the same time, but the story is the same either during your tour in Nam or my tour and you know it.

Woman and children need to be respected and protected. You know as well as I do, I only do it when there is a need for someone I love or like very much. I am sick of the bullshit in this society that allows assholes to hurt woman and children and I should add; when someone wanted to financially hurt my brother, Alan…Well, I just can't allow that to happen. When someone fucks with my world – I fuck with theirs. I'm just killing slimy slugs. I am the prosecutor, jury and judge in one neat package. Hey, be thankful, the local county police department just started publishing the pictures and addresses of all the child molesters in this area. Don't worry; I'm not going to go after them. Too public – too easy to get caught – not my deal. And to answer your question…with this one - makes only four. And this one is the last. I am getting nervous about getting caught."

"Okay. I'll cover for you. How do you want to do it?"

"We are going out fishing for the afternoon and evening. We will come back about eleven with lights on. We will make enough noise leaving and you make plenty of noise coming back. Make sure you yell my name, like I'm going to the house. We load the boat on the way out and then make a stop at the marine dock for fuel, beer and bait fish. We make a commotion, so everyone hears and sees us and remembers us at the marina. On the way out to the inlet, I get off at a dock I know, and I leave you there. You and the boat head out the inlet and go way out in the ocean to fish. You have a good day fishing, stay away from other boats and don't make contact with anyone. I should be back by ten or eleven, so I'll try to be on the dock waiting for you. Let's just keep it real simple. Any questions?"

"Na, sounds simple enough. Too bad you won't supply me with a woman to keep me busy."

"No complications my friend - no complications. Keep the radio on channel eleven and if there is a problem I will call you. If I am not on the dock at eleven there maybe problems. Just keep your mouth shut and go back to Maine. Grab a cab from the downtown cab stand and don't talk to anyone. Just go home. If all goes well, and it will, we will have a drink at eleven. Guess what – tomorrow is the eleventh. Good omen!”

"God, you make me nervous."

"Okay, we have a long day fishing tomorrow. Let's get some sleep."

Chapter Fourteen
Just a Normal Day

Thursday started as a normal day. James went to work while Alan readied the boat. His boat was a Silverton 33-foot cabin cruiser. James kept it at a dock on his property which was on Manatee Pocket. The Pocket was a harbor right off the intercoastal waterway with direct access to the Port St. Lucie inlet which led to the ocean. People around the Pocket knew James and his boat.

James told everyone he was going fishing and left the site well before noon. He went home and helped Alan finish getting the boat ready. They took the boat down the harbor to one of the marina gas docks. They made a lot of noise as they brought the boat to the dock. James purposely brought the boat in cockeyed to the dock and then had to make three attempts to bring the boat in properly. Alan on the bow, throwing lines that missed the dock boy by a mile. Finally, when the boat was tied up to the dock the dock boy laughingly asked if they had ever been in a boat before. A long conversation ensued with the dock boy and the man who pumped the gas into the boat's tanks. James and Alan went to the marina store and bought beer, ice, sandwiches, bait and some fishing equipment. Joking, making more noise than necessary and flirting with the girl behind the counter. They invited her to go out for a day of "fishing" with them. She refused but James was sure she would remember them.

They left the dock and headed for the inlet. Once out of site of the Pocket, James quickly swung the boat toward a private dock and brought the boat in. Alan took the helm and James jumped on the dock and quickly disappeared while Alan, never stopping, turned the boat back into the channel and out the inlet to the ocean and went out of site.

James walked a path through a small clump of woods which led back almost to his house. He got in his car and drove over to the next town and the yard where Bruce kept his equipment. He left his car and took the truck Bruce had left for him. He put some made-up magnetic signs on the truck with "Leon's Painting" which had a false telephone number on them. He drove to Naples and arrived about five fifteen and made a stop at a 7-11 for a case of cold beer. He then drove to Roger's apartment and arrived at five thirty. He stayed in the truck and beeped the horn. Roger came out and jumped in the truck.

"Hey Roger, good to see you again. Here, have a beer. I picked some up a few minutes ago."

"Oh Leon, I was gettin worried you wasn't goin to show."

They exchanged pleasantries as James left and started driving out of town. James started talking about the job and slowly drove out of town while they drank beer. They downed about two beers each when James said he was lost and had gone the wrong way. He swung around and finally found the right road. It was totally deserted as he expected. He knew where he was the whole time. He drove till he found the orange grove he wanted. He swung off the road and into the grove.

"Hey, where we goin Leon?"

"Oh, this beer got me good. I've got to drain my pet weasel." He pulled up between some trees, so he wouldn't be spotted from the road. "I'll be right back. You need to go?"

"Na, I'm cool. I've got a big tank and can hold half a case before I come up for air."

James wandered off into the grove. He waited a few minutes, pulled the gun from his pocket, checked the rounds and yelled at Roger. "Hey Roger – come here. You've got to see this!"

Roger got out of the truck and made his way to where James was. They were separated by the drainage ditch.

"Over there Roger! In the drainage ditch, check it out."

Roger went over to the edge of the ditch and looked into it. "I don't see nothin."

James approached and got to about 10 feet away from Roger. As Roger turned toward James, James fired a shot hitting Roger in the left knee. Roger fell to the ground, rolling half way into the drainage ditch and howled.

"Holy shit! You shot me! What the fuck you do that for? Oh my God you shot me! You shot my knee! Help me I'm bleedin!"

James calmly said, "Shut up you miserable fuck."

"What are you doin? I'm bleedin, help me I can't walk! Help me!"

"Roger, get use to it and enjoy your last few minutes on this planet."

"Leon, what the fuck are you talkin about? I haven't done nothin to you. Are you crazy?"

"Shut up Roger and I'll tell you. Look you miserable piece of shit. You are just a rotten human being. You stole over thirty thousand dollars from me. Then you fucked my wife."

Roger was pleading and crying, "Leon – Leon. What are you talkin about? I just met you the other day. I didn't steal any money from you. I don't know your wife. Stop it you're makin a mistake!"

"Shut up Roger. I'm not Leon, I'm James and you just stole thirty thousand from me. You have been keeping my wife, Susan, drunk, fucking her, letting Mexicans fuck here like some whore you own just so you could get a rock and then you continually beat her up. Now you are going to pay me back. You understand now? You fucking piece of shit!"

Roger looked confused and then his mental light bulb started getting brighter. "Huh, you're James, Susan? - thirty thousand? – No, I didn't – honest! Stop, please stop and let's talk this over – please help me. We talked on the phone – everything was cool – you said so."

"Too late Roger – If you had thirty g's on you that might be one thing. But then I would still have to deal with what you did to my wife, the other women you have beaten up and all the other crap you have done in your stinking, miserable life. You crossed the line with the wrong person."

"You said she wasn't your wife anymore."

"Just a figure of speech. You're just a miserable piece of crap but not for long."

Roger started pulling himself out of the drainage ditch with one hand while holding his bloody knee with his other hand. "Help me please! We can work this out, just gimme a chance – please!"

"Stay where you are Roger!"

Roger tried to pull himself up to a standing position.

James shot again, hitting Roger in the other knee. Roger howled and fell down on the top of the edge of the ditch. "I said don't move Roger."

Roger was howling, holding both knees. Whimpering he said, "Please stop, please, please stop. I'll do anything you want – I'm sorry, I'm sorry. I'll pay you back, honest!"

"Roger, you've led a miserable life. Didn't you think it would catch up with you someday? Well today is the day it is all catching up to you. All the miserable, rotten things you've done to people – today is the day – today is your day of reckoning. Today is pay back day from all the people you have hurt – sorry about that," said James coldly.

"You can't kill me, please don't. You'll go to jail, you don't want that. Just help me, I'll never say a word, I'll pay you back...I'll do anythin...please...stop...com'on man...please..." Roger reached slowly for a large rock thinking James hadn't noticed it.

James fired another round hitting Roger's hand. He howled more. "Please stop - please!" Roger was bleeding from both knees and now his left hand was a bloody mess.

"You shouldn't have reached for that rock Roger. Now, I only have three rounds left. Let's see where shall I aim next? I'm a pretty good shot, wouldn't you say Roger? I learned how to shoot in Nam. Good training provided by good old Uncle Sam. You know Roger, I've killed better men than you and I didn't even know their names. They were just faces and bodies. I feel sorry I had to do it but with you, I am just enjoying this with a great sense of satisfaction and happiness. This is what it is all about. Ridding the world of vermin like you. You're a miserable piece of shit."

James heard a car go by on the road. He waited and listened. The car never stopped and finally was out of earshot. "Now Roger, the next

138

bullet is for my wife. You're going to love this one." James moved to his left, raised the gun and shot at Roger's groin. Direct hit. Roger yelped and howled, spurting blood from between his legs.

"Aw gee whiz Roger, only two bullets left. Let's see, where should I put them?"

Roger looked up at him with both hands holding his groin and both knees bleeding. Gasping, panting with blood squirting out of many places covering Roger and the ground around him. "Please James, let me live – please let me live. I promise I won't tell anyone. I'll say it was a huntin accident – please let me live!"

"Sorry Roger, too late to stop now. I decided a long time ago you were going to die and now is the time. Where would you like the last two bullets? I think one in the head and one in your black little heart. You have any preference which goes where and which one first?"

"Please stop – please stop! I don't want to die, please, please."

"Sorry Roger, it's just your turn to die. I think the next shot is for your heart, you might still live for a few moments, then I'm going to put a shot right between your eyes. Then your pain will be over and all the pain you have caused others will be avenged. It's time Roger. Anything you'd like to say? Would you like to confess your sins? Hurry Roger, I'm tired of this and I have to get out of here before somebody hears or shows up - sorry."

"Don't do it – please don't do it – please…"

"You're boring me." James was transfixed. He was flashing back to Nam. He took careful aim, fired the fifth shot hitting Roger just to the side of his heart. He was still barely alive, gasping for air. James smiled and laughed a low chuckle and took a few steps closer. "In Nam, that is what we call a sucking chest wound Roger. It's almost a definite killer, but I owe you one more. Say bye-bye Roger." As Roger looked at James' face, James took careful aim and shot the last bullet at the top of Roger's nose. He slumped over, dead and lifeless. James just looked at him for a few seconds then leaned over and couldn't feel any pulse in Roger's neck. He was dead, very dead. James took a small plastic bag of pot he had brought with him and carefully wiped his finger prints off the bag with a handkerchief. He put it in Roger's hand for a second and then very carefully inserted it in Roger's jeans. James rolled the body down into the drainage ditch by kicking it with his foot. James looked once more at the body lying at the bottom of the ditch, he then turned and went back to the truck. James smiled as he thought of something from Nam. Then he said out loud, laughing; "Probably should have put the honey on him and let the ants make it really painful for him."

He drove back to Stuart. He turned the radio on, sang along with the songs and drank a few beers along the way and felt wonderful. James came upon a river and pulled off the road just before the bridge that crossed it. He walked to the middle of the bridge on the sidewalk which ran along one side. He looked around carefully to see if there was anyone in sight. James then threw the gun into the river. He went back to the truck hopped in and drove away. He drove carefully so as not to get stopped for any reason or attract any attention. He went to Bruce's yard, exchanged vehicles, locked the gate and drove to his house. He arrived at 9:30.

He picked up the portable marine radio and called Alan. "Allee, Allee in free." James went to the shower to wash and change. He carefully put his clothes in a plastic bag and then put them in the trunk of his car to dispose of later. He took a shower and dressed. He poured himself a drink and went down to the dock to wait for Alan and his boat.

It only took a few minutes before Alan arrived. They tied up the boat and decided to wash the boat down the next day. They headed for the house and sat down with a drink.

"How did it go?" Alan finally asked.

"No problems. How many fish did we catch?"

"Just some small ones – a couple of small redfish and a lot of barracuda. We threw them all back. We spent the day talking and drinking beer."

They talked long into the night going over all the details of what James had done. They decided how to spend the rest of the weekend. James was going to work on Friday for a short while and then they would hang in the area for the rest of the weekend, have some food and drink and then Alan would go back on Sunday morning.

Early Saturday morning James and Alan sat down over a pot of coffee. "James, you can't keep doing this...You are going to get caught...I am really worried..."

"Look I won't do it anymore. I just had to do this one...too many reasons not to do it. He was a bad person and bad people should not live in this world...at least not in my world. I'll stop. I'm getting too old and I could make a mistake. People are killed all over the world and their murderers get away with it most of the time. It is usually a crime of passion or one that is witnessed, that is when and why they get caught. Just sloppy murderers," James chuckled. "People who intentionally plan ahead are the ones who get away with murder. People should be allowed to be in this world without fear. All my acts outside of Nam were justified. Nam was a war which is different than intentional murder. Wars are just stupid political murder and should never take place.

You should have seen how badly that guy hurt my little Nutan. She was just a young girl, not a whore. He beat her almost to death and what for? His pleasure...the sick fuck. He had no right to do it or reason. She will never walk right again or use her left arm. I had to leave her there. It broke my heart."

"Well you could go back and get her," Alan suggested.

"Ya, but the past is the past. I flash back there all the time, but I don't want to go there ever again. If I had tried to bring her back here I might have gotten caught. It might have raised too many questions. I gave her a lot of money before I left and sent her some after I got back to the states. Still do, but after the war I lost contact...it's best to leave it alone. I'm wrong but that's the way it went down. Now your situation was different. That guy was just trying to screw you to a wall. How did you get so deep in debt to him?"

Alan stuttered, ... "Well I...it just happened...I thought...if I just borrowed the money...my deal...the fishing camp would make enough money to be able to pay it back...but it didn't, you know...we've talked about it enough."

"Ya, but it didn't – so therefore someone had to help you. We have talked about this too much. I don't want to beat a dead horse. It doesn't bother me, it was easy. I made him give me back all the papers you signed and then he fell down the stairs and died. Terrible, terrible accident. He was just a leach, a parasite…a Shylock, who did this to many people. I hope some of the other people he tried to fuck were helped by his death."

"But, it was just business after all…" Alan interjected.

"Whose side are you on, yours or his?" James shot back. "What…are you having a change of heart?... Little late my friend…Was he not the son of a bitch who was going to take away everything you own?...all your hopes?…all your dreams? For what - a few dollars?"

Alan hung his head as in shame. "Ya, you're right. It was best. I owe you…thanks."

"I did it for you because we have been friends for a long, long time and you are closer than a brother, and no one is going to hurt my brother. Please remember, he was doing it to many people. He would screw his mother if there was a nickel in it for him."

"What about your secretary's husband, the one in Houston? You have never said much about that one."

James got up, grabbed their mugs, went to the kitchen and poured another round of coffee. He returned to the porch and quietly thought about the question. "Well, Phyllis was my secretary and a very good one. She was married with two little children. Her husband was a concrete truck driver."

"Were you doing her?" Alan interrupted.

"NO! I wasn't. He was a bad drunk and use to beat her and the kids on a regular basis. She never said anything about it and kept it quiet, but I had my suspicions from some of the marks I noticed. Then she was out sick for about a week. When she came back I put my hand on her back while I was talking to her. She jumped and screamed from my touch. That's when I found out he had set her on fire and her skin was all burned off her back. He had gotten drunk, got pissed at her and sprayed her with lighter fluid then set her on fire. Somehow, she got the fire out but not before her back was pretty well damaged. She went to the hospital; got treated saying it was an accident of some kind. It was never reported as anything else other than an accident."

Alan was cringing from the story.

142

"That's when she told me the whole story. He had always beaten her and the children whenever he got drunk. She lived accepting it because she had no family nearby. He always took all the money she earned and told her that if she ever told anyone, he would kill her or the kids. She was afraid because he was so violent. That was the norm, and then he got really drunk that night, sprayed her with the lighter fluid and set her on fire."

Alan was shaking his head in disbelief, "Then what did you do?"

James lowered his voice. "Well I – we found out that her husband had a one hundred-thousand-dollar insurance policy through his company. After a lot of discussions, I convinced her she would be better off without him and especially if she was a hundred g's richer. I forgot to pay her one Friday and called her house that night and as expected he answered the phone. I told him I had to go that way and I would meet him to give him her check. He was a greedy bastard. He jumped at the chance to get out of the house and get money to go drinking with. He met me at a quiet stretch of country road as agreed in Tomball close to where their driveway met the road where they lived. I gave him the check, he turned away and I knocked him over the head. I took the check back, left him partially in the road and ran over him. I had rented a car for the occasion. The Tomball police never put two and two together. They came by and questioned me as her employer; general stuff. They didn't seem too interested. They just thought he was a drunk, got out of his truck to take a piss, fell down, hit his head, knocked himself out and then got run over by a hit and run."

Alan jumped with, "Couldn't they trace the tire marks or the car or something?"

"I don't know, but they never put it together. There are a lot of tires in Houston and the Tomball Police are way under staffed and it just went as a case unsolved. I guess they believed it was a hit and run but they really didn't have any leads. Phyllis buried him, collected the insurance and moved her and her kids back to her family in St. Louis. End of story. It's been over ten years, so I don't think anything is going to come of it." James spoke easily and without emotion.

"Wow, you got really lucky on that one," Alan whistled.

"So that's all of it...all four. There is not going to be any more. Now you know the whole story. I was worried for a while about the Phyllis deal but that's gone by the boards. She kept her mouth shut. On this one, I need to be ready to answer a few questions. I was out fishing with you, and I don't think anyone saw anything. There isn't much to connect me to that turd. They might be able to connect me through Susan, but with the restraining order it appears I was just trying to help her and stay legally clear of the situation. Com'on let's go grab lunch at Shrimpers."

*****

At the end of the next week James called Susan to check up on her. She was sober but seemed sad. "What's the matter?" he asked.

"Oh, the police came by to ask me some questions. Roger was killed in a drug deal gone wrong they said."

"Good. Now you don't have to worry anymore about him. Serves him right. You okay?"

"Ya, he didn't do me any favors."

"What else did the cops ask?" James asked.

"Nothing much. Just asked if I knew anything. I said no, and they left."

"Look, Susan, I am going on a vacation for a couple of weeks. I am going to Brazil to visit some friends. I need to get away, I'm tired."

"Oh! Can I go with you? I'm not working yet, and we could have some fun. Take me with you. Who do you know in Brazil?"

"No, you can't go...it is sort of business...a fishing trip." James chuckled and thought, 'there isn't enough booze in Brazil if she starts to party.' He quickly tried to get her off the subject. "Will you be okay for a while?"

"Ya, but I want to go, pretty please..."

"I said no and that's the end of it. I am sending you some money to get you by. See if you can mend some fences with your family while I'm gone. See if you can get some money from them. I can't support you for a while. You kind of ruined that my dear."

Susan got quiet again. "I'm sorry about that. I'll see if I can get back in their good graces."

"Okay, you behave and don't drink. Make it happen." "I will," she said, but if you change your mind about Brazil...

James hung up.

Chapter Fifteen

Freedom to Brazil

James worked for two more weeks after the Naples incident and finished the job site. He attained all the final county approvals and closed out most of the houses in the subdivision. He threw a large party for all the companies and the workers who participated on the project. It had been a good project for all. Very few problems and everyone made a nice profit. James' projects always did well, he made sure of it.

James had another session with Ray. He had been getting together with Ray about every three weeks. He would not speak of the murders only referring to his work, his attitude and his depression which seem to be gone or at a minimum on the wane. Happiness was returning to his life and he credited Ray with helping him down the road of obstacles. The drugs lifted the fog he had complained about and the anger that was in his mind was changed to positive enforcement in his career path and hopefully in his personal life.

James booked his flight to Brazil. He held the final meeting with the developer and turned over the project to Ben and the main office. They would be responsible for any items that might arise while he was gone. Ben could run the project in the field. He could now leave the project, take a vacation and finish after he got back. The hard work was done. It would take three or four weeks before all the final bills and warranty work got done and that didn't need James' attention. James was tired.

He was looking forward to his vacation and being reunited with his new love – Vera - his Queen of Brazil. He packed for a day and did odds and ends so he could leave. The next day he drove to Miami and took an eight-pm flight to Sao Paulo. He flew on TAM, a Brazilian Airline. Everyone on the flight was Brazilian so he couldn't talk to anyone because his Portuguese was so weak. He didn't try. He drank for about three hours, ate some food and quietly sat thinking of the past few months. He finally drifted off to sleep. About six-am the stewardess woke him and served him breakfast. He started feeling anxious and was looking forward to seeing Vera. The plane came into Guarulhos Airport at eight-am. He gathered his stuff, disembarked and went through customs stopping in the duty-free shop for some perfume Vera had asked him to pick up.

After customs, he turned the corner and there she was, blond and beautiful in a sexy red dress, high heels and a beautiful welcoming smile. They ran towards each other and embraced. Their kissing didn't stop. Their hands started to grope each other and then they realized they were in the middle of a crowded airport. They finally stopped, laughed and went to get James' bags. After retrieving his bags and getting some money exchanged, they walked to where Vera had parked. They got into the car and started kissing again. Vera pulled a lever on James' seat and pushed the seat back.

"I want my pinto now!" she smilingly demanded like a pouty little kid. "I have to welcome my pinto to Brazil!" She unzipped his pants, undid his belt and pulled his hard penis out of his pants and proceeded to take him deep down her throat and would not stop until he came which did not take long. After, she put his penis back in his pants, put him all back together smiled and said, "Welcome to Brazil meu querido! Now go Sao Paulo, I show where live."

They headed into the morning traffic maze of Sao Paulo. She guided through the traffic like a NASCAR pro, swearing at people while telling James how much she loved and missed him. He didn't know whether to laugh or crawl in the back seat for protection. He had not experienced traffic like this since Saigon. She finally pulled into her hi-rise in the Villa Mariana. "We nao stay long, you just see then go, okay?"

She had a three-bedroom, two bath apartment on the fifth floor with a nice view of the city from the balcony. Vera grabbed a few things threw them in a suitcase and she happily screamed "We go Guaruja – Vamos!" Back down to the car and with smiles and giggles they left for Guaruja, eighty-five kilometers to the south. Vera didn't stop talking the whole trip. She talked about everything and anything pointing out different things to James as they drove.

James was fascinated by the change in scale of the vehicles as compared to the US. All the cars were smaller. They ran on gasoline which was an ethanol blend, or they ran on alcohol. The gas guzzling

SUVs of the US didn't exist here except for a very few. Hundreds of motorbikes and motorcycles zipped between the cars and quickly sped past them, one and two people per bike, carrying packages, equipment and things for delivery. A person in a car couldn't dodge them, you just had to pray that they would miss you and amazingly they did with only inches to spare.

They left Sao Paulo and began the trip through the mountains down to the seaside town of Guaruja. James was amazed at the engineering of the elegant roadway through tunnels in the mountains and over bridges held aloft on huge, tall, concrete pylons. The lush green mountainsides were filled with copious amounts of beautiful purple and white flowers with waterfalls sprinkled about.

Traffic moved easily over the four-lane highway, built as well as any in the United States. There was another four-lane highway of traffic heading back to Sao Paulo, completely separated from the one they were on. The two roadways went over and under each other in a twisting dance of love weaving through the mountains. Whoever had designed this was a genius. His ears were popping as they went from the twenty-seven-hundred foot elevation of Sao Paulo down to the sea level of Guaruja. They went through different industrial and residential areas. James' head was spinning with awe and amazement of the sights, aromas of the flowers, the beautiful countryside and most of all - the love emanating from his Queen.

At the end of the highway the city of Guaruja popped up. In a split second it quickly went from super highway to city traffic. The road swiftly became crowded with cars, trucks, buses, motorbikes and bicycles. There were more motorbikes and bicycles than cars. Strange road signs and signal lights with buses racing cars, cars racing buses, dodging trucks with people on mopeds, motorcycles and on foot, all defying accidents with their very lives at stake. They were all changing lanes rapidly as if they were little midget cars. You could easily reach out and touch the car or bike to either side and there was no room left in front or back. It became a dizzying site.

Vera's driving was amazing, moving in, out and around cars, buses, bicycles and people. She shifted gears effortlessly, gently squeezing James' leg with each shift, weaving through traffic while swearing at the other vehicles in Portuguese and speaking to her love in Inglis. She pulled into the Golden Beach Hotel high-rise, waved at the guard and sped up the narrow serpentine ramp to the third floor. She guided the car into a space. James took a deep breath when the car finally stopped and silently said a big thank you to God. They unloaded, quickly found the elevator and went to the 16th floor. She led them down the hallway and then unlocked the door to a unit she had rented for them.

James dropped the bags and went to the balcony. The view was spectacular. The beautiful blue green ocean with rolling waves splashing onto the golden sandy beach with the green flowery mountains on each side and small islands scattered just offshore. His senses were devouring the scene in front of him. People half-filled the beach which was dotted with umbrellas, tables, lounge chairs. Surfers were playing on the waves and bright sunlight was flooding the scene below with fluffy white clouds overhead. He was fascinated by the scene.

"James, you nao want look me?"

James turned and saw Vera with only her hi-heels and a big smile. Her body was amazing. It was perfect. She was something out of Playboy. Her long blond hair, beautiful face, perky large breasts and long exquisite legs. It made James very happy. They made love on the balcony, sitting in a chair, on top of the table, standing at the rail and finally in the chaise lounge. They were like two rabbits coupling in every position they could conceive. Finally, they climaxed together…then stopped, and just held each other shaking from the passionate intercourse. They fell asleep holding each other in the warm breeze of the Brazilian spring.

They awoke in the early evening, showered and went to the restaurant, "Combinati," located on the first floor. Over a delicious longostino dinner they discussed their vacation. Vera had planned a route around the state of Sao Paulo to show James all the wonderful spots she knew. They would start with a few days of beach and fun in Guaruja then head out on her planned road trip. Vera had left her sons Leonardo and Cassiano with their father, Paulo, for the next three weeks while she and James traveled. Then, when they returned to Sao Paulo, they would pick up the children and bring them back down to Guaruja for a family vacation.

During the first few days in Guaruja they went to the beach, mainly to rest from the intense love making of morning, noon and night. They would stroll along the boardwalk, eat and have coffee in sidewalk restaurants, peruse the shops for everything from lingerie to ice cream, constantly laughing and talking. They were in a world of their own.

Vera had arranged for Tango lessons with Aldo and Sirlee, two local dance teachers. After two lessons, Vera became intensely jealous of the pretty Sirlee dancing with her man and flirting with him while she taught him the Tango.

Because of it, they had their first spat. James had heard how Brazilian women get very jealous, but he didn't see this coming. Vera skyrocketed with a wild temper tantrum of thoughts that James was trying to have an affair with Sirlee. James was totally innocent, but after their second dance lesson, Vera cried torrents of tears through dinner and after withheld sex until he swore he would never go near Sirlee again. She locked him out of the bedroom; crying and screaming at him. It was two-a.m. before she would unlock the bedroom door and allow James to calm the situation and make love to her. She relented but was still angry and jealous with him. Just before James entered her vagina, she rolled on her stomach and made him enter her in her ass. Just as James was starting to enjoy her tightness, she started crying again. James disgustedly gave up, got out of bed and decided to pour himself a drink. He went to the balcony and thought about the total realistic pain of loving someone too much.

On the fifth day they headed out for Ubatuba. They found a cute little pousada, the Hotel Elexsior on the beach and settled in for a few days. The rooms were more utilitarian and on the same idea as a motel, but the food, drinks and staff were excellent. They were happy in their little love nest.

One night as darkness fell; they were walking along the beach. Vera stopped and looked at the waves rolling in. She ran into the surf and stood there as the waves hit her, knocking her over. She laughingly called for James and they played in the surf. Vera took off her wet clothes and threw them on the beach. James did the same. They played and romped into the darkness. With a full moon rising in the east out of the ocean and shining down upon them, they reached the water's edge and made love with the waves crashing over them. After they finished, they looked up to find two couples quietly watching them in the dark, twenty feet away. The couples applauded then moved on. James and Vera were at first embarrassed then laughed and sat there letting the waves roll over them holding each other tightly.

Their next stop was Campos do Jordao, a cute little village in the mountains made to resemble a Swiss Alpine village. The town was very romantic and full of couples holding hands and strolling all over the village. They shopped for clothes and for gifts for James to bring back to his friends in the states. There were plenty of restaurants to try and plenty of shops to look in. Before dinner they would stop at an open bar with tables on the sidewalk. They would have cocktails there while a guitarist played and sang with always a special love song for Vera. Even the Brazilians were enthralled by her beauty.

They were in a shop late one night as it was about to close. Vera was talking to the sales girl about clothes. Vera came to James and said, "This girl muito nice. Do think she sexy James?"

James panicked and wasn't sure what to say. The girl was very cute and sexy, but he felt a trap coming on. "Darling, yes she is - but not as beautiful and sexy as you."

"She like you and me. She nicer than beetch Sirlee, she go hotel com us."

James puzzled was still not sure what to do next, but he did realize it was best to say and do nothing. The girl shut off the shop lights, locked the door and walked back with them to their hotel room. The girls chatted in Portuguese and laughed along the way. They entered their hotel room and when James turned around they were kissing.

"James, ela nome Renata. She my gift for you. You can love her. No more Sirlee, OK?"

This was becoming confusing to him as he stood frozen in place. Renata solved the problem by going to him and starting to take off his clothes, then Vera came over to help her. Finally, James decided he might as well play. All the clothes started to fly and the three of them ended up in a pile on the bed. Renata turned out to be very versatile. James took her from behind while she went down on Vera. They played and switched into many different positions for the next three hours. James sat out for a while just to watch and because he was tired. Finally, Renata got dressed, kissed both goodbye and left. James just sat there in amazement.

"James quando voce quero em outra woman – tell me – I get – no more Sirlee – OK?"

"Yes dear." James wasn't sure how to figure this, but he thought why should I complain?

*****

They traveled from beaches to mountains and from mountains to cities. Vera showed James the Brazil she loved. The winding roads were full of beautiful vistas everywhere with cute and quaint shops full of happy people everywhere. They stayed in hotels and pousadas, eating in restaurants, from street vendors and on the beaches. James enjoyed the Brazilian diet. She varied it to show him all the different fruits and vegetables he had never seen and tasted. He loved the way they included rice and beans with every meal. The meats, chicken, pork and beef, all had a different taste than he was used to in the states. The breakfast was about the same everywhere they went. There were lots of cheeses and breads to go with the fruits and coffee. She took him to chocolate factories where Vera tried to buy everything in the store. They stopped at roadside vistas where they took pictures of each other with the beautiful Brazilian countryside behind them.

She took him dancing at night. She taught him the Samba and the Forro and he never dared to mention the Tango. Many nights they danced till five am in the morning, laughing and playing with each other. They also had some quiet nights just listening to guitar players and small bands play and sing.

James had forgotten the world he had left and was totally absorbed in this new culture and this new world. For the first time in a very long time he was relaxed and at peace with himself. His past was just that – his past and his conscience was clear. He felt he had done the right thing by Susan and helped her by getting rid of her problem once and for all. His new life was very pleasant and pleasing to him. His new love was fun, interesting and seemed very devoted. He wanted to go forward with this relationship.

Vera took him to a Brazilian motel. She drove to a drive-up gatehouse, spoke to the girl and left her license with her. Vera pulled the car around to the back of the motel and into a single garage. They got

153

out and Vera hit a button and the garage door came down. "These places Brazilians go to make love. You take wife, lover, girlfriend or prostitute here. Muito private, yes?"

They entered into an immaculate room which had a king size bed, padded headboard, mirrors on the walls and ceiling and a huge flat screen TV on the wall facing the bed. The room had its own huge bathroom with a hot tub and robes for two. There was a beautiful view of the mountains and you could not see anyone else or any of the other rooms. Vera got on the phone and said something. A few minutes later a bell went off and Vera retrieved a bottle of champagne in a bucket of ice with glasses from a cabinet in the room. "No one see no one," she chimed. She grabbed the remote control and surfed the channels till she found pornographic movies. Vera left it on a movie and all you could see and hear were two people fervently making love. She changed into some very sexy, blue lingerie. They had two glasses of champagne then started making love. She seemed to keep one eye on the movie and kept trying to copy whatever the starlet in the porno was doing. James loved this all-out attention and complete involvement with lovemaking. He had never had a woman who pushed the envelope with sex the way Vera did.

At a break in the action she turned to James, "You like motel? Rent by hour. When need to go way from family, come here, easy, nao cost, muito happy. After a few hours they spent time in the hot tub. After, Vera ordered another bottle of champagne and a pizza. James was amazed by the whole system of making love in a Brazilian motel. They stayed for almost two days and nights making love, napping, eating, drinking and bathing. When they left in the car, Vera paid a hundred reais at the guard gate and retrieved her license. James calculated it cost about ninety US dollars for the room, two bottles of champagne and snacks. He was impressed as to how acceptable and easy the whole system worked.

They left and drove for an hour ending up back in Sao Paulo at Vera's apartment for a few days. She gave him the tour of the city and its vibrant nightlife. She took him to the financial district, to the top of the tallest building, a tour of huge towering cathedrals built in the early 1500's, museums, wonderful restaurants and shopping in the chain stores and among the many street vendors. James was amazed by everything he saw. He was impressed by the culture and the complexity of the world's second largest city of over seventeen million people.

She made dinners for them deftly displaying her culinary skills. She massaged him and made love to him continually. James could not believe her caring and love that she showed and demonstrated to him. He thought if they had a permanent relationship and she demonstrated only ten per cent of what she was showing him now, he could be very happy – very, very happy.

On the fifth day Vera went and picked up her two children from her ex-husband, Paulo. The four of them were all to go to Guaruja for a family vacation. James wanted to meet the children and spend time with them and Vera as a family unit. By this time, James had determined that this was the last step before finalizing a plan to bring them all together and move them to the United States as his newly adopted family and the new love of his life. He and Vera had discussed this throughout the weeks he was there. To be sure, there were still some problems to be worked out. Moving countries was not an easy thing to accomplish. With each day he became more resolute that this was what he wanted for the rest of his life. He was in love, although shocked by his desire to make this relationship work permanently.

Even though he was just officially divorced for a few months, his relationship with Susan had ended years before and he knew this. The years he had spent trying to nurse Susan back to sobriety wasn't a relationship, it had just been work, and he had failed. He was surprised by his own desire to get married again. Vera had convinced him that this new relationship was everything he wanted. She was perfect in every aspect of their rapport. Marriage had been mentioned many times and discussed with great anticipation and excitement. The meeting of the children was the last step in James' mind before he would make it official.

They returned to the apartment to meet James. He could sense something was wrong. The boys, Leonardo and Cassiano were polite little gentlemen, twelve and eight years old. They walked to him and offered their hands and said in perfect English, they were happy to meet him. Yet, they were quiet and after meeting James quickly went to their respective rooms with a tremendous air of silence. This was not how James had thought they would act. James was puzzled. He looked at Vera and something was different and wrong about her. They talked quietly but she kept her distance from him and wouldn't go near him. She gave the boys orders of what and how much to pack. She then spent considerable time in the kitchen and then retreated to her bathroom for the longest time.

She emerged from her bedroom and James finally realized she had yet to take off her large sun glasses. "Take off your glasses," he said. She ignored him. "I said – take off your glasses Vera!" She did turning away from him as she did. He went close to her and grabbed her arms turning her to face him. He looked carefully. She had caked makeup all around her left eye. He looked closer and could see her red and bruised eye and face almost hidden by the makeup.

"Who did this?" James asked as if he couldn't guess. She wasn't forthcoming with an answer. "I said, - Who did this?"

"James, it nothing. It accident, please forget. I did not see his hand coming. It accident."

"Like hell. That's not an accident. Why did he do this to you? Why?"

"No James, it accident, really."

"Bullshit Vera. Why, what was the reason for this?

"Okay, we have fight. He drinking and mad because you here. He hit...forget...we forget."

"He has no right to hit you. I am going to go see him now."

"Please James, no more. We all go Guaruja. Forget. We go - family vacation, please. No more trouble, please forget, we go Guaruja now, okay?"

James thought for a few seconds then said, "No Vera. Here's what we are going to do. We will pack the car and go to Guaruja, but on the way, we are stopping to see your ex-husband. I just want to talk to him for a minute. Understand?"

Vera stood there for a minute and looked at James. She finally understood James was not to be moved from his position. She turned and started getting the boys ready and packing their bags. James went to the balcony and tried to decide how he was going to handle this situation. Within twenty minutes everyone was ready to go. They loaded the car and started driving with James at the wheel. He took the wheel because he was determined to do what he wanted. He turned to Vera and told her to start giving him directions to her ex-husband's business. Vera kept pleading for James not to go to see Paulo, but James was determined to talk to him. As they drove James kept asking questions about Paulo. Finding out about the situation he was about to walk into.

Paulo owned a small bar not far from Vera's apartment. As is with most small bars in Brazil, the front of the bar is open to the street. They arrived and parked across the street from Paulo's bar. From the car Vera pointed out Paulo. James left the car and told Vera and the boys to stay in the car, he would be right back. James got out of the car and walked into the bar. James surveyed the room and the bar. There were three men at one end of the bar drinking and talking to Paulo who was behind the bar. James walked to the empty end of the bar and stood there. Paulo looked up, noticed him then walked down the bar to him. He was taller, heavier with a more muscular body than James. Paulo had a rough, tough appearance to his face and looked mean and nasty. He had an unkempt, shaggy look needing a shave and shower. His dirty shirt and pants were stained with work and use. As he got closer, James took a deep breath and wondered if he was biting off more than he could chew.

"Oi," said James. "Eu quero falar com voce."

"Oi," said Paulo curiously eyeing James without an expression and without any thought of politeness of welcoming someone to his bar.

"Voce fala inglis?" James said in the pigeon Portuguese he had learned.

"Um pequeno," said Paulo.

"Don't you ever hit Vera or your sons again or I will kill you."

"Chupa meu caralho gringo!" retorted Paulo angrily as he suddenly realized to whom he was talking.

James didn't know what Paulo was saying but he realized it wasn't Happy Birthday. He wasn't sure if Paulo understood what he had said but by the reaction he had understood enough to cause that mean sneer. James just stared at Paulo for a few seconds then flashed a smile at Paulo and walked out of the bar. He could feel Paulo's icy stare on his back. James went back to the car and drove away. Nobody in the car dared to ask what had happened and there was silence for many miles.

Chapter Sixteen
Learning a New Life

They arrived in Guaruja after a very quiet ride from Sao Paulo. James pulled into the Golden Beach Hotel and parked the car. All the bags and toys were unloaded and taken to the apartment. Everyone settled in their respective rooms. It was mid-afternoon, and James realized he needed to change the mood of this group. He told everyone to change to something casual and they would go have a late lunch. They wandered down the sidewalk which ran along the beach and James picked out a restaurant he had been to before with Vera. As lunch progressed James slowly started asking questions of the boys about their schools, their sports and what they liked. They slowly warmed up to James and started talking to him while watching their mother for her reactions. As Vera laughed more and loosened up so did the boys. By the end of lunch, the boys were starting to ask him questions about the United States and what his life was like there. After lunch they strolled along the boardwalk. James suggested ice cream cones for all. By the end of the ice cream cones the boys had accepted James and had decided to like him – because their mother did, they did. James suggested they go change so they could all go to the beach for a late afternoon swim. Everyone excitedly agreed.

They played in the surf of the ocean, laughing and enjoying each other's company. The rolling waves would knock them over and they would laugh at each other as it occurred. All of a sudden James noticed a large bruise on Cassiano's bottom. The bathing suit would slip down when the waves would hit him and knock him over. Cassiano would just get up and adjust his bathing suit as a normal reaction. James watched him carefully and decided to investigate this at another time.

They returned to the apartment with everyone taking showers and resting. The boys played quietly in their room and James and Vera enjoyed a glass of wine on the balcony. Vera was proud of her two little gentlemen and James agreed with her about them, how she had raised them, especially how intelligent they were and what an excellent command of the English language they had. They eventually wandered downstairs and had dinner at Combinati. The waiters and the owner recognized James and made a fuss over him, making sure James and his new family were comfortable and received excellent service. After a large heavy meal, they returned to their apartment. The boys watched TV while James and Vera talked. The boys went to sleep. James and Vera waited a respectable length of time for the boys to fall asleep, checked to make sure they were and then went to their bedroom and quietly made love.

The hotel breakfast room was at the top of the building. As the new family walked in they were greeted by Sirlee, who also owned half of this food concession. As Sirlee approached them, James squeezed Vera's hand, looked deep into Vera's eyes and shook his head. Sirlee greeted and kissed everyone and then seated them at a table. James realized that Vera was watching his eyes. James made sure he was watching only the boys and Vera. During breakfast it started to rain. James suggested after breakfast they go to the Aquarium.

The Aquarium was a big hit with all. The boys were looking to James to answer question after question that they had. James was able to answer most. But the ones he could not, he said they would have to get a book. After the aquarium they had lunch in a small sidewalk café. The rain clouds disappeared while they were at lunch and the sun returned. They went back to the apartment, changed and decided to go to the beach.

James decided to take Leonardo for a walk. James turned to Vera and said to her that he wanted to talk to each of the boys individually. He said he would start with Leo while Vera kept Cassiano occupied. Vera understood, agreed, smiled and went off to play with Cassiano, while James and Leo strolled along the beach.

James slowly started talking with Leo about anything he could think of with no general direction. They talked about soccer, surfing, the aquarium, the differences between Sao Paulo and Guaruja. After James was sure Leo was comfortable he asked about Leo's relationship with his father. Leo went silent. James decided to change tactics.

"Leo, I am in love with your mother. And I know you do not know me very well, nor does your brother. I would like to be friends with you and your brother. I would like to ask your mother if she will marry me and live with me in Florida. I would like you and your brother to come to Florida, live there with us and go to school there. I know this is a big step, very exciting but also it can be very scary. I am not trying to take you away from your father. You only have one father, so I can only be your friend. You are old enough to make up your own mind – that is why I am now talking to you man to man. If you do want to come to Florida, we can do it in one of two ways. One, you could stay here with your father and go to school just as you are doing now and when you are on vacations come to Florida and stay with us. Or two, what I would like, you can live with us, go to school in Florida and on vacations come back to Brazil to be with your Dad.

These are things I would like you to think about. You can take as long as you want. I will answer any questions you have about me or anything else you want to know about me. You do not have to make up your mind until you are sure you know what you want to do. These are important decisions everyone will have to agree on; you, your brother, your mother, father and me. I only want what is best for all. Do you understand?"

Leo walked along in silence kicking the sand and looking for small shells not saying anything. Finally, he stopped and looked at James with a long stare. "If Cassiano go, I go. He nao go, I nao go."

"That's fine with me Leo. We will all sit down and discuss. You can discuss alone with Cassiano. You should also discuss with your mom – without me around. Okay?" James was sensing fear coming from Leo, fear of what he did not know.

They reached the end of the beach and turned around walking back. James changed the subject talking about anything again trying to make little jokes and befriend Leo. By the time they reached their spot on the beach they were laughing and kidding each other. They met up with Vera and Cassiano and the four of them returned to the apartment. James decided to wait to talk to Cassiano later.

For dinner they went out for pizza and then returned to the apartment. Vera seemed frisky and James was tired but horny for his new love. He decided to see if he could get the boys to bed a little early. He let them watch TV for a while and then told them to get ready for bed. The boys seemed to be taking a long time in the bathroom. James decided to find out why and walked to the bathroom. The door was open a crack and suddenly he could see Cassiano bent over with his pajama bottoms down while Leonardo was looking at Cassiano's ass. Cassiano's ass was covered with red welts, hand prints and bruises. James held back and decided not to interrupt. The boys talked quietly, and it sounded to James

161

that Leonardo was reassuring Cassiano. James went back and sat with Vera not saying a word about what he had seen.

*****

James was in awe of Brazil. He loved everything he had seen. He thought the people were kind, gentle and most of all relaxed. They smiled, laughed and seemed to treat everybody with respect. The diet was different and better than the States. There was more emphasis on fresh vegetables and fruit with very little fried foods. All of the food was cooked to order and fresh all the time.

He quickly realized Brazilians had a special, national religion - it was the beach or "praia." With his cautious eyes he quickly realized the women of Brazil were gorgeous. There was nothing better than to go to the beach. Not much was left to the imagination. The bikinis were all they wore, the smaller the better and the women always wore the smallest they could find. They covered their nipples and vaginas to be sure and to be in good taste but there was a lot of skin exposed on purpose. They were everywhere; smiling, laughing with a flirtatious air about them. Brazil is a happy place seemingly existing without the pressures which are present in the United States. The women took excellent care of themselves. Their bodies were in great shape, hi-heels were standard issue for all, hair, nails and makeup were all deliberately cared for to make them as attractive as possible. They liked men and wanted them – it was obvious.

He had to be careful around Vera; she was always watching his eyes. There was a streak of jealousy in her which he could not figure out. It was because of her two-way attitude; jealous but maybe if he wanted, she was willing to arrange for them to have an additional woman with their love making. This was an unexpected feature of their relationship he loved. What could be better? Although at this point he did not dare to bring up the subject – he thought better to let her take the lead. Every man's ego always wants to have two women in bed with him, even though a man's desire and ego are much greater than his ability. On the other hand, this feature could be dangerous he thought. When an attractive woman walked by them, she watched him. Vera would then walk to him

162

and asked if he liked her. James learned a pat answer – Yes, she is pretty or yes, she is sexy but you my dear are so much better! Or even better was to say – I'm sorry who? Or I didn't see her. These answers seemed to satisfy Vera and all remained calm.

James bought trucks and cars for Cassiano to play with on the beach. They played together building roads and tunnels and just having fun with the toys in the sand. Leo watched carefully, noting how his brother was enjoying James. It was simple child's play and through it Cassiano was bonding with James.

James finally took another walk with Leo. They walked for a long time talking about the United States and what could be and what were the possibilities for Leo. After James gained the momentary confidence of Leo, he gently spoke. "Leo, you are a great brother to Cassiano. I am not here to hurt you in any way and I can help you and Cassiano. Sometimes as we go through life things go wrong or things are not what they should be. Sometimes people do things to other people they should not. Sometimes people cannot protect themselves from other people doing terrible things to them or others. Maybe the person doing the terrible things is bigger and stronger. Sometimes people need help, but it is hard for them to get help or even ask for help. I know what is wrong and I know you and your brother need help. Let me help you and your brother. I can protect you and Cassiano. I cannot do it unless you tell me what is really happening. Is your father hurting you and Cassiano?"

Leo acted as if he had been hit with a lightning bolt. He stopped and looked down not saying a word. He then started walking again and started to cry quietly as he walked with James. They walked for a long time without saying a word; just the quiet sobbing of Leo broke the silence. Finally, Leo stopped crying.

"Leo just tell me, and it will be between you and me and who knows I might be able to help...somehow."

Leo looked at James with tears in his eyes. Then suddenly ..., "Please don't tell...Promise?"

"I promise, just tell me and maybe I can help. It will be between you and me."

"Pai did to Cassiano. He do to me when I young. Now he only does to Cassiano."

"Did what? You have to tell me, and we can make it stop and help Cassiano and you from ever letting it happen again."

"He drink muito then he take Cassiano to room and put thing in him. Cassiano not like but he hit and slaps him. He hurts Cassiano cause Cassiano nao like and tries to fight with him and make him stop. He hits him and hurt him more when Cassiano want him to stop. He did to me for many anos, then he stop doing it to me - then he start doing the same to Cassiano. He locks door so I cannot stop. Please do not tell Pai I mean Mai. She nao listen. She believe Pai, Cassiano fall down and hurt self in rear. She laugh and say it okay. Please stop so Cassiano stop hurt and cry."

"Okay Leo, I promise this is between you and me and I will make sure it will never happen again. What he is doing is wrong and I will get him to stop hurting you and your brother. Don't say anything to anybody including your mom. I will fix it and it will never happen again. Okay?"

"Okay, por favor help Cassiano – it hurt him bad. Please nao tell Mai – she nao listen." Leo was sobbing and feeling the pain for his brother and himself.

James also felt pain for both boys. He tried to console Leo as they walked along; reassuring him again and again he would fix the situation and not betray Leo's trust. James was trying to come up with his own plan and trying to decide what to do. He abhorred abuse of women, children and animals. They were defenseless when men took their anger or their sick and twisted pleasures out on them. He was driven to right the wrongs men caused to the people James loved. Men used their strength to inflict pain, control their victims for their own pleasure and to satisfy some sick perverted, twisted, ego driven, inner need.

He had seen so much of it in his life. It really came to his attention when he was in Nam. Men use war as a cover for their meanness and greed. To him, his actions were not sick like those who preyed on others. He recognized his way as direct correcting action, he had to fight, protect the down trodden, the oppressed, for those who did not have enough strength to be able to combat those who preyed on them. Men used their size, strength, anger and rage to bully and hurt the innocent; the women, the children and the animals. He knew he was wrong in some moral sense regarding the way he rectified these problems by assuming the power of being the judge, jury and executioner. As long as he acted only on what he knew was true and not for his own benefit - then losing a few bad people in this world wasn't going to stop the earth from spinning. Morality is created and judged in one's own mind, not just by some rules written and decided by others but by each individual with each decision they make. Through the years James had examined many thoughts as to the formation of societies and the laws man creates to control those same societies. If everyone lived by the 'Golden Rule' that would be fine in his mind.   But in modern societies there is too much greed and self-indulgence. He always said out loud: 'There aren't enough genes in the gene pool' or 'There aren't enough people swimming in the gene pool.' There is a mean streak in men...that in some...runs very deep.

Vera's ex-husband Paulo had assaulted James' love, Vera, and hurt her children through battery, sexual assault and rape. He had demonstrated a machismo that made James sick. There was no reason for his actions and James could tell through this machismo, Paulo controlled his victims' lives. The victims were at Paulo's whims and desires. They had lost control of their lives to his powerful, sick desires.

When James thought about the situation, his mind would snap back to Nam. He decided to change this situation. The same way he had done when Lieutenant MacDonald had brutally beaten and raped James' Vietnamese girlfriend and others because they would not submit to MacDonald's sick, twisted, drunken desires.

He thought back on his other indiscretions; when he lived in Houston, there was Phyllis his secretary. Phyllis was a very quiet, capable and nice person who worked well with James. He decided to protect her and that is why he killed her husband. Creeps like her husband should be banned from this earth. Phyllis seemed to be always on edge and tried to hide her tragic home life from James. However, through time and talking, James became her protector. His mind had flashed back to Nam seeing Nutan lying broken in a hospital bed when he saw Phyllis' oozing burned back. James lost it quietly and could only think about destroying the bastard that did this to her. His mind became obsessed with ridding Phyllis of her problem. She was better off alone than being with this piece of slime. There was no earthly reason to allow this person to breathe another breath. When these thoughts came to James, there was no way of turning him in a different direction or turning them off.

Just like when Alan was threatened with financial disaster by a crooked attorney and was about to lose all his possessions and be forced into bankruptcy, the attorney was pushed or fell down two flights of stairs and died because of the many injuries to the head from hitting the steel and concrete steps on the way down. He had been beaten and robbed by a person or persons unknown. It was common knowledge the attorney was a shyster and had financially ruined many people. Alan was saved from this money grubbing attorney by this incident.

Then of course there was Roger and his unfortunate demise by a drug deal gone wrong. At least, that is what the police had said and what had been reported in the newspapers. Putting six bullets in him was the answer that brought peace and calm to James' mind.

James did not want to do any of these killings, but to him these situations just couldn't be ignored. The police rarely solve any crimes. They only solve the easy ones. The legal justice system protects the criminal at the expense of the victim. James knew, psychologically speaking, he should not kill, but controlling his emotions and actions were beyond his ability. He could not accept seeing the people he liked and loved hurt. Why not save everybody the time, trouble and cost of unsolved crimes and half-baked justice. The mafia polices themselves, the CIA, FBI, and even police departments take care of their own problems their own way. Many other groups and individuals kill instead of going through the system, why shouldn't James.

Now, another situation presented itself. Was it right for Paulo to beat his ex-wife? Was it right for Paulo to rape his children? What made it worse was the fact no one was doing anything to stop him. No one was raising a finger against him. Even Vera did not seem overly concerned. She must not even realize it was happening. James flashed that it was unconscionable. According to Vera, Paulo was not a good father to the boys and when his drinking got out of hand he became violent. They had divorced because of the beatings, his philandering, his poor economic performance toward his family and his meanness caused by the alcohol. Vera said she was lucky because her family helped her get away, but by law Paulo still had rights to the children. However, the law and Vera did not know or care about his taking sexual advantage of his sons. It was just a dirty little secret. It was a secret James had discovered. James could not stop his thought patterns of getting rid of the problem, his way, his easy way, his right way.

Vera was saying to him that they had to get permission from Paulo to allow the boys to leave Brazil. "We need nao upset him or make mad. He say nao and boys stay here. Please James – nao make Paulo mad. He ruin plan."

James decided that the secret Leo had entrusted with him would stay secret. He was sure he would not let it continue anymore. His new wife to be and new step sons needed a fresh start and a way to get away from this monster. James would extract justice his way – quietly and completely. He just had to figure how to do it. He certainly needed to be very correct in his actions because he had heard of the horror stories of Brazilian jails and he had no desire to be caught as a gringo and end up in a Brazilian jail.

The days went by and the new foursome grew nearer together having happy times and learning about each other. The boys grew closer to James even acknowledging how great he was and how much they liked him. He spent the time talking with them and playing with them, getting nearer day by day. Vera saw what was happening and liked James even more. She said the only problem now was Paulo.

Vera was worried Paulo would block the boys from leaving Brazil. James mentioned he thought Paulo was physically hurting the boys. Vera was either not aware or was in denial. She said a little spanking would not hurt them and the boys were always blowing things out of proportion. She would always come back to the fact that Paulo would try and prevent the boys from ever leaving Brazil for a visit to the United States.

James decided the best course of action was to eliminate the monster. Eliminating Paulo would also remove any blocking of allowing the children to go or visit the United States and also stop all the child sexual abuse the boys were suffering. James decided with Vera, she should spend the day with the boys, alone without James near. They would be able to talk freely to each other about going to America. He would go sightseeing on his own. Since they were to return to Sao Paulo on Thursday, they picked Monday as the day they would have this separation. He told Vera he was going to Ubatuba for the day.

Chapter Seventeen
Once Again Into the Breach

When the day came, James went north heading for Sao Paulo instead of east to Ubatuba. He arrived in the city about ten am. Once he was in Sao Paulo, it took James over an hour to finally find the address. Driving in Sao Paulo was a definite challenge. He drove around the area of Paulo's bar. He then practiced finding his way back to the highway. He did it three times. He then found a little restaurant far away from Paulo's bar where he had lunch. He was as careful as possible not to attract attention. He pointed to items on the menu and said as little as possible. He kept his face down and faced the wall or shielded his face with his hand.

He finished lunch and drove back to a mall he had seen. After parking, he went in and looked for a hardware store or a home furnishing store. He found a store similar to a Home Depot. He went in and bought a roll of wire; thin, strong, flexible, stainless steel wire, two wooden handles like those used to start lawn mower engines and a handful of washers. He returned to the car and while in the parking lot, he took a piece of wire about two and a half feet long and fastened a lawn mower handle at each end, fastened tight by wrapping the wire through a bunch of washers and around the handles. When he was through he had made a garrote. He had learned of this weapon while in the Army. It was developed centuries before and had been used in most wars and in thousands of assassinations. The idea was to sneak up behind the intended victim, slip a loop of the wire around the victim's neck and snap the wire by quickly pulling tight on the two handles. The wire would then cut into the neck, crush the windpipe and kill the person without their being able to make a sound. If you didn't pull fast enough, or with enough force, or you didn't surprise your intended victim you could botch the deal and end up as the victim instead of being the assassin.

He drove back to the area near the bar and waited till dark. He then moved the car closer to the bar, so he could watch what was happening inside the bar. It was an open-air type sidewalk bar. It was easy to see everything that was happening. Being a Monday, there was very little business. Paulo was the only person working in this small establishment. There were a few men who stopped by to have a beer, it looked like a slow night, as James expected. The customers left after two or three beers. James counted as Paulo drank eight or nine beers while he waited for more customers. By ten pm no one was in the bar and it looked like business was done for the night. Paulo started sweeping the floor and cleaning up.

There was an alley to the side of the bar which contained a dumpster. James had a hunch that Paulo would probably go to the dumpster at some point. When no one was in sight, James went and hid behind the dumpster, sitting on the pavement and waited in the cool, damp air. He took off his shoes and jacket. He didn't want anything to impede his actions. Shoes are noisy on pavement and the jacket could restrain his arms. It was almost an hour of quietly waiting behind the dumpster before he heard the sound he had been waiting for. The side door of the bar, which was on the alley, was unlocked and opened. James went to a crouching position and readied his weapon. He heard Paulo's footsteps coming down the alley and walking to the dumpster. Paulo opened the dumpster and threw a bag of garbage in and let the lid slam then turned and started walking back to the door.

James took a deep breath counted to three and with catlike moves quickly came from behind the dumpster going up behind Paulo. Paulo was almost ten feet away from the dumpster. Before James got to him, Paulo must have heard something because he stopped and started to turn. James was next to him and slipped the wire over his head. Paulo realized he was being attacked and started to push James away. He realized there was something around his neck, grabbed the wire and got a hand between the wire and his neck. James tightened the wire, Paulo's hand was stopping the wire from hurting him.

James was on Paulo's right side and it was his right hand between the wire and his neck. He was swinging wildly at James with his left fist and arm. As Paulo turned to his right to get a better swing at James, James would move to the left. They twirled around in this dance of death, both grunting sounds of anger as they spun. Paulo couldn't get to James and James couldn't snap the wire hard and fast enough to kill Paulo. The groans of effort from both men filled the air. They were locked together and the person who gave up first would lose.

James finally decided on a move he hoped would work. If it didn't he could easily lose his life against the younger and much bigger Paulo.

He slacked off on the handles, quickly slid to his right and rammed his knee into Paulo's balls. A huge moan came from deep inside Paulo as he doubled over. As he went over, James snapped the handles with every muscle in his body. Paulo fell to the ground and started to twitch. James kept the pressure on until Paulo gagged and went limp. James closed his eyes and pulled tighter; wanting to make sure he was dead. It seemed like an hour before James loosened his grip. He looked down to see he had cut four fingers off Paulo's hand. The wire had gone through Paulo's neck cutting everything all the way through to the spine, which was the only thing he had not cut. The body twitched and kept moving in jerky motions. The blood was spurting everywhere, on him and spraying all around forming a huge pool on the ground. James watched it until it stopped. In the huge pool of blood were Paulo's four cut off fingers and Paulo's head lying in it with more blood gushing from the head and the neck of the now still body.

James relaxed and finally took a deep breath looking down at the limp, dead figure on the ground, the handles still in his hands. Now he had to get out of there fast. He tried to undo the wire, but it must have lodged into a vertebra in Paulo's neck and it wouldn't come loose. He started to panic. James had to take the weapon with him – no evidence must be left behind. He had pulled so tightly the wire had tightened around the washers and the handles. He finally found an end to the wire and had to unwind it from the washers and the handle. As he was doing it, a couple walked down the street, James froze; they kept walking not looking down the alley. James finally got one end loose and with considerable effort was able to pull the wire through the neck and become free.

James gathered his jacket and shoes from behind the dumpster, telling himself to keep calm and think – think – think it through – carefully. He scrambled to the car and started to leave. Looking back at Paulo, he saw his bloody footprints from the body over to the car. Too late, he had to leave now as fast as he could. He drove off and as he drove he noticed blood all over his clothes, arms, hands and everything he touched. He was dripping blood from his clothes that had been soaked in Paulo's blood. Paulo had spurted a lot of blood from the neck and now it was dripping all over the car with his every movement. He had to think of what to do to avoid getting caught or being noticed. He made his way through Sao Paulo traffic and back onto the highway that would take him back to Guaruja. He finally came upon a small lake by the side of the highway. He pulled the car off to the side behind some shrubs and when the traffic abated he made his way to the edge of the lake.

He quickly walked to the lake and washed himself as best he could, then his hands, face, socks, shoes and his bloody shirt. James was scared. This had not gone as easily as he had expected. There was a lot of blood in the car and on the outside of the driver's door. James took off his shirt soaked it in water from the lake and washed down the outside of the car as best he could. He got back into the car putting on the jacket with his bloody handprint on the back of the jacket and drove barefoot back to Guaruja. He had to go through a toll booth. He pulled far enough through the toll booth, so he had to reach back to give the attendant the money, so the attendant couldn't see directly into the blood splattered interior. He pulled into the Golden Beach Condos and waived at the guard as he quickly went by and up to the parking space.

James climbed the stairs to the sixteenth floor not wanting to take a chance being seen by someone in the elevator. The climb was difficult, but his adrenaline kept him going not allowing him to stop. He went to the apartment and let himself in. Everyone was asleep. The door to their bedroom was open a few inches and Vera called to him.

"James, why you late?"

He put his head into the dark bedroom. "Honey, I'll tell you in a minute. I have to go back to the car. I left stuff and the keys in it; but first I really have to go to the bathroom. Go back to sleep and I'll wake you when I get back." In the bathroom washing again to get off all the blood he had missed at the lake and cleaning himself as best he could. James grabbed a towel, wet it and walked to the kitchen and grabbed some dish soap. He then returned to the car via the stairs. He scrubbed and cleaned the car as much as he could see. He threw the towel in a dumpster and went back to the apartment. He was breathing very hard after the trip up and down the stairs, but he was on a mission on automatic mode.

James took a shower, gathered his clothes and shoes, went into the darkened bedroom throwing his clothes and shoes under the bed. Vera stirred when he climbed into bed. She awoke and started to talk to him. He just hushed her and told her to go back to sleep, "We will talk in the morning darling – just go to sleep – I love you – very much." He kissed her, and she turned over and went back to sleep.

James laid awake all-night thinking about every step of the way from the previous day. He went over everything two or three times. Finally, as it all made sense and he had an answer to every question, the sun started to shine, and he drifted off to sleep.

"Good morning darling," said Vera bringing him a cup of coffee in bed.

James sat up and took the cup and tried to wake up.

"Why you late? Where were you? Where you go?"

James realized he had to come up with all the answers to calm her and make sure she wouldn't have any questions. "Darling, I went to Ubatuba, walked around, had lunch in that cute little restaurant we liked on the beach then went window shopping. When it got dark, I had dinner then I decided to drive back. Well, I got on the wrong road or missed a sign and I must have driven a long way before I realized I took the wrong road. I started to turn around and the car got stuck on the side of the road in a mud puddle. It took me a long time to get the car unstuck, and then I turned around and had to go back to Ubatuba to start again. I got all greasy, dirty and wet because I fell into the mud puddle. The car is all dirty and wet and I have to have it cleaned today. That is why I was so late – it was just a big mess."

"James… what window shopping? You buy windows?"

James broke out in laughter. "No dear. Window shopping is looking not buying.

"You nao buy me present?" She said with anger.

"No dear, I am sorry, I did not."

Vera grabbed his coffee cup in a huff, mad that he had not brought her a present, and went to the kitchen to refill their cups. She never mentioned anything about his day trip again. She just seemed to pout like a small child and remained somewhat distant to him for the rest of the morning. James just smiled inwardly and realized that his story was plausible, and she believed it. While she was in the shower he scooped up his clothes into a plastic bag and placed them in a dumpster on one of the parking floors.

After breakfast at the top of the building, with another session of making sure he did not look at Sirlee, James told Vera to take the boys to the beach while he got the car clean. He went across the street to the supermacado and bought cleaning supplies and some towels.

He then approached a man, he had noticed many times before, who was without a job and just hanging around the area. He waved a fifty reais bill in front of him and motioned to him to follow me saying in his best Portuguese, "Anjudar-me." The man followed with a big smile at his good fortune. James opened the car and pointed to the dried mud and blood, pointed to the rags, supplies and showed him where the water spigot and hose were. "OK?" said James, the man nodded and went to work.

James watched for a few minutes then decided to go get another cup of coffee at the roof top restaurant. Sirlee saw that he was alone and greeted him with a big hug and a kiss on the lips. They talked while James had two cups of coffee. James was trying to figure a way to get Vera to like Sirlee. He thought she would be fun in bed and it would be a great threesome but realized his wishes were not going to come true.

He returned to his car washer to check on his progress. The man was doing an excellent job but was far from finished. The car was a lot messier than he had first thought. He walked to the beach and sat with Vera while she read and kept a mother hen's eye on the boys while they played by the water's edge. They chatted for a while about what to do for the rest of the trip. James started to relax and decided everything was going smoothly. He went and bought a caparinia, the Brazilian local drink of pleasure, at a vendor's beach stand and returned.

"Why you drink James?"

"Just relaxing my darling – just relaxing a little early today." James smiled and felt good inside. After he finished the caparinia, he excused himself and went to check on his car cleaner.

The man was finished and waiting for him. It looked like a brand-new car. James inspected the car very carefully, found a few spots the man touched up immediately and James breathed a sigh of relief. He gave the man his fifty and added ten more, patted the man on the back and said, "Bom, obrigado." The man thanked him and went on his way with a big smile but a smile not as big as the one on James' face.

174

James changed and went back to the beach and spent the rest of the day with Vera and the boys. His attitude had changed. He was totally relaxed, enjoying the afternoon and then James went deep into thought. How many more of these monsters are out there? Is the world made up of people who abuse and people who are abused? Is there no middle ground where people can just exist and go through life without suffering pain and anguish from the hands of others? The jails are full of abusers. The cost of keeping people in jail is an enormous burden on civilized society, who pays for their incarceration. There are many more that should be in jail or mental institutions, but will never get there. The penalties for their actions hardly fit the crimes they commit. Penalties are not severe enough. Most criminals are never rehabilitated. They return to society just to continue committing crimes.

He felt strong and justified for doing something for the people he loved and for ridding the world of another monster. No longer would these young children be threatened, abused and raped by a sick pedophile. Nor would Vera have to suffer any more physical or mental abuse from a man she hated. What good had Paulo ever done in the world? He had hurt people physically and mentally. He had held people hostage to his sick mind. The world is a better place now that he is gone. Most importantly, no one would stand in the way of James bringing his new family to the United States.

*****

The foursome finished the last three days and headed back to Vera's apartment in Sao Paulo. James was positive the group would be a unified family. He knew not to bring the subject up now for very shortly the shit was going to hit the fan. It did not take long. They were at Vera's for less than an hour when the phone rang. It was a friend of hers. She took the phone call, happy at first and then she went very silent, listening intently. She quietly asked a few questions and then hung up the phone.

She looked at James with a somber look on her face and motioned him to join her on the balcony. She then closed the sliding glass door, so they were alone. "James, Paulo murdered other night. Found him alley

175

next bar, neck cut open. Don't know how tell boys. This terrible. We marry six years. Nao good way die. What should do?"

James was silent just watching her reaction. There was something wrong with her reaction. He didn't know what and this was puzzling to him. He finally put his arms around her as she barely showed any emotion. "Vera do you want me to tell the boys? Do you want to tell the boys, or shall we tell them together?"

"James, you help tell boys." She turned and went to get the boys. They all returned to the living room and sat down.

She told them in Portuguese, so James didn't know what she was saying. He watched their faces for a reaction. No reaction from either, their faces were just blank. After she was through, Cassiano asked if he could have an ice cream and Leonardo asked if he could watch TV. Vera nodded to both requests and the boys left the room.

Vera turned to James. "Why nao sad?"

"Honey it just hasn't sunk in yet. All the excitement of the trip, it's been a long day and they do not realize yet the implications. Give it time. They will react later. Is there a funeral?"

"Nao, burn yesterday."

"Oh, cremation."

"James, what have dinner? Pizza ok?"

He nodded, smiled and that was the end of Paulo.

Chapter Eighteen

Back to the USA

James stayed with Vera and the boys for the next five days. Very little was said of Paulo. James talked to each boy individually and tried to gauge their reaction. Leonardo said he was happy because Paulo could not hurt Cassiano anymore and Cassiano didn't react, just nodded, not saying a word. A peaceful existence returned to the home.

During the next few days James and Vera discussed the future and how they were going to handle it. James still had a few more months of his project to wrap up then he could get more time off. They agreed James would return after those months, take the time off and they would marry. With Paulo gone, nothing was blocking them from taking the boys to the states. Vera was excited that she and the boys were going to be United States citizens. They discussed the plans and that it would take some time with Brazilian paperwork, passports and visas. They would make it all happen in time. Their relationship was becoming more objective and it seemed to James that their romance seemed to be on the wane. James noticed the change and started to feel Vera had reached a plateau mentally with what she wanted. The discussion of a green card and American citizenship became more and more dominant in her planning each day.

A female Military Policia detective, Andrea Araujo, came to the apartment. She asked Vera a few questions about Paulo and discussed the incident with her. Then she gave a cursory questioning of James. Her Inglis was perfect and her beauty was spectacular. James was amazed at her language ability. She spoke as if she had lived in the United States her whole life and majored in English at Harvard. He was short and sweet with his answers, saying he really didn't know anything and he couldn't speak Portuguese, so he was unaware of what was going on around him verbally. He didn't know Paulo and they were all in Guaruja when it happened. James was a bit nervous but controlled his thoughts well. It was hard to do because she was extremely attractive and pleasant to him. He felt strangely attracted to this beautiful woman. She looked deep into his eyes with her gorgeous, piercing brown eyes. He found it hard to concentrate but managed to quickly dismiss the interview. Andrea thanked them and left.

The interview had made James very anxious. There was nothing they could do to Vera, but a little snooping by this detective could be detrimental to James. He came to a quick decision to beat a hasty retreat to the States and safety. James booked a flight out on the next plane available. Two days later, Vera took him to the airport. The goodbye at the airport was one of a long-married couple. They discussed their future contact via the phone and on the internet. They kissed; he boarded the plane and began the long flight home. As the wheels left the ground in Sao Paulo, James smiled and breathed a huge sigh of relief.

*****

After a few days of relaxing and catching up on personal matters, James got a visit from Beth. She came by without calling. James answered the door. She wore a trench coat, high heels and was carrying a large bottle of champagne.

"You didn't tell me you were home! Oh, boy! Have I been horny for you darling!" She opened her trench coat wide, revealing a black teddy.

"Beth, come on in. We need to talk."

"Talk, bullshit. I'm gonna fuck your brains out and mine too. After - later - we can talk if you still have the energy." Beth started pushing James toward the bedroom.

"Beth – WAIT! – I have to tell you something. I'm going to marry Vera. I decided while on this trip that…"

"I don't think you will my little killer! Now let's fuck – I'm as horny as a two pussied whore."

James went white as a sheet. "What di-did you s-say?" James tried to recover but he couldn't. His voice had gone up an octave and he had a stammer.

"Shut up and get in the bedroom. We'll talk about this later after I'm completely satisfied." Beth continued to push him into the bedroom. "My time is now, and you are now going to make me happy – very happy. If you don't, I will spill all the beans you are hiding. I know everything."

James didn't know what to do – play along – pretend it wasn't true – say something – don't say anything. He decided to pretend to forget what she said. "Okay my little red head – let's do it. You want it and now you are going to get it. I could use a good blow job."

"Oh - no, killer. No blow job for you tonight. I just want you to fuck me till your cock falls off. I'm in charge tonight. You are doing me, I am not doing you!" She walked into the bedroom with James nervously close behind. Beth took off her trench coat and let the teddy drop to the floor, then she jumped on the bed. "Hurry up honey; I'm real, real horny."

James stripped down mumbling quietly, "I don't know what you're talking about but let's get it on."

Beth just smiled, chuckled and pulled him onto the bed. She then grabbed the sides of his head and pulled it to her waist. "Start!" she commanded.

James lowered his head and started on her. He found it hard to concentrate. He was thinking what to say – what to do. He was nervous and was not into what he was supposed to be doing.

"James – come on, you can do better than that. Come on, give me that wonderful tongue – make me happy baby! If you don't I will make you very sad."

James tried harder and Beth started to enjoy what James was doing. She started to move her hips a bit and move her legs farther apart. She closed her eyes and started to breathe harder. Suddenly she whimpered, she started to climax and tried to pull away. James just kept going and wouldn't let her go. Beth tried to pull away, pushing with her arms and grabbing the sheets with her hands. She was trying to get away, but James wouldn't let her go. He just kept going harder and harder.

Beth climaxed, and James never let up. He didn't miss a beat. He wanted control.

"Okay – okay – stop – stop – stop. Let me breathe for a second," she pleaded.

He suddenly stopped and let her go, rose up on his knees and smiled down at her. "Okay, now let's fuck that sweet pussy."

"Wait a minute James – STOP! - just give me a minute. That was a little intense. You did good baby. I see you didn't lose your touch. That was good – really good."

"Come on you wanted it. Now I'm horny. Spread those legs and welcome me home properly." James was now angry and decided to fuck her with a vengeance and give it everything he had. He pushed her legs apart and fell forward on her, then guided himself into her. It was angry sex for him – no love – just mean, hard fucking and he could care less. He was tearing her up and was out of control. He reached behind her and started shoving as many fingers as he could up her ass. It was painful for her. She looked up at him with fear on her face. He was hurting her with his thrusts, she didn't dare stop him.

Then she finally screamed, "NO! NO! Aahhhha, Stop!" Beth wasn't enjoying it.

He didn't stop he just kept thrusting and rubbing harder and faster.

"Aahh – aahh – aaahhh - - - please stop, okay – okay – please stop, you're hurting me!"

He wouldn't stop. He was going to keep going, holding back on his climax. Hurt her - was in his mind. She knew something, and he wanted to fuck it out of her. Scare her until he was in control. She was in pain. Finally, after minutes of pounding, nature called, and he shot his load with a final shove as deep in her as he could go. James stopped, pulled out and rolled off to the side. He was wrong, and he knew it. His anger was out of control. In a split second he had gone from a protector to a perpetrator of violence and it was directed at her.

She threw her arm around his chest, buried her head into him and pulled herself tight to him with her whole body shaking. "Oh my

God James, that was very intense. You hurt me baby. Please don't be like that. Don't do that anymore. I love you. You can't do that to me – that hurt." She started to recover. "I guess that's why your mine – all mine from now on. You make me crazy. I love what you do to me. Darling, you have to be a little easier on the equipment. Now that you're mine, all mine, anytime – anywhere – just mine. Shit, I don't even have to share you anymore. Oh baby, don't worry everything is a secret between us. I'm not going to tell anybody."

James looked at her with a mean hard twisted face. "Just what the fuck are you talking about?"

"Oh honey, I know everything. I know you killed Roger and the others. It's okay, I won't tell a soul. You had your reasons and you were right. It's our little secret. You don't have to pretend anymore. It's okay – I love you. It never has to be mentioned again."

James wasn't sure what to do. How did she find out? Was she guessing? Someone must have said something but whom? "You don't know what you're talking about. Roger who?"

Beth sat up in bed happily smiling and said, "Look James, one time and one time only. You killed Roger. I have it on tape. You killed the others. I have that on tape too. You had long discussions with Alan and I got to hear every word. If I didn't have the proof I wouldn't have said a word - but I do. I want you and now I have you. You now belong to me and not to that Brazilian bimbo. You will do as I say because if you don't, I will send the tapes to the police and you, my love, will spend the rest of your natural days in a little prison cell. Oh, I know you would try and make me believe all sorts of things and deny it, so I brought you a copy of the tapes. Wasn't that nice of me? And in the spirit of our new love, I am going to excuse all those nasty thoughts and comments you made about me."

James mind was racing, and a hot flash took over his body. Deny, deny, deny was his first thought. No wait, hear her out – stay calm.

"I have thought everything through very carefully and I do realize your first thought is to get rid of me. However, I have taken precautions so that will not ever occur. There are a few copies of the tapes in various locations I have left with friends. If I should come up missing or dead, they have instructions to proceed to the nearest police station and deliver them. So, my dear, it is time you started appreciating me. As to that South American whore, she's history!

We are going to start formally dating and after a respectful amount of time, we will marry. I will get rid of that Bozo I live with and we will become the happiest couple in town. The kids are young, well behaved and you will grow to love them. Any questions?" Beth leaned back against the headboard with a big smile.

James couldn't believe what he had just heard. He swallowed hard and realized the game was over or was it? He went quiet. He needed time to think. He also realized he must play along with this bitch until he could find out more – a lot more. Tapes, how could she have tapes? Where did they come from? What does she know, what does she really know? She must know something, or she wouldn't have taken this stance.

"Ya, I have quite a few questions. Please tell me where you got these tapes?"

"Well, do you remember when you gave me a key to your house a long time ago? You asked me to drop some papers and some packages off at the house. When that happened, I just made a copy of the key. Now my boyfriend isn't good for much, but he is smart about electronics. I had him teach and show me how to plant microphones and a voice actuated tape recorder. I hooked one up and also tied it into your house phone, you know, like a tap on the line. The rest was easy. I just changed the tape once a week and I know everything you have said for the past two months. Whenever you worked late, I stopped by and changed the tapes. And boy, you've said a lot," she said with glee in her voice.

"Where are these microphones and tape recorder?"

"The recorder is above the ceiling in the hall closet and the microphones are in every room except the bathrooms – I thought I would give you a little privacy," she chuckled. "I'm sure I didn't miss much. You are such a bad boy. I should spank you and don't worry I'm going to do that too, but you'll like that. Now, about the pictures I took. That was easy too. When I knew you were going to fuck that whore you go out with, I just took pictures through the window. That wasn't necessary, but I just thought it would be fun and I am always curious to see what you are doing. Thank God you like to fuck with the lights on – it made it so much easier – some great shots – really hot. I've even jerked off to

182

some of them while I thought of you. Don't worry dear; we are going to be very happy, you will see.

James slowly started to recover, "Beth, these tapes and pictures are dangerous to have around. They worry me the most. I can understand you are black mailing me but if they fall into the wrong hands I will be gone and even you will not have me to play with. Where are they or who are they with?"

"James, don't worry your pretty hard-on about it. They are all in safe PLACES. With people I trust, and they know what to do, just in case you think you can get away with another murder. And four murders James, aren't we the busy little boy. I do have to applaud you for what you have done and your reasoning behind everything. Very admirable of you to get rid of all that vermin in the world. There's a few I would like to get rid of too. Maybe you can do it for me. Wouldn't that be fun? You and me – we could call ourselves the Lone Ranger and Tonto."

"You're crazy."

"James, I may be crazy but now I have what I want – you. And you, my darling, are going to do what I want from now on. No more murders James. We are going to be model citizens. It's okay, you will like, just give it a chance James and our life together will be a bed of roses." Beth was acting like a kid on Christmas morning. James got up without saying a word and went into the kitchen. She yelled after him, "Bring us some champagne so we can celebrate."

James just stood quietly in the kitchen. He was in trouble and for the first time he was scared of the consequences. He didn't know what to do. He realized now was not the time to make a decision about anything. He decided to play along, gather information and don't fight the river. This was too big, too important to move quickly and stupidly. She wasn't bluffing, and a hot temper would get him nowhere. He returned to the bedroom with the champagne, two glasses and a big smile.

"Darling, maybe this won't be so bad after all. I could get use to you very easily. Certainly, you love sex as much as I do and that's half the relationship. And, we have already worked together for over half a year now and that's worked out pretty good. It could be worse – you could hate my guts and then I would be in a lot of trouble. Okay, I surrender to your arms and your charms," he said with a big smile.

183

Beth looked at him wondering if he was serious and telling the truth. A look of shock came across her face. She paused for a few seconds and then smiled a big grin. "Well, you are taking this better than I thought you would. Don't worry; we are going to be very happy together. Now when are you going to tell that Brazilian bimbo?"

James opened the champagne with a large pop. "Beth, don't worry about that. It will happen soon enough. Right now, let's celebrate and oddly enough, I am free now to make some good decisions and I think I will like you more and more. Freedom comes in many forms and although you are kind of forcing me, it's a good choice. You are cute, intelligent, funny, have a great body, you love sex and most importantly you like me."

"Sorry James but there will be some rule changes. No more extra women, just me. I was willing to share, but now you are only for me. You will only fuck me and if you get restless, I have stamps already on the envelopes the tapes are in. Get it my love? ...Get it?"

"Okay, I got it," James added with a big smile.

Beth smiled and nodded, "But of course my darling. And please remember you have to be a good boy and behave yourself." Beth put her champagne glass down and started kissing James. They played in bed for two or three hours, then Beth had to go home to her boyfriend and children. James treated her like the greatest love in his life and told her he couldn't wait for her to return tomorrow night. James needed time to get his thinking around this problem. This was a time bomb ready to explode in his face and he was worried, but he did not let it show to Beth.

As she left she told him to leave the recording equipment alone. After she left, he immediately searched the house for the microphones and the recorder. They were everywhere she had said. He took them all down and placed them in a pile. There was a recorder and seven microphones. He then played the copies of the tapes she left for him. She wasn't kidding. It was all there; his voice, telephone conversations with everyone, and all the conversations he had with Alan when he had come to town. There were hours of recordings. It was all the damaging evidence needed to get him sent to the electric chair. James was sick and mad. He found a hammer and viciously attacked and killed the pile of equipment making it a mound of pieces. He saved the tapes.

184

James called Alan but could only leave a message to call back. He wandered the house trying to come up with answers to this problem and what to do about Beth. He had to play along with her until he could come up with the answers. He knew he had to get his hands on all the copies of the tapes. How many were there and who had them?

Chapter Nineteen

Life on Fire

James went to work the next day. He arrived very early and searched the office for any microphones or recorders but found none. He was satisfied she had only bugged the house. Nothing was said between them during the day. Beth arrived in the morning very happy. She came into the office and gave him a kiss on the cheek then smiled and went about her work. The day was underway, and the office was too busy to talk. They both went about their normal routines.

Later in the morning, Alan called. "What's up Killer?"

"Got a problem." James walked outside the office to avoid being heard. He then told Alan about the trip, about Beth and what had happened.

"Oh fuck, you are in trouble. Another one? And she knows. I can be down there at the end of the week. Are you sure of all this? God dam it – I told you this would happen."

"Ya, I'm sure and don't come down yet. Let me do some more work on the problem. I have to get closer to her and find out where these tape copies are being hidden. I think that's the first order of business. I'll give you a call later and don't call me at the house. I am pretty sure I removed all the equipment but I'm not positive yet."

"Okay but be careful. This is serious shit. Talk to you later."

James returned to his office and started working again. During the afternoon, whenever they were alone, Beth would make small talk about their new love and what a wonderful couple they made. She was giddy and excited. James tried to avoid any talk saying that is was best not to talk during the business day. She agreed after he consented to see her back at his house after the day was over.

James got to the house and Beth was already there. "Beth, I thought it over and this could be a good thing. I think you do love me and

187

surely, I need someone in my life. There is much to do so let's not rush. There would be problems if the office knew about us. We need to be careful, go slowly and figure out how to handle this. Maybe you need to find another job because if the office doesn't look favorable upon our marriage, I could be out of a job. And we certainly need my salary to support us dear."

"My little genius…good thinking darling but what I was thinking is this - I should just quit and you support us in the style to which I want to be accustomed to," Beth laughed. "Darling, you make enough money for all of us and since I have your balls in a ringer, I want to relax and become a wonderful stay at home wife and mother. I've worked hard my whole life and I want to take it easy – just like a rich bitch. Besides, I have you as my personal slave. You decide not to agree with me or fuck me in any way, you will end up at the grey bar hotel for life. Let's get that clear right now. Do you understand me, my sweet husband to be?"

"Oh, I understand you completely. Besides, I am getting tired of this craziness I have done and want to settle into a calm, normal life. This might just be the answer I am looking for. Do you think you can just love a normal man?"

"You bet your sweet bippy, darling." Beth made them a drink and they sat on the porch and continued the discussion.

"I mean I have done things which I think are for the betterment of mankind. It is more for the betterment of a few women and children, which in turn, hopefully changed their lives for the better and rids the world of some lousy people. I have only killed because these creeps have picked on defenseless women and children. Nothing upsets me more than some asshole hitting or hurting a woman, child or animal."

A quizzical look came across Beth's face. Her tone was soft and caring, "When did you first start doing this and why?"

James looked pensive, paused and started telling his story with a blank stare on his face while remembering. "It started in Nam. We killed so many women and children there it made me sick. I was against the war to begin with and I just couldn't believe that all of them were guilty. We were gun happy over there. They were just pawns caught up in a war they didn't want. The Vietnamese were having a civil war, first fucked over by China then the French and then the Americans. We didn't have any reason to be there except President Johnson needed a boost for the economy and Robert McNamara was his war minister who concocted this whole thing which killed over fifty-eight thousand Americans. I was so pissed about how terribly badly we conducted ourselves. Try to explain the death of those soldiers to their parents. What a waste, what a waste.

It really hit me when a guy in my unit beat the living shit out of my Vietnamese girlfriend and almost killed her because she didn't want to fuck him. She wasn't a whore, just a normal person trying to get through life – her life in a war zone. I guess I snapped. I was tired of the war, tired of the carnage, the waste of life and the stupidity of killing rice farmers and their families along with the enemy. There was no reason to hurt my girlfriend, my Nutan. No reason to beat her to a bloody pulp and permanently disfigure her.

A month later we went and destroyed a village. Before that firefight, the Lieutenant that beat Nutan was still bragging how he took care of Liberty's woman. Somehow, he was shot and killed by friendly fire. An accident…"

Beth quickly asked, "Did you kill him?"

Liberty went silent.

"Did you?" she repeated.

Liberty looked at her, shrugged and a slight small smile crossed his lips. "I don't know but I am glad he died. He was a mean prick. He had no right to do what he did to her. No right what so ever."

"What about the others you killed?"

"Look, I killed but only after I was sure the person I was killing deserved it and I felt they would do more harm to others in the future. There are lots of rotten people in this world. I don't know…men should not go through life hurting others and getting away with it. The legal system sucks and only barely protects people after a crime is committed. Most men get away with it. Women and children either are too afraid and don't report the crime or are afraid that the person will keep hurting them, so they never speak up. I have seen too much of it. I have even had men brag to me how they beat the shit out of their wives or children to keep them in line. Absolutely disgusting.

189

That fucking pig my ex-wife hooked up with deserved it. He had a record as long as your arm. Constantly beating up women and using them, stealing their money. He really pissed me off. She is sick with alcoholism and he took advantage. He struck too close to me, hurt her and stole my money. I don't get mad, I get even. Then, that fuck head in Brazil. He was fucking his own sons in the ass. How sick is that. Pedophile extraordinaire. Anyone who does that should get the worst done to him. It is against the law for one thing and he was doing it on a regular basis and not getting caught. I decided he shouldn't and now he definitely won't do it again."

Beth was surprised, "What fuck-head in Brazil? You didn't tell me about that. What did you do now? Oh my God, I'm marrying a serial killer. James, this has to stop. You have been lucky up to now, but the tide could turn at any time. Tell me about this one."

"I'll tell you later about that one." James realized he had just made a big slip. "Don't worry my dear wife to be. I have decided not to do it anymore. I have been careful not to get caught and I don't want to end up in jail. I am not going to kill anymore because I could get caught. Eventually the odds will turn against you or you get sloppy and leave clues that could get you caught. Look you uncovered everything. Someone else could too. Time to mind my P's and Q's. No more killing, no matter what. So as long as you keep my secrets, I guess I will behave myself and live a righteous life with you by my side."

Beth smiled, and happiness came into her voice. She seemed to ignore what he was saying, and her mind was on a different track. "That's what I wanted to hear. I want to live a good life and we can be very happy together, you will see. When shall I move in? I have to dump Bill and get rid of him. He is a nice guy but as exciting as watching paint dry. Our sex life is non-existent even when he tries. I can't even feel him inside me. He is too small compared to you. You make me cum over and over again. That's why I want you. You take me to a different world. My body shakes for hours after we make love. I can't wait to be with you full time. How about I move in next month?"

"Darling, I am glad to hear all that but that is way too soon. I have to end the relationship with Vera and stop her from coming to the states. Then, I want the next project to start so the company will not interfere once I have started it. I want you to help me get it started and then you will need to train your replacement. Also, we still have a lot to do to get ready for your move in here. You have to do the break up dance with Bill and give it a little time. Things don't always go as smoothly as you imagine. We also need to figure out how we are going to live like a family. Your two boys will have to go to a different school. There is a lot to arrange and think about. I also need a little time to wrap my brain around it. The school year ends in about four months. I think it would be better if we wait till summer to put it all together."

"I hope you are not back peddling on this deal," Beth said questioningly.

"No – no. Just relax. It will all happen. I can't and won't rush it. We still have to be careful. Don't worry, just go find a good baby sitter so I can rock your world and we can have fun dating while we are getting ready. Relax baby, go make us another drink before I practice making you climax," he said laughing. He realized that he was taking control, the way he liked it. She would fall in line and do what he said.

Beth smiled, kissed him and headed to the kitchen.

*****

James finally got a night alone. He was mentally exhausted. He just wanted some alone time. He had a few drinks and then grilled a steak. He couldn't take his mind off of how to get the tapes from Beth. He had to play along, make her happy and keep her happy until she gave him all the tapes. He had to also make sure she didn't hold any back. She wanted marriage and would probably, at a minimum, hold back on the tapes until the marriage was consummated. How could he get the tapes before marriage and then not marry her, yet keep her quiet afterward? Killing her never entered his mind – just the recovery of the tapes. The marriage will never be. He would just have to figure out how to avoid the union. The happiness he had found in Brazil had now vanished like dissipated smoke.

James groaned out loud as the phone rang not wanting an intrusion to his thoughts, "Hello."

"James OK? You nao email or call. I miss you. What wrong? James, you nao love Vera nao more?"

"Hi honey. I'm sorry. There has been a lot happening at work and there aren't enough hours in the day. I still love you and miss you very much. How is everything on your end?"

"All tudo bem. I excited, boys excited. I do all paperwork with government. I wait for them. I not finish my project. Boys finish school Decembro, then come to you. James come visit your summer? Miss you. You want Vera come visit now? James, Military Policia detective woman who see us, she come ask more questions about Paulo and us?"

"I remember. Why? When? What did she ask?"

"She ask where we are that night. I say we in Guaruja. Then say, where you go in car day you go Ubatuba? I tell her Ubatuba – yes? She here week ago."

James mind raced. He went silent trying to figure out what this meant. "James, I do OK?"

"Yes dear. Everything is all right. Is that all she asked?"

"She ask about marriage. Then she go. When do Vera see James – soon?"

"Yes dear, I will plan a trip to see you soon. I have a lot of work I have to get done. I will plan a trip soon." They chatted for a while and spoke of love and missing each other, James was preoccupied and concerned with why the detective showed up and was asking questions again. He tried to break off the conversation as soon as he could, promising to call her soon. He put the phone down, took a big gulp of air and made himself another drink. He started going over everything he could think of about killing Paulo. Good God, could they have found a clue? Maybe they were just following up. How did they know about James leaving for the day? What did Vera say? He silently sat there and thought for hours. He finally came to the conclusion that he would never go back to Brazil again. There is no extradition to or from Brazil and none through the US. He was safe – with that one. After James reached that conclusion he stumbled off to bed. His head was spinning, and he felt pressure in his head. What else could go wrong?

James finished the week and hopped a plane to Portland, Maine Friday afternoon. He called Alan and told him to meet him at the airport. His head was still spinning. The ride was long but finally landed and he found Alan in the airport. They grabbed his bag and went to the closest bar for a drink.

James filled Alan in on the latest developments as Alan cringed and listened. "I think I am safe on the Brazilian deal, but I still don't know what to do about Beth. I have to do something, and I have to do it fast and I still have Vera and her kids in the not too distant future. This is developing into a big mess. What do you think I should do?"

"I told you this was going to blow up in your face and it is, but not the way you thought. Instead of the legal side you have the love side as a problem. If you don't solve the love side problem, then you will have a big legal problem and guess what? You will be in jail."

"Oh, knock that shit off. I don't need an 'I told you so speech.' I need answers and a way out of this mess. Come up with something worthwhile," James said sternly.

"Okay, I'm sorry. You're going to have to get those tapes and you may have to kill her. She does have you by the balls."

"I can't kill women."

"James, you may not have a choice. She is very dangerous to you and your personal freedom. You will always have to do what she says, whether you like it or not. That is until you get your hands on those tapes or get rid of Beth."

They left the bar and drove to Alan's lodge, talking the whole way but no answers came forth. They spent Saturday and Sunday trout fishing and constantly talking. Monday came early, and Alan drove James back to Portland to catch the plane. They went their separate ways without an answer.

Alan called that night with a possible answer to the problem. "Look, I think what you have to do is convince her that because she knows all about it, she has become an accessory to the crime, thereby making her guilty and just as vulnerable as you, especially since she is not married to you at the present moment. What do you think?"

James thought for a moment. "You may have something my friend. You just may have something. She is now definitely involved, right up to her eyeballs. They only thing left is somehow to prove, or be able to prove, she had knowledge for some time and could have come forth. And the bottom line is – It wouldn't make a difference – we would still both go to jail." They went over it a few more times and James decided it was well worth a try, if only to force her to give up the tapes. It was a start. James hung up and felt much better about the situation. Now all he had to do was figure out the best way to present this to Beth. He must draw her into a situation she could not get out of and put herself in jeopardy.

He thought about going to see Ray, but that was out of the question. The situation was way too deep now, and he dare not reveal the true facts. Best not to be in a position where a slip of the tongue could take place. No need for Ray to know what he had done even though it was in the past. Silence can be golden.

Chapter Twenty

The Detective

The week went past. James still could not decide the best way to present the concept to Beth without pissing her off. She had stopped by the house twice after work, but only for sex. She was determined to solidify her place in James' life. She talked incessantly about their marriage and living together. James was tired of her constant chatter. He spent the rest of the nights trying to come up with a plan to force Beth to release the tapes. As he was wandering about the house one night, James came upon the shattered parts of the taping system Beth had installed. Beth had even made snide comments about what he had done to her recording devices. She had said that no one was ever going to be able to use that pile of crap you made. Then the idea hit him. What was good for the goose was good for the gander. James would install new microphones and a recorder. He would tape Beth talking about her knowledge of the murders. This was not any good in court, but it would prevent her from saying she never knew about the murders and she never had prior knowledge of all instances or at least direct knowledge after they occurred. He wasn't sure this would work but it was worth a try, since Beth just liked to chatter so much. She might just chatter her way into talking about the whole situation. It might end the whole discussion about James being guilty, because she would not be able to go forward with an accusation without putting herself in jeopardy. She would still demand marriage from James, of that he was sure. He had to start somewhere. Maybe the answers would come as the scenes played out. Take the first step, one step at a time.

James looked forward to the weekend. Some peace and quiet would allow him to set up the recording devices and get ready to tape the conversations he wanted to have with her. Saturday, he busied himself laying out the microphones and running the wires in the attic. As he was installing the equipment, he barely heard the knock on the door. He stopped with a start, then crawled across the attic and came down through the attic access hole and down the step ladder. He had a lot of loose insulation stuck to his clothes. James brushed it off then went and opened the front door.

There stood the gorgeous police detective from Sao Paulo he had talked to at Vera's apartment. A rush came over James. He recognized her. He suddenly had a strange nervousness and a shaking in his knees. "Oh hello...Miss...ah - ah" pretending not to remember.

"Lieutenant Andrea Araujo," she filled in the blanks for James.

"Well this is a shock...Come in...What are you here for? ... Oh my God, is everything alright?" James stammered.

"Thank you. Everything is fine. I just stopped by to ask you a few questions."

James laughed nervously. "Um...you just stopped by from Brazil to ask me a few questions? They don't have phones in Brazil anymore?" James, as nervous as he was, thought she was even more beautiful than he had remembered.

Andrea walked in about ten feet turned and faced James. She laughed as she started answering his questions. "Relax Mr. Liberty. I came to Miami to take a course the Florida State Police are offering. While I am here, my superiors and I thought it would be a good idea to follow up with you on a few details about Paulo Fantinato's murder."

"Like what are you referring to? Please, let us sit down, come in, follow me." James led her to the porch and offered her a chair. "Can I get you something to drink?"

As she sat down she smiled and said, "Thank you, water would be fine."

James was starting to recover from the first nervousness he felt in his gut. He went to the kitchen and slowly got two glasses of water. He was trying to figure what this was all about. He told himself to stay calm and cool. He then returned to the porch and put the water down.

"Thank you," she said with a smile. "You have a lovely home with a great view of the harbor. Mr. Liberty..."

"Call me James, please."

"Okay James. Please call me Andrea. Well, let me start from the beginning. We believe Paulo's death resulted from a robbery and as a result Paulo was killed because he fought back or something like that. However, we do a very thorough investigation, and there are a few details that are unanswered, which leaves us very curious until we have all the answers. Please excuse me; my English is not very good."

"Please," James said in a shocking way. "Your English is excellent, if I did not know you are from Brazil, I would say you sound like you are from Ohio or someplace in the Midwest. Matter of fact, your English is better than most Americans. You have learned well."

"Oh, thank you," she said with a smile, and a slight blushing was apparent. "I have studied your language for many, many years. I have tried to become as proficient as possible. It has opened many doors in my career, and I really enjoy the ability to communicate. My department always wants me to be the interpreter for them, and as a result I even get to travel to the United States for training. I get to teach my fellow officers all the new techniques I learn. Oh, I also get to shop here and enjoy myself," she smiled and laughed at her own good fortune.

James noticed how proud she was of herself, and how attractive and sexily coy she was. She seemed to be a very happy person. "Well, that is wonderful. Please tell me exactly why you are here and how can I help you?" James said in a very elegant tone.

"Well...this is, how do I say, very intrusive and embarrassing. While I have been in the United States I have been lucky enough to have access to all the data bases around this country. One of my assignments was to investigate your background – only as follow up..."

"Excuse me, Andrea, my background?" James started getting nervous again.

"Yes. The more we find out about you the more we, or should I say, - I wonder about you."

"I am getting lost...I am getting confused."

"Please James; let me explain all and then all will become apparent." She stopped and sipped her water, then took a deep breath. "At first, we thought it was just a murder due to the robbery, but with the strange relationship and your involvement, and then after the background check I did on you, it really brings up so many questions. Especially, about your involvement."

"Lieutenant, I really don't know where this is going, but I do not like what I am hearing."

"Oh, please, relax James. This is all really unofficial, and no one in Brazil knows what I have found out and at worst case, there is nothing we can do anyway. You know – with no extradition allowed between our two countries. I just cannot understand the whys of this case, especially with your background and that is why I became curious. And, the more facts I came across, the more I became confused and wondering about you. So, this is why I came to see you"

James was now very nervous. "Please Andrea, what are you talking about?"

"Well, let me be straight forward with you. One of the most interesting facts in this case is that you went for a drive and were away for a long time the night Paulo was killed. You left the Golden Beach Hotel alone early and did not return until late at night, actually, early the next morning. This in itself is no big thing. Then, when I started doing a background check on you, I came across some interesting things in your past. You see, as I said, when I come here for training, I have access to the wonderful data bases you have in the United States, and I can start putting things together."

"You have lost me my dear. I do not have any idea what you are talking about," said James trying to be as dumb as possible.

"The computers in your country and all the data bases make it easy to learn about someone, and how you say…connect the dots. I do not think I am the first to do this or maybe I am…I do not know. All the notes from different investigations around your country of your different policia departments can be accessed. When I do a name search on you, many investigations come up where you have been questioned. Mr. Liberty, you always seem to be so close to many murders in your life." She shifted in her chair and crossed her long legs exposing a lot of leg towards James. She did it very slowly and watched James' eyes follow her legs. "I have had access to your Department of Army file and found out you were involved with a murder in Vietnam. Excuse me, or should

I say, questioned about – what they say…a friendly fire?… I do not know about this…maybe you can explain."

James swallowed hard. He thought this bitch may look like just a beautiful woman, but she is smart…too smart. Time for me to be smart – watch out. This may be a trap. "Andrea, I do not care for your implications. The incident in Vietnam, which I do not expect you to fully understand, happened during a war. The person who was killed in my unit happened while we were engaged in a hostile mission. Either the enemy or someone from my company accidently killed this man by not shooting correctly, and as a result he died – thus if it was done by someone on our side it is called 'friendly fire.' I and everyone else in my company were found not guilty, and no one was charged with any crime. Do you understand?" James was trying to hide his nervousness. He was trying to sound as nonchalant as possible.

"Well I guess that explains it." She paused for a moment. "Next, I found out you were questioned by the Houston Police about your secretary's husband being killed in an accident? Someone ran over him many times until he was dead. It does not sound like it was an accident – more like murder."

Oh Jesus, thought James, this bitch is dangerous. "Yes, it was a very unfortunate accident. If I remember correctly, he was run over by a car or a truck. I think they said it was a hit and run. I really do not know all the facts. I never knew him, just his wife. My poor secretary had two children and was left without a husband to support them. Terrible! I just tried to support her in her hour of need. How did my name come up?" James felt himself flushing, and a warm sensation came over his head with a shortness of breath. It seemed best to him to keep the answers very short and non-committal.

"You helped her talking with the policia about the incident and because you did, your name was in the reports when the officers questioned her, so you must have been there at some time with her. You must have been very close to her?" Andrea said this with a look of concern but ended the sentence with a cute, sexy smile.

"Wait a minute – Just because someone has an accident somewhere in this world does not mean you should insinuate I had something to do with it. And if you are inferring that there was some sort of a relationship with my secretary, let me assure you, it was strictly business. And the interview with the police, you are referring to, took place in my office during the normal work day." James tried to put some anger in his voice to avoid the nervous stuttering that was apparent.

"Nao. Nao. It was just interesting to me that your secretary got a lot of insurance money from this accident. It was good for her, yes?"

"I guess. She moved back to wherever she came from and I never saw her again." James then quickly excused himself to go to the bathroom. He went to his bathroom, shut the door and sat on the edge of the bathtub. His breathing was rapid, and perspiration collected on his forehead. He was trying to accumulate his thoughts. How could this Brazilian bitch figure this all out? What should he do? She had not even gotten to Paulo's murder. He took deep breaths, splashed his face with cold water, toweled, looked in the mirror and tried to relax. He tried not to take too long, so as not to raise suspicion. Returning to the porch, he sat back down, noticing she had undone another button on her blouse, exposing more cleavage. "Can we get to the point, Andrea? I don't care for what you are saying."

"I am sorry to upset you," she said sweetly and with an air of concern.

"I am not upset," he blurted out. He thought: Oops, I said that too quickly and with too much anger, calm down James, calm down.

"You came here to discuss Paulo. Can you get to the point, please?"

She smiled. "Oh, yes I will. I also learned you just happened to be with your friend, Alan French, when he was questioned about a business connection he had. The man he was involved with came to a tragic death. He accidently fell down two flights of stairs and died, how terrible. You were his – how they say - alibi for when it happened."

James just looked at her. He stared into her eyes. His mind was racing. "Look – is any of this your concern? I am getting sick and tired of this, and I think maybe you should talk to my lawyer. For some reason you are fishing – for what I do not know. I do not like this intrusion into my privacy. If I have done something wrong, then I am sure the local authorities would have come to me long ago, but they have not, and I am not guilty of anything." James was going to pieces very quickly. He was trying to figure out how to end this questioning.

"Nao, nao, nao, please James. All of this just fell into my lap by accident. It is of nao concern to us in Brazil. I could not even do anything anyway. I am not accusing you. It is just background which is leading up to my questions. I mean no harm and I cannot do anything, please believe me. Please, just let me go on. There are just a few more things."

James was in a panic. He felt a huge urge to run away from this woman. He froze for what seemed to be a lifetime. He then smiled and laughed. "I am thirsty and hot. I think I will have a beer – cerveja to you. Would you care to join me?" He rose quickly and started toward the kitchen.

"Yes, that would be delightful," she answered with her sexy smile.

James went to the kitchen and retrieved two beers and glasses. His mind was spinning. If he threw her out, it would look suspicious. He felt the walls closing in on him. Could Beth be involved? No, this was too complicated for her to do this. If he continued – he had to continue. I have to throw this girl off track. She can't do anything to me but she can tell one of her American police buddies. I have to get on her good side. Time to conquer this bitch. Use all the charm, turn off the nervousness. He returned and poured a beer into her glass with a shaking hand. She watched his hand shake, then looked up into his eyes and smiled.

"You are such a handsome gentleman. We Brazilian woman love a gentleman. I would love to find a gentleman like you to be with. You are caring and kind. Why are you not married?"

James sat down and smiled at her. "That's nice. Can you get back to business?"

She feigned naiveté. "Oh, that is right - you just got a divorce, not too long ago. I am sorry to hear that. You seem to have a lot of bad luck. That reminds me. Your ex-wife's lover was murdered. What a coincidence. Or did you not know this?"

"She mentioned it. She has poor taste. It is probably good someone killed him. From what I know, the man had a very long record of crime. My ex-wife is very sick. She suffers from alcoholism and as a result she makes some very bad choices. I hope she gets better soon. Now, how did I get connected to this?"

"That would be good for her. Did anyone ever question you?"

"No. No one ever asked me about it."

Andrea smiled again, and looked at James. "It is probably a good thing they did not question you. Your name was mentioned in one of the police reports as being the ex-husband. You helped her file a restraining order against him. And when I did the name search – up you popped again, amazing." She then paused and said, "That brings me to Paulo's death, or should I say murder."

"Good, that is what you came here for, correct?" James was starting to lose it again. How the fuck did this bitch unravel his whole life and put all of this together? She must know – she must know. She has done this all by herself – but how and why? Who else knows? Who has she told?

"What we know is - Paulo was a very bad person. He served time in our prisons twice: once for stealing and once for attempted murder. It was sad because it was a little boy he almost murdered after he raped the little boy many times. In our system, these crimes would keep him in jail for the rest of his life. But he had a very good lawyer, who got him a very short sentence."

"I didn't know any of this." James said gathering himself for what she was here to find out.

"He was a known homosexual. When he got out of prison the second time, he married Vagner."

"Who is Vagner?" James was now very puzzled. "Look, how and why would Vera ever get mixed up with a queer like Paulo, if in fact he is a queer? This is not making any sense what-so-ever."

Andrea stared at him in disbelief. She froze. "Maybe - Could I have another cerveja, por favor?"

James looked at her quizzically, said yes, and went to retrieve two more beers. He returned and poured her another beer. He sat down, but the air in the room had changed. His mood quickly went from

202

nervousness to trying to figure what was really going on, and what she was trying to say.

"You really do not know, do you?"

"Know what?"

"About Vagner."

James just looked baffled. "I don't know a Vagner..."

Andrea lowered her head, lowered the pitch in her voice and softly said, "Ah...umm...Vagner is Vera."

Silence covered the room. She stared at James. James looked at her in disbelief. His mouth fell open. He could not move. Finally, he recovered and managed to say emphatically, "Your nuts! You don't know what you're saying! You're crazy!"

"Well at first, I was surprised too, nao it is true."

James was now in more shock than the whole meeting had produced. He was almost screaming at her. "Lady, you're nuts! I know better. I have been with that woman many times. I have been over her body with a fine-tooth comb, and that is no man, and I know women. You're crazy!"

"James, I am sorry to be the one to tell you. I thought you knew. I had no idea, honest."

"How could this be? You're crazy!"

"Nao, it is true."

James was stammering. "But she is the mother to those two boys. How do you fake that? Tell me!

"I am sorry to be the one to tell you this. She is not the mother, she is the father. Vagner was originally married to a woman by the name of Inah. Inah ran off with someone, we are not sure with whom or why. She left Vagner with the two boys who were very young at the time. At the time, he was a college professoro and became very famous for his research. Vagner then turned gay or should I say was gay. Vagner's wife then left him and shortly after that, Paulo was released from prison, and began an affair with Vagner. Then Vagner went through many operations to turn himself into a woman. Why this all happened, no one seems to know, we can't figure it out. There are many questions. Maybe Vagner, I mean Vera can fill you in on the answers. You must remember, Brazil is the plastic surgery capital of the world. Many women and men are altered – a lot. I must say, they did a great job on him/her because I never would have guessed it myself. She is now a very beautiful woman. They then married, like any male-female couple and lived that way. Paulo then adopted the boys. After five years they divorced. Paulo use to physically abuse her, which caused the divorce apparently."

James could not believe what he was hearing. This was the woman he loved. The woman he was going to spend the rest of his life with. He had forgotten all about the murders and the investigation. He felt foolish and duped. Why had Vera never mentioned it especially after the amount of time they had spent together? How could he have gotten so deep into a relationship, and never have a clue about the woman he had fallen head over heels in love. James was silent, just looking down at the table in front of him.

"Please James, I am sorry to tell you this. I really thought you knew. I understand how hurt you must feel. I take it you are not a homosexual?"

"Fuck you bitch!" James angrily retorted. "I'm not gay, never have been and never will be. It is something you just know. Boy, have I been lied to. I do not know what to do." James went silent again.

They sat there for a while. Not a word was said.

Finally, Andrea broke the silence. "I am truly sorry. However, I must still ask you the questions I came to ask. May I, are you alright?"

"Ya, fuck you, go ahead. What else could make this worse?" he said hopelessly.

"Did Vera have anything to do with the murder of Paulo?"

"No," he answered in anger.

"Did you have anything to do with Paulo's murder?"

"Certainly not, and I am pissed about the whole way you have investigated this, and my background. I have always done the right things in life. I am not the bad guy. I am the good guy. You waltz in here accusing me of killing everybody from Julius Caesar to President Kennedy. I think I have answered your questions and I think it is time for you to leave. I have nothing more to say."

"Okay and I am sorry I brought you this news. I thought you knew and I still have to ask the questions. I am sorry."

"Just leave me alone please. Just leave."

"I'm sorry." She paused, waiting, but then seemed to give up. "Don't get up I can find my way out."

She quickly left. James sat at the table in awe, not knowing what to do. He went to the bathroom and threw up. He went back to the porch and sat there in silence until night came. At some point in the night he stumbled to his bed and eventually his mind stopped talking and he fell asleep.

Chapter Twenty-One

Too Many Problems

Sunday morning arrived. James arose, with his mind swirling in disbelief. He had a pounding headache. He was confused and did not know what to think next. What should he focus on? The problem with this detective, the problem with Vera – Vagner, the problem with Beth were all connected and one false step on his part would be the end of him.

How could Vera fool him the way she had. That made him sick every time he thought of it. He felt foolish he had fallen in love with a man. He knew instantly he could not go forward with this relationship with Vera. This was the end. He had to fix the rest, but at least that group of problems would be gone from his life. The situation of getting rid of her was easily done and controllable. This, however, might be good. He could get relief of her, her children, and all the problems of bringing them to the United States. At least, that would eliminate having two women at the same time. Vera didn't know about the murders so the danger level she created was minor and by dumping her, it would not increase his risk regarding the murders.

Now Beth was a different problem. He didn't want to go forward with her. She was the one forcing the union. He had to be careful here because he still had to get those tapes at a minimum and that had to be done quickly. He could hold off the proposed marriage, but the tapes, those dam tapes.

The detective presented a unique problem. She had information no one had ever been able to put together. What was she after? If she didn't think Vera/Vagner killed Paulo, then was she intimating that he had? Was she just trying to be a Sherlock Holmes? What was in it for her?

James decided he just needed time to work this through. In the interim he should go back to the present plan of trying to tape Beth, so he thought the best thing was to get back to the project of wiring the house with the microphones. He realized he had way too many problems and no viable solutions. It was best to try to work through what he knew. But his main concern was now for the Brazilian detective. He still had to find out if she had told anyone. He worked through the day. In the late afternoon the phone rang. The Brazilian detective called.

"Hello James, I just wanted to call you and tell you how deeply sorry I am for telling you what I knew. Are you alright?"

"Yes, Andrea, I am okay. I'm sorry I fell apart. It was quite a shock to my system shall we say. I will be fine. It will just take some time to adjust. How can I help you Andrea?"

"I was just checking on you. I can understand how you feel. You are too strong a man to allow this to bother you. You will get through this; it is not the end of the world. You will be better off for knowing. I am just really sorry I was the one to tell you. Anyway, since I am up in this area for another few days maybe you could tell me where there is a good place to eat?"

James suddenly saw an opening. He had to find out what this woman knew and her intentions. "Well, where are you staying?"

"I am staying at a place called the Ramada Inn."

"Look Andrea, why don't you have dinner with me? It might help me if you were to tell me more and I need to get some food in me anyway. So why not have dinner with me, my treat."

"I don't want to be a problem to you."

"Relax, no bother, I will pick you up at seven. What room number are you in?"

"Well if you are sure James."

"Yes, I am sure. Now, what room are you in?

"I am in room 201."

"Okay, I know where you are, and I will see you at seven. See you then." He quickly hung up.

At seven James pulled into the Ramada parking lot and made his way to her room. He had a plan in mind. He knocked on her door and she opened it. She was dressed in a beautiful blue summer dress and high heels. She was prettier each time he saw her. James had a strange feeling come over him. He felt more interested in this woman than he had with Vera. He briefly felt confused and then realized he was here on a mission.

"Wow, you look beautiful."

"Thank you," she cooed.

James smiled. "Before we go any further, I would like to ask you a question."

"Sure, what?" as a quizzical look crossed her face.

"Are you sure you are a woman and not a man or have ever been one?"

She started laughing, "Yes, I promise I am a woman and have always been."

"Okay, let's go. Stuart is a small town and goes to bed early. There is a nice restaurant downtown I think you will enjoy." He guided her to his car and as he opened her door for her, she looked appreciative.

"Well thank you. A woman doesn't get this kind of assistance in Brazil."

"What do men in Brazil do? Drag their dates behind the car?"

She started laughing and then asked, "Am I a date?"

"No, but I am amazed to find out that I think chivalry is dead everywhere in the world."

They chatted as James drove to downtown Stuart to the Riverwalk Café. It was one of his favorite restaurants and he ate there often. The hostess greeted him warmly and gave them his favorite table. The Riverwalk was a small and red brick walled cozy place with large glass windows. From their table they had a great view of the St. Lucie River as dusk was falling.

"This is elegant James. I love it. I hope the food is good."

"I think you will enjoy. They haven't killed too many people here," he said dryly.

They laughed and talked as if it were a date, which is what James wanted. James ordered a bottle of wine and they bantered their way through two glasses each, after which they chose an appetizer and an entrée. They both let their guards down and were talking and laughing more like lovers than adversaries on issues that had brought them together. James was trying to find out as much information as possible about Andrea, and what she knew. In his mind it would be best to talk about anything and everything. Just keep the conversation flowing; don't dwell on any one item which might slow, stop or raise suspicion about what he was trying to find out.

He inquired about her life. She was young. She admitted to twenty-nine, but James thought she may be shaving a couple of years. Andrea was from a well to do family in Rio. Andrea had gone to a university, and after graduation decided to get into police work. She was now disappointed with the work, and wanted to change her career. She had now decided to follow in her father's footsteps, and become a lawyer. Andrea was a beautiful woman. She had long, wavy, brunette hair with streaks of blond which hung six inches below her shoulders. Her beautiful wavy hair framed her oval face with large almond shaped, deep brown, almost black eyes. Her slim body was very curvy with large breasts which she didn't mind exposing. They seem to be exploding out of her lacy red bra. On the ride there he had noticed her lovely rear and legs. It seemed as if the dress was always exposing one of her shapely legs, and showing lacey thigh high nylons. She was wearing hi-heels which made her about two or three inches shorter than James. He couldn't help but wonder why all these Brazilian women were so beautiful. Her makeup accented her eyes and beautiful red lips exquisitely. Her finger and toe nails were well shaped, and the color matched her lipstick. She wore long dangly earrings with plenty of gold and diamonds which matched her necklace which plunged deep into her cleavage.

Another bottle of wine appeared as a gift from the owner, who waved and winked at James. He approached and said, "James, how do you always seem to find the most beautiful women in the world?"

"Just a lot of luck and an ability to kidnap. Thank you, Steve for the wine and if you keep ogling this woman I am going to tell your wife. How is the beautiful Sharon?"

"She is fine, and I will not tell her you were here. Every time I mention your name her eyebrows and ears seem to perk up." He turned toward Andrea, "Watch out for this one honey, he is very dangerous, don't believe a word he says."

Andrea almost choked on her wine. "Oh, I really do know he is very dangerous," as she smiled and looked knowingly at James.

Introductions quickly came, and Steve was his charming self. They chatted for a few minutes then Steve said, "Just watch yourself in the dark corners honey. I'll see you later, work calls."

"Steve, work maybe calling but you will never ever find it. Now go away or I will never bring her here again," James laughed as Steve made his exit to the kitchen.

"It's so easy to like you James," Andrea said sexily.

"Well, I will let you, now that I am a free man again."

"Well under the circumstances, I think I should keep my distance."

"Now that you brought it up, let's talk. Do you actually believe all the crap you mentioned yesterday or are you just playing detective?"

"To tell the truth James, I do like you. I liked you when I met you in Sao Paulo. You do scare me, however. You seem to always be near a murder. I do not judge, I just investigate. On the good side, if you did do all those things, they seem to be justifiable murders, if there is such a thing. Still they are murders, but there are a lot of people who probably deserve what they get. I see a lot of it. My job is to find the murderer, no matter right or wrong, regardless of what I personally believe.

My work is not what I expected it would be when I originally got into this line of work. I mean it has been fun...no not fun...at least interesting. The down side is there are too many undesirable types in this line of work. The men you meet are not the type of guys you want to bring home to the family. That is unless your family is in the bank robbing

211

business. So, to me, while I'm young, I want to switch and try my hand as a business type lawyer working for my father – take the easy road for a while."

"I understand. That is probably a very intelligent move on your part. I would encourage that: working for daddy is usually best – faster promotion rate too. But getting back to my situation: you must understand I just happen to have been near or close to situations when they occurred. Everything is just circumstantial...Wrong place at the wrong time. Tell me something. After you are through turning my life upside down, who should I expect next to follow up with all these silly accusations? Who have you told so far and when are they going to try to throw the book at me?" he said jokingly to her.

"Well James, I am not suppose to be telling you this, but I think I am drunk enough. No one, but me, put all these pieces together." Andrea was smiling and so proud of herself. "Pretty good detective work, wouldn't you say? I am the only one who knows so far. I would not accuse anyone of anything until I have positive proof. To accuse someone of a crime, you have to be doubly sure of the facts. I did not tell anyone on the American side. I am suppose to tell my supervisors in Brazil when I get back what I have learned. I don't think I am going to tell them anything about you because if you did do it; there is nothing we can do anyway. I personally believe you, and you are too nice a person to commit murder. People who murder are usually scum, and have a dim view of life. Additionally, I took a course about how you can tell if someone is guilty just by watching their eyes. I have determined you're not guilty. You are very straight forward and are always looking at me and not trying to look away. Besides, the extradition laws between our two countries really suck and no one is going to worry about the loss of Paulo. He was a creep, so why even try to make a big issue out of it. Now, if Vagner/Vera did it, then that would be a different story, but he/she didn't. The only thing is that Paulo was a bad man and the world is a better place with him gone. That's as far as I'm concerned. Boy, that wine is good. Can I have some more?"

James immediately filled her glass. "Well, to tell you the truth, neither Vera, whatever, nor I did the killing. Sorry, you will have to keep looking. However, I will tell you something. After learning the background from you, I believe Paulo was abusing the boys and Vera was turning a blind eye to what he was doing to them." James noticed the wine was having an effect. He needed to plant little correct thoughts in her brain.

Andrea was starting to slur her words. "That does not surprise me. Well, are you going to tell me the truth about the others? I am curious, you know, just to see if I am on the right track." She broke out in laughter.

"Well, put the handcuffs on me honey. To tell the truth, you are totally wrong on all but one."

There was a huge sudden spark of interest from Andrea. She could hardly contain her exhilaration. "Which one did you do? Wow, I'm excited"

"Calm down. Not exactly...the truth is that it is possible that I or quite a few other people could have been responsible for the death of the officer in Viet Nam. In a firefight it is too hard to tell what is really happening. You just shoot and spray your bullets – you don't take careful aim."

She looked as if all the air had gone out of her balloon. "Oh, that one doesn't count. I thought you were going to tell me that you were responsible for one of the other murders. Now, I am disappointed."

"You sound as if you want me to be a murderer. Does that excite you?"

Andrea started giggling as she spoke, "Ya, a little. I guess there is a part of me who wants a bad boy to love."

"So, you won't love me unless I'm a *Bad Boy*? You can still put the cuffs on me – that might be fun."

"No, it's just a silly girl's fantasy. Oh, I thought you were going to tell me a secret. Now I will have to fantasize differently." She giggled when she spoke.

"Well, I too will have to fantasize differently. Fantasies are wonderful. If you actually live out a fantasy, you can go create a brand new one. Now, I will have to look for a new love for my life. It may take a while to get over the fact I was sleeping with a man. Just the thought turns my stomach and makes me sick," mused James.

She was totally sympathetic with his situation and sadly said, "Oh no James. Don't think like that. You were fooled. Anyone would have been fooled. His – her surgery was so perfect, he actually did become a woman."

"I feel like no woman would ever want to sleep with me again," James said this tongue in cheek, fishing for how Andrea would respond.

"You are being silly. You are a very desirable man. Any woman would love to make love with you."

"Well, I think it is going to be hard to get this out of my mind. It is different for a man than it is for a woman. A man has to perform. He has to become erect. A woman just has to lie there and receive. When a man has a mental problem, like I have now, it may take a while to get over it."

"Yes, you are right...but a good woman can help you get over it quickly. A woman who understands what you have been through will help you get back on the horse, so you can ride again." Andrea reached over and held his hands with hers with a very compassionate look on her face and she looked like she was almost going to cry.

James spoke in a very downtrodden way, "That is easy for you to say. What am I suppose to do go around saying – Gee, I was sleeping with a transvestite or a woman who was a man. Now I want to sleep with a woman again. How is that going to sound to the average woman on the dating circuit? And furthermore, what if I cannot perform in bed? Maybe I will never be able to get over it."

Andrea was looking very concerned and begging him, "You are making much too much about this. Besides you do not have to tell a woman this, all you have to do is jump into bed and try."

James wanted to seem sad to her and on the verge of tears as well, "I don't want to fail. No man wants to fail. This worries me, I guess eventually, I will figure it out with enough time and therapy," he smiled, paused and demonstrated he wanted to get away from the subject. Quietly he said, "Let's eat."

While they ate, James kept gently probing Andrea, asking again if she had told anyone about her investigation. Asking again if anyone from the American police departments had wondered what she was doing with all the data she was collecting. She kept reassuring him, that no one knew about what she was doing. She said she would never reveal to anyone the information until she could prove her case. Why would she let someone else steal her glory? He kept her wine glass full and pretended to be drinking with her. Andrea became a little chatterbox. She was proud of her work; even though James could see she was somewhat disappointed she could not prove he was a murderer. James filled in with questions about her life in Brazil. He was falling in like with her. Her gentle easy ways made him feel wonderful. He made many comments on how smart she was, how impressed he was with her education and her communication skills. By the time the check arrived, Andrea had probably consumed the most of three bottles of wine. When they stood to leave, she laughed as she almost fell over. James caught her before she went too far.

A cute little giggle came from her and then a slur of words, just barely distinguishable. "James, you mus help…. me to the car. I thin I had oooo too much wine. Pleas don't think bad of me. I so sorry I put you through all that. It was not – not - not right of me. You believe me. I did not know you were unaware of Vagner, I mean Vera. We all get fooled now and then. You're a really great guy… and I can clearly see that. I like you... and like I said earlier... if I could find I guy like you, my life would be very happy."

James ushered her to the car and into her seat. He got in and said he had better take her back to the motel. "Well, I can see and tell you are a wonderful woman and I am surprised you are not married." With a big smile he said, "If I was a guy who slept with women instead of transvestites I would grab you in a heartbeat."

She laughed heartily at his comment, "You would?" she said beaming a huge smile.

"For sure! I would love to have a woman like you in my life."

Andrea leaned over and kissed him on the cheek. "Oh, thank you, that makes me feel so much better. And you forgive me?"

"Ya, nao problema my dear. I'll figure it out eventually…I hope."

When they got to the motel, he had to put his arm around her waist to steady her as they slowly walked up the stairs and to her door. They got to the door, and she fumbled for the key. He took it from her and opened the door.

James made a little bow and tilt of the head toward her and very elegantly said, "Well, Ms. Araujo, I had a wonderful evening and I very much enjoyed your company," emphasizing each word.

"James could I have a kiss goodnight? I really like you."

"My pleasure."

She quickly wrapped her arms around him, pulled herself close and kissed him. After a few seconds her tongue darted into his mouth. The kiss lasted for much longer than he expected, she wasn't letting go of him.

"James, help me to the bed. I had too much wine, I am dizzy." He walked her to the bed, and then she drunkenly motioned for him to sit next to her. "I know this is rather sudden...since I am aware of your prob...situation...maybe...I could help you, and see if I can get you over it. You see, I have a plan. Do you find me attractive?"

"More than you can imagine," was his slow reply. "More than you can *ever* imagine."

"I want to try to fix you," as she turned, wrapped her arms around his neck and kissed him. "Is it okay? Do you want to try?"

James never said a word, he just started. They kissed for a while then slowly started to feel each other's bodies. They fell backwards on the bed, and slowly started to fumble with their clothing. James had her breasts in his hands and was kissing her nipples. She took a deep breath, held it as she reached down, unbuckled his belt, unzipped his pants and reached into his pants. She pulled her head back in shock as her hand grabbed his hard penis. She beamed a huge smile as if she had personally just solved the problem of world peace. The clothes started coming off faster as she was anxious to make love to him. James had to slow her down because he wanted to play with her body and it was a beautiful body as he had noticed before. He realized the wine was having a strong effect, so before she faded he mounted her. As they rolled together on the bed

216

she pulled him on top and inserted the head of his cock into her vagina while wrapping her legs around him.

James slowly thrusted forward, little by little, inch by inch. She was very wet, but he kept moving slowly going a little deeper each time with each thrust. Every time he went deeper her eyes would open wider. She focused on his face with her mouth open and slowly nodding and with each push saying, "Yes…yes…yes…more…more…" Suddenly her back arched and she let out a moan from somewhere in her body, but she couldn't get it all out. She kept catching her breath. She suddenly froze solid in place as he went faster and faster. She started climaxing, closing her eyes and rolling her head from side to side. She didn't stop. They made love for fifteen or twenty minutes, then at the end, they climaxed together. Andrea was trying to catch her breath. She was gasping, acting as someone had stolen all the air in the room and she couldn't breathe. They lay there holding each other in silence.

She finally calmed down and was the first to say something and with a big smile, "Oh my God…AMAZING…Good job baby…never been *there* before." She laughed again, "I knew I could fix you. That was wonderful. Did you enjoy?"

James smiled lovingly at her. "Yes, I did. Thank you, that was wonderful. But maybe you are the only one I will be able to do this with? Maybe, I will only be able to make love just to you for the rest of my entire life. The Japanese have a saying – If you save a man's life, you are responsible for him forever."

She looked up at him like a helpless child in love and slowly and sweetly said, "Okay." She paused for a few moments and then said, "James, please spend the night with me."

They took a short nap. James woke up and slowly started to make love to her again. They climaxed and fell asleep again. In the morning they took a shower together and made love in the shower.

The next morning James called Beth at the office. "Beth, cancel my appointments and have Ben take over the inspections for the day. I am taking a sick day and I will see you on Tuesday."

"Wonderful, I'll be right over with some chicken soup and a blow job. Great!" She was excited with the news. "I wanted to take the day off anyway. I had a lousy weekend with numb nuts and the kids. I'll suck those bad, bad germs right out of you."

"Hold it, hold it Beth. I said I was taking a sick day, not a day at home in bed. I have things to do."

"Like what?"

"Like, I'll tell you later. It's important and I am not at the house today. So, handle everything and cover for me, Doctor…Dentist…something like that. I'll be back tomorrow."

"You're not going to kill somebody again, are you?" she said with a laugh.

"No! God dam it! Stop thinking like that. I said those days are over," he said angrily.

Grudgingly she agreed. "I'll swing by after work."

"Don't, I won't be there. For once, do as I ask, and I will see you tomorrow. Goodbye," as he put the phone down.

James turned and saw the smiling face of Andrea. "Okay, my dear. I'm off for the day. Now, let's see if you are the real Mother Theresa or not. Come dearest and heal the sick. Let's see if you can raise the dead again."

"James, if I raise the dead one more time, I'm going to be dead. I think you are fine. Matter of fact, I think this doctor has announced a full recovery of the patient. And the patient is doing very…very well as he has demonstrated to this doctor. You do not love women James; you kill them with your love. Oh God, please love me forever. I have never felt this way making love. I have climaxed before but nothing like that, and all that fluid when I came, I have never squirted like that - nothing even close. If that was a climax - then I have never climaxed before. I don't know what I have been doing, but I only want to do *that* from now on."

Andrea was jabbering and slightly dazed, "I wasn't sure it was going to be this way, but – wow - it is and I don't believe it…James, please be mine…If you don't, I will still love you forever…What is wrong with me?....James don't love me...we are worlds apart...I must tell you – I was right - you are the one...The one, I have always been waiting for..."

"My dear...this is just a one-night stand, however, you, my dear, have the power to love me in a way I have never been loved before. That was rather amazing. Do you want to continue this debauchery?"

"Do you see me making a move toward the door?"

"It's your room, why would you leave?"

Andrea was laughing and smiling, "Oh yes, right...you've got my head so twisted I don't know where I am...what country I am in...what language...I speak...oh the hell with it...take me James...take me anyway you want to...I'm yours."

Andrea was in the bed. James had been standing naked at the foot of the bed. He dove onto the bed next to her. They both laughed then kissed. "Hey James, if you are still crazy in the head, I don't think I want to know you when you are sane. I mean, are you always like this? – A love making machine – you have to stop and give me a break. What...do you star in those porno movies? I think my pussy fell out a few hours ago and I don't know where it is. It left me because it was tired. Do you see it anywhere?"

"No," he said, "I am not like this all the time. I must say you do bring out the best in me. It's like when you are kid and you get a new toy at Christmas. You just want to play with it forever. Too tired my dear? Now remember, if the front door is locked you can always go around and get in the back door. That's always open."

"Too late for that my dear. You ripped off the screen door in the back a few hours ago, if I remember correctly. Tell you what, James, how about you going down on me again, that was so good and maybe I can get back in the mood. It's either that or take me to the hospital, so I can rest. James, before you turn that wonderful monster loose again, tell me...am I really only a one-night stand?"

"Look my dear." James turned quiet and somber with his tone. You live in Brazil, I live in America. After what has happened and under the circumstances I don't think I ever want to go back to Brazil again. It has just caused a bad taste in my mouth. You are beautiful, intelligent and very sexy. I could go for you in a big way but even though I would

219

love to see it work, the odds are against it. And even if…well, I need some time. This is all very sudden. Maybe I could be your Americano lover when you come to town and we will see where it goes from there."

Her mood changed in a brief second to one of anger and hatred, he could see it on her face. Andrea started to cry. She became inconsolable. She got out of bed, sat in a chair and cried a flood of tears. James stayed in bed and just watched her. She finally regained her composure then burst into tears again. She finally stopped and looked at James with an inquisitive stare.

James thought for a moment then decided to say, "Did I say something wrong?"

"Oh, you're just a God dam son-of-a-bitch!"

"Hey, I'm the one who has been through hell here, not you. Give me a break!"

"Ya, you're right but you are wrong!" she snapped.

"How's that?"

"I have a plan. A plan I have been working on since I was first assigned this case and I met you. I was not sure until I could spend some time with you. Unless you come to Brazil and be with me, I am going to turn over all my information to the Florida State Police. There are too many instances which prove you may have done all those murders. When I found out yesterday you had no idea about Vera, I realized you had been fooled but that made you more desirous. I wanted you. I wanted you when I first saw you in Sao Paulo, but I was not sure. At that time, you were just some kind of weirdo freak because you were with that man/woman, but for some strange reason you excited me. I could not figure out why you were with her. Now, after all I have found out, I am sure you did not know. But the facts are still the same. I know you did those murders…not maybe…but for sure. I am positive. But it is okay because you didn't do the murders for any personal gain. You and I think alike, I can tell. There is a lot of scum in this world and you are just trying to help out Mother Nature by doing some house cleaning. I don't think you have done anything wrong, but the rest of the civilized world would not agree with you or me."

James felt a strong change in the wind. 'Oh no,' he thought, 'here it comes. She has been stringing me along the whole time. Let her lay this all out. I know what is in my head, but I don't know what is in hers. Let her keep talking – don't react. This bitch is a whack job.'

It didn't matter, she was not going to be interrupted, "I could not be sure until I tricked you into sleeping with me. After last night, I wanted to see if we were sexually compatible. We most definitely are. And you thought I was drunk last night," she coyly said. "Women are so much smarter than men. Not only are you better than I imagined, you are definitely the one I am going to spend the rest of my life with. *TA-TA-TA:* don't say anything – I know what you are going to say: you are older than me, blah, blah, blah…but I don't care and it doesn't matter. You are the one I want and after making love to you – wow - you are never going to be with anyone but me. So here is the deal I am offering you: You move to Sao Paulo to be with me. I am almost finished with my law degree. Then, after I get my license to practice, we will move to Rio where my family lives and I will join my father's law firm. Then we will have a happy family and live happily ever after. I don't think you will like the option…*The option is – you go to jail for the rest of your life."*

James just looked at her with his mouth wide open. "You're *nuts* lady! A plan? This is no way to select a husband! You just decided this all by yourself? I don't even know if I really love you. I like you, but it is way too soon to even say the word love, let alone think that this is a sure thing…You don't even really know me." He could not decide what to do. Should he murder her on the spot? Tell her how crazy this all was, or should he go along with it…?

"James, close your mouth. Love… A woman knows these things. She feels them in her heart. It is just the feeling she gets right away and recognizes it. It is an automatic thing. You will understand it later in the relationship. I am going to give you one minute to decide. This isn't a court of law. It is the court of the heart. It is reality and the way I want it. I don't care what you think. This is your future. Besides you will be safer in Brazil. If anyone should ever piece all the facts together like I did…you *will* go to jail. You're crazy to stay in the United States. You will be safer in Brazil.

You will be very happy with me. This is my life, your life, our life together. Don't worry honey; you are going to make a great daddy to our three children. Oh yes, I want three children. I will make you very happy

221

and you will love Rio. I - we already have a great house on Ipanema beach and you will never have to work. You will just be my wonderful husband and the wonderful father to our children. Time's up. What do you want? And, oh by the way, murder in my country is the same as yours. There is no statute of limitations, so you're screwed either way and I might add – forever. I can protect you in Brazil. All I have to do is delete a few records and you will be as innocent as a new baby. And by the way – if you are thinking of murdering me – think again...too many people know I have been with you tonight, and...there is that pile of evidence I put together...Well?"

"Well what?" James stared at her in disbelief, he couldn't move. He was frozen solid, thinking this woman was nuttier than a pecan tree.

"James, your answer," she said with a smile.

James had never felt so silent in his life. The silence to him was deafening. The whole world had collapsed again. His soul had vanished, he died inside...he was not of this plane.

"James, your answer."

James paused then laughed, "Whatever happened to just plain fucking?"

"That's another reason I love you – You have a great sense of humor. If it makes you feel any better...you can make love to me again."

"Darling, I am going down to the Tiki bar by the pool and have a drink – alone. Don't worry, I can run but I cannot hide. I will be back after I figure whether I am going to commit suicide or not. Is there any thought in your head that I could be innocent?"

"Not in my lifetime darling. You can go to jail, or you can have a wonderful life with me."

"Well you're wrong. I am innocent, but the way you have me set up, you put my neck in a noose. Life is a little more complicated than you describe. There are some problems I need to think about and there are quite a few details you do not know about. I will come back with an answer for you...shortly. Why don't you take a little nap and I will go and decide."

"Okay," she off handedly answered. "Take your time, but if you aren't back in an hour...well you better be."

James quickly dressed and left. His head was swimming. He wanted to leave her with a little doubt even though she was totally on the right track. The Tiki bar by the side of the pool had just opened. There was no one there but the bartender was setting up. He had the place to himself with the bartender. "Pour me a triple."

"A triple of what?"

"Anything you can put your hand on. Make it scotch, water side."

"Little early for serious drinking," the bartender mumbled.

"That's okay; I have a serious problem, thanks." None of your fucking business, James thought.

James pulled out his phone and called Alan.

"What's up killer?"

James ignored his comment, "You're not going to believe this one. I don't even believe it." He went on to lay out all the details of what had happened in the last two days.

Finally, James was through and he let Alan speak. "Holy shit! Where do you find these crazies? You've attracted more nutty broads than the free clinic at the state mental institution. I don't know if that cock of yours gets you in trouble, or gets you out of trouble. You can't marry both of them, or should I say all three of them. Two of them have you by the balls, and the third one is just waiting for one of them to loosen their grip so she can grab on. Actually, you only have to worry about the two, Beth and Andrea. Vera is out by default, that is unless you have started liking men. If I were King Solomon, I would just cut your cock in two and give them each half and your ball sack goes to number three. How the hell are you going to do this one? Who else is going to show up? Well, the only quick solution I can think of is to find another country to go to that doesn't have an extradition agreement with the United States and Brazil. Boy, when you do it, you really do it. How about

Switzerland? I'm not up on my diplomatic relations but I'll check that out for you.

Another answer is to pick one of them and marry them. If you marry Beth, Andrea will really screw you. If you marry Andrea you may have a chance, but somehow you have to get Beth to give up, give you the tapes, promise not to squeal on you and let you go. But if Beth gets pissed she can pass the information about Paulo to the Brazilian police and even then, Andrea can't protect you."

"Alan, the main point is - I don't want to marry any of these nut jobs."

"Friend, I haven't got any answers, I'm just trying to deal with these crazy questions you bring to me. Maybe, put them both in a room and let the stronger one win by killing the other. Well in any event...stall as long as you can...we're bound to come up with something...I'm sorry pal; this whole scenario is out of fantasy land. I don't believe it is happening. I just thought that someday someone would just catch you murdering people and put you in jail. You think they are nuts – you're nuts too. You can't go around murdering people, no matter what you think is right or wrong. All of these crazy broads are wise to you and the odd thing is - You've got them lined up to marry you and two of them know you play Robin Hood murder man. This conversation is absurd. Hey, do you really like this Vera at all...you man fucker," by this time Alan was laughing so hard he was about to split a gut. "Sorry man, but this is the most ridiculous and weirdest thing I have ever heard."

"Shut the fuck up. You would have fucked her/him too if you had seen her. There's another problem – I've got to get rid of her too. Okay, let me get back to you. I have to go and get back to number three now."

"Hey – I've got it. Why don't you cut your dick off and become a woman – then none of them will want you."

"Look Alan – go cut your own dick off. See if you would like it. Ya, right, that's a good plan. Let's see, if I did that - then I would have to marry you."

"You are one, disgusting man fucker! I'm not fucking you and you are not fucking me – I'm straight. Talk to you later – man fucker.

Stay out of trouble, please. Just play along with her. Tell her you will marry her. Let's get everybody confused."

James sat there and had another drink. He was tired, disgusted and felt the world coming down on him. There's got to be an answer – somewhere. He headed back to the room and knocked on the door. Andrea let him in.

"Darling, have you decided to accept my generous offer?"

"Andrea look, I like you a lot especially for the very short time I have known you, even though this has been one hell of a shock. Number one, I did not commit any murders. Number two, I have a career here and a life. Number three, we really need to talk a lot about our future – that is if we do have a future. Number four, maybe we live here in the States, if we do get together as a couple. And then there are another hundred reasons. My point is – we need time. Time, to work out a lot of details. You really don't know me; this isn't being fair to you or me..."

"James, I've been studying your whole life for more than a month. There is a fine line between crime and legality. How and when we cross the line is a matter of opinion. You have crossed it many times and you still believe you are on the legal side. I know everything about you. You have been my special project. The more I studied you, the more I found out, the more I wanted you. I see something in you, well I see a lot of things, and I know now you are the man who fits into my life. I know what I want, and what I want is you. And most important you are also a gentleman. The other thing that is most important and was the deciding factor was you fit my body. When you are inside of me you are hitting something in there that has never been done before. You make me orgasm like crazy. It drives me wild."

James started smiling, "Ya, well that's nice but I haven't been studying you. I just can't drop everything and run off to Brazil because you say so and because you *think* you have something on me, like murder. And, *I am innocent*, by the way. And then the thought crosses my mind, why does this woman want to marry a man whom she believes is a murderer. This fact in itself does not make sense. Someday you will know I am not a murderer and you tricked me, but it will be too late, and you will be in a marriage you may regret, then you will have to apologize to me and no one will be happy." James suddenly switched gears. "But it's okay, because we will have a lovely family by then. If it's worth doing,

225

then it's worth doing well and proper. You are going to have to go back to Brazil soon. I can come down there and spend some time with you and then you can take a vacation and come back here. That way, we really get to know each other, and it will give us time to make good decisions, not rushed ones. You know what I am saying is only right. I still have to break it off with him/her, Vera, which won't be hard to do. Yes, we can make it as a couple, but we need time…you don't even know that I snore," he added with a smile and a laugh. "You just can't tell me we are going to get married and throw me over your shoulder and take me back to Brazil like I am some kind of a piece of meat. I can see you now walking into your parent's house throwing me on the floor and saying, 'Gee mom and dad, look what I got on my trip to the states…pretty good, huh.' Andrea, we need some time…you might even change your mind, who knows?" James stopped talking, sat on the edge of the bed and waited for her answer.

She paced around the room slowly not saying anything, not smiling, just looking up and glancing at him with every time she turned direction. "Okay that makes sense, but if you try to not go through with marrying me I will drop your folder on someone's desk that will make your life miserable. I have to go back to Brazil on Friday. When can you come down to see me?"

"It will be soon. Remember, I just got back from taking a vacation. I have more time coming to me. The problem is; it's a day to get there and a day to get back. I'll try to squeeze out another week. When I go away, I have to get the project covered so I have to plan it all out, so it takes extra time to arrange. I will be there as soon as I can, promise. We can talk by internet and by phone. Let's have a love affair my dear. I want the romance, the love, the caring and all the fun we can have. Let's plan it…I want to meet your family, see your house, I want to court you. I don't want just sex…stick it in…climax…roll over… sleep…and then that makes a marriage. I want to find out about you the person, you the woman, your mind, and especially your body," he said with a sexy lilt in his voice. "I want to play your body like a rare Stradivarius. Don't worry, we can marry very quickly. But first, let's enjoy each other – let's enjoy."

"Okay," she answered reluctantly. "I thought at first you were trying to get out of it. I think you are sincere. I will give it a try but just you remember what I said. One false step and I will turn over all my notes to my friends in Florida."

226

"Now let me show you my dear," as James pulled her into his arms, kissed her and laid her down on the bed. She easily succumbed to his arms with a smile and molded her body to his. He took his time gently kissing her, feeling her, exploring her body from her mouth, to her neck, her breasts and finally arriving at her vagina. He heard her gasp as he slowly worked his magic on her, playing her lower body with his lips and tongue, while his hands gently squeezed her breasts and nipples. She moaned deeply and grabbed the sides of his head forcing him to stay right where she wanted him to be. He knew this is what she liked best. She held him there firmly till she shook from a massive climax. She then completely relaxed and went limp. James slowly raised himself and moved up on her until he was face to face lying on top of her. "My turn dear," he whispered in her ear. He pushed her legs farther apart and guided himself into her. He moved gently at first then quickly picked up speed with his rhythm. James climaxed shortly after he started, kissed Andrea and tightly held her wrapping his arms around her. He kissed her face and her eyes, then he rolled to one side, and James smiled to himself. He was back in control; unfortunately, he realized it was from inside of the insane asylum. But at least he could enjoy - his day off.

They spent the day together. It was early afternoon before they managed to get out of bed and go have lunch. James had calmed her into totally believing he belonged only to her and her master plan of capture and domination over him was complete. They went to the harbor and walked the docks in the warm sunny afternoon looking at the boats bobbing in the water, whispering words of love and speaking of their future together. In the late afternoon, he took her back to his home. After he made a trip to his medicine cabinet, they made love again. Then he cooked some steaks while she made a salad. It looked like quite a nice domestic scene. They ate dinner on the porch while the sun was setting, with Andrea totally content.

Andrea had to work the next few days in Miami. James suggested they get to bed early and she could go along in the morning. He set the alarm, but come morning he was already awake before it sounded. He had an erection and crawled on top of her before she awoke. He pushed her legs apart and was inside her before she knew what was happening. He whispered in her ear, "Darling this is the way you are going to wake up every day from now on - with me inside you. Just as I am yours, you are mine. Now let's practice making the first baby." She had tears of joy streaming down her face while holding him tightly as he thrusted until he climaxed. She didn't climax. She didn't care and neither did James.

227

After their love session, they showered and dressed together. She was ecstatically happy because she believed her dreams were coming true. She watched his every move with worship and admiration like a love-sick puppy. She fixed some coffee and muffins. He took her back to the Ramada. He helped her pack and put her in her car with the promise he would see her Thursday afternoon and spend the night with her before she left for Brazil on Friday. He would put her on the plane at Miami airport Friday morning. She thought he was being a gentleman. He was just making sure she was going to be definitely out of town and on her way back to Brazil.

Chapter Twenty-Two

Suicide or Not

James wanted to take another day off, but it was not in the offering. James' cell phone started ringing early and often. Vera called twice, there were many calls from sub-contractors and his main office kept calling. Beth was hovering and kept coming into his office especially when he was on the phone. She was always trying to find out who was calling and why. The nosey bitch! He thought, doesn't anybody understand my life is on fire. It was hard to concentrate on work or his personal problems. The day seemed to drag on forever. Finally, five o'clock rolled around.

"Another day, another dollar," said Beth, happy as a clam. "Let's go to the house, Baby, I want to hear about your day off. I am very curious."

"Let's not. I have to go to the main office and meet with the big boss now. Then, I think we will probably go out for drinks and dinner. So, my dear, let's plan for tomorrow."

"James, you and I haven't had any sex in almost a week. I'm real, real horny and I want to find out what you did yesterday."

"Well, it's not going to be tonight, it's going to be tomorrow night. Now, I have to get to this meeting and I do not have time to stay and explain everything to you. If you love me, you will be my good little Honey Lamb and work with me on this and not bug me."

"I love it when you call me Honey Lamb. How about a quickie in my office? Almost everyone is gone, and we can lock the door."

"You know I don't like quickies. When I want to make love to you, I want to do it right. So be a wonderful Honey Lamb and let me do what I have to do. Thank you and with that I bid you adieu," and out the door he quickly went.

James ran to his car as fast as possible and left the site not knowing where he was going. He finally decided to drive to the next town, Jupiter, and find a way to lay low. He needed time to think. His phone kept ringing, so he finally shut it off. James finally found a quiet bar down on the water. He ordered a drink, slowly sipped it and tried to figure out a plan of attack.

With each different approach he would find a dead end. He had reached an impasse. Every avenue he tried to explore only made more problems. Either Beth or Andrea would cook his goose either way he turned. He felt he had made a mess of his life. He had done the wrong things to a productive life. He was now going to pay for crimes that, in his mind, weren't crimes. His head hung low. Why had he done it? It seemed like the right thing to do. Now, it didn't seem like a good idea. Was he up for this challenge? He had to be, because somehow…he had to get his ass out of this mess.

The only easy answer he came up with was to get rid of Vera. He could do it with one phone call and it had to be done. By getting rid of her/him, Beth and Andrea would both see it as a step in the right direction. With that done, it would also relieve him of the time it was taking to deal with her and then he could devote that excess time to the other two problems. So, then there would be only two… progress!

Wednesday night he would have to deal with Beth and then Thursday night he would have to go to Miami and get Andrea on a plane to Brazil Friday morning. By assumption he realized that Beth would want a return engagement on Friday night or Saturday morning. So now, he had to come up with a story which would keep Beth satisfied.

Divide and conquer. Keep them separated. The important thing was they didn't know about each other. Their paths had never crossed. Beth was unaware of Andrea and visa-versa. Since Beth didn't have her taping equipment anymore, she wouldn't find out about her. Together, they kept him confused and off his game. He had always thought that he liked smart women. Now, he thought what he really needed was a woman with the I.Q. of a peanut. By getting Andrea back to Brazil he would have more time to deal with Beth. This might work after all. But he needed to keep them in the right places.

He thought back to the first meeting with Vera. That was just going to be a quick fun relationship. Something that might get him out of his shell from the depression he had suffered from his marriage with Susan. Instead, it had turned out to be the start of nightmare. He mused; maybe he could re-marry Susan and that would get him out of this crazy situation. He chuckled out loud as he thought: Was a sharp stick in the eye better than a bullet to the head? No, let's not bring her back into the mix. That was about five years of hell he did not want to repeat. She was finally out of his life and did not want to see a re-run of that movie again.

Who was the most dangerous to him? Probably Beth was. Andrea was right. If he went to Brazil and married, then the United States could not claim him for any of the murders in the states. However, if Beth told the Brazilian authorities about Paulo, he would be screwed and even marriage couldn't protect him. Which was worse, a US jail or a Brazilian prison? No contest, the US was a better bet. However, if Florida or even Texas took precedent for the murders in either of those states, both were capital punishment states. If he went to Maine and pleaded to the murder he committed there, then that was the best answer because they didn't have capital punishment. However, would Maine want to get rid of him and dump him back to the other two states to stand trial there as well? Which state would want to bring him back for an additional trial and which one would be the final state to end up with him? This was far too complicated to figure out; too many things could happen and go against him.

Then it occurred to him: If he pleaded guilty to murder for the killing in Vietnam, then the Army would have jurisdiction, which would place him in a Federal prison or military prison. At least there probably would be no execution, but he was not sure. Either way he sliced it, he was going to do jail for the rest of his life at a minimum. The whole thing didn't seem fair to him. All he had done was protect women and children by getting rid of some nasty people who went around hurting women and children.

Now, because two women got smart and greedy, he was going to have to pay a handsome price – his freedom. How could two women react in such a way and why did they want him even knowing what he had done? Why did they want a murderer in their lives? The main point was – he did not want to go to any jail, for any reason. Somehow, he had to figure this out so he would remain the way he had always been – free.

Maybe he could ask for mercy from both of the women. They were both nut jobs. Maybe they might see that neither could win, and then ask for mercy. If somehow, they could see that neither of them could win, then maybe one or both of them would give up their claim on him. No, probably not. One would hold out for the other and the last one standing would claim him as the prize. Besides, they each still had the evidence in hand.

Beth's tapes could not be used in court but could be used for the state to find the evidence and prove their case. With Andrea, the state would just follow the leads she had come up with in her search. Either way he was screwed.

Maybe…one should die…which one? Maybe…they both should die. That wasn't his style. He shouldn't think like that, but when you are backed into a corner all bets are off, and he was definitely in a corner. Neither of them had done anything wrong, but they were both crazy. He was a good lover and a good catch for a woman, but this was going a little too far for normal human beings. There are a lot of men out there. How and why did these two crazies with obvious psychiatric disorders focus on him? Obviously, these women were not normal.

With Beth he could easily understand how she could get emotionally attached. They worked together five days a week. They were in close quarters. It was easy to learn about the others life. She wasn't happy with her own personal situation and wanted to improve her life and lifestyle. Financially it was a win – win situation for her. She was living in an apartment with her two children and a boyfriend she had grown tired of at a minimum. She was bored in life. When women get bored in life they make changes. Some change the furniture – some change the men.

Okay he could kill Beth. It would have to be Beth. It was too difficult to kill Andrea. Get the tapes back and do her in. No that wasn't appealing…she was a mother, but if he got the tapes back from Beth, it would leave him a clear field to kill her and end up with Andrea. Getting the tapes back would be the problem. He was sure that after all Beth went through to make the tapes, she would not just hand them over. One of the questions going through his mind was – Why did Beth make the tapes in the first place?

He had a few more drinks but the answers were still not coming, and the liquor was starting to cloud his thoughts. His mind was spinning around and around and going nowhere fast. Just like a car stuck in the snow with the wheels turning…racing…spinning…but nothing happening…no progress…not a drop. He decided it was late enough and he could go home without being hassled by Beth. He paid his tab and drove home. He settled in and decided to do what he could to relieve some of the pressure. He called Vera.

"Hallo"

"Vera, this is James."

"Hallo my dear. How are you? It good hear your voice," she was elated to hear from him.

"Vera, we need to talk…"

She interrupted, "Yes, much to talk about…"

Very somberly he started "Wait. This is very important. Over the past few days I learned you are a man and not a woman. You have lied to me all along and I cannot have this. I must not see you anymore. I am very hurt by all the lies. Our romance is over."

"James, this is not true. I am woman – you know this, she quickly and emphatically said.

"NO! - Vera, stop it. You are a man."

"James, it true I am woman. I have muito operations. Now I woman. Doctors fix everything so I am woman. I look like woman, yes? I act like woman, yes? I think like woman, yes? And I love you James. I be your wife. Stop James, I love you. You are everything to me. We plan, we come Florida and marry. I am woman for you. I was woman for long time now, then I find you and I love only you."

"Vera, that's all well and good but I cannot marry a man. And you were wrong not to tell me. If you really loved me you would have told me. I cannot marry a man."

"I nao man! - I am woman! I have pussy, I have breasts, I have bunda, I real woman. You fuck me, you know I real. Am I not good for you? Do not I make you feel wonderful? We wonderful together, right James? Oh James, pleazzze nao tell me this…I love you…We are good together, yes?" She was starting to beg.

233

"Vera stop! It does not matter, I cannot do this, you are a man and not a woman and I do not care how many operations you have had, you are still a man to me."

She became very angry and emphatically said, "No man, I woman. I do because what I want. I want be no man, I want be woman. James, I love you, STOP, I make best woman in world for my James. I only want you. Love me pleaze, I love just you."

Vera, I'm sorry I just can't do it. To me you are a man and I don't want a man, I want a woman. You are a wonderful person. I really thought we were hitting it off together. This fact has thrown me for a loop. I cannot do this. To me you are a man, no matter what you say.

She went silent for a few seconds then confidently said, "You have to love me...You have to marry me...Nao worry...I promise nao tell nao one about Paulo, I promise, honest, promise."

"What are you talking about?"

"I love you and you must love me and you marry me..."

"No Vera, the part about Paulo. What did you mean about Paulo?"

"I promise never tell any you kill Paulo. I nao tell Policia woman, sim. I love you, I never tell, promise."

"I didn't kill Paulo, Vera. Not me, you're crazy!"

"It's OK, I never tell you do. Policia woman say I kill Paulo. I do not. I with boys in Guaruja. You go Ubatuba. Nao, you go Sao Paulo kill Paulo. I know you go Sao Paulo, nao Ubatuba. I tell policia woman you go Ubatuba. It's OK, I never tell. It good. He was muito mau homme. You did for me. You did for boys. I thank you, muito, muito obrigado...it good."

James mind was whirling but he realized he didn't want to dwell on this subject, best to just pass on it as quickly as possible and get back to the problem of getting rid of him/her. "Vera, I did not kill him. It does not matter. I can't love you anymore. You are a man! It is over between us. I am sorry you are a nice person - you will always be a man to me and I cannot marry you."

"James, you love me, marry me or I tell Policia you kill Paulo."

"You can tell them anything you want. I didn't kill Paulo and, I don't love you anymore. I am not going to marry you and I am finished. Goodbye!" James slammed the phone down. He was in a sweat. How did she find out? Just guessing? He couldn't believe what just happened. This was supposed to be the easy part, getting rid of him/her. Now he was back to three problems.

He sat for a while finally thinking: there are too many options… this would not be fixed tonight. He took a shower and went to bed. He lay there in the quiet but not able to sleep. He could not sleep, his mind focused on only one thought. The one thought that he had not given any credence to before…but now was the only thought. The way out…logical…what did it matter…His only thought…*suicide*.

Chapter Twenty-Three
Trying to Make a Decision

The next day went smoothly at work but James found it hard to concentrate. His thoughts kept drifting back to the problems at hand. He kept going back to his thoughts of suicide. He wanted to talk to somebody. The only person he could talk to was Alan and he was out guiding a fisherman in the Maine woods. He then decided to talk to Ray. He called Ray and got through to him but didn't know where to even start the conversation. James was confused and not sure what he should even tell Ray. His mind was spinning. Ray tried to convince him to come to the office, so they could talk. Finally, James refused because this was one situation he had to work out for himself. Ray didn't even know about the murders, so why try to drag him in now. James decided to stay at work, but his mind was exploding.

"Darling, what's wrong?" Beth wanted to know half way through the day. "Don't worry you're going to get laid tonight," she happily told him. "Only three more hours and I will take all that crabbiness out of you."

"I'll tell you later. Thanks anyway for trying to cheer me up. I'm going to go inspect something," as he walked out of the office and headed out on the site, with no intention of doing anything. He walked around blindly just thinking and walking. He was snappy to everyone; people quickly noticed and left him alone. No matter what, he had to keep his composure. He tried to rationalize that suicide might not be so bad after all. He had a good life and ending a bit early wasn't the worst thing. Why stick around for a bunch of crap. Why stay for a life jail term or allow someone else to take his freedom from him? Just end it early, avoid the misery.

He felt like a circus juggler. Here he was juggling balls as fast as he could, and someone kept throwing more balls at him, more balls than he could handle. But he was forced to keep adding the new balls to the others. If he didn't add them to the mix…the whole thing would blow up like a huge bomb if he dropped even one of the balls. Panic was setting in, but he knew he had to fight that emotion. He had come too far to lose it now. He went home early, and Beth arrived just after five. He had turned on the recording equipment to be ready for its first test. Until he made his final decision he must keep going, playing each and every angle.

She walked into the house. "Okay, what's up? What has your panties in a wad?"

As they went into the living room James very seriously said, "Sit and listen, Honey Lamb. I have had a visitor. Her name is Andrea and she is from Brazil. She also just happens to be a police detective – lieutenant or something like that. Somehow, she seems to have figured everything out about the Paulo murder except what truly happened. She firmly believes that Vera did it. Now, I told her it was impossible because she was with me most of the time. I don't know if she is acting or what. Now swallow hard on this one…Quite by chance, she investigated me and has somehow connected me to the three murders in the states and the one in Nam. At this time, she doesn't think I did them just that they just happened around me. She tried hard to get me to slip up and say something that might incriminate me."

"Oh shit," Beth turned white as a sheet. "What can she do? What is she going to do? Where is she now…"

"Hold it, just let me finish. You will hear everything. She called early Monday morning and gave me a rough idea of what she wanted to talk about, so I agreed to meet with her at the Jupiter Police Department. I had to go there, and she interrogated me for hours. Not in a hostile way but trying to pin everything on Vera. I carefully went through the whole procedure and even went to lunch with her. She is working with the Florida State Police down in Miami. She asked me to make a statement on Friday morning. I am going to do it because it would look suspicious if I don't. I don't need any hassle at this time and I think she is too stupid to come up with any real evidence. Hopefully, she will not tell the police here what she knows. So, I am driving down tomorrow after work, spend the night there so I can be there early as agreed. Then make the statement she has asked for and then get back before noon."

"Oh, this makes me nervous."

James laughed. "Makes you nervous? What about me? Do you see how dangerous it is to have evidence lying around? If anything falls into the wrong hands – even by accident – I will swing from a very tall tree."

"Ya, I see what you mean," said Beth in astonishment.

"I also took the time to go see a lawyer afterwards and get some advice. There's not much she can do to me because there's no extradition to Brazil."

"What's extradition?"

"It is an agreement between two governments to not allow criminals to hide or be in each other's country. They will give or send them back to the country where they committed the crime. In this case it saves my ass regardless, even if they think I did it. The US nor Brazil would not send me back to the other country for punishment because there is no extradition treaty between them. However, if it became an issue then both countries would have to make sure by means of an investigation. In either case any investigation would draw attention to me and I really don't need that…at all. I do not need anything blowing up in my face. Which brings me to a point: You have to give me all those tapes you made." James said it with a very serious tone.

There was a slight pause from Beth as she stared at him. "Like hell! They are the only insurance I have you are going to marry me and do everything you said you would. No, I won't! I will give them to you on the honeymoon, maybe and maybe I won't. You would then get rid of me. I want to be protected here and the tapes are my only protection. I'm not some silly, stupid bimbo you can push around."

"Beth, first tell me, why did you make the tapes in the first place?"

Beth thought for a moment then got very sheepish, as if she had gotten her hand caught in the cookie jar. She proceeded to speak softly and slowly measuring her words. "Well, I really liked you from the very start. I realized I would never be able to have a man like you. You are smart, good looking and very kind. Here I am stuck with guys like numb-nuts boyfriend. I got fucked over by my first husband and now I'm stuck with two kids and no child support. Well, I do get some child support from the state, however, there's never enough and it comes late and well, it's just a royal pain. There is never enough money to do anything and I want something more out of life.

Then, I saw the way you treated that drunken wife of yours, and I wondered how that stupid bitch of a wife of yours…sorry…got so lucky and never appreciated it. It made me mad, since she was never going to recover, and I could tell that or at least I thought it. I wanted a chance to have you as my man. Why not go for it and maybe I could get your attention? I first used the sexual harassment issue but knew I couldn't get that to work forever. I knew I had to have an angle, so that's when I came up with the plan to tape everything you said. Then, I might be able to find out and learn more about you so I might be able to figure out how to land you, the big fish in my life. I was going to be perfect for you, so you would want me. I would always be one step ahead of you. While you were away, I was amazed when I found out about the murders. Then I knew I could do it. I had all the evidence. I could make you do everything I wanted. The Brazilian bimbo just got in the way. But after you got back…well you know the rest."

James listened intently to every word she said. He then looked directly into her eyes and took her hands in his and said, "Beth, that's not the way to do it. Not the way to my heart. Even if there had not been the murders – that's just not the way to my heart. I can appreciate your attempts and your plan, but you only got yourself in a lot of trouble."

"How's that?" she questioned.

"Well, the fact of the matter is; by doing it the way you did, you made yourself an accomplice to murder. If anything ever happened to me, you would go to jail too. Now you are an accomplice to murder and you tried to extort me. I don't think any judge would like the way you are thinking. And if something ever happened to one of the people who has a copy and the cops found it or even if I gave them my copy…let me put it this way…they would not give us adjoining cells."

"I didn't think of that," she sounded very worried.

"Look Beth, Honey Lamb, you are going to have to trust me. How many copies are there and who has them?"

Beth hesitated for a moment. "There are five copies. I have two and my brother and sister each have one…plus the one I gave you."

"I want you to get them back and hopefully they didn't open them. If they did, we could be in serious trouble. I know you trust them, but you never know what other people will do. Go get them back and then we will destroy them. We will go on as planned because what you don't understand is that I *do* like you and a life together could be fun. Of course, we will have to keep me out of jail. I'm tired of all this and I have been lonely for a long time." And with a big smile he looked at her, "I think you will make a very good wife."

Beth just looked at him then tears ran down her cheek. "I will be a very good wife, you will see...Oh I love you so much." She got up from her chair and threw her arms around his neck. "Can we make love now, please?"

They spent the next three hours making gentle love. Beth went home at nine and James just smiled and went to bed. Finally, he thought, at least something might be working.

*****

James drove to Miami, and met Andrea at her hotel. They spent the late afternoon talking about their future, then went to dinner. James was careful not to appear anxious. He just kept trying to question her to see what she had done with all the information she had collected.

"Oh, my dear, don't worry. I have it in a safe place. It is in the room and I will give it to you. I'm not worried because I can always duplicate all of it. But, it is probably best you take it and destroy it. We wouldn't want it falling into the wrong hands, now would we? Of course, if you do not come to Brazil or try to dump me, or worse, you know very well what will happen. I am so excited James. We are going to be very happy together."

James' mind went crazy for the rest of dinner. How could he kill her after he got the paperwork? She had sealed her own fate. If no one knew what was in her possession then they wouldn't be looking for it, if she turned up dead. But too many people had seen them together from the desk clerk to the waiters – just the whole staff. This wouldn't be the time or place, but it was very tempting to him.

"Andrea, tell me something. Why did you fixate on me? Why me? You are so very beautiful, intelligent, educated and from a rich family. You can have any man you want. Why did you choose me, especially when you found out what you think I have done? Even though - I didn't do it."

"Darling, I have had to work very hard my whole life. I worked my way up the career ladder in the Federal Policia. Then I decided to study law and become a lawyer. I always wanted to become a mother and wife. There has never been enough time to accomplish all of it as quickly as I wanted. So, all of a sudden, I realized I am getting older and the switch to becoming a lawyer is about to happen. All my career dreams are coming true, so now it is time to concentrate on the family side. About this same time, you just happened to show up in my life.

A woman chooses a man. Men go around thinking they are in charge, but they are not. If the woman doesn't want the man she will not spread her legs for him," she said laughingly. "Now, I must admit, I think most Brazilian women would love to marry a rich, handsome, American man. They are an exotic breed to the Brazilian woman, however they rarely have the opportunity to find and meet them. And the language barrier is still a big problem, but I think the desire is there usually. But you my dear, just fell into my lap.

The more I found out about you, the more curious I was. Sometimes, when you see or meet a person you know you want to take it to the next level. You made me hot between my legs. You were with Vera, who even I was attracted to, I know him/her whatever…But, after I found out she had been a man, I was very confused about you. So, the curiosity started and since I was assigned the case, my curiosity kept me thinking about you. Your background was interesting and easy to follow. I was able to use my connections in the states to find out your history even before I left Brazil. By the time I got to America, I just wanted to see if you were a good lover or just some freak who liked people like Vera. Then I found out more about you being the bad boy you are. Now I know; you are a good person with a good heart and a really great lover."

James listened intently then interrupted, "So you decided to force me to love you and force me to go to Brazil and marry you? Andrea,

don't you think forcing me is a bad thing? You are a very smart woman and very beautiful. You can have almost any man anywhere you go. You have no problem finding men or attracting them. But you know; when you force something to happen, most of the time it is not for the better."
"Thank you for the compliments and you are right, I can have most men. But James, it is so different to have a smart, handsome, American man for a husband in Brazil. It is a status thing for Brazilian women. I know you do not love me now. In time you will because I am good for you and you make me happy. I love to talk with you. There has to be something between rounds of sex. The mind is the sole stimulation for sex. You are so patient, love to talk and fun to talk with, although in the future there will have to be more talking and less sex. If I let you have your way all the time, I will be a very tired, old woman very quickly. And, yes James, I am forcing you. This is the way it is, and a woman knows these things better than a man. Men think with their lower heads. There is never enough blood to fill both heads at the same time. Women think with their hearts first, then their emotions, then their brain and finally they think about sex."

James chuckled at her words. "Darling you barely know me, and I am older than you. I have already had children and don't think I want to go through that pain again. I do have a career here that I like and have no desire to raise three kids and not have a job and live in Brazil…"

"Stop James. We will live in Brazil. We will have three children." She paused. "There is something I haven't told you yet."

"And what is that?"

A huge smile came across her face. "My family is just not rich, they are very wealthy. They own many farms. My father, whose main business is the law firm he owns, does not have any sons. Both my sisters are married. My father thinks their husbands are idiots and they are. He will not let them touch anything in the family businesses. He also likes to invest in American businesses. So, you could work with him for a career. You don't have to raise the children; there will be plenty of maids to take care of the children. I want to travel and see the world. We have our own aircraft to take us anywhere. My dear, I am not only forcing you to join me, I am buying you at the same time," she chuckled, "and I am positive you will enjoy your new life with me. I am tired of working and proving to myself that I can do anything I have to and want to do. Now is the time for me and you. I will not work hard, nor will you and we will have a wonderful life."

James went deep into thought. Just when he thought he was coming up with answers, someone throws him a new curve ball. Maybe he should wait on his decision to get rid of this one. Andrea had painted an attractive scenario. The problem was still all three women had him cornered in some way because they all still had the information to put him in jail forever, somewhere.

They finished dinner and went to the room. "Now for desert, my beautiful wife to be."

"Wait James, let me dress for you." Andrea went into the bathroom. Five minutes later she re-appeared in beautiful black lingerie and hi-heels. "Now James, this is desert, you like?"

"Oh, I like," as he started toward her.

She pushed him away. "No James, I am in charge tonight." She went back to him and slowly started to remove his clothes. First his shirt came off. Andrea started kissing him all over his chest, neck and arms. She then loosened his belt and let his pants drop. She smiled and dropped to her knees and started kissing him taking him deep down her throat. She kept sucking him till he came to full erection. James moaned, and she pushed him down on the bed. She mounted him sitting on top then inserting him into her. She rode him slowly at first then continually going faster and faster. She never took her eyes off him, watching every facial expression. Suddenly she squealed and climaxed, but never stopped the motion. She saw that his expression was changing, and he was about to climax. She went faster and faster until he couldn't hold back anymore. James exploded, and Andrea just smiled and shortly came again. Finally, she just stopped and looked at him. "James did I do that well?"

"Yes dear, very well...very well indeed," he answered with a wide grin.

"James, you do a great job. Good job, baby, good job. There will be lots more in Brazil. I want to keep you happy all the time. When are you coming to Brazil?"

"As soon as I can wrap things up here, I'll be down. Darling you took the life out of me. Give me a kiss and let's go to sleep and get up

244

early." She snuggled up next to him and drifted off to sleep. James lay there pretending sleep, wanting to find an answer to his many dilemmas. Soon he gave up and went to sleep.

The next morning, they had breakfast from room service. They chatted about her trip back to Brazil. James tried to keep the conversation light. Andrea kept bringing the conversation back to their future life together. With each sentence James cringed inwardly, not knowing whether to kill her or keep her. It seemed like a pretty good bet to keep her. If Beth or Vera opened their mouths and exposed him, it wouldn't matter, off to jail he would go. There wasn't an answer. Just play along till an answer presented itself. As promised, Andrea gave him the file. Finally, they headed for the airport and once there James held her in his arms and whispered all the things she wanted to hear. Finally, her flight was called, and he had to leave her after she had checked in and had gone through security. As she walked slowly backwards towards the departure gate, she cried with tears running down her cheeks. James headed for the parking lot with the file and began the hundred-mile ride north back to Stuart. Things were slowly turning in his favor. Patience is a virtue; slowly grind away till you achieve the finality you want.

James went to his house first and read each sheet of paper Andrea had collected on him. He sat at his desk and shredded each and every one.

Chapter Twenty-Four
Who to Kill

Beth was on him like a duck on a June bug as soon as he hit the trailer office. "Well, how'd it go?" with great inquisitiveness.

"I told the truth, I told them you did it." James started laughing. "I told them you flew to Brazil and killed him. They will be coming by later today to arrest you."

"Fuck off. No, tell me the truth what happened?"

"Nothing, I made a statement saying nothing. I didn't know anything about the murder of Paulo and Vera was with me and her children when the incident occurred."

"You should have told them she did it," Beth diabolically interrupted.

"Look Beth, I want to keep this as clean as possible. They seemed satisfied with my answers. I think they will just probably close the case. Hopefully, they will not ask anyone any more questions. The last thing I want is anymore talking about the situation, by anybody. The least said the better."

"Okay darling, you're right, now we can get on with our lives. I never did like those Brazilians. I could never figure out why you liked them. I mean, what is so great about them as compared to good, old Americans? Tell me."

James thought for a few seconds. "Well, there is nothing wrong with American women, however there are a lot of differences. The Brazilian culture is different. They are a lot more relaxed than uptight Americans. They haven't had the economic advantages we have had, so they depend more on social contact. They are an older country than we are. They appreciate and honor older people or seniors. They are not as uptight sexually. They never had Pilgrims and Puritans forcing their moralistic behavior on others…"

"You mean they fuck like rabbits."

James chuckled, "Yes they are more open sexually. The women take care of their bodies and looks; their hair, makeup, dress a little sexy, show a little more skin and most important, they take care of their men. They appreciate men; they are more respectful and can get very jealous and protective of and for their man. It is not a bad thing it's just different. Once you go outside the US, you find that women don't seem to have an ax to grind against men like women in the US do. Maybe it is because other nations aren't as advanced, and men are valued more because women haven't achieved enough financial freedom yet. Women in the US are very much aware the courts are, for the most part, on the female side, and divorce can be a lucrative deal for them. That, in itself, keeps everybody in America on edge. American women have more financial freedom at their fingertips.

Brazilian women work for the life; always trying to make a life better and make their relationships better. And to be honest, all women around the world are better at relationships then men. The Brazilian women seem to be happier, regardless of the sex. They seem to look at life differently. They are not in competition, they work together. They use their minds as opposed to men who are constantly using their muscles, power and rage to force things to happen. Men aren't cooperative with other men. They don't even talk to each other in a bathroom. Men go to war when they are not in agreement. Men fight – women resolve.

Most important of all, Brazilians are happier. They laugh more, have less pressure and enjoy life more. Women in the US seem to be in competition with men and each other for that matter. The cost of having a good life in America is greater than anywhere else; therefore, it spurns more competition and creates the monetary race we seem to have here. The almighty dollar seems to rule our thoughts, our lives and sex is something we have to do as opposed to a wonderful thing we can do. A good sex life is good for the mind and the body. The release you get from climax helps keep the tension out of your life. Americans worry too much about having sex and the men are in constant turmoil of trying to get a little bit. The women are in constant turmoil of not letting them have any. So, if the sex is easier to come by, it allows everybody to be more relaxed. If you know it is easy to come by, then you are more relaxed. Does that answer your question?"

248

"Ya, thank God that doesn't apply to me. I'm a horny little rabbit, right? I mean, I'm like those Brazilians, right? I mean, I am better than those Brazilians, right?"

"Yes dear you are. No tension with you." James turned away from her and rolled his eyes. "Now let me finish my work so we both can get out of here for the weekend."

"James, when are we getting together this weekend?"

"As soon as you bring me the tapes. I'm tired of all this bullshit and I want to put it all to bed quickly. So as soon as you bring me the tapes, the sooner you will get back in my bed."

"Okay James, you will have them tomorrow afternoon and I will have you."

*****

Beth showed up as promised on Saturday afternoon and handed James the tapes. "Here are all the tapes honey. Now, you just remember your promises to me."

"Don't worry; I remember each and every one. You are going to get exactly what is coming to you." James felt a sense of relief and now wondered what he was going to do. "Now, do you swear to me these are the only copies."

"Yes, James, I love you and I will do everything you say from now on. I have given you all of them."

"Okay my dear, hop in bed for a good time."

James went through the motions. Trying to satisfy all these women was wearing him down and taking its toll on him. He was getting very tired of women. After Beth left, he spent the rest of the afternoon burning each and every copy of the tapes.

He was not sure if he could kill these three women. It wasn't his style. Their only fault was in trying to pressure him into a marriage. Yet, they all had him in a vise, and were all trying to tighten it and squeeze him. What had been the purpose of the killings in the first place? Was he becoming just a crazed serial killer? The present problem was these women were putting him in jeopardy. In the past there had been a definite reason for the killings, and very little direct connection back to him for the killings. Each man he killed was vermin. He had never killed a woman and found the very thought distasteful. But if he didn't kill them, he would be the one to suffer. Each of them was threatening his freedom for their own greed of wanting him. They were backing him into a corner and forcing him to react to save himself.

At least he had acquired the written and taped proof of his misdeeds. He could kill Beth then take a trip to Brazil and kill the other two. It would be better to kill all three and start fresh. He didn't want to, but they were not giving him a way out. Eventually someone else might put the pieces together and find him, but that was a chance he would have to take. He could give up and go to jail or worse...be executed...No, he wanted to keep going, trying to stay a step ahead of the law - alive and free. He really wanted to stop killing. He could not find peace, not now. In his mind he was crossing the line from do-gooder to just your average crazed serial killer. But doesn't self-preservation come first? Maybe suicide wasn't such a bad alternative. James was sick of the whole thing. He was tired and wanted it all to end. How had it started? The Army...Yes, the Army had made him the murderer he was.

Chapter Twenty-Five

Suicide or Accident

The small church was full. There were people standing in the back. There were well over two hundred people in attendance. The minister finished the prayer and nodded to Alan. He stepped forward to the podium, took out some notes and looked at the crowd.

"Accidents happen without notice or planning. Is that not the true meaning of accident? Something we cannot plan for, something that enters our life without forethought or planning. Something we just cannot see on the road of life, something that jumps up and bites us. Sometimes easily – sometimes hard. Accidents can bring happiness and also bring much sorrow. And to see all of you here for the same reason, makes me realize just how much pain this accident has brought. We are all sharing the same pain and grief. I am grateful to see you all. Most of you I do not know. Today we share equal thoughts of happiness and joy of having known the same person. And today we also share the deep sorrow of losing that same person.

He was a wonderful person. He had an extraordinary life. He and I grew up together, went to school together and stayed in close contact with each other at every turn. He only had thoughts to make the world a better place. By seeing so many of you here, I realize you feel the same way. He made friends, many friends. I have never met or talked to anyone who didn't like him.

He served his country and served it well. He offered his life at a time when others would not. He put himself in harm's way so that others would not have to. He did this without fanfare and without notoriety. Many of you don't know he was awarded three Purple Hearts and a Bronze Star for his heroism. He never mentioned it... it was just something that happened in the past. He never talked about himself – never bragged. He just did what was right. He always tried to do the right thing.

He returned to civilian life and rose to the top of his career field, making many friends along the way. He was honest to a fault. He supported his friends and always lent a hand when necessary. He was in a position where he had to make decisions. If you were on the receiving end you may not have always agreed with him, but you knew his decision was as fair and just as he could make it. And you had to respect him for it.

He was not perfect as none of us are. He attempted to come as close as possible. He had so much more to give, yet God has other plans for us than the ones we make. He had plans which will never be realized, sadly never realized. I will miss him…there is a hole in my heart that will never be mended, never healed. This hole will always be a reminder of our friendship. I don't think I can ever go through another day without thinking of James. He was my friend, confidant and proudly I say my brother, not by blood but by choice.

I will spread his ashes in the places he loved. And when I do, I will do it thinking of him and also thinking of all of you. We share this pain of loss. We will miss James. And I know God realizes what a wonderful person James was and what a wonderful soul he will share heaven with. Adieu my brother."

Alan was choking up with tears pouring from his eyes. He had gotten through the speech he had prepared. He slowly folded his notes and walked slowly making his way to the back of the church. The minister took the podium again and led the group in a hymn, the Lord's Prayer, and some final words about James. Then he offered condolences to all, said Amen and all exited.

Everyone filed out slowly, talking to others in hushed tones. Everyone was sad. As they filed out they came to Alan, who was at the back of the church. Telling him that he had made a fitting tribute to a good friend and how sorry they were for the loss of James. As Alan shook their hands, hugged the few people he knew, he was constantly looking for the three he needed to see.
Four showed up.

He knew they would be at the end of the crowd. One by one he greeted the four. They were not together but separated by others in the crowd. Each one introduced herself to him except the first.

Susan got to him first and hugged him crying. She was a mess. She was drunk and barely able to walk. "Oh my God, Alan. This is the worst thing that could have happened. I tried not to drink before this, but I couldn't help it. If I had known this was going to happen I would have given up the dam booze long ago. He was so good to me…I didn't do right by him."

Alan tried to say the right things, "Susan he loved you so very much. You should stop the drinking just to honor him, and in that way you will."

"Oh, I will, I am staying at the Holiday Inn. Will you call me there and we will get together and catch up before I go back to Ocala? I have to catch my cab now; he has been waiting for me."

"Ya, I will. Just let me get through this and I will call you later and we will get together." Alan wasn't sure she heard him as she stumbled toward the waiting cab. He just shook his head. He felt deeply sad for her as he watched her walk away. A few more people greeted him and shook his hand. Then he quickly realized that Beth was in front of him.

"Alan, my name is Beth and I was James assistant." She was crying and could barely get the words out.

"Oh yes, we have spoken briefly before. You were the very first person I called after they told me. He always had so many nice things to say about you." Alan leaned forward and whispered in her ear. "I know what James and you were planning. He was excited about your future together and spoke of it often. I am sorry those plans will not go to fruition. This is a tragic loss for all of us. My heart is broken knowing the pain he went through at the end. I just hope he didn't suffer."

A flood of tears emitted from Beth at his words. "Can we get together and talk? You are the only person who really knows everything. I need to talk to someone badly and you are the only person I think I can talk to."

Alan smiled, "Yes, maybe there is somewhere nearby we could have a drink? I think I need one."

"Let's meet at Shrimper's, it was James' favorite place. How about in an hour?"

"Okay, I think I will be through here by then, don't worry if I am a little late. This is the first time I have done this and to bury my best friend…"

Beth nodded, "I will see you there. I will wait." She started crying again as she walked away.

After a few more people went through the line, Andrea came upon Alan. She introduced herself to him. She was tall, beautiful and strong. She was dry-eyed.

"Andrea, it is so good to finally meet you. You were the very first person I called after they told me. I know you and James were only together for a short time, but he said it was the best time he had ever had. He was excited about moving to Brazil with you. He was excited about you, now I know why; you are so beautiful. James raved about you."

Andrea stayed very professional as she spoke, "Mr. Alan, I am at a deep and profound loss. Yes, we did not have much time together, yet it was wonderful. Thank you for calling me and letting me know. Can I get together with you after this event?"

"Yes definitely. Where can I reach you?"

"I am staying at the Ramada. You can reach me there."

"Okay, would you like to have dinner tonight?"

"Yes, that would be wonderful. I would like that. Please call me. I am in room 207."

"I will." Alan held his breath as she walked away from him and he thought, I better be careful with this one.

A few more people went through the line and at the end of the line was Vera. She was sobbing and finally reached Alan. She threw her arms around him and hugged him tightly. "Oh Alan, James speak best of you. I, Vera. This greatest loss of my life."

"How could I not know you. You are the beautiful flower of his life. We spoke on the phone. I called you as soon as I found out. You were the very first person I called after they told me."

"Oh Alan, I nao go to life without him."

Alan leaned forward and hugged her. "Oh Vera, I understand. It will be hard for all of us to get through this and we will," Alan answered reassuringly, but he was nervous. Was he hugging a man or a woman?

"Let us dinner tonight?" she asked.

"Uh, uh…tonight isn't a good night with all these arrangements and stuff. You understand. Let us have dinner tomorrow night. That would be better and then we could spend some time talking."

"Bom. I stay Pirates Cove. Will call and tell when?"

"Yes, I will. I will call you tomorrow and let you know what time."

Vera started crying again as she started to walk away. Alan let a sigh of relief and returned to speak with the minister. After a brief conversation he left the church and headed to Shrimper's to see Beth.

Alan found her sitting by the deck. She had a drink in front of her and was crying, staring out over the harbor. He went to her side, bent down and gave her a kiss on the cheek.

"Oh, Alan, thank you, thank you so much for coming."

"Not my pleasure but my duty and honor my dear." He ordered a drink to the passing waitress and then sat opposite her. "These are always hard and difficult times to get through. How are you holding up?"

Beth sadly smiled, "I can't stop crying. He was my world. He was going to marry me and take care of me. He was the greatest man I have ever met. We were in love, deeply in love. God has taken him from me. I want to go find him and be with him even if he is dead. Alan, how can life be so cruel? He told you we were in love? He told you how much he loved me?"

"Yes Beth, he loved you deeply. We never had a conversation without him telling me how important you were to him. He told me that he was going to end it with Vera and marry you. I knew that Brazilian thing would never work out. He did tell you about his bad boy side?"

"You mean the killings?"

"Shhh," as Alan tried to quiet her down as he looked around to see if anyone had heard their conversation.

"Alan, I know all about them. He told me everything. It was okay, he did them because they had to be done. He was very brave to do that, and risk being caught." She leaned forward and in a low voice, "Killing those men was the best thing for him to do. They were bad people. I'm glad he did it, I was very proud of him. Not many people would have that initiative."

"Beth, you must never speak of this again. Let the memory of James be without sin. This has to be a very deep and dark secret and you can never speak of this. If word got out, you would be ruining his reputation. You should never speak of this to anyone. Yes, you know and I know, but let us promise to let it go no further."

"You are right Alan. I won't, and it will not go any further, I promise. You are a good friend to him. You're right, we should honor his memory." Quickly switching the subject, she said, "I saw that Brazilian bimbo there. What did she say?"

Alan paused for a moment, "She is very upset. Of course, she would be. I know James never told her he was breaking it off, so she still believes she was going to marry him. I don't think there is anything wrong in letting sleeping dogs lie. She is going back to Brazil and will be sad for a long time. We know the truth, so what does it matter? Just let her go back to her country and drop it. I hope you weren't planning on talking to her."

"No! I don't want to even talk to that slut. It drives me crazy just to think James fucked her. I mean, he even said I was better in bed than her, he told me," she said proudly.

Alan's devil horns popped up. "Yes, James said you were very good in bed. He said I should be so lucky as to have a woman like you. Beth, if there is anything I can do to help you through this time, please just ask. I am here to comfort you, so at any time you want to talk just let me know.

"Well Alan, thank you but comfort me? - The way you said that it sounded like you are trying to have sex with me. I hope that isn't in your brain. No one can ever replace James."

"No! – No! – No! Don't be silly. I'm just here as James' friend and I am here in respect of him. Please Beth, if you need anything just call me. I am here for you.

"Okay and thanks."

"Now, let's have another drink and I will tell you about some of the times James and I had. We were pretty wild together; we made a pretty good team." Alan ordered them another drink and told her stories to fill the time. After the second drink, Beth said she was too sad and wanted to go home to cry. Alan paid the bill, walked her to her car and sent her off. He breathed a sigh of relief. He headed for James' house to wait for his dinner date with Andrea.

Alan had arrived three days before the memorial service. He had spent the time getting with the church, the minister and the florist. He had brought James with him in an urn for the ceremony. He arranged for the sale of the house and put the boat in a consignment yard to be sold. He then started to pack up James' belongings. He had a pile of boxes by the front door. Alan was just jamming stuff into each box. No care was given to any item, just shoved into a box. He would have plenty of time to figure it all out.

He called Andrea and gave her a time when he was to arrive at the Ramada. He was short with her. She was suppose to be the smart one. Alan wanted to be sharp with her. He arrived at her door five minutes late. He had to catch his breath when she revealed herself from behind the door. She looked beautiful, Alan was aroused. Andrea was ready to go, so they quickly headed for his car. He went downtown and pulled in front of the Riverwalk Café.

Andrea sternly said, "I can't go here. I had dinner here with him right there. I'll be a crying mess. Just go somewhere else. There – there's a spot to park - right in front of the Black Marlin Restaurant – perfect! Go there!"

The Black Marlin was small, quiet and cozy. The hostess led them to a booth which was the last open table. The high backs on the booth

257

seats gave them plenty of privacy. Alan asked what she would like to drink, and she ordered a Margarita and he added a 'me too.' The drinks came quickly. They were finally left alone to peruse the menu.

Andrea dropped her menu below her face and stared at Alan, then firmly with a smile asked, "Okay best friend! … Where is he? Where's he hiding? He is the sneakiest bastard! This was a pretty good idea!

"Andrea your crazy. He died in the accident. He's dead. I wish I could tell you otherwise, but he is dead…"

"Don't give me your bullshit!"

Alan raised his voice, "He's dead, D-E-A-D," he spelled with great sternness. "You're wrong, I'm devastated. I just lost my best friend and you want to play police interrogation. Accept it! – He's dead!"

"Are you really telling me the truth?" she asked quietly.

"Yes – he's dead and I miss him. We were friends for almost thirty-five years…," Alan started to choke up.

"Okay, I had to be sure. James was capable of anything. What a man! He spun my head around. I don't know what I'm going to do…what a waste…I'm devastated," she said matter-of-factly. "I had hopes he would be alive. He made my life complete. Did he tell you about me?"

"Oh yes! He was very…well he told me he was in love with you and moving to Brazil with you. He seemed to be crazy in love with you. This was real fast for him, but James had a good eye for quality…I hoped it would work out for the both of you…he needed a good woman in his life…and I can see you certainly fit the bill. You're gorgeous!"

She gave Alan a perfunctory thank you. "I wanted him and at the same time I could protect him. He was a very busy boy. Were you a part of his killing people?"

"No!" he said in a shocked manner. "I never participated. He did everything on his own."

"I could never have turned him in. He was right if he did those killings. I became fascinated with him. We made a good couple. He – we could have had a great life together. I was just surprised he was taken in by Vera. She is beautiful. Better living through plastic surgery, I guess. Even I thought she was a woman until my investigation. You do know everything, I take it?"

"Yes. James gave her the nickname 'the Queen of Brazil,' he just didn't know until the end how right he was. Oh, he knew because you told him. I think he was in disbelief. He never would have gone through with a marriage, that's for sure, but wow was he amazed. I am amazed, but you are even more beautiful and natural I might add."

Andrea started probing again. "And you didn't have anything to do with the murder he did in Maine? I mean you must have known."

"Stop it Andrea. If he did that, he did it on his own and without my knowledge. That was the way he was. He just did it without discussion and without collusion. If he did that, then I never knew he was going to beforehand and he never said anything after. I mean I realized somewhere in my mind that he must have done it and it was wonderful he did it for me...But he never mentioned it. He didn't talk about it."

Andrea smiled. "Okay, I believe you...right. Don't worry I'm not going to get you arrested for anything. These secrets will go to the grave with him. What are you going to do with his ashes? Oh, and I want to go through his things. Can I meet you at the house tomorrow?"

"I will spread his ashes in a bunch of locations. Some, here in the water and then some up at my lodge. He loved it up there. You could go through his things, but I've already packed everything. I am going to ship it all back with me. I will go through it and sort it out. Is there anything in particular you were looking for?"

"Well, I wanted some photos and I don't know...something of his I could keep as a reminder. But if you have already packed everything, will you send me some photos and find something I could have?"

Alan gave a warm smile of thoughtfulness and caring. "Yes, I will my dear. I'll put together a nice little package for you and send it to you. Promise. Tell me, what is a beautiful woman like you going to do now? I mean, you're so beautiful, I was amazed that James had gotten so lucky."

"Thank you," she said. I don't know, I guess my quest to find the right man for me will go on. I was positive he was perfect for me. Sad isn't it? You think you find the right person and then something terrible like this happens. Tell me again what happened."

"Well there isn't much to tell. James came up for a weekend. We fished, drank a little and had a few laughs. He was talking about the upcoming changes. Going to Brazil, ending his job and career here, he was happy. He had found this gorgeous woman...you. He was at peace with everything. He just wanted to go, be with you and start this phase of his life. He even said you two were going to have three children. Sunday, he had an afternoon flight. We had a long breakfast and as he started to leave it started to rain. He took the back road through the mountains to get to I-95. He must have hit a wet patch or swerved to avoid something. Don't know. He went off the road and it was about a 1000 foot drop. I guess he knew what was happening but couldn't do anything about it. The fear he must have had...I don't like to think about it. The car hit and exploded. I hope he passed out before impact. He must have been already dead when it exploded...before the explosion and fire. There wasn't much left when they finally got to him. Just a pile of bones. They tell me it was a mess, just charred remains. They gathered up as much as possible. I took the remains that were left and finished with a proper cremation."

"Was there a thorough investigation?"

"Thorough? Ya, I guess so...like what do you mean...there wasn't much to investigate."

"Well did they match dental records? How did they determine it was James in the crash?"

"I don't know what they did. The police called me within hours. James had given my address to the rental car company and the police just showed up to confirm everything. There wasn't much to investigate. They just sort of realized it was him. They found some of his stuff and there was no one else in the car. Sort of obvious. I couldn't even identify him by just his bones. There was some luggage in the trunk that didn't get burned. That's how they put it together. I helped the guy at the funeral home make the final determination. Is that what you mean?"

260

Andrea watched Alan's eyes and mannerisms as he spoke. "So, there wasn't a dental record match?"

"I don't know Andrea, maybe there was. The whole thing has been very, very painful. I tried to do everything right. Should I have done something else?"

"No, that's okay. I guess it all matches. It's just my thorough police brain at work."

They ordered another drink and dinner. Eventually they stopped talking about James and pursued other subjects during dinner. After their dinner, Alan took Andrea back to the motel.

"I hope you come up to visit me in Maine," as he got her to her motel room. "Do you want me to stay with you for a while? We all need to be comforted by this tragic loss. Can I hold you? The grief is over whelming. Let me comfort you."

Andrea smiled, "No, that's okay, thanks anyway. Now, don't forget the package you promised me. Thanks for everything." She quickly kissed him on the cheek and disappeared into the room, rapidly shutting the door.

He stood there for a second trying to figure out how James always got into their pants and he couldn't. He just took a deep breath and went to the car and back to the house to sleep.

The next day Alan finished packing and called Susan. The front desk said she had already left. He inquired politely as to how she left. They said they had called a cab for her to take to the airport in West Palm Beach. He thought that was all for the best. He loved Susan. She was his favorite, but he was always sad to see her in such bad shape. He asked the clerk if she was sober when she left. "Most assuredly sir," was the reply. "I checked her out myself." That made Alan feel better.

He handled some more of the details and got ready for the meeting with Vera. He was tired and wanted to get all this over with. He wanted to go back to Maine. He knew he would have to return at some time in the future. Most of the problems could be handled by phone. He had delayed the memorial service for James so that everyone had plenty of notice, since at least two of the people would be coming from Brazil.

He wanted to make sure the word got out and the service would be well attended, which it was.

He called Vera and gave her a time he would pick her up. She was crying on the phone. He found it hard to understand her between the crying and the language barrier. Finally, she understood he would pick her up at seven.

That night he knocked on her door. After what seemed to be a long wait she answered the door. She was wrapped in a towel and was dripping wet from the shower. She was all apologies saying she was late because she couldn't stop crying. She went to hug him but as she did the towel slipped exposing a breast. Alan just looked in amazement. The breast was perfect. She giggled a bit, apologized again and went to the bathroom to dress. Alan sat on the end of the bed to wait.

Vera called out to him, "I had champagne little refrigerator, help self...you want?"

Alan poured himself a rum and coke and returned to the bed. As he gazed around the room he noticed the bathroom door was slightly open. As he looked in he could see Vera toweling off in the reflection from the large bathroom mirror. Her body was perfect. She was beautiful. How could this be a man? No wonder James had been fooled. Alan was fooled, and he knew the secret. James had told him how good in bed she was. His thoughts went to thinking that she might be fun to bed down. No, that was crazy. She's a man, or is she? He had never seen a body as beautiful. It was straight out of Playboy. She slowly dressed and put on her makeup. If she knew he was watching either she did not know or did not care. She finally came out and apologized again.

"I sorry Alan, just cry. I miss him muito. He best man I ever had."

Alan rolled his eyes at her response. "That's okay. You're set now so let's go to dinner. Why don't we just eat here at the hotel? I saw the menu on the way in and it seemed pretty good. Do you have any objection?"

"Nao, good; but I nao hungry."

He led her to the restaurant and they were seated near the window overlooking the harbor. Alan ordered a margarita and Vera

262

ordered a martini. They chatted but all Vera seemed to want to do was sniffle and drink. She finished the first martini in three or four sips and asked for another. Alan ordered another for her and told the waitress to make it a double in a larger glass.

"Alan, you James friend, why happen? I lost meu husband. I don't know what I do. He love me and I love him. I nao believe happen. It bad dream and I nao wake up. Tell me he love me – please tell me."

"Vera, James loved you deeply. He was going to marry you and bring you to this country and your boys too. This was a terrible accident. It will take a while but someday you will be fine. Sometimes we lose people for no good reason. I am sure you will always remember him; he was a great person and my best friend. I don't know how I got through that memorial service. I was choked up and crying so hard inside. I know how you feel Vera."

He went to order their dinner but Vera sort of waived the waitress off by ordering another round. With each sip she seemed to sob and sniffle more. She was not holding her alcohol well and seemed to be getting sloppy. Vera had a very low and loose cut dress on and when she moved Alan could watch and see her nipples. He had to work hard to look her in the eyes. Those beautiful breasts were dancing for him and it was hard not to get excited. By the time they ordered an appetizer and a main course she had ordered her fourth martini and was downing them faster than the bartender could keep up.

"Alan, you think me pretty? James say I best looking woman in world. What you think?"

"Vera, I must admit you are very, very beautiful. James was very right. I wish I could find a woman like you. You are picture perfect. Maybe someday I will find someone like you." Alan was thinking – like hell - I want a real woman not a re-manufactured man.

She toyed with her shrimp cocktail and ignored her dinner while Alan tried to eat. He was distracted. Every time she moved he watched her body hoping to get a better look. She managed to swig down two more martinis while he was eating.

"I think I drunk. Because I miss him muito. Want him back," she started to cry again.

263

"Vera, please calm down. I know you're upset but we cannot bring him back."

"Alan, nao replace James, he best man ever have. He muito good in bed, you know?"

Alan added smugly laughing, letting the alcohol get a hold of his tongue, "Well I never went to bed with him. I heard he was good in bed but my dear, I taught him everything he knew."

"You better than James?" she asked unbelievingly.

"Yes, I am much better in bed. Women have told me so."

"Maybe someday I try make love to other man. But what if nao good? Make me worse than before or better than after? Right?"

Alan was confused and found it hard to follow what she was saying or meant. He was fascinated by this woman/man? The more he drank the better she looked and the hornier he was getting. She kept exposing herself. Alan found her very sexy. He found it hard to think of her as anything but a woman. He started rationalizing in his mind. Why not? If James did it with her, then why not? It must be pretty good to fool James and he said it was the best sex he had ever had. Who would know if he did her? She was getting very drunk, this would be easy. At least he would be able to nail one of James' women. What are friends for? The more he drank the easier the rationalization became.

"Oh Vera, you will find another love. There are plenty of men in the world. They are like buses. If you miss one there will be another one along in a few minutes. You will just have to try a few out to find one you like. Oh, you're empty –Waitress could we have another round, please?" By his calculation she had over eight double martinis and he had over five margaritas. One more should do it. This way I can always claim I was drunk he thought.

They had been talking for over two hours while the alcohol flowed. They had just about finished the last drink. Alan paid the bill and suggested he had a lot to do tomorrow and he should go. "Let me walk you to your room Vera."

"Oh good," she said, "a gentleman. Yes, walk me to room. I find nice Brazilian girlfriend for you. You will like Brazilian women. They

264

are fun." They went to the room with both of them weaving in their tracks. She found the card key and opened the door. "You come in?" Alan was already in the room before she finished the sentence.

Vera started to cry again as she sat on the corner of the bed. She looked at Alan with tears running down her cheeks. "Alan, you hold me. James left my life. I want kill me."

"Vera, there, there." Alan sat next to her on the bed and put his arm around her. She put her head on his shoulder. "Vera, relax, I have you. I will comfort you. It's okay, go ahead and cry. I know exactly how you feel. We want to be near someone when we go through such a tragedy." He just let her cry for a while. When she had settled down, he slowly turned her head toward his face. "My dear, we can comfort each other in honor of James. He would want us to be happy. He would want me to comfort you by making love to you in his memory." He then slowly kissed her on the lips. She responded and then pulled back.

"Nao Alan, James nao like."

"Vera, James is not with us anymore. He would want me to make love to you, to comfort you. We must go on and I really do want to comfort you. This is a terrible tragedy for both of us. Besides James would want us to be happy and comfort each other. There is nothing wrong with what we are doing. We are adults and both hurting. Please comfort me and I will comfort you." She seemed dazed, the alcohol had taken effect.

Alan kept kissing her on the lips, cheeks and neck. His hand slowly dropped down to her breast and he started squeezing and feeling for the nipple. She was slow to respond.

"Nao, James nao like, nao please."

"It's okay Vera. James would like. Let me comfort you. He would want us to be happy and love just like he loved you and you loved him. This will be special, just for us, to make us happy." Alan slipped her shoulder straps off, so he could expose both breasts. He was kissing her and feeling both breasts.

"You sur?" she slurred.

"Yes, it is okay for us to be happy." He laid her back on the bed and started kissing passionately. His left hand slid down the inside of her dress until he found her panties. He pulled them to one side and inserted a finger in her vagina. She moaned softly while she kept sobbing. After he rubbed her vagina he knew it was going to happen, he pulled her dress over her head and then pulled her panties off. He quickly took off his pants and got on top of her. He wanted to get inside her before she objected. He knew once inside her she would keep going. He quickly inserted himself.

"Oh James, James I love you."

Alan didn't care what she called him, he was inside and going to get his rocks off. He noticed she felt wonderful to him. She was tight and well lubricated. He slid in very easily. She didn't respond much at first. She cried and kept calling James' name. Finally, she started moving with him. Her legs wrapped around him and she pulled him deep inside her. Alan couldn't wait any longer and exploded, then stopped moving.

When she realized he was done, she raised her self-up on both elbows. "I nao cum, Alan. You make me cum, please. Use tongue."

Alan sobered up fast when she spoke. He was indecisive. Should he go down on her? All of a sudden, she was a he in his mind. He started using his fingers on her.

"Nao Alan," use tongue, she implored.

Alan didn't know what to do. "Let me rest a minute Vera," was all he could come up with.

"I pretend you James – do what James do."

Alan slowly lowered himself into position and started licking her. Slowly at first. He could not get the idea that she was a man out of his head. His only thought was that he had turned queer and he was really sucking some guy off. He started to back off, but she was ready, wrapping her legs around his shoulders and putting both hands on the back of his head so he couldn't move his face. He finally gave in and started licking harder. Vera came screaming 'James – James' the whole time. After she came she let him go.

266

They laid there not saying a word. Finally, she turned to Alan. "Now you go home now. I love James nao you," she said with an edge in her voice.

Alan didn't say anything. He put his clothes on, bent down, tried to kiss her on the cheek but she turned away. There was nothing more, so he left. He was more confused than ever. 'Does this make me a queer?' was his only thought.

He found the car in the parking lot and started to drive home. On his way, he was about to pass Shrimpers, but decided he would go in, have a drink and think about what he had just done. He sat at the bar and ordered. He was quietly deep in thought, drunk and halfway through his second drink when a guy came in and sat next to him.

"Mind if I sit here?"

"No, go ahead," said Alan not really paying attention.

"Hi, my name is Doug. What's yours?"

"Alan."

"Nice to meet you. You a local or on vacation?" he asked trying to start a conversation.

Alan noticed a slight lisp coming from Doug. Oh great, he thought – God, are you trying to convert me? "Look uh...Doug. I just finished burying my best friend of thirty plus years. I just need some peace and quiet."

"Oh, that's terrible. You poor man, oh, I know and understand your pain. Let's get a table. Please let me comfort you. I know just what you need. I will make you feel wonderful. Let me help you with your pain and sorrow."

Alan snapped and reacted alarmingly, automatically to his words. He swung as hard as he could, hitting Doug in the side of the face with a left hook. It knocked Doug off the stool and onto the floor. Alan threw a twenty on the bar and walked out stepping over Doug's legs as he left, saying to the bartender, "Fucking fagots – Comfort me – bullshit!"

Alan retreated to the house. He poured himself a big glass of vodka, took a large swig, rinsed his mouth with it and spit out. He did it a second time. He was mad at himself for touching that woman/man. He was sick, how could he have gone to bed with her? Too late, no one saw it – it's okay. Who's gonna tell?

He spent the next day finishing all the loose ends. He had done all what was expected and then some. He arranged for all the boxes to be picked up by a shipper. The truck and two men showed up taking all the boxes and the furniture which was to be sold. Alan was left with a house void of personality. James did not exist anymore. His stuff was gone. James' memory was alive but fading. He took care of some last-minute details and headed to the airport for a flight back to Maine.

Chapter Twenty-Six

Time Goes By

Over a year later Alan headed to the airport in Portland. He waited at luggage arrival. People came and went to pick up their bags at the carousel. The time dragged on for almost an hour as he paced the floor. He was tapped on the shoulder. He turned around to find a bald man with a full unkempt beard dressed in well-worn dirty jeans and a shirt that looked like he had slept in it. He looked, stared and decided he was getting hit on by a panhandler for some money. He reached in his pocket and handed the bum some loose change. He turned away to keep walking and the panhandler grabbed his shoulder. He turned back to the man, "Hey! That's all the change I have, get lost!"

"How about twenty bucks you cheap bastard?" came the reply.

Alan recognized the voice and smiled. "Well you got me," he said laughing. "Beautiful, really beautiful. I couldn't have recognized you if I had fallen over you. Good to see you again. I was beginning to believe you were really dead. Come on let's go. Great outfit – No one can recognize you if I can't." They walked to the car, threw James' bags in the trunk, left the airport and drove back to the lodge, arriving at dusk.

They sat at the kitchen table drinking, making dinner, eating and talking just like old times. The large kitchen was illuminated with propane gas lights. Since the temperature was cool outside, Alan started a fire in the old large black wood stove to keep the room warm. Electricity and other modern conveniences were not available deep in the woods. They laughed and joked and spoke of old times of their long relationship. They each had to make trips to the nearby outhouse in the chilly night air.

They had finally worked through their old friendly banter. "Well, catch me up. There must be a lot of news. A year plus of silence is hard to do," said James.

Alan started to report the past year. "James, it is so good to have you back. A lot has gone on. Everything has gone pretty much the way you planned. The first month was the toughest. Getting through your funeral was tough. You had a couple of hundred people at the ceremony. Everyone was sad, a lot of tears. You have, or should I say *had* a lot of friends. There were your kids, all your women and even a blind guy, quite a turn out. Most signed the book that was at the church. They sent it to me, I'll show you later. It took me a few days to pack everything up and then ship it here. I put it all in storage except for some minor things. Each girl wanted something to remember you by. So, I put together some pictures and some of your shirts – girls always want shirts – anyway, some small crap stuff, made up the packages for each of them. I got a thank you letter back from each of them. They thanked me and all boo-hooing about you. I saved them for you.

The insurance policies paid off pretty quickly and it all went to the trust fund you had. I paid all the bills out of it and all of the expenses. They finally sold the boat two months ago and that went into the trust. Well, not all. I had to keep some cash to pay me back."

"Pay you back for what?" James said kiddingly.

"Well, the worst thing was your Nam buddy Richie Hegeman. I thought the deal was finished. He came to me two months after the accident. He said there were some police that came back and some private detective people who were asking a lot of questions. He didn't give me a lot of details about who they were and what they asked. He is pretty tight lipped. He wanted another five thousand to keep his lips sealed. I wasn't sure what to do because I thought it was kinda shitty of him to make the deal and then double the price after the fact. I wasn't quite sure what to do. I finally decided to give him the money because I didn't want him to open his mouth and blow this thing wide open. So, it cost you a total of ten thousand for the body."

"That's okay. You did the right thing. It's was a good deal at twice the price. Heg can be trusted. He kinda underbid the job in the beginning. I was in a rush to die," said James chuckling, "and we didn't have the time to really think it through as to what the ramifications could be. There was more work and effort on his part than he anticipated. I think he was just trying to be a good friend. The major problem these days is…you just can't walk into any Seven-Eleven and pick up a good dead body," James laughingly said with educational wisdom.

"There is about $200,000.00 left after all the expenses and what I sent you. Other than that, it's been a quiet year. Occasionally, someone who knew you asks about the accident or how I'm taking it, or what a pity to lose you…that kind of stuff. But the good news is that no officials or police have been around or asking about you.

"Good. Everything seems to have gone smoothly. Tell me about my girls. How did they take it?"

Alan made them another drink and sat back down with a big smile on his face. "Well, Susan made it to the ceremony and sad to say she was quite tipsy, left quickly, took a cab, thank God. I was suppose to get with her and have dinner but she split fast. I checked with the room clerk and he said she was sober when she went to the airport the next day. So, all you can do is keep your fingers crossed on that one."

James hung his head and went sad. "I thought she was going to be the last one. I thought we were happy, but she went and had that affair and is continuing to have that affair with Mr. Al Cohol. Ripped my heart out. Things sometimes just don't go the way you want them to go. I guess there isn't an answer…"

"Ya, there are always the sad things that happen in your life that you can't forget. Like Nam…you can't forget it…it never leaves you…no matter how much you want it to."

James straightened up, "Your right…Nam never goes away. It's with you every single day. Okay now let's not get maudlin here. Hey, how about my other three loves?"

"Well, I must say James they were good fucking, sorry you couldn't be there."

"You fucking bastard! You fucked my girls?" James indignantly snapped.

"Ya, but the girls only. You couldn't anymore, you're dead. I fucked them right after the memorial service. Someone had to comfort them. What did you expect? Better me than someone you don't know. They were all torn up with grief. I only fucked Beth and Andrea. Susan was there but I couldn't do her. Too much history there and besides, she cleared out early. But I couldn't fuck that man. I don't know how you got fooled. It's easy to tell she's a man. Fucking a guy would send shivers up my spine."

271

"You are a rotten bastard. I guess it doesn't matter. You're right; I certainly have crossed those girls off my list. But at least it gave you a chance to screw real women instead of that right hand you date in the outhouse. But I am surprised they jumped in bed with you so quickly after my death. Kind of hurts my feelings. Which one did you like better?"

"Oh, Andrea was probably the best fuck, but I must say that little Beth tries real hard to please. It was a one-shot deal anyway and it was just a quickie. It is something that has no future so it's best to just forget about it and get on with life. Don't even want to talk about them anymore. Well James, what do you want to do now?"

"After much thought, I think I want to follow the original plan. I will spend a year here and then decide. Just think of me as a fishing guide. I want to keep a real low profile for a while then decide where I want to go and what I want to do."

"We'll move your stuff into the Lobster Shack cabin. It's small. I'm sure you'll like it. It's good and private and sort of off the beaten path. And very close to the outhouse I might add."

"Ya, that's fine. I'll settle in."

They spent the rest of the evening trying to find the bottom of a large bottle of scotch.

*****

The summer season started and James, now named Ben Herd, became a fishing guide. He kept to himself unless one of the guests needed a guide. He kept his distance from everybody. Some of the people who came to the lodge had known James from before but failed to recognize him now. Ben became the quiet fishing guide, no fanfare, he stayed away from the drinking and mixing with the guests. The summer was quiet. The lodge was a good place to hide.

On Labor Day weekend, he was walking along the Carry Road, a deeply rutted path through the woods. He saw a female with fishing gear coming toward him. As she got closer he realized it was Andrea. He couldn't avoid her. At first, he just tried to walk past her, not saying anything. She moved to get in his way. They both stopped and looked at each other.

"James."

"No, my name is Ben."

"That's a great outfit honey; I almost didn't recognize you."

"You've got me confused with someone else lady."

"James, you can change your appearance, but you can't change your voice and besides I would recognize you anywhere."

"Lady, you've crazy." He tried to walk away.

James, stop it. Come back here. What do I have to do - turn you in? The game's over for good. You're mine and you know that. Now talk to me."

James turned and faced her. "Okay, now what?"

"Kiss me, I love you my crazy man."

He moved toward her. They both dropped their fishing gear at the same time. They hugged and kissed. They sat on a log and talked.

"I knew you were still alive. That accident was too convenient. And Alan couldn't tell a lie if he wanted to."

"Why did you fuck him?"

She laughed. "Fuck him? I wouldn't even if he was the last man. Did he tell you that?"

"Ya."

Darling, stop your silliness. Now time has passed, we can go to Brazil and get married, even though you're a man with a different name," she was laughing.

"Andrea...look I think it would be best if I stayed hidden for a while. I don't think I should go to Brazil. Too many people that could ask questions. I would stand out like a sore thumb down there. I want to put more distance between me and the murders and of course my death. It's going well now, and I don't want to rock the boat. I will go to Brazil when I think the time is right. I want to stay hidden. You found me, maybe someone else could."

"Don't worry my dear, everything will be alright. Besides you have to do what I say, or you will go to jail, remember? This was a good ploy. Your dying got you out of everything. It certainly got you out of the pickle you made for yourself. It was easy for me to figure out and realize the mess you were in after seeing the other girls at the memorial service. They were crying their eyes out. There was a bunch of them. I don't think you told me about some of them. You had more of a stable of them than even I knew. But, if you start connecting the dots...I couldn't believe Alan. He was lying with every word that came from his mouth. And having the accident take place in Maine, with no one around, come on...then inviting all those people so they could witness an urn at a memorial service. Your plan was excellent. One thing, whose body was it?"

James was getting uneasy. All the plans and the past two years were down the drain. He had run away from all three of the crazy nuts. Now, he had been found. Andrea was ruthless in her pursuit. How had she found him? "Darling, an old Army buddy of mine from Nam owns a funeral home in Portland. For a few dollars you get a body. If you leave enough identification around, it kills most of the questions that come up. Then my friend in the funeral homes certifies the identification that Alan provides. Easy!"

"That is...unless someone found out...and she didn't get what she wanted. Then you could still get turned in and go to jail. Now what do you want my dear...me or jail?"

"Andrea, I give up - I am all yours."

"That's what I wanted to hear."

"How did you find me?"

"For the past two years I have been coming to the US about every other month to look for you. I went to different cities and paid a lot of detectives but with no results. I came here first but you were smart enough not to come here…too easy. I quit my job, so I could spend the time looking for you. My father is having a fit over all the money I have spent to find you. I hired more detectives than you could ever imagine. I looked in about ten different states. All the states you had mentioned in conversations. I never found you. Where were you?"

"I went to Seattle, Washington. Big enough of a city to get lost in and easy enough to hide."

"Do you have a girlfriend?"

"No. I decided to stay away from women for a while. I only seem to get in trouble around women."

"Good. That will make things very easy. From now on I am the woman you will serve. You just do what I tell you to do, and everything will be fine. One step out of line and you will not like a Brazilian jail. Here are the rules: You touch another woman – Jail. You can't make me pregnant – Jail. You can't get along with my family and especially my father - Jail. We live in Brazil. We spend our days and our nights together. We do everything together, no exceptions…Do you understand me…dear?" She was happily laughing as she spoke.

"Yes." James was thinking about her rules and possessiveness. His thoughts told him, this cannot work. Being tied down totally in life to this woman was not what he had in mind. He wanted to be left alone. He did not want a woman who was constantly holding a gun to his head. Then again, what choice did he have? Maybe it would be all right. Maybe he could learn to be with this woman. A fresh start – a new life…

"James, go get your things and bring them to the lodge on the lake and be quick about it. I am staying there. I have a cabin, number five. Meet me there. We will spend the night there, then tomorrow we can get you a passport and we will go back to Brazil as soon as possible. So, go hurry dear. I'll be at the cabin. While I am waiting for you I am going to the dam to try to catch one of those famous trout you told me about." She got up to leave, bent down, kissed him and started down the Carry Road, back to try her luck fishing at the dam.

275

Chapter Twenty-Seven

Unexpected Future

"Ben, how ya doin?"

The words caught Ben off guard. His back was turned away from the Carry Road while he was cleaning some fishing gear. It was Bob, the local game warden walking up to him. "Hey, you scared me. I'm good and, how are you?" Not waiting for an answer, he asked with a chuckle, "What's up Bob, caught anybody stealing fish?"

"Naw...I'm doin pretty good...Yup. Ya know, we finally found that woman who disappared a couple of weeks ago...Yes sa." Bob's heavy, thick, Maine accent was calmly relaying the local news.

"Really, she alive?" asked Ben inquisitively."

"Naw...Drown...Yup...Ya know we found her bawdy down in Lake Umbagog. Pretty easy to figure what happened. Yup...must have fallen in by the dam. She was stayin in one of those cabins by the dam...And, she must have been tryin to fish and fell into the riva...Yup. The current musta takin her down the riva. The rocks really banged her up...Yup. A fisherman found the bawdy floatin over on the faar shore...Yes sa." Bob stopped talking and waited a while.

When Ben didn't speak, Bob started talking again. "Ya know...if you don't fasten dem waders propberly, then waater gets in thar and acts like an anchar...Yup...Yup. At least, that's what we think happened...Yes sa...And that's what we told the people who wer lookin for her...Yup. She came from Brazil – Wow...Ya know that's pretty faar from here...Yup."

"Wow. That's too bad. I guess some people should just never travel," said Ben turning back to working on the fishing gear. He didn't want Bob to see his tears.

"I heard you was leavin us."

"Ya, for a while Bob. I have to go back to the real world for a while. I need to go talk to a blind man for a while."

Bob looked confused and started scratching his bald head, "Well...Yup...see ya latar...Yes sa...see ya latar...Yup." said Bob turning and continuing to walk up the Carry Road.

Ben finished cleaning the fishing equipment. After putting it away, he went to his room and continued to pack. Alan came by with a couple of drinks, sat down and made small talk.

"Ya know Ben - James whoever you are" he said laughing, "I hope you are making the right decision. Andrea finding you was a streak of luck on her part."

"No, not really. Eventually she would have found me. It is just terrible what happened. I think it is time for me to go make peace with the world. Too many things have happened in my life for it to be considered normal, average or even mundane. The past thirty years has not been what the average American goes through. I just caught the lucky train. I never got to do what I wanted to do when I started out, but I am left with what I have done and what I have created. I guess that is all any man is left with after it is all over."

"Ya, your right, but I don't think this is fair to you. I don't agree with your thinking or your choices. Please reconsider."

"No Alan, it is time. It will be okay because there is not a lot of time left. Time controls everyone's life completely. From the moment you are born you are racing towards death. So, best I take off, get everything done and spend some time with the blind shrink. Then and only then will I leave. I figure two to three weeks. Hey pal – you can visit ya know. You act like this is the end."

"Well, after all that has happened – Murder doesn't go away."

"Alan, I think it is best. I'm all packed. Let's go put a dent in that bottle before dinner."

****
278

James flew to Florida. He was careful to wear a disguise. He rented a car and a hotel room in Jupiter, ten miles from most of the people he knew. He made an appointment to see Ray. Oddly enough he had an open slot the next day.

The office girl announced Alan French to Ray. When James entered, Ray greeted him as a new client.

When James started talking a quizzical look followed by a big grin grew on Ray's face. "James, it is so good to find you're not dead. I thought I was just welcoming a new client when you first came in, but I remember voices well. Oh, I am so happy you're not dead. This is quite a shock and quite a wonderful event."

"I'm glad I'm not dead as well. There is a lot to tell Ray. I don't think we can do it in an hour. Do you want to have dinner tonight?"

"Okay, yes, but please sit down and tell me a rough overview. I went to one nice funeral for you. I am confused, but so happy you're alive. Then over dinner tonight we can get down to particulars."

During the next hour James glossed over the most relevant points and brought Ray up to speed. He didn't mention any murders.

Later, James picked out a restaurant which was out of the way and didn't have much traffic. Ray was dropped off by his secretary. James selected a table way off to one side hidden behind some plants. They finally got settled and ordered cocktails. "So, Ray, let me tell you the rest of the story...the whole story...and nothing but the truth." James proceeded and started from the beginning in Viet Nam." At some point they ordered another drink and then dinner. James was still talking all the way through dinner. Finally, by the end of dinner James was done with his story.

Ray sat quietly listening, occasionally asking a question. At the end there was dead silence from both which lasted a good three or four minutes. Ray finally spoke, "James, that is one hell of a story. My problem now is that all my clients past, present and future are going to be very boring, dull, dreary and monotonous. From now on I will keep my sunglasses on while in session. That way they won't know I'm sleeping through their mundane, uninteresting, small minded lives.

You know James, you are morally wrong in the modern world. I applaud you as a vigilante, but I can't applaud you as a Christian. If anyone ever finds out or figures it out they would still have to find you. They could still charge you with murder because there is no time limit. And you are right with time everything does fade away. People don't remember and from your narrative and with consideration to the people involved past and present, I don't think anyone cares to figure it out. The people you have removed are not at the top of anyone's list. They are just fodder in the cesspool of life. Still, you should not do this anymore for fear of being caught, or being killed by someone stronger, more prepared, or someone who might get the advantage over you. And you must remember you still have people who may want to hurt you, especially the people who didn't get there needs met. That, in itself, is a dangerous situation and one you must be very, very mindful of.

I think you are doing the right thing by getting out of town and starting a new life. All people move on. You must be careful of no matter where you go because there is always something somewhere which can hurt you and I must say where you are going could hurt you at any time. My only thought is you may want to change your destination and the reasons for a change in the destination. I am glad now I did not know the details and even if I had there would have been nothing I could have done. You were totally protected from me unless you had told me in advance regarding a murder or two. Even then I think I would not have done anything to disrupt you in any way.

So, my friend, please change your ways. Stay on the straight and narrow and be very careful in life. Oh, and stay out of jail," he said with a laugh.

"Ray, I will and thanks for everything and allowing me to use you as my sounding board. It is my intention to stay as straight as an arrow. I believe my choice of the Queen of Brazil as a final partner or at least a partner who offers the most for me, at this time, is best. There are many issues I have to deal with, and sometimes the choices seem wrong or at a minimum questionable, but I think I can live with this. She makes me happy, certainly takes care of me sexually, and seems to comply with my wishes. She is a beautiful woman, so I can't complain. And if things don't go as I have planned there is always divorce, and I am not afraid of that. I have been through it twice now, so a third time would not scare me. I will get out if necessary, hop on a plane and come home. I think I am doing the right thing. If not, I will change. That is the nice thing about life - at any time you want you can change anything and everything. If anything does happen, I am sure you will hear about it or at a minimum I will let you know."

They had another drink and talked about a variety of things. James paid the bill and took Ray home. They agreed to stay in touch. James said goodbye and headed to his hotel.

James got up in the morning, packed and headed to the airport. He was a bit anxious, second guessing himself, wondering if he was doing the right thing. Apprehension takes many forms, but he had made up his mind and was ready to go forward. He had time to kill at the airport and wandered about going from bar to restaurant to bar just to kill time. Finally, the announcement came, and he headed for his plane. Usually, he slept on planes, but he couldn't. The past few years reverberating in his head, trying to make sense of it all. Careers won – careers lost – love won – love lost – people he loved – people he hated – there were no easy answers.

The flight seemed like it would never end. He drank, he ate, he thought about the past and he thought about the future. He decided he was a person who did not look back, only forward. You must live in the present. But the present quickly becomes the past. You must live in the future. From the moment you are born you are racing toward death. Try to make the most of the future is what one needs to do.

There was turbulence as the plane dropped from its apogee. He laughed to himself – How ironic it would be if the plane crashed. The plane finally landed, and as it did his body let out a huge release. He felt safe. He felt safe like he had never felt safe before. He felt safe and a calmness entered his body, and a smile crossed his lips and his mind. He waited for most of the people to disembark, why fight the river? Finally, he exited the plane and made his way through the necessary maze till he reached the waiting area.

There she was the Queen of Brazil – beautiful and with a huge smile. They kissed and held each other as to never let go ever. They chatted for a while and finally she said, "James, I thought you would never get here. I am so happy to have you in my arms again. Why do you keep calling me the Queen of Brazil? Don't worry, I am a regular certified woman."

"Just something silly I thought of, but to be truthful, you are now my Queen of Brazil. There is no other woman in the world that I love or care for. You are the woman I am devoted to and I will work for your love and trust every second for the rest of my life. I think of no other woman, I see no other woman and I will never be with another woman. You have my being; my heart and my soul so please take good care of it. Before I came here I decided that my life with you shall be complete as long as I am with you and only you. My love for you is never ending and I am devoted to you for the rest of my life."

"Oh James, that is so beautiful. I love you too and I knew that you would love me. You calm my fears and I feel your devotion to me. My heart belongs to you as well and I will never do anything to disrespect you and I am devoted to you forever. Want to know something crazy? – I was thinking that they made a mistake and you found my helper Karen in the river alive and you would show up and bring her with you. I am still sick from that tragedy. She should never have gone fishing. I still have nightmares about losing her and to such a terrible end.

"Sorry I couldn't bring her to you Andrea. She was a very nice person and very loyal to you. Accidents do happen. Just hope they don't happen to us.

Andrea, all I want to do is love you forever. Now let's gather my things and go meet your family. Let's get this over with as quickly as possible so we can be alone. I am very anxious to get you alone and get our new life started."

THE END and NEW BEGININGS